A Liver Bird Sings

Carol Fenlon

Published in 2019 by FeedARead.com Publishing

First Edition

A CIP catalogue record for this title is available from the British
Library.

Chapter One

Bernadette McCann peered over her brother's shoulder as he eased the battered old van close to the kerb. John gripped his rollup between his teeth and blew a cloud of smoke as he cut the engine. Bernadette waved the smoke away as she looked up at the blank windows of the middle flat in the three-storey block.

'Is that it, Mam?'

Maureen McCann turned in the passenger seat and her tired eyes crinkled as she smiled.

'That's it, Bernie. Our new home. No more sharing. Our own front door.'

Bernie fought back tears. This place looked like an alien planet with its square blocks of flats plonked in the middle of swathes of grass. A road ran through the middle but ended in a brick wall with a footway through to the busy East Lancashire Road. Bernie saw a green bus flash across the gap and she wished she could jump on it and fly back to the crowded streets, shops and terraced houses of Toxteth. How would she ever get to see her boyfriend George and her best friend Aggie? It was the end of the world. She mouthed the words of the Skeeter Davis song and it made her want to cry all the more.

She turned to look through the van's rear windows, over the heads of her two little brothers and her younger sister Teresa. A group of children was playing at the far end of the street, which turned into the big housing estate they had just driven through.

'Let us out, John,' Matty shouted. 'We want to play with them kids.'

'You're going nowhere,' Maureen said firmly. 'We've got to get settled in before your da gets here. It'll be dark before you know it.' She looked up at the sky. 'What time is it?'

John looked at his wrist out of habit. 'How should I know? Me watch is in the pawnshop till Friday.' The van door squeaked as he got out. 'Come on then yous, let's get this stuff unloaded.'

Bernie pushed back thoughts of her old home and jumped out of the van and into her new life. She lined up her brothers and sister while John and her mother began unloading. In the late afternoon sunlight, the shabbiness of their furniture struck her as each piece was dumped on the pavement. She felt hidden eyes boring into her back as she loaded the children with small items. She looked round uneasily but saw no one although net curtains twitched at the window of a ground floor flat on the other side of the street.

She felt better when John lifted out their stylish new television and set it beside their old sofa, where it looked about to walk off on its spindly legs. Again she wished herself back in Toxteth, where everyone else was like them. What kind of people lived in this place?

She picked up two kitchen chairs and followed her mam up the couple of steps into the lobby of the flats.

A skinny little woman in a nylon overall bobbed out of a door on the ground floor.

'I'm Mrs Farrier – Kathleen.' Her faded blonde hair stood up in a quiff and she had an anxious look but her eyes were kind and she had a welcoming smile. Bernie saw a girl of about her own age peeping round the open door.

'This is me daughter – Annabel. Maybe I could make you a cup of tea?'

'That's very kind,' Maureen set down the bundle of bedding she carried. 'I don't think our gas is on yet. I'm Maureen McCann, me daughters Bernadette and Teresa and me two lads Matthew and Anthony. Me older son John's outside with the van.'

The younger children gawked in silence. Bernie stared at Annabel. She had a washed out look like her mother. Her long limp hair was almost white blonde and she was slender like her mother but less bony. She smiled suddenly at Bernie and her face lit up so that Bernie couldn't help smiling back.

'I'll put the kettle on,' said Kathleen, 'and if you go and let yourselves in, I'll send me son Peter out to give you a hand. Me husband Tommy is still at work.'

Maureen led her family up the stairs, the key to the new flat clenched in her fingers. She opened the door with a flourish then they all stood on the threshold, feeling like outsiders who didn't quite belong there. The boys pushed past their mother and ran down the narrow hallway, ducking in and out of the doors along the passage.

'Look, look, we've got our own lav.' Matthew yanked the chain experimentally. 'And a bath,' they chorused. The others trooped in to have a look.

'Do you think it works?' Teresa edged towards it as if it might bite.

'Of course it works,' Maureen ran her hand along the enamel rim. 'Needs a good clean but once we get the hot water sorted…'

'Bagsy first go,' Anthony shouted, 'ooh, the water's freezing.'

'We'll never get in there,' Teresa said, looking in the tiny square mirror over the sink. 'Not once our Marie gets here.'

Bernie laughed. It was true her elder sister would hog any facilities for primping herself. But there would be no more humping buckets of water from the shared bathroom on the floor below and no more boiling them on the kitchen stove. Still, that didn't make up for leaving everything she'd ever known behind.

'Stop messing with those taps,' Maureen remonstrated but the boys were already in another room, chattering like monkeys.

'Ah, look at this. Can we have this one, it's got aeroplanes on the wallpaper?'

'Is this our room?' Teresa pulled timidly at Bernie's hand. The room was overshadowed by huge pink roses on the wallpaper that hung in strips here and there. Maureen came in and saw Bernie's expression.

'Don't you worry love, we'll soon have it spick and span. Come on, let's get on with moving the stuff. Where are those boys?'

She glanced out of the bare window. 'Here comes your Aunty Joan with our Polly. Honestly you wouldn't think that girl had just turned twelve. Look at her skipping along showing her knickers like a five year old.'

A few moments later Polly flew into the bedroom. Her dark blonde pigtails swung as she examined the room.

'Is this ours? Oh it's fab. Where's our beds?. Where's Mam?'

She darted out, squeezing past her aunty Joan. Bernie followed her but the hall was full of Aunty Joan, with John and a big fair-haired boy around her own age, manhandling a bedstead between them.

'I've brought some firewood.' Joan delved in her enormous shopping bag. 'I don't suppose you thought about it. Have you got coal Maureen?' Her sister looked blank. 'You need to get the fire lit first, this place is damp as a Dutchman's armpit. Have a look in the coal hole.'

Maureen fiddled with the keys and they all rushed to the back door to step out on the tiny balcony. Maureen looked in the coal cupboard while the children hung over the metal railings, gazing at the view of a similar block of flats to their own.

Maureen shovelled up the bit of coal she found into a battered bucket presumably left there for the purpose then while she and Joan lit the fire, Bernie and the other children ran up and down the stairs helping John and Peter to carry their possessions in. They worked without stopping except for the few minutes it took to drink the hot sweet tea that Annabel brought up on a tin tray decorated with a picture of Queen Elizabeth and Prince Philip.

Bernie wanted to talk to Annabel but John thrust a sack of clothes in her arms and Kathleen called Annabel in for her tea. Bernie's legs ached from running up and down the stone steps but she'd caught the excited mood of the rest of the family. For a while she forgot about her old home, distracted with thoughts of how she would arrange her corner of the bedroom and how she might make friends with Annabel. The big blond boy brushed past her in the hallway. She blushed as she squeezed by without looking at him. At the bedroom door she turned to peep at him but he had already gone and in his place a beefy red-faced woman with bright orange hair strode towards her.

'Don't be staring at me like that, girl.' The woman stopped, hands on hips 'What's your name?'

'Bernie,' Bernadette mumbled. She felt frightened even though she had no idea who the woman was.

'Where's your mam?' The woman swept past her, into the living room where Maureen was holding an old newspaper up against the fire to draw the flames.

'I saw your sticks out on the pavement – blocking the pavement they are in fact an' I says to myself, 'that's the new family moving into the Bensons' old flat, gawd help them.' I hope they've fumigated the place for you. I've lived in this street longer than anyone else here. Not in this block of course. We're in number 47 up the street – and on the ground of course, these stairs is no good for my legs.'

She sat down on the kitchen chair that Joan was about to climb on in order to put up the net curtains.

'Have you not got a cup of tea to offer your new neighbour?'

'We've no gas yet,' Maureen apologised. 'If I can find a pan, I'll boil up some water on the fire.'

'On the fire?' the big woman exclaimed. 'On the fire? Yous aren't tinkers, are you?'

Maureen bit her lip at the insult but Joan put down the curtains and advanced on their visitor.

'No, we're not tinkers and I'll thank you to mind your manners. Who might you be anyway?'

'I'm Mrs Hanson, Rose Hanson,' the woman said. She seemed to puff up like a bullfrog and her bosom swayed under her pink jumper. 'We're respectable folk. My husband has a very important job with the Prudential. And what does your man do then?' She looked at Maureen.

'He's a – a- second-hand dealer,' Maureen stuttered.

Mrs Hanson stared. 'Second-hand dealer? You mean he's a totter? My God, I knew it. I says to myself when I saw you pull up, 'there's a totter's van if ever I saw one."

'And what of it?' said Maureen. 'It's an honest trade.'

'Hmph!' said Rose Hanson. 'Well, I suppose it's better than those layabout Bensons that were here before yous. An' you'd better watch out for those Jacksons on top of you. Dirty lot they are and watch your washing line. They'd steal the eyes off a corpse when you wasn't looking.'

A screech of brakes put an end to the conversation. Mrs Hanson peered out of the window.

'God bless us, who's this?'

Bernie looked out of her bedroom window at the sound of the car. The kids from the end of the street were clotted together in an awestruck group, admiring the turquoise and white two-tone Ford Zephyr with its white-walled tyres. Bernie could see Matthew and Anthony already at home amongst the group and she smiled at their ability to make friends quickly. It wouldn't be so easy for her small sister who had such a shy nature. She looked down at Teresa's wispy blonde hair as the child craned to see over the window sill.

'Oh, it's only our Marie,' she put her arms round Teresa's neck and cuddled her. The car belonged to her sister Marie's boyfriend, Jimmy. As they watched, the passenger door opened and Marie got out managing to look elegant despite her tight skirt. She slammed the door and tottered into the block of flats as the car zoomed off with the knot of children in pursuit. It was all right for Marie, Bernie thought, she wasn't cut off from the boy she loved. Once again tears welled up.

She wiped her eyes, hearing Marie's stiletto heels striking the stone steps as she came up to the first floor. Maureen had also heard her and called out.

'Marie, come in the back. Mrs Hanson, this is me eldest daughter, Marie. And I haven't introduced meself. I'm Maureen McCann and this is me sister Joan.'

Polly took advantage of the distraction to slip out of the back door.

Mrs Hanson looked Marie up and down. Marie leaned against the door and looked straight back. She chewed her gum, then glanced around the room.

'God it's freezing in here.' She pulled her pale blue cardigan closer round her shoulders. 'It's a bit of a dump, isn't it?'

'A dump? I'll have you know this is a very select neighbourhood,' Mrs Hanson jumped in. 'An' we ain't never had the likes of totters here before.'

She glared at Marie who pulled a sulky face and patted her beehive. She turned her back on Mrs Hanson and disappeared to inspect the rest of the rooms.

'Well' Mrs Hanson looked at Maureen. 'I bet that one's a handful.'

'She's a good girl,' Maureen said stoutly.

'She should show respect for her elders.' Mrs Hanson folded her arms across her chest. 'An' I wouldn't let a girl of mine run round in a skirt like that. No wonder she's got a feller in a flashy car running after her.'

'That's enough,' Joan said. 'No one asked you to come in here and insult us.'

'Well, I only come in here to be neighbourly – help you out like and this is what I get.'

'I'm sure no one means any harm.' Maureen tried to soothe the situation. 'Look, the fire's lit now. I'll boil a kettle and we'll all have a nice cup of tea.'

'It's too late for that now,' Rose Hanson snapped, but she looked mollified. 'Mr Hanson will be home soon and I have to be getting his tea.' She looked out of the window. 'It looks like the gas man is here for you.'

'Oh Lord, has John brought the stove up yet?' Maureen ran to the kitchen, giving a sigh of relief when she saw their ancient gas stove among the chaos of bundles and boxes dumped in the room.

She followed Rose to the front door.

'I'll come for you tomorrow and show you where everything is, the shops, the doctors. I'll be here nine o'clock sharp, after the kids have gone to school.'

Bernie could see that her mam wasn't keen on having Rose's company the next day, but the thought of getting the cooker connected filled her mind so she hastily agreed.

'Who's the old bat?' Marie kicked off her shoes and rubbed her feet. Their mattresses were piled in the bedroom and she plumped down on top of the heap. 'God my feet are killing me, walking round that bloody shop all day will be the death of me. Oh yes, Modom, that really suits you?' She pulled a face and laughed.

'It's all right when you're getting staff discount on your clothes,' Bernie pointed out.

'Yeah, you're right.' She looked round. 'God what a mess. I've got to get changed and be ready by half-past six. Jimmy's playing at the Clarence tonight so he's picking me up early.'

She made no effort to help unpack, but started rummaging in the bundles of clothes for her evening's outfit. Bernie thought about asking her if Jimmy might take her back to Toxteth to see George but decided against it. No one knew about George and she didn't trust Marie to keep it secret, at best she would torment her unmercifully if she knew.

Bernie went back out to help John carry the last few things in, leaving Teresa to start unpacking their clothes. Polly had long since disappeared; Bernie could see her at the end of the street with a group of big girls.

Maureen looked anxiously at the kitchen clock that John had just hung on the wall. 'I didn't realise the time. Are you picking your da and Vinny up?'

'They said not to bother. I dropped them off at the Crown. They're getting a lift down, said they'd be here about five.'

'Heaven help us they'll be here any minute.' Maureen glanced at the gas man who was connecting the ancient cooker.

'Here's ten bob.' She extracted the note with care from her well-worn purse and held it out to Bernie. 'Tell our Polly to find the nearest chippy and get fish and chips for your da and a sausage each for everyone else and enough chips to go round, and plenty of salt and vinegar mind, and tell her not to be dawdling back with them or they'll be cold. And then you come straight back and help me get the kitchen sorted out.'

'Kettle's boiling in here,' John called from the living room as Bernie ran down the stone steps to find Polly.

Annabel was just coming out of her front door, slipping some coins carefully into the pocket of her jeans and she smiled shyly at Bernie.

'I'm going to the van for some milk. I'll show you where it is if you like.'

'Okay, but I have to look for me sister Polly, me mam wants her to go to the chippy for our tea and I can't be out long, me da'll be home.' Bernie glanced through the open door behind Annabel, hoping for a glimpse of her brother but there was no sign of him.

'It's not far, and the chippy's just round the corner from there.' The two girls fell into step together. 'Will you be going to St Anthony's? That's the school I go to.'

9

'I don't know.' Bernie felt sad, remembering her old school and her mates from St Xavier's. 'I expect Mam'll keep me off till next week to help get the place sorted out.'

'It would be nice if you come to our school – maybe we could walk there together.'

Bernie smiled in reply. She didn't feel quite so bad. She would have at least one friend when she joined the new school.

'I'll be leaving school next year anyway,' she told Annabel, 'me Aunty Joan works at the Meccano and she'll probably get me a job there.' She broke off suddenly as she saw a gang of girls jostling on the next corner. In the middle she could see her sister's unmistakeable blonde plaits flying.

'Hey, what's going on?' she broke into a run, leaving the startled Annabel to follow her.

Bernie tried to pull her sister out of the group. The other girls fell back but Polly was too busy with her opponent, a dark-haired girl much bigger than herself, whose arm she had twisted up her back while her other hand pulled viciously at the girl's hair.

'What're you doing? Let go.' Bernie grabbed her sister by the back of the neck.

'Don't you ever say that again,' Polly hissed in the terrified girl's ear, then let go of her with a push that sent her flying into the other girls.

Bernie dragged Polly away. Her sister's face was scarlet and her breath came in ragged gasps.

'This is me sister Polly. She's only been here five minutes and she's causing trouble already.'

'Wasn't me! 'Polly shouted. 'She called us names. She said we was all totters.'

'That's Katy Sullivan,' Annabel said, casting an admiring glance at Polly, 'she's a right bully. Her mam's Mrs Hanson's sister. They think they own the street, that's what me mam says.'

Bernie shook Polly's arm, 'Mam says you're to go to the chippy for our tea and I'm supposed to go back and help her, but I can't leave you on your own now, I'll have to come with you. Will you show us where it is?' She looked at Annabel.

'I'm not scared of them,' Polly swung her plaits, 'Just let her say it again.'

Polly was unshaken but Bernie was subdued as Annabel led them to the nearby big red mobile van where milk and all sorts of necessities could be bought. If this was what happened on their first day, what kind of welcome were they going to get from the other kids in the area?

Annabel took them to the chip shop and as they came back, Bernadette saw her looking up and down the street and she wondered if she could stand up for herself against Katy Sullivan.

'Why did she call us that, anyway?' Polly said as they turned into their street, clutching the hot greasy bags of chips.

Bernie saw her da and Vinny Mack get out of an open truck parked at the kerb and go into the block of flats. The truck was full of old copper water tanks and scrap metal and it was badly in need of a coat of paint. She couldn't see the driver for the clouds of exhaust it blew out as it pulled away. She also saw Rose Hanson peeping from the window of a ground floor flat on the opposite side of the street.

'I think I know,' she said hurrying past that relentless gaze.

Chapter Two

'Where've you been for God's sake?' Maureen pounced on Bernie as the girls came into the flat. 'Your da's here already and no tea waiting.' She ran round the kitchen gathering plates, bread and butter, finally seizing the hot chips and throwing them into the oven. 'Get some knives and forks out and set two trays for your da and Vinny.' She thrust two plates at Bernie, then began to cut thick slices from a loaf on the table.

Bernie hunted round in the bags and boxes for cutlery. She could hear her father washing in the bathroom, prior to going out for the evening to his favourite pub. He did this six nights a week and even moving house would not make him change his daily routine.

'Here, take this in to Vinny.' Maureen put a tray into her hands containing a portion of chips and a sausage arranged on a plate, with two big doorsteps of bread and marge. Vinny Mack was sitting on their sofa watching Joan hanging the living room curtains.

'Why, ta very much, Bernie,' he took the tray from her. His Errol Flynn moustache went up and down as he spoke. 'Getting a big lass eh?'

Bernie felt uncomfortable. Last New Year when Vinny Mack had been drunk he had tried to kiss her in the back of the van as they had all been coming back from a party. She remembered the horrible beery smell and the touch of the bristles prickling her face and she went over to steady Joan's chair as she climbed down.

Her da appeared in the doorway, his face red from scrubbing with carbolic soap and his curly hair still wet and gleaming. His belly bulged over the thick leather belt round his waist and he was buttoning the cuffs of the clean white shirt Maureen had managed to find him.

'What kind of food is this?' he said, watching Vinny Mack wolf his chips. His voice was jokey but held a warning grumble and both Joan and Bernie stiffened slightly in response.

'We've had no time to get anything ready,' Joan spoke up, 'and the gas man's only just been.'

'Leave the girls alone, Joe,' said Vinny Mack round a mouthful of sausage. 'It's good grub.'

'You wouldn't know any better,' Joe said. 'Shop-bought rubbish,' he muttered as he turned away. Bernie wondered why her da always looked

for things to grumble about; for the rest of the family chippy chips were
a rare treat.

'Why do you have to give Vinny Mack his tea?' Matthew asked loudly
as he watched his mother sharing out the food.

'Hush now,' Maureen, looked towards the closed living room door.
'Your da expects me to give him his tea when he comes back from work.'

'Why can't he get his own tea?' Matty's voice was even louder.

'Hush up and eat your chips.'

The younger children needed no further bidding. There was only
room for the four of them at the table, Bernie and Joan stood by the
kitchen sink, while Maureen stayed by the stove. John had gone to eat
with the men in the living room.

'Where's our Marie?' Maureen, looked into the oven. 'Her food's
going to be dried up.'

'You can have my sausage, Mam,' said Bernie, seeing the few chips
her mother had on her plate. 'I'm not very hungry.' She ducked out of
the kitchen to summon her sister but before she reached the bedroom
door Marie wafted out in a cloud of Goya's *Black Rose*, her hair so stiffly
lacquered, it looked like a hat. The skirt she had on was even tighter than
the one she had been wearing earlier, with a split up the back that
showed the flesh above the backs of her knees.

'I haven't got time to eat all that,' she said. 'Just give me a cup of tea.
Jimmy'll be here any minute.'

'Your da'll have a fit if he sees you dressed like that.' Maureen poured
tea.

'Da's already got a cob on 'cos his tea wasn't ready.' Bernie looked
enviously at Marie's high heels and promised herself next year, when she
got her first pay packet, she would buy a pair just like them.

Maureen sighed. 'I've got a nice bit of steak for his supper, that'll put
him in a good mood.'

'Mam, lend me half-a-crown till Friday,' Marie said, eating chips with
her fingers.

Maureen looked aghast. 'Half-a-crown? I've hardly a sixpence to me
name. What do you want it for?'

'I've no dinner money left for the rest of the week.'

'What you spend it on I don't know. Too many clothes and too much
make up.'

'I got to look nice going out with Jimmy.'

13

'That stuff you wear's old fashioned any way,' Polly butted in. 'Everyone's going to be mods now and no one's going to wear them stilettos, you'll be the only one, antwacky Annie!'

'What do you know you stupid eejit!' Marie glared at Polly.

'It's true, I saw it on telly. Mods are gear, and ride round on scooters. People like you go out with greasy rockers on motorbikes.'

'You cheeky little cow!' Marie leaned over to give her sister a slap but Maureen pulled her back.

'Jimmy likes the way I look,' she said sulkily. 'He's going to be famous, one day soon.'

'Famous my foot,' Maureen laughed. 'And I think your money's going on ciggies, I'm sure I can smell smoke on you half the time.'

'I never smoke,' Marie, turned bright red. 'It's just all the smoke in the pub, it gets in your hair and everywhere.'

'Just let me catch you,' Maureen warned.

'Here,' Joan took a two-shilling piece from her purse. 'That's all I got. You can pay me back on Friday.'

'Thanks Aunty Joan, I'll give it to Mam, soon as I get paid.' She grabbed the florin and tucked it into her handbag.

'Antwacky Annie,' Polly taunted and slid under the table as Marie made a grab for her, where she hid behind the boys' legs, making them giggle.

'I'll swing for her,' Marie hissed, 'and what are you two laughing at?' She groped under the table, her face flushed, yet not a strand of her stiffly lacquered hairdo moved.

Just then, the sound of a car horn blasted from the street.

'That's Jimmy,' Marie grabbed her bag. 'I'll get you later,' she hissed under the table.

'Don't let your da see you. And don't come in late,' Maureen warned, but Marie was already gone.

'Can I have her sausage?' Polly asked surfacing like a diver coming up for air.

Once Joe and Vinny Mack had left for the pub, Maureen organised the rest of the family to put the flat to rights. Joan had gone home to her own family and John disappeared to catch a bus into town where he'd arranged to meet his mates.

If only I could do the same, Bernie thought. It was Wednesday and she had no chance of getting any money until Saturday when her mam usually gave her a shilling or two if she had it to spare. If she had some money she could call George's aunty, the posh one with her own phone, and leave a message for George to meet her. Her spirits sank as she

14

worked her way through the endless tasks of making up beds and putting away clothes, then cleaning the bath but she couldn't help smiling when she saw how delighted Matt and Anthony were, splashing in the soapsuds. Teresa followed them but there was no hot water left for Bernie or Polly.

'You can have one tomorrow, Bernie,' her mam said, doling out cocoa to the younger kids, all cuddled up in their pyjamas on the sofa. Their pink, shiny faces and the damp hair curling round their heads, made them look so sweet. Bernie thought how lovely it was going to be, not having to trek to the public baths and come back damp and shivering through cold streets.

'You've been a good help today,' her mam said, once the others were in bed.

It was the best time of day, Bernie thought, when she was alone with her mam. Maureen put her feet up on the rickety coffee table, rummaged in her overall pocket for her packet of Woodbines and lit one up. They watched *Take Your Pick* just like they used to in their old home and the smell of cigarette smoke, mingling with the scent of her father's steak and onions in the oven, was so familiar that Bernie almost imagined herself back there. Tears came and she brushed them away.

Maureen got up and poked the dying fire. 'Have to get some coal tomorrow,' she said. 'That Annabel seems a nice girl, do you think you might make friends?'

Bernie nodded, picked miserably at her skirt.

'You're missing Aggie, aren't you?' She went over to Bernie and sat beside her, putting an arm round her shoulders. Bernie leaned against her warmth, breathing in her mixture of Woodbines and talc. She couldn't stop tears leaking out.

'You'll still be able to see your friends. You can write Aggie a letter, ask her to come for tea one day. I'll give you the money for a stamp at the weekend.'

'Thanks Mam,' Bernie dried her eyes but she was thinking of George rather than Aggie. Her mam didn't know about George. Bernie was too terrified of her da finding out if her secret was shared.

'You're worn out,' her mam said, 'You'll feel better tomorrow, wait and see.'

Bernie went to bed early, too miserable even to listen to her beloved radio. She heard John come in and then her father and she lay listening to the sounds of her mam fussing round with his meal. Marie hadn't yet come home and Bernie couldn't settle. Gradually the flat quietened and all she could hear was her sisters' even breathing as they slept heavily, despite the strangeness of the new room.

Bernie wept silently into her pillow. Toxteth, Aggie and George were only on the other side of the city but they might as well have been in Timbuktu. She thought of the sweet kisses George had given her only last Saturday at the teenage pictures; she could almost still feel his warm lips on hers and she squeezed the pillow as she would have liked to squeeze him.

She wondered if she could cadge some money from John so she could phone George's aunty. She resolved to ask him the next day but once that problem receded she began thinking about Rose Hanson and the way she had tried to boss her mam about and then there was Katy Sullivan…

She fell into uneasy sleep. A dragon with bright orange hair barred her way to the phone box where George was trapped inside. She woke suddenly in a sweat, almost screamed as a shadow passed over her.

'SSSHHH!' Marie hissed, climbing up to the top bunk in a cloud of stale perfume. Bernie peered at the alarm clock on the chest of drawers and saw it was ten past one. Mam must have left the back door open for her.

The bunk over her head creaked and groaned, Bernie heard the scrape of a match, saw a brief glow, then smelled the smoke of the cigarette.

'I'm trying to sleep,' she hissed, 'me da'll kill you if he catches you.' She reached up and thumped the underside of the upper bunk.

'Oh piss off,' Marie retorted, tossing and turning so the bunks rocked like a ship in a storm.

Bernie rose and went to the toilet, another new indoor pleasure. Through the open living room door she made out the slumped shape of her father, sleeping in his armchair, his teeth chattering and grinding as they always did. She wondered what he dreamed about as she padded back to her own bed.

The next morning Bernie leaned on the bedroom windowsill, looking out at the street below. Through the gap at the end she could see the early morning traffic rushing along the East Lancashire Road towards the city. She was alone in the bedroom; Marie was putting on her makeup in the bathroom while the younger girls banged on the bathroom door shouting at her to let them in.

The back door slammed suddenly and she heard her father's heavy footsteps going down the stone stairs, followed by John's lighter steps, then he appeared in the street below where Vinny Mack waited in the van. Another man came out of the flats and hailed her father who turned in surprise, suspicion etched on his features.

The stranger's voice floated up to Bernie. 'I'm Tommy, Tommy Farrier... live on the ground floor.'

Joe looked at Tommy's outstretched hand but didn't take it.

'Nice to meet you,' Tommy said uncertainly. 'If we can do anything to help you settle in, just knock.'

'Thanks,' Joe said gruffly, 'got to get to work.'

He turned away and climbed into the cab next to John. Vinny Mack drove off leaving Tommy Farrier with his hand still extended in greeting.

Bernie burned with embarrassment. Why was her da always so grumpy? She loved him but the whole family had to tread carefully when he was home. He was never violent but his raised voice struck terror into them all. Why couldn't he be kind and friendly like her friend Aggie's da?

The door banged again and Marie appeared in the street a moment later. She put her nose in the air as she passed Mr Farrier and clattered off towards the main road. Despite the morning chill she wore only her cardigan over her tight black dress. The dress was the standard uniform for the assistants at Miami Modes dress shop where she worked on London Road in the town centre. It accentuated her curves and Bernie could see Mr Farrier watching her as he followed her out of the street and across the road to the bus stop.

'Bernie!' her mother yelled. Bernie sighed and went to the kitchen where the younger kids were eating cornflakes.

'Caught the milkman downstairs,' Maureen said through a mouthful of hairgrips as she yanked a hairbrush through Polly's rambling curls.

'Owww!' Polly sprayed a mouthful of cereal and milk over the table.

'Look what she's done, all over my uniform.' Teresa started to cry.

'Never mind.' Bernie grabbed a dishcloth and started rubbing at the stains on Teresa's jumper.

'Stop that giggling,' Maureen shouted at the twins who were red in the face with laughter. They subsided but continued to snigger into their hands.

'What's so funny?' Maureen demanded, snapping elastic bands on the ends of Polly's plaits.

The boys didn't answer but carried on eating, rolling their eyes at each other.

Maureen finished the hairdressing and began sorting through a pile of coats and blazers that were bundled up in a candlewick bedspread.

'Come on you lot, get your coats on, we're going to be late.'

Polly stood up and promptly fell forwards, crashing into the table and knocking Teresa out of her chair and onto the floor. The twins collapsed in fits of laughter as the two girls howled. Bernie, looking under the table, saw that they had tied Polly's shoelaces together.

'Look what they done, Mam,' Polly screamed. She pulled off the shoes and threw them at her brothers. Bernie tried to keep a straight face as she picked Teresa up and dusted her down but Maureen's flashing eyes sent a dire warning to the two boys who skedaddled out of the kitchen with Polly in hot pursuit.

Once her mam had taken them all to school, Bernie tidied up the kitchen. After washing the dishes she fetched her transistor radio, sat down at the kitchen table, tuned into Radio Caroline and began to sing along to the latest hits.

If only she could be a famous singer like Cilla or Lulu, all her problems would be over. She'd buy her mam a big house and she'd be able to get the bus into town, to see George any time she wanted. No, if she was really famous as Cilla she'd be able to have a big car with a driver to take her wherever she wanted.

She was still daydreaming when the back door opened and her mam came in with Rose Hanson.

'I don't believe it,' Maureen huffed, taking a pint of milk out of her shopping bag. She struggled out of her coat and sat down. 'Put the kettle on, our Bernie, while I try to think. What am I going to do?' She gazed at Rose who settled herself gingerly on a wobbly chair.

'What's up Mam?' Bernie fetched clean cups and spooned tea into the tin teapot.

'Turn that flaming noise off,' Maureen said and Bernie ran to save her precious radio before her mam started fiddling with it.

'Kids have got to have new uniforms,' Rose Hanson said. 'Ain't you got no proper milk?' She peered askance at the bottle of steri on the table. 'We always have fresh.'

'We haven't got a fridge,' Bernie said and could have bitten her tongue when she saw the shamed look on her mother's face.

'Well!' said Rose and shook her head.

'It got broke,' Maureen said, 'when we moved. Joe'll get us a new one.'

Bernie looked at Rose's smug face. Why did her mother have to lie to this woman? 'What's wrong with the kids' uniforms?' she asked to change the subject.

'Headmistress says they're the wrong colour. They got to have grey ones and they got to have them by next Monday or they can't go to school.'

'You'll have to ask your husband,' Rose pronounced and took a big sip of her tea.

'I got a little bit put by,' Maureen said slowly. She got up and went out of the room. After a few moments she came back with two pounds and a ten-shilling note in her hand. 'I was saving it for Christmas.'

Bernie knew all about her mother's hidden savings, scrimped and scraped from the meagre housekeeping. She'd seen her often enough with her fingers poking inside one of the Three Graces, the hollow statues her da had brought in one day and insisted they keep on the mantelpiece. Her mam thought no one knew about the money and that was fine with Bernie. It wouldn't do for Marie to know and if her da found out he'd be sure to cut the housekeeping down even more if he thought Maureen saved anything out of it.

Rose pursed her lips. 'There's a second-hand clothes shop on the Broadway. We can get the bus down there after we've sorted you out with the doctor and the dentist. We might find something there and I can show you where the market is, the shops there are cheaper than round here.'

Maureen looked relieved and Bernie thought that perhaps Mrs Hanson wasn't so bad after all. At least she was trying to help them even if she was a bossy busybody.

It was an exhausting day, first the doctor's, then the dentist's to register the whole family, then there was the coalyard to visit and the small row of local shops.

'You got a washing machine?' Rose asked.

'We always went to the wash house back home,' Maureen faltered.

'Don't keep saying that, this is home now,' Rose marched them towards the shops. 'There's a laundrette here.'

Maureen bit her lip, 'I bet it's expensive.'

Rose turned on her. 'Well what are you going to do?'

Maureen was silent.

The bus rumbled up and they all got on, Maureen carefully counting out the coppers for their fare. Rose didn't offer to pay her own and squeezed into the seat next to Maureen, leaving Bernie to sit behind them. Bernie didn't mind, she was thinking about the phone box she'd seen on the corner by the laundrette and how she was going to get the money to use it.

The journey to the Broadway was short and the first thing Bernie noticed when they got off the bus was the swimming baths. Her mam might give her the money to take the younger ones in the school holidays to get them off her hands. They had some success in the second hand shop, finding a grey pinafore to fit Teresa and two pairs of grey shorts for the twins.

'They'll have to manage without jumpers or blazers for now,' Maureen sighed, 'at least it's not cold yet.'

'What about Polly?' Bernie asked.

'I'll think of something,' Maureen said.

'I'll be okay anyway,' Bernie said, 'St. Anthony's uniform is the same colour as my old school. I saw Annabel going to school in hers this morning.'

Broadway market was full of interesting things: fruit and vegetables, fashion and nice underwear, stockings and makeup that Bernie knew she could never afford for herself. Most of her things came off her da's rag and bone round, plus a few cast-offs from Marie when she was feeling generous. Occasionally her mam would get a Provident cheque and they would all troop down to T.J. Hughes's in town. Everyone would get new shoes and if there was enough left over, something nice to wear. There would be a long gap while her mam paid the money back. Bernie thought it seemed an awful long time since the last one.

'I'll take you up to Kirkby market on Saturday, if you like,' Rose said when they were on the bus going home.

'I can't,' Maureen said. 'We always have a stall on Greaty on Saturdays.'

Bernie knew her mam looked forward to her Saturday mornings on Great Homer Street market. John would drive her to set up the stall on which they would pile all the stuff her da had collected through the week that was too good to be weighed in at the scrap yard but not good enough to take to antique dealers. Standing on the market was too demeaning for her da, who would spend the morning in the cafés on the dock road with Vinny Mack, until the pubs opened. Bernie also loved the market and haggling for bargains if she had any cash but she was often left at home to mind her brothers and sisters.

'Greaty!' Rose sniffed. 'It's full of darkies and tramps scrabbling over old rags.'

Maureen turned pink but didn't say anything. Bernie gave a hefty kick to the back of Rose's seat.

'Oh sorry,' she smiled as Rose's angry moonface turned towards her. 'My foot got stuck.'

Back at the flat, Bernie helped her mam set the rooms to rights and put everyone's clothes in their proper places. The coalman came and by three o'clock the place felt like a cosy home. Peace didn't last for long however. Bernie had just started peeling the potatoes for tea when the back door banged open and Polly crashed in with a snivelling Teresa in tow. The twins followed, shouting, 'Biff…Bam…Biff,' as they pretended to wallop each other.

'Blow yer nose,' Bernie said as Teresa sank onto the opposite chair at the kitchen table.

'What's up with her?' Maureen asked.

'She got teased at school.' Polly tore off her old red blazer and dropped it on the floor.

'Don't do that, pick it up and put it away proper. 'Who's been teasing her?'

'Was it that Katy Sullivan?' Bernie asked.

Teresa shook her head, hiccupping with tears.

'Nah, she's not in our school. Don't know who she was but it doesn't matter, I splattered her anyway,' Polly said.

'Don't you go causing trouble already,' Maureen unwrapped a packet of lard and tipped it into the chip pan.

Polly flounced out to the girls' bedroom. The twins could be heard shouting and play-fighting in the living room then there was a sudden silence.

Maureen cocked an ear. 'Your da must be on his way up,' she said and the next moment the back door opened again and Joe came in with Vinny Mack.

'Where's our John?' Maureen said.

'I sent him to weigh in some copper.' Joe headed for the bathroom.

'I made him some sarnies.' Maureen looked reproachfully at her husband.

'He can have them when he gets back. They ain't gonna go cold are they?' He grinned at Maureen but there was a hint of irritation on his face. 'Go and sit down Vin, Mo'll bring you a cup of tea.' He disappeared into the bathroom and Vinny Mack winked at Bernie before ambling into the living room where he started chaffing the twins.

Bernie listened to her da humming as he got ready to go out for the evening with his pockets full of cash from the day's takings on the round, whereas she couldn't even raise pennies for the phone. Presently he yelled for a clean shirt and Maureen scurried to fetch it.

'Bernie, take these teas and the butties through,' she hissed as she pulled the freshly ironed shirt from the maiden.

Bernie took the tray through to Vinny Mack, keeping out of grabbing range.

'Ta, Bernie luv,' he said, trying to look her in the eye as she set the tray down. She kept her gaze averted. 'Why couldn't they fetch their own blasted tea?' she thought. 'Why do they have to be waited on hand and foot?' She went out in silence; she would never have dared to voice her thoughts to Vinny Mack, let alone to her da.

After tea, she caught a few quiet moments alone in her room. She turned on her radio and got out the notebook in which she wrote the lyrics of the latest songs so she could practise for her dream of stardom. Sandie Shaw's *Always Something There to Remind Me* came on and she struggled to scribble the words down but lost concentration halfway through, thinking about performing barefoot like Sandie. Were her own feet pretty enough to do that? She kicked off her shoes and pulled off her socks to examine them when Marie came in

'What are you doing?' She sat down at the dressing table and began powdering her nose.

'Nothing,' Bernie said, hiding the notebook. She watched her sister's face in the mirror. Maybe she could tap her for the money for the phone but it was unlikely; Marie never had any money. Still, it was worth a try.

'Marie…' she began.

'Can't stop,' Marie said, standing up to pull off her work dress and slip on her new Crimplene two piece. 'Meeting Jim.'

Bernie followed her into the hall. 'Lend us a tanner, Marie,' she said.

Marie turned and laughed. 'Get lost,' she shouted. 'I haven't got a tanner and if I had I wouldn't lend it to you.'

Bernie turned back as Marie went out of the front door to avoid meeting her father.

'What's up?' Vinny Mack came down the hall towards the toilet. 'What you want? A tanner? I'll give it yer.' He fished in his pocket. 'Here, get yourself some sweets.' He dropped a shilling into her hand, pressing her up against the wall as he did so.

'Thanks,' Bernie squirmed away. She didn't want to take his money but her need to phone George overcame her distaste.

She went out, the shilling burning a hole in her pocket. She called for Annabel and the two of them headed for the paper shop where Bernie planned to buy sweets to share and get change for the phone.

'Who you phoning then?' Annabel couldn't imagine phoning anyone except for the time her Aunt Linda's baby was coming and her husband had to phone the hospital.

'My boyfriend.' Bernie saw that Annabel was impressed. She puffed out her chest. 'His name's George.'

'Does he go to our school?'

'Don't be daft, he lives in Toxteth, where I used to live and anyway he's left school now. He's seventeen, he goes to work.'

'Work?' Annabel's eyes widened. 'Where?'

'The Post Office in Victoria Street, sorting the mail and he goes to evening classes so he can get promoted, see.' Bernie would rather he was a pop star or at least played in a group like her sister's boyfriend but she knew that even working in the post office would sound really grown up to Annabel. 'We'll probably get engaged soon,' she held out her left hand and admired it as if the ring was already on her finger.

Annabel was awed into silence.

'But don't you tell no one,' Bernie said, 'me da'd kill me. Even me mam doesn't know.'

'You haven't…' Annabel hesitated, '…have you?'

'What?' Bernie was still lost in the dream of the engagement ring.

'You know…it…you haven't done it, have you?' Annabel dropped her voice to a whisper and glanced around.

'What do you take me for?' Bernie flounced away.

'Oh, I didn't mean….' Annabel ran after her. 'I just wondered you know, what it was like….'

She was saved from further embarrassment as they came to the paper shop and Bernie was so excited about getting change for the phone that she forgot to be offended.

They came out of the shop with a sherbet fountain each. Bernie opened the door of the phone box. 'You can't come in,' she said to Annabel. 'You wait outside.'

'Oh please,' Annabel stammered.

'No,' Bernie said, 'we'll be saying, private things, love things.' She swung the heavy door shut and dialled the number. George's aunty answered after a number of rings.

'Hello Mrs Ryan,' Bernie said in her best voice. 'It's Bernie McCann here, George's girlfriend.'

'Oh hello Bernie,' said George's aunty, 'how are you settling in your new place? George isn't here you know luv,' she went on without waiting for an answer.

'I just wondered if you could give him a message? Could you tell him I'll meet him at the post office on Saturday when he finishes work? Half-past twelve, isn't it?'

'I think so dear, yes I'll let him know.'

The pips went and she was gone but Bernie blew a few kisses into the mouthpiece and rolled her eyes for Annabel's benefit before replacing the receiver.

'Oh, he's so sexy,' she said, coming out of the phone box and fanning her flushed face.

'You've kissed him then?' Annabel asked between sucks on her liquorice straw as they began to walk home.

'Of course…and more,' Bernie eyed her friend to be sure she got her meaning.

'What's it like?' Annabel asked and Bernie stopped in her tracks.

'You don't know? Haven't you been kissed?'

Annabel hung her head. 'Well, not really,' she admitted, 'only by Christopher Byrne at last year's Christmas social at St Mark's and that didn't really count 'cos he's only ten.'

'How old are you?' Bernie asked.

'Thirteen and a half.'

'Well, you don't know much for a thirteen-year-old, do you?' She was about to launch into a description of George's romantic attractions when they turned the corner and saw a group of lads on the pavement.

Bernie barely noticed the rest of the group. Her eyes were riveted on the tall figure in the middle, lounging against a lamp post. Dressed in black jeans, red shirt and black leather jacket, with an Elvis quiff to match, he clearly dominated the other boys who fell back as he moved forward to block the path.

'Well, who's this?' he drawled, then wolf-whistled softly and reached out a hand to detain Bernie. She tried to dodge out of his way but the other boys had flanked him on both sides, watching to see what would happen next.

The tall boy's eyes raked over her. She felt as if he was stripping all her clothes off just with his gaze.

'Well?' he demanded.

'She's Bernie,' Annabel said nervously. 'She's just moved in our block.'

The boy's face darkened. 'One of the ragman's kids?' he said, dropping Bernie's wrist and making exaggerated gestures of brushing dirt from his hands. 'Ugh!' He turned to someone in the crowd and called, 'Farrier, you shouldn't let your sister hang round with totters. She might catch something.'

Bernie reddened but before she could answer back she saw Peter emerge from the rest of the boys.

'Leave them alone Jacko,' he said quietly and Bernie saw the other boy's fists bunch. Peter stood his ground. 'Come on girls, I'll walk you home,' he said, taking Annabel's arm.

There was a tense moment then Jacko shifted, allowing them to pass. As they moved away, he called after them, 'Fancy yourself, Farrier? Better get some flea spray in.' There was a guffaw of laughter from the others.

'Take no notice,' Peter said and they walked in silence to the end of the road.

'Why did he say that?' she asked, once they'd turned the corner.

'He can say what he likes,' Annabel sucked the last dregs of her sherbet fountain, now the danger was over. 'He's cock of the estate,'

'He's got a dirty mouth like his mother,' Peter said. 'Rose Hanson thinks she's better than everyone else round here.'

Surely there were two sides to Mrs Hanson, Bernie thought, coming round pretending to be their friend and calling them names when she went back to her own family.

'Is he in your school?' she asked Annabel. She couldn't bear it if he was already spreading lies about her before she even started school.

'No, he's left, didn't pass any exams. Shows you how bright he is,' Peter said. 'He works in the butcher's in Kirkby precinct, comes home stinking of blood and meat.'

Bernie giggled. They were in their street now and she felt safe with Peter.

'Don't worry,' he told her as they entered their block. 'He won't bother you any more, I'll make sure of that.'

The way he looked at her made her stomach flutter as she ran up the stairs, but the feeling disappeared when she reminded herself that she would see George on Saturday.

She wanted to tell her mam what had happened but when she got in, Mrs Hanson was sitting at the kitchen table, all smiles, having a cup of tea with Maureen. Polly was twirling round wearing a neat grey pleated skirt and blazer.

'It fits a treat,' Maureen's face was flushed with pleasure. 'Oh Rose, I can't thank you enough.'

'Don't mention it,' Rose replied. 'Always happy to help a neighbour. It's my niece's old uniform, she's gone up to the secondary now and there's no one to pass it on to.'

Bernie was silent. How could she tell her mam about Jacko with his mother sitting there? She felt confused; how could Rose be so helpful and friendly yet at the same time be saying such hurtful things about them to her family.

Lying in her bed, she longed for George's arms around her, his warm fingers touching her neck, her shoulders, but she kept seeing Jacko Hanson's ugly sneer and hearing his horrid words. She began to cry softly into her pillow so as not to wake her sisters. If only they could go back to Toxteth where everyone was friendly.

She was still awake when her da came in, his voice echoing round the flat, rough with drink. Why couldn't he get an ordinary job, work in Ford's or somewhere nice, then no one would be able to look down on them?

Thankfully it was raining on Saturday morning so Bernie's mam wasn't standing at Greaty market. Once Marie had left for work, Bernie raided her makeup, picking the lock on the old dressing-table drawer with a hairgrip.

'She'll batter you if she catches you,' Polly observed as Bernie dithered between Hot Ice Pink and Scarlet Fever lipstick.

'Well, she won't, will she?' Bernie plumped for Scarlet Fever and sat back to admire the effect. She wondered if George would like it and she got that fluttery feeling in her stomach again. She gave herself a generous dab of Marie's *Black Rose* perfume before backcombing her hair and cementing it firmly in place with Marie's hair lacquer.

She left home with a two-shilling piece from her mam in her pocket – just enough to pay her bus fares and maybe a coffee in town. She planned to window shop at the big stores and the little fashion boutiques along Church Street and Bold Street before going to meet George. Marie had taken their only umbrella so she contented herself with tying a rainhood over her hairdo.

Town was already busy when she got off the 19a bus in Church Street. Despite the rain, people bustled along the street and as she lingered outside C&A's shopfront, admiring the models in the windows, the smell of fresh coffee wafted down from Cooper's Food Hall at the bottom of Lord Street, making her mouth water.

She wandered through the treasure trove of C&A, stopping in front of a plaster model wearing a lemon cotton smock trimmed with broderie anglaise and bell-bottom jeans. The smocks were lined up on a nearby rack. She could just try one on but she didn't dare. She would want it so badly and the assistant would expect her to buy it. She looked enviously at the girls and women flocking into the changing rooms with armfuls of clothes to try on. Most of them carried shopping bags bursting with things they'd already bought.

Bernie left the store, thinking that maybe her da would bring home some really nice cast-offs from the posh houses he trawled on his round. Occasionally there would be some trendy stuff amongst the old ladies' frocks and dead men's suits and the family were allowed to pick through it before the rest was weighed in as rags. Bernie imagined rich young girls throwing away once worn outfits, thinking nothing of going up Bold Street and spending five guineas on a new frock, fawned on by someone like her sister. But next year she would leave school and get a job, until she could pursue her singing career, then she too would be able to buy new clothes.

She bought her weekly copy of *Valentine* in W.H. Smiths then sat in Littlewoods' café under a pall of smoke, amid the crowd of families. The occasional wails of babies and toddlers punctuated her daydreams as she dawdled over the romances and fashion pages of the magazine.

George was always happy when he finished work but today he seemed moody. Bernie thought she'd imagined it however, when he hugged and kissed her as usual, but once settled in their favourite café by Lime Street station, he turned solemn.

Bernie chattered on about her window shopping but she could tell he was paying more attention to the radio behind the counter where the commentator was discussing the upcoming football matches. George was an Evertonian, blue through and through, and Bernie just had to live with that. She told him about the beautiful lemon dress, adding, 'Well, next year I'll be working too,' in case George might think she was hinting for him to buy it for her.

'What do you want to do?' George finished his beans on toast. He pushed his chair back and lit up a cigarette.

'I want to be a singer.' Bernie rested her chin on her hand and looked into the future.

George spluttered with laughter.

'But I can sing.' Bernie stared at him.

'Don't be daft. You want to get something steady.'

'I'm not being daft,' Bernie said. 'Steady? What do you mean? Like the post office?'

'Dad says the post office is a good career. I'll get promoted, once I get my exams.'

Bernie remembered how she'd bragged about this to Annabel but now it just sounded boring.

'You want something nice and clean, not factory work and not something where you're standing up all day like in a shop; something where you can get on a bit.'

'I will have to get a job first,' Bernie conceded, 'so's I can get some money for clothes and stuff. I'll have to look nice if I'm going to sing in public.'

George sighed, tapped his cigarette in the ashtray.

'I thought I might try for the pools,' Bernie said. 'Littlewoods isn't so far from our new house.'

'That's a great idea,' George's face lit up. 'Just the ticket for you – or you could take a secretarial course.'

Bernie smiled but she felt like a crushed butterfly.

'What's the matter?' George said. 'You look like a week's wet washing.'

'Oh, nothing,' Bernie said. 'Can we go to NEMs, listen to records?'

'I thought we'd go to the pictures,' George said, 'get out of the rain. *The Pink Panther's* on at the Odeon.'

George was paying so Bernie didn't have much choice. Anyway she enjoyed the kissing and cuddling in the dark. She lost track of the film halfway through when George's hand strayed onto her breast over her shoulder. She opened her mouth to his kisses and her blood ran hot, flushing her with the desire to go further but it was dangerous territory. When she felt his other hand on her knee, a picture of her father's face, bloated with rage, flashed in her mind. That, together with the thought of having to confess to their priest, Father McKenna, turned her emotions stone cold. She pushed his hand away, heard him sigh, then he lit up another cigarette. They watched the rest of the film in silence, his arm draped casually over her shoulder. This she liked, it was a comfortable, snuggly feeling.

'This is no good, only seeing you now and then,' George said as they walked to the bus station.

'I know,' Bernie said, 'but we can talk on the phone and maybe you could come up and meet me?'

'Mmm,' George said absently.

'What about next Saturday?' Bernie said, even though she had no idea if her mam would let her go.

'Oh, I don't know,' George said, 'You best ring Aunty in the week. I'll leave you a message.'

'Okay,' Bernie agreed but she sensed coolness in his voice. Was it because she'd pushed him away? Was he going off her?

She was reassured when he pulled her close at the bus stop and his kiss was as firm and warm as ever. She let him open her coat and slip his hands inside, holding him tight as his hands brushed her breasts and slid under her sweater to tingle the bare skin of her back. She gasped at the cold and the shock of his skin on hers, then the bus bell jangled, the conductor grinning at her as she broke away and jumped on.

She waved from the window but George had already disappeared into the crowds on Paradise Street. She stared through the window unseeing, wondering if she should have let him go further?

Chapter Three

It was two weeks since the McCanns had moved into their new flat and Bernie was settling in to the routine of her new school but at half-past eleven on Thursday morning she was sent home as her throat was so sore she could barely speak. She felt herself alternately going hot and cold and dreaded a bout of the severe tonsillitis she'd had in the past.

Her mother was at her part-time job at the greengrocer's shop back where they used to live, so Bernie felt for the spare key that lived behind a loose brick in the coal hole. It wasn't there and this surprised her. She tried the back door handle which turned easily

'Mam, are you there?' She paused then her heart quickened as a hasty rattling and rustling came from her own bedroom. Should she face the intruder, or turn and run?

The door opened and Marie came out, quickly closing it behind her.

'Why aren't you at work?' Bernie cried.

'Why aren't you at school?' Marie spat.

Bernie stared. Marie's face was beetroot red and her hair was all over the place. She was wearing her dressing gown but the buttons were done up all wrong and Marie was always so fastidious.

'I got sent home,' Bernie croaked, 'I can't swallow. I need to go to bed.' She moved towards the door but Marie blocked her way.

'You can't come in,' she blustered, 'I – I've been sick. You'll have to go and lie on the couch.'

'I don't want to. I want me own bed. Let me in Marie. You don't look sick to me.'

She lunged under Marie's arm and the door flew open to reveal Jimmy in a pair of Y fronts, frantically tugging on his jeans.

Bernie looked at his smooth muscular chest, at the rumpled bed where Polly and Teresa slept and at the self-satisfied grin on Jimmy's face, then turned accusing eyes on her sister.

Marie pulled her into the room, and pushed her against the wall, grabbing her neck and squeezing it hard so that Bernie began to choke.

'Don't you say a word to our mam or you will have a sore throat.' She let go and Bernie fell on her bunk, coughing.

Jimmy reached for his shirt. 'She's not going to say anything, are you Bernie?' He smiled at her but his eyes were full of menace. Marie turned away and began straightening their sisters' bed.

After they'd gone, Bernie lay on her bed trying to listen to her radio but her mind was full of the sight of Jimmy in his underpants. What if her mam had come home early, or worse still, her da? It didn't bear thinking about – and what if Marie got caught for a baby, like Janet Rogers, a girl at Bernie's old school?

She tossed and turned until her mam returned from work at three o'clock, then she got up, appearing silently in the kitchen.

'God's sake, Bernie, you frightened me to death.' Maureen took off her coat and untied her headscarf. She took a loaf and a box of eggs out of her shopping bag and only then noticed her daughter's flushed face and brilliant eyes. 'You look terrible. What's the matter?'

'Sore throat,' Bernie whispered. 'Sent home.'

'Open up, let me see.' Maureen took Bernie's face in her hands and peered down her throat. 'Hmm, you'd better get to bed. I'll pick the kids up and get some aspirins and yellow lemonade. If it's no better tomorrow you'll have to go to the doctor.'

Bernie got into her pyjamas and climbed into bed with her notebook and radio. She hoped she would be better the next day. She was having an audition for the school choir the next afternoon. Soon her mam and the kids arrived home and she could hear them clattering in the kitchen. Polly came in with a mug of hot lemonade. 'Mam says she's put an aspirin in it and I'm not to disturb you. I'll just get me clothes and get changed in the bathroom.'

The hot lemonade soothed Bernie's burning throat. She started writing down the words to, 'Something Tells Me I'm Into Something Good,' when it came on the radio but she dozed off before the song finished and only woke up because of a terrible din coming from the bathroom.

The noise was so bad she couldn't hear her radio so she got up and went to investigate. Matty and Anthony, stripped to their underpants, were stamping up and down in a bathful of soapsuds and dirty clothes, executing a Red Indian wardance. They were having such fun they never noticed Bernie come in and her attempt to shout them down came out as a strangled whisper which they didn't hear.

'OWWWW!' howled Matty as Bernie sank her nails into his bare shoulder. 'MAM!' he shouted, 'MAMMM!!' but Maureen was too busy frying chips to hear him.

Bernie shook him as hard as she could but his soapy skin made him slippery and he slid from her grasp and sat down in the water, his fall cushioned by the soaking clothes. 'We're doing the washing for Mam,' they cried in unison, backed up now against the taps to evade Bernie's clutches.

'I can see that,' Bernie hissed, 'Just shut up.' She went back to her room and

lay on her bed, jotting down words to her favourite songs as they were played, and thinking about George. She hadn't seen him for two weeks. Maybe he was going off her. Maybe she hadn't let him go far enough. She'd wanted to, her body had cried out for him to touch her but all she saw was her father and the figure of the priest. She'd had to confess that lustful feeling anyway and felt so dirty for it, sure the priest knew who she was and was condemning her behind the grille.

She felt under her pillow for her little purse and checked that there were enough coppers for her to phone George's aunty. She would do it the next day, when she felt better and maybe he could get a message to Aggie. Bernie was worried because she'd sent Aggie a letter over a week ago, spending precious pennies on the stamp but there'd been no reply. In three weeks it would be her birthday and she wondered what George would buy for her, hoping it might be the locket and chain she really wanted.

'Bernie?' her mam shouted, 'Someone to see you.' The bedroom door opened and Annabel peered round it. It was good to have some company and she enjoyed listening to the day's events at school but then Marie rushed in.

'What's she doing here?' She looked venomously at Annabel.

'She's come to see me. I'm sick, remember?'

'You will be if you don't keep shtum.' Marie ripped off her coat. She sat down at the dressing table, and taking the little key from her handbag, opened her makeup drawer and began repairing her face. 'Don't forget,' she pointed her mascara wand at Bernie in the mirror and drew a finger across her throat. The two girls watched in silence as she relocked the drawer and left the room.

'What was all that about?' Annabel asked.

'Can't tell you,' Bernie said. 'It's a secret. Do you like the Kinks?'

Bernie got up later to find her mam getting ready for a session of bingo. 'Now don't let Matty and Anthony stay up late,' she warned, checking her purse for her bingo money.

'I won't Mam,' Bernie had no intention of putting up with the twins a moment past their eight o'clock bedtime but for once she was glad of them snuggled up with her and Teresa on the couch. Polly was busy cutting out fashion pictures from Marie's old magazines in the kitchen and all was quiet, the twins exhausted from their exercise in the bath. Bernie noticed Teresa was sucking her thumb, a habit she had grown out of a couple of years ago but she was too tired to think about it and, lulled by the noise of the television and the warmth of her brothers' and sister's bodies, she dozed on and off.

She woke to find Teresa shaking against her and she opened her eyes to see tears gleaming in her sister's eyelashes.

'What's the matter?' she whispered, anxious not to wake the twins who had fallen asleep on the other end of the sofa.

'Nothing.' Teresa rubbed her eyes.

'Come on, tell me, is it school?'

Teresa nodded.

'Don't you like it? Or is that girl still bothering you?'

'It's all of them,' Teresa whispered, 'they all hate me.'

'Oh come on,' Bernie said. 'You must have some friends.' She realised she hadn't seen Teresa playing with anyone except Polly and the twins since they'd moved here and she couldn't remember seeing her leave the flat unless one of the family was with her.

'Don't worry, we'll sort something out,' she rocked her sister until they were both soothed into a half-slumber. Bernie wondered whether to tell her mam or to try and sort it out herself but her thoughts lost shape, as her mind edged towards sleep. She was only dimly aware of laughter from the telly when a new noise shook her awake and Marie and Jimmy came into the room.

'Out.' Marie jerked a thumb at the kids, Jimmy grinned and arranged himself in the armchair as the children got up and trooped to their bedrooms. Marie had disappeared into the girls' room and Bernie got up and followed Teresa. Marie was on her knees fishing under the bunks for the little locked suitcase where she kept her treasures. She emerged with a tiny tin of Nescafé and a small packet of Cadbury's chocolate shortbread biscuits.

Bernie started climbing into her bunk but Marie said ,'Don't go to bed yet,' her voice layered with unaccustomed sweetness. 'Come and have a cup of coffee with me and Jim.'

Bernie stared. Marie never, ever shared her precious coffee. She followed her sister to the kitchen but Marie turned a smile on her as she filled the kettle. 'Why don't you go and sit down. You're not well. Go and talk to Jimmy while I do this.'

Jimmy had moved to the couch so Bernie sat in her da's armchair. 'Hiya Bernie,' he drawled and she knew he was thinking of that morning and how her face must have looked when she caught them in the bedroom.

He snickered and she felt her face flame so she pretended to watch the TV news but she was conscious of an uncomfortable silence.

Marie came in with the coffees and the biscuits arranged on a plate The coffee was watery; the little tin had to last a long time but Bernie was too nervous to take more than a sip.

'Have a biscuit,' Marie urged. She sat down next to Jimmy on the couch and smiled up at him as he draped an arm over her shoulders.

'Throat's too sore,' Bernie muttered. Normally she would have savoured such a rare treat but all she could think about was why they wanted her here. Her stomach clenched and she wished her mam would come in and put an end to her discomfort.

'About this morning,' Marie said. Jimmy snickered again. His fingers played deliberately in the lacquered strands of Marie's hair and he watched Bernie watching him do it.

'I won't say nothing.' Bernie flushed.

'We're getting engaged anyway, see,' Marie said. 'At Christmas – it's to be a surprise – so no one's to know.' She gazed up at Jimmy but he took his arm from her shoulder and picked up his cup.

'Da'll kill you,' Bernie said.

Marie tossed her head. 'Why would he?' she said. 'I'll be seventeen in March.'

'And our mam'll go mad. Are you having a baby?'

Marie turned red. 'Of course not, you cheeky cow. Anyway, even if I was, so what? Me'n' Jim'll be married, won't we?' She looked at Jimmy but he got up and changed the TV channel to a boxing match, lingering in front of the screen with his back to them.

The back door banged and their mam came in, pulling off her coat and headscarf.

'Oh, hello Jim,' she said. 'You know what, someone one won a hundred pounds on the Link. I never have that kind of luck. If I did have a big win, you girls would get such a treat and we'd all have a real holiday to Blackpool or somewhere.' She shrugged her shoulders. 'Bernie, you'd best get to bed before your father comes in.' She headed for the kitchen to check on the steak in the oven. 'And you best make yourself scarce,' she smiled at Jimmy who rose lazily to his feet.

'Right on, Mrs M.' He put on his jacket. 'Night Bernie.' Bernie caught the meaningful look he gave her.

She went into the bedroom and crawled into her bunk. Marie came in to primp her hair in the mirror. 'Here,' she handed Bernie a half-used lipstick, 'you can have this, it'll suit you better than me.'

'Thanks,' Bernie whispered but Marie had already gone. Bernie got up again and peered out of the window to see Marie emerge onto the street with Jimmy. She watched as they clinched under the streetlight outside the block then ducked down as Marie turned to run back up the stairs. Back in bed, she tucked the lipstick under her pillow, reached for her purse and counted the money in it. Not enough for a trip to town to see George.

In the double bed, Teresa was crying softly, the noise masked by Polly's snores. Bernie sighed. Something would have to be done about the bullying.

'Happy birthday, kid,' Marie pressed a brown paper bag containing something heavy into Bernie's hand.

'Aw thanks,' Bernie flushed with pleasure. She couldn't remember Marie ever giving her a birthday present before. Marie ducked her head, checked her hair in the dressing table mirror.

Well, I got to go, late for work. See you.'

'See you.' Bernie fumbled to open the bag as Marie disappeared. She uncovered a jar of Lily of the Valley bath salts, almost full.

She tucked the gift under her pillow and joined the family at the breakfast table.

'Happy birthday Bernie,' the kids chorused. Even Teresa wore a smile although her wan face stood out in contrast to the twins' ruddy complexions.

'These are for you.' Polly pushed forward a little pile of hand-made cards.

Bernie sat down, smiling as she opened each one, done on sugar paper with wax crayoned flowers and messages. 'To our best sitter,' the twins' card read and Bernie hid a giggle at their apt mistake.

Teresa's card was carefully lettered, 'To Bernie, my sister and freind.' Bernie looked up to see her watching. Her big eyes were always sad.

'Thanks Treez,' Bernie said, patting her hand. She was pleased to see her face light up.

'We made them last night,' Polly said, pushing her own offering forward. Bernie opened the card and read the message, 'Best sister and much bester sister than our Marie.' She shut the card quickly so her mam wouldn't see and shot Polly a mischievous glance.

'This is for you too, I saved up for it.' Polly passed her a small tube wrapped in more sugar paper on which she had coloured a pattern of stripes. Inside was a packet of 'Lovehearts' sherbet sweets.

'Coo,' Matty said, 'Girls don't give them to girls. Your boyfriend should give you them.' The twins dug each other in the ribs and giggled.

'They're lovely,' Bernie said, knowing how little money Polly ever got. The mention of boyfriends made her wonder if George had remembered her birthday and her heart fluttered. 'Has the post been yet Mam?' she asked but Maureen shook her head.

'I suppose you're expecting your usual card from your nan?'

Bernie nodded although she hadn't even given her nan a thought.

'It'll be here when you get back from school. This is from me and your da.' She took an envelope from behind the bread bin.

Bernie opened it to find a proper birthday card with 15 emblazoned on the front in bright pink. 'Thanks Mam,' she said, disappointed that there was nothing inside and no sign of any present.

'Now you're to come straight home from school,' Maureen said. 'I've got a cheque from the Provi to spend and we're going to town to buy you a two-piece.'

'Oh Mam.' Bernie sat down. She'd never had a new suit of her very own. Dazed, she looked at the other kids, saw Teresa's lip start to quiver. 'But…' she said, thinking how Teresa relied on her to pick her up from school and avoid the bullies.

'Polly can bring her home,' said Maureen.

'But I want to play with me mates,' Polly protested.

'You can do that when you get home,' Maureen said. 'Now come on Bernie, get ready. You don't want to be getting detention for being late.'

Bernie rushed to get into her uniform, breakfast forgotten. Today was going to be the best birthday ever.

'Happy birthday. This is for you, me dad gave it me but I saved it for you.' Annabel handed Bernie a Mars bar as they walked to school.

'Ah thanks,' Bernie stowed it in her blazer pocket. 'I wasn't expecting anything you know.'

'Well, you are my best friend, aren't you?' Annabel said.

'Yes,' Bernie said thinking with a pang of Aggie. She watched as Annabel rummaged in her satchel.

'Oh and this is off our Peter.' She handed over a pink envelope. Inside was a card with a red rose on the front. 'Happy birthday to someone special,' the message read. Inside he'd just written, 'Happy birthday from Peter.' Bernie turned it over in her hands, looked questioningly at Annabel.

'He fancies you,' Annabel giggled.

'Get away,' Bernie flushed.

'He does, I can tell.'

Bernie stuffed the card in her bag. 'Come on, we're going to be late.'

She couldn't wait for school to be over but she was disappointed on arriving back at the flat to find that no card had come from George or Aggie. Still, all that was soon washed away in the excitement of getting ready for the trip into town. It was Marie's half day but she was sulking because she had to babysit the other kids and see to her da, John and Vinny Mack when they came in off the round.

Bernie got a gruff, 'Happy birthday,' off her da and she almost fainted with surprise when he gave her a ten-shilling note.

Together with the ten shillings her nan had sent in her birthday card, it made a whole pound and when John gave her another five bob, she began to feel rich. She felt happy till Vinny Mack tried to give her a birthday kiss while slipping her a half-crown.

'Come on Bernie,' her mam rescued her and hustled her out of the back door.

On the bus Maureen said, 'He's no better than he should be that Vinny Mack. Has he been bothering you?'

Bernie squirmed with embarrassment. 'Not really,' she muttered.

'They're all the same,' Maureen huffed. 'Dirty bugger and him old enough to be your granddad.'

'You won't tell me da, will you?' Bernie clutched at Maureen's coat sleeve.

'Jaysus no,' her mam said, 'there'd be a blood bath for sure. No, I'll have a quiet word meself. He won't bother you again. Let's forget about him anyway, we're out to enjoy ourselves.'

They spent a magical hour rooting through the clothes rails in T.J. Hughes's fashion department before Bernie settled on a wonderful tweedy Norfolk jacket and matching pencil skirt.

'But it's seven guineas,' she whispered.

'I promised you a treat, didn't I?' Maureen said, 'Go and try it on.'

37

It fitted perfectly and Bernie watched in a dream as the suit was carefully wrapped in tissue and handed over in a posh carrier bag. The remainder left on the Provident cheque was soon spent on wallpaper and paint for the much- needed decoration of the flat.

'You haven't bought yourself anything, Mam,' Bernie said as they enjoyed a cup of coffee and a cream horn in the Kardomah café.

'I don't need owt girl,' Maureen said. 'This is treat enough for me.' She licked cream off her fingers and her face brightened with a lovely smile. 'You enjoy yourself. You're only young once.'

Bernie hugged the carrier bag to her chest all the way home. She resolved that once she left school and went to work she would treat her mam as often as she could and when she really got famous, like Cilla Black or Dusty Springfield, she would buy her mam a nice bungalow and take her on holiday to France or Spain.

When they got home, Bernie put on her new outfit to show Annabel.

'Don't you get it messed up,' Maureen said. 'It's for best, not for playing around.'

'Playing around?' Bernie said indignantly. 'I'm fifteen now, not five our Mam.'

'Well, mind you just stay in the street,' Maureen said, turning to help Marie who was up to her elbows in soapsuds and banging the dishes fit to break them.

'How come she gets everything?' she cried but Bernie didn't hear her. She was already halfway to the bedroom, her mind on how she was going to look in the new suit. Polly and Teresa were pasting pictures in Polly's scrapbook. They watched open-mouthed as Bernie put on the suit and preened in front of the mirror.

'You look like a pop star,' Teresa said.

'I will be one, one day,' Bernie said.

'This will be you.' Polly held up a cut out of Lulu, making the paper legs jig in a dance. They all started laughing, then Marie came in like a thunderbolt.

'It doesn't suit you,' she said. 'Not your colour at all.'

Bernie looked in the mirror. It wasn't true. The soft oatmeal coloured fabric set off her dark hair and brown eyes perfectly.

'You're just a jealous cat,' Polly said, jumping back as Marie made a grab for her. Marie's fingers caught in her hair, now loose from its daytime plaits, and she pulled hard.

38

'And you're a cheeky little cow,' she yelled as Polly howled.

Maureen appeared at the door, wiping her hands on a tea towel. 'Stop that,' she shouted. 'Marie, why can't you just be happy for Bernie, you're spoiling her birthday.'

'Oh pardon me,' said Marie, flouncing to the door. '*I've* always had to pay for everything I've got.' She stalked out and locked herself in the bathroom.

'Go on, off you go, you look lovely,' Maureen said to Bernie, 'Back in by ten mind, you've got school tomorrow.'

'I won't be long, Mam,' Bernie said. She skipped down the stair to the Farriers' flat, Marie's jealousy already forgotten.

'Why look at you,' Kathleen Farrier exclaimed. 'What a grown up young lady.'

'Can Annabel come out for a bit, Mrs Farrier?'

'I don't see why not. She's finished her homework. Here, I've got something for you.' Mrs Farrier handed Bernie a small paper bag full of jelly babies. 'Happy birthday, Bernie.'

'Ah thanks Mrs Farrier.' Bernie didn't really like jelly babies but thankfully Annabel appeared and saved her from having to elaborate.

The two girls sat on the low brick wall outside the block of flats. Bernie told Annabel all about the birthday treat and Marie's outburst while Annabel ate the jelly babies. 'I wish I had an older sister,' she said.

'You can have her and welcome,' Bernie said.

'Not one like her,' Annabel said. 'Isn't she nice sometimes though?'

Bernie thought about the lipstick Marie had given her and the jar of bath salts but the gifts were outweighed by all the horrid things she did.

'She's always bad-tempered,' she said. She was about to tell Annabel how disappointed she was that she hadn't received a card from George or from Aggie but Peter suddenly came out and said, 'Annie, Mam says you have to go in.'

'See you in the morning Bernie,' Annabel jumped up and scurried off.

'Thanks for the birthday card,' Bernie said.

'Did you like it? I chose it special for you.' Peter sat down on the wall next to her. There was a fizz of something electric in the air and Bernie felt nervous She couldn't think what to say.

'It's lovely,' she offered at last.

'You look lovely,' Peter said.

Bernie felt heat rush into her face. The tips of her ears tingled. She stared furiously at her lap, aware that Peter was trying to catch her eye.

He shifted awkwardly, narrowing the gap between them. 'I – I wondered if you'd like to come to the pictures one night…' His words tailed away into silence.

Bernie sneaked a glance at him under her eyelashes. He was staring away from her down the street.

'I've already got a boyfriend,' she said.

'Oh.' He didn't move away from her but something changed in the way he held his body – the space between them was now a barrier. 'I'd better go in,' he said, getting up.

Bernie didn't move.

'We're still friends though?' he asked. She looked up to meet his gaze and nodded.

He went away, turning back at the lobby entrance to say, 'I do like you Bernie.'

She sat on in the dark for a few minutes after she heard his flat door slam then she went up the steps to her own home.

The kids were snuggled up on the sofa with their cocoa, watching Z-Cars while her mam was ironing the next day's school clothes on the dining table by the living room window.

Bernie changed into her pyjamas, carefully hanging the new suit in the wardrobe. She went to the kitchen to make tea for herself and her mother when a collective groan went up.

'Bernie have you got a bob for the telly?' her mam yelled. She came out to the kitchen rooting in her purse. 'I forgot to get some while we were out.' Bernie knew she only had her untouched birthday money. 'It's gone off right in the middle,' Maureen complained. 'I'll never get them to bed now.' Bernie could hear the children already whining and fidgeting; In a minute Matty and Anthony would start a fight. She went into the living room and they all looked at her hopefully like a row of little birds.

'Okay, I'll fix it.' She fetched a hairgrip from the bedroom and in less than a minute she'd picked the lock and opened the coin box on the back of the TV.

'Our Bernie's going to be a burglar when she leaves school,' Matty shouted.

Good humour was restored as Bernie removed a shilling from the box and slipped it through the coin slot in its lid. The programme miraculously returned and the kids settled down with an audible sigh.

'How much is in it?' Maureen asked.

Bernie counted. 'Eight bob.'

'Give us five,' her mam said. 'Tide us over till pay day.'

Bernie was immediately stung with guilt, thinking how much the tea and cakes at the Kardomah must have cost.

'You can have five bob out of my birthday money, Mam,' she said but her mother shook her head.

'That's your money Bernie. The TV man's not due till next week, I'll have it back by then and anyway we might run out of shillings again.'

Bernie handed her the money and relocked the box.

'Don't tell our Marie how to do that,' Polly said. 'There'll never be anything in it.'

'And don't give her any of your money,' Maureen said, accepting the cup of tea Bernie now brought her.

'Mam, I'm going to have an early night, I'm tired.'

'All right, sweetheart.' Maureen turned off the iron and sat down in Joe's armchair. Putting her feet up on the arm of the sofa, she sipped her tea and felt in her overall pocket for her Woodbines. 'Have you had a nice day?'

'It's been wonderful,' Bernie said, bending down to kiss her.

'Night Bernie,' the kids chorused.

She lay on her bunk, her tranny tuned to Radio Caroline, practising singing softly along to the records. She was due to have the missed choir audition the next day and she really hoped to get in. Even though the songs the choir had to sing were pretty boring, she knew it would be good training for her voice and would help her on her way to stardom. Somehow she needed to start singing somewhere where she would get noticed. She thought about how nice Marie and Jimmy had been to her recently now she was part of their secret. Maybe Jimmy would give her a chance at singing with his group but she didn't have the nerve to ask him. Perhaps she'd mention it to Marie first. After all, they owed her something for keeping quiet. She thought about Peter asking her out and her thoughts turned to George. Of course he wouldn't send her a card because he knew she hadn't told her family about it. He would be keeping her birthday present for when they next met. She was more upset about not hearing from Aggie but she forgot about her as she sang along to the radio and imagined a future filled with fame.

She was quite lost in a daydream of being spotted by Brian Epstein when Polly and Teresa came to bed. Their endless chatter and bickering irritated her so much that she got up and padded to the kitchen.

'Can't sleep with all that row they're making,' she said, fetching a cup of water. 'Wish I could have a room of my own.'

'I know love,' Maureen said. 'Maybe one day, you never know what's round the corner. It's better than where we were before though.'

'Yes,' Bernie said sadly.

'Come on what's up? Haven't you heard from Aggie?'

Bernie shook her head. For a moment she wanted to tell her mam about George but thought better of it.

'You know sometimes, friends drift apart when their lives change,' her mam said. She was ferreting in the kitchen cupboard, didn't see tears spring into Bernie's eyes.

'But we've always been best friends,' Bernie whined, wiping her eyes on her dressing gown sleeve.

'I know but…' Maureen hesitated. 'You know, it's a fresh start here and you've got Annabel, she's a lovely girl.'

'Peter asked me out to the pictures,' Bernie said.

'Oh did he now?' Maureen leaned back against the cooker 'Well, he seems a nice boy, and we know his family. You like him?'

'I s'pose,' Bernie said.

'I got no objections. It's only the pictures anyway; he's not asking to marry you.'

Bernie giggled.

'Get this down you.' Maureen ladled out a good helping of onion gravy from the casserole she'd taken from the oven and set the dish on the table with a slice of bread. 'Anyway, you could go and see Aggie if you wanted, you've got enough money now.'

Bernie picked up the spoon. Her face brightened. 'I could go on Saturday.'

'But we'll be at Greaty, unless it rains,' Maureen reminded her. 'Better go Sunday. If you like, I'll call at theirs on my way home from work, tell them you're coming.'

'Would you Mam? I'd love to see her.'

'I'll go tomorrow. Don't you worry. Now eat up birthday girl.' She looked at the kitchen clock. 'I don't know what time our John's going to land in. He's never home these days. I don't know where he gets to.'

'He goes back to Toccy,' Bernie said between delicious mouthfuls. 'To see his mates.'

'I just don't want him getting into trouble,' Maureen sighed. 'Young lads his age, who knows what they get up to?'

'Our John wouldn't do anything bad,' Bernie defended her brother, 'but Mam, something needs to be done about Teresa.'

'She's still getting bullied?'

'It's them Sullivans,' Bernie said angrily.

'But they don't go to her school, they're both in yours.'

'They pick up one of their neighbour's kids at the primary. And Katy and Morag have turned all the kids round here against us. I can't protect her when she's in school, can I? Our Polly's always fighting her corner, so are our Anthony and Matt for that matter. Can't you do something Mam?'

Maureen held her dog-end under the tap and threw it in the bin. 'Look, if I go up there and start telling the teachers off it'll only make things worse. The kids'll have it in for her worse than ever. There's only one way in this situation and that's to stand up for yourself.'

Bernie knew she was right but how could Teresa ever stand up to the Sullivans and their cronies? She was such a mouse.

'You'll just have to sort it out between yourselves,' Maureen went on.

The back door opened and John came in on a gust of cold wind. 'What's up with you two?' he said, then without waiting for an answer, 'Is there any of that onion gravy over Mam?'

'Sit down,' Maureen said laughing and the mother-daughter conversation was over.

Bernie was still awake long after her father had come home and the flat had settled to silence. There was too much to think about: her lovely birthday, the new suit hanging in the wardrobe, going to see Aggie and hopefully seeing George. Teresa – she would have to take a stand over Teresa. Her mam was right, she would have to learn to stand up for herself and she and Polly would have to teach her how. She felt under her pillow for her little purse, now fat with her treasured birthday money. She would leave a message for George with his aunty to meet her on Sunday at Aggie's.

She thought about Peter and whether she'd been silly to turn him down with George blowing so hot and cold. Sunday would be her chance to find out where she stood with George. She was nodding off when she heard Marie creep into the room.

'Hey, Bernie.' Marie began shaking her shoulder.

'What?' Bernie tried to roll away.

'Lend us half-a-crown till Friday.'

'No,' Bernie muttered. 'Mam says I'm not to.'

'Come on, you're loaded. You can't spend it all before Friday.'

Bernie remembered Marie refusing to lend her sixpence to phone George. 'Get lost,' he muttered and turned her back.

'Bitch,' Marie pinched her shoulder hard then climbed up to the top bunk, rocking and rattling it as much as she could. She was soon asleep and Bernie too slid towards sleep. Sometime in the middle of the night

she woke to use the lavatory. When she returned she took a half-crown from her purse and reached up to place it on
Marie's pillow.

Chapter Four

'What'd you say to our Peter last night?' Annabel asked on the way to school the next morning.

'Nothing. Why?' Bernie avoided looking her in the eye.

'He was real quiet, seemed a bit down. He spent all night in his room playing his guitar.'

'He plays the guitar?' Bernie's ears pricked up.

'He's dead keen on it,' Annabel said. 'He's looking to join a band.'

'Our Marie's boyfriend's in a band. It's called Strawberry Jam.'

'That's a daft name,' Annabel said.

'I know.'

'He's got a part time job in Hessy's,' Annabel went on. 'So he got a discount on the guitar and they're letting him pay it off weekly.'

'Oh,' Bernie said, 'I thought he was at sixth-form college?' She was impressed. Frank Hessy's shop was the place where all the local musicians hung out.

'It's just a Saturday job but he reckons when he's finished college they'll take him on, especially with him studying music. But working in the shop's just something to fall back on. He really wants to be a professional musician.'

'He asked me out to the pictures,' Bernie said slowly. Peter had suddenly shot up in her estimation.

'You said no, then?'

'Well, there's George, isn't there?' Bernie said, but in her mind Peter had acquired a glamour that now seemed sadly lacking in George.

'Wish someone would ask me out to the pictures,' Annabel said as they turned into the school gates.

At home time, Katy and Morag Sullivan were at the junior school entrance when Bernie and Annabel arrived to collect Teresa and Polly. As usual, the twins had already run off to play with their mates.

'What are they doing here?' Bernie hissed as she saw the Sullivan girls.

'They'll be picking up their neighbour's kid, Sandra Wilkinson, that one there with the red hair.' Annabel pointed.

Bernie saw a skinny ginger-haired girl coming out of the doorway just behind Polly and Teresa. Bernie waved and Teresa's face brightened but as she neared the gate the red-haired girl caught her up and gave a vicious tug at her ponytail. Polly rounded on her but as Teresa jerked her head back Katy Sullivan stuck her leg out and Teresa fell over it, flat on her face.

Morag laughed and Bernie's reaction was instinctive. She jumped on Morag's back and got an armlock round her throat. Polly let go of Sandra and grabbed Katy, swinging her round till she lost her balance. In a moment there was just a pile of fighting bodies, thrashing arms and legs.

A crowd of children gathered to watch as well as a few mothers who flapped about in distress.

'What's going on here?' a male voice bellowed and Mr Gardner, the top form class teacher ran up and dragged Bernie from the top of the scrapping heap.

'Look what she's done,' Morag howled, showing torn stockings and the collar almost ripped from her school shirt.

'They started it,' Bernie yelled as she struggled in Mr Gardner's grasp.

'I don't care,' Mr Gardner shouted, holding the two girls apart. 'Get up you,' he yelled at Polly. 'We don't tolerate this kind of behaviour on school property – or anywhere else for that matter. I'll be speaking to the Head about this and no doubt she'll want a word with your mothers.'

'Nothing to do with me,' Morag retorted, 'I don't go to this crummy school.'

'Oh, don't worry, we'll be having a word with St Anthony's as well. You..' he pointed at Bernie, 'get your sisters home.'

Bernie grabbed Polly and the weeping Teresa and set off home. Mr Gardner wisely kept Morag, Katy and Sandra back and as Bernie scurried away she saw Mrs Bellman, the headmistress crossing the playground towards the commotion with a face like thunder.

The next afternoon Bernie and Annabel waited a little way from the school gates but there was no sign of Katy or Morag. Polly and Teresa came running across the playground before any of the other kids came out.

'I got a letter,' Polly pulled a crumpled envelope out of her bag. 'It's for our Mam.'

'It'll be about the fight,' Bernie said gloomily.

'Can't we chuck it in the bin?'

'Don't think so,' Bernie said, 'they'll only send another.'

Indoors she changed out of her uniform and had started the hateful chore of peeling the potatoes when there was a rentman's knock at the door and Rose Hanson marched in without waiting for an answer.

'Oh there you are.' Arms wrapped around her capacious bosom, she stood by the back door. 'Where's your mam?'

'She's not back from work yet,' Bernie muttered.

'Well you're not getting….' Rose was nearly knocked off her feet as the door opened and Maureen bustled in.

'Oh, hullo Rose,' she squeezed past and dumped a string bag full of vegetables on the table. 'Mr Soames let me have some fruit and veg cheap, end of day. You can have a few oranges if you like.'

Rose seemed to inflate. 'As if I'd want anyone's leftovers,' she hissed. 'And don't pretend you don't know what I've come about.'

Maureen looked blank but her smile faded. She shrugged off her coat and picked up the kettle. 'Shall I make us a cup of tea?'

'No thank you,' Rose said, 'I'm not here for socialising.'

Bernie's gaze went to the envelope propped up on the teapot. 'It's about this,' she said, handing her mother the letter.

Rose launched her attack right away. 'Our Morag's got a black eye, and you should see our Katy's new blazer, the sleeve's ripped right out.'

Maureen looked up from reading the letter. 'Bernie!' Her eyes were accusing.

'It wasn't our fault Mam,' Bernie began.

'Brazen,' Rose said, 'absolutely brazen. Our Morag and Katy were only doing a neighbour a favour and they get terrorised at the school gates, not to mention all the other children.'

'Polly!' Maureen roared. Her forehead pleated in a frown and her eyes flashed as she skimmed through the letter.

'But Mam..' Bernie said.

'Quiet!' Maureen shouted and Rose gave a smirk.

'Heaven knows I've done my best for you and your family and this is how I'm repaid. I'm telling you Maureen, if you want to fit in round here, you need to control your kids.'

Maureen's eyes flashed but she bit back a retort as Polly came in, downcast but defiant.

'They started it,' Polly said before anyone else could speak.

'You see,' Rose shrugged.

Maureen turned to Bernie. 'What were you thinking of?'

'Like animals they were,' Rose interrupted. 'Frightened all the little kids. Mr Gardner had to pull them off.'

'But..' Bernie tried to get a word in.

47

'Our Morag and Katy were terrified. They're too scared now to go and get Sandra.'

'She hit Teresa,' Polly butted in.

'Don't lie,' Rose leaned over her. 'Sandra's the quietest girl in the street.'

'My kids don't lie,' Maureen said quietly, 'whatever they have or haven't done.'

'You're not going to let them get away with it?'

'I'll deal with this myself,' Maureen said, 'and you better do the same with your nieces. I've had enough of them bullying our Teresa.'

'I might have known,' Rose gasped, clasping her bosom as if wounded.

Maureen rolled up her cardigan sleeves. 'I think you'd better go, my husband will be home soon. Bernie, Polly, go to your room.'

'Well! Once a totter, always a totter,' Bernie heard Rose say as she and Polly left the kitchen. Teresa had cried herself to sleep so they lay on their beds straining their ears but could only make out a low mutter before the back door banged, then silence.

The two girls scrambled to the window to see Rose emerge from the flats and march away. The next minute their mother flew into the bedroom in a fury.

'What was you thinking of?' she shouted, swiping at Bernie's head with the wet tea-towel she had in her hand.

'Owww!' Bernie yelled, 'Mam, you said we had to stand up for ourselves.'

'Not like that, not where everyone can see in the school playground.' Maureen whipped the towel at Polly who cowered back on the bed. Teresa, now wide awake, sobbed behind her.

'Making a show of the whole family in front of all them teachers. And where was the twins? You was supposed to look after them.'

'They'd already gone off with their mates,' Bernie wailed but it was useless to protest once their mam's anger was up. The three girls clung together trying to avoid the towel until Maureen's temper was spent. At last she calmed down and took pity on them.

'You should be teaching her to look after herself,' she pointed at Teresa. 'Anyhow I don't know why you can't get on with those girls. We've got to live with Rose and the other neighbours.'

'It's all because of me da,' Bernie wanted to say but didn't dare.

Polly glared but Bernie sighed. 'I'll try, Mam,' she said although the thought of sucking up to the Sullivans turned her stomach.

'At least keep it away from school, just walk away.' Maureen got up and went back to the kitchen. Bernie wished it was that simple. If only they had never come to live here.

'In here a moment, please Bernadette,' Mrs Meredith called from the music room door.

Bernie turned leaden feet towards her. Her face still burned from the ticking off she'd got from the headmaster about the fight. Her heart sank. Whatever the music teacher wanted it wouldn't be good news.

'I can't believe what I've been hearing about you Bernadette.' Mrs Meredith closed her door once Bernie entered.

Bernie bit back a denial. 'Sorry,' she muttered.

'Well, what are we going to do with you? Such a promising singer as well.'

Bernie saw her hopes of getting into the school choir disappearing. She was too choked to speak.

'You passed the audition with flying colours.' Mrs Meredith picked up a violin and twiddled the tuners. 'The choir travels to perform at concerts all over Merseyside, you know that, don't you?'

Bernie nodded miserably.

'Our reputation depends on the girls' performance – and their good behaviour.'

Bernie hung her head, tears brimmed over and ran down her face, tickling her hot cheeks.

Mrs Meredith handed Bernie a tissue from a box on her desk. 'Against my better judgement, I'm going to give you the benefit of the doubt. I think you were provoked.'

Bernie's head swung up, her eyes filled with disbelief.

'But you must never ever let anything like that happen again, do you understand?'

Bernie nodded, smiling through her tears. The next magical words tossed her from despair to bliss in an instant.

'All right, off you go and be here for choir practice after school, next Tuesday.'

Bernie couldn't wait to tell her mam her news when she got home from work.

'Oh Bernie luv, that's wonderful.' Maureen sat down, eyes round with surprise. 'Just think – my girl in St Anthony's choir.'

Bernie doubled in pride.

'You're a good girl,' Maureen said, easing her shoes off. 'Best get those spuds in water. We're having mash tonight not chips.'

Deflated, Bernie pulled out their big saucepan and began washing the potatoes she'd just finished peeling.

Maureen sat back and lit a Woodbine. 'You might get on the radio, or even on the telly. That'd be one in the eye for them round here that think they're better than us.'

Bernie didn't tell her mam that she had far wider ambitions. No one made money from singing in a choir and St Anthony's was only the first stepping stone of her career – if all went as planned. Her daydream was interrupted as screams and shouts broke out from the living room where the twins were tormenting Polly and Teresa.

'SHURRUP,' Bernie yelled, so loudly that Maureen jumped.

'Don't shout like that,' she said, rising to sort out the squabble. 'You'll damage your vocal chords if you're not careful.'

Bernie grinned and got up to light the gas under the potatoes.

'There's a pack of sausage in my bag. Put them under the grill, there's a love. Oh, by the way, I've seen Aggie's mum and you're invited for tea on Sunday afternoon.'

On Saturday morning Aunty Joan took Polly, Teresa and the twins to Walton Hall park, leaving Maureen and Bernie free to man a stall on Great Homer Street market. Bernie couldn't wait to spend her birthday money and there would be fun at home that night as they planned to celebrate Hallowe'en early so that Sunday night would be left for getting ready for school. And on Sunday she was going to Aggie's for tea. It was going to be a fab weekend.

Great Homer Street sported a carnival atmosphere with people thronging the street as John turned their van into the market and peered round for a pitch.

Bernie helped her mam to set up their paste table and arrange the assortment of ornaments and tableware her da had sifted out of the round that week. John dumped the boxes out on the floor and drove off, his mind on bacon butties with Joe and Vinny Mack in their favourite caff on the dock road.

'Mam, can I go have a look round?' Bernie eyed the shoe stall further up the aisle where a clutch of women and girls were haggling with raucous cries like seagulls fighting over fish.

'No you can't,' Maureen snapped, still feverishly unpacking. 'I'm going round first. I got to find school things for the kids.'

Sulkily Bernie arranged the china, cutlery and pots and pans. By the time she got to have a look, all the bargains would be gone.

As soon as the stall was set up, Maureen disappeared, leaving her to deal with the customers who picked over the goods, quibbling over halfpennies. Normally Bernie took pleasure in selling, chatting to people and feeling the weight of coins growing in the pocket of the heavy apron she wore. However, today it seemed that her mother was never coming back. It was too bad of her to be so selfish.

Although it was bright, the promise of winter was near and Bernie's fingers and toes began to nip with cold. At last her mother returned triumphant with carrier bags stuffed with old school shirts and blouses.

'Can I go now?' Bernie said petulantly.

'Aye okay. Give me the pinny.'

Bernie stripped off the apron and Maureen smiled when she felt the weight of the money. 'Don't be all day,' she said, 'Our John will be back soon and he won't want to be kept waiting.'

The market's nearly ready to close, Bernie thought bitterly. Already she could see one or two stallholders packing things away. She headed for the shoe stall; at least there was still a huge heap of footwear on display.

Now she was beset by choice. Peep toes or sling backs? Stilettos were out and granny heels were in but Marie was still wearing stilettos and there was a beautiful red pair with pointed toes. She looked at them, thinking her mam would never let her wear them because her dad would go mad. She picked up a pair of brown granny shoes that would go great with her new suit but she kept the red shoes in her hand, finally deciding to buy them both. ' I'll hide the red ones and put them on when I get away from the flat.' She giggled to herself as she thought of her plan as she wandered on, fingering second-hand dresses, jumpers and bags.

The traders were packing up in earnest when she spotted the red boa hanging from an old clothing rail. It had a few bald spots and a dark stain on one end but it looked just like one she'd seen Twiggy wearing in a magazine photo and it matched the red shoes. No amount of haggling could get the price below five shillings so she paid up reluctantly but

51

once it was in the bag nestling next to the red shoes, joy and satisfaction filled her.

She imagined herself in her new finery but as she turned the smile froze on her face. At the end of the aisle she saw George walking away from her. Even though his back was turned, there was no mistaking him, she knew his figure so well – and he had his arm round the waist of a girl, her head hidden by a large grey velvet hat.

Bernie ran after them but they'd turned the corner and by the time she got there they'd disappeared into the crowd of people leaving the market.

Skeeter Davis, *The End of the World*. Bernie's pent up tears fell freely as the song played on her radio. It was as if the disc jockey played it especially for her and she just knew Skeeter had suffered the exact same heartbreak she was going through now.

'Something Tells me I'm Into Something Good,' came on next so she turned the radio off and wept into her pillow. Could she have been mistaken? she kept asking herself all afternoon, but in her heart she knew what she had seen.

'BERNIE?' her mam shouted and the ensuing racket told her that the rest of the kids were home. She hoped no one would notice how upset she was. Thankfully they were all too excited to bother about her. Even Teresa had some colour in her cheeks after the picnic they'd had in the park. Everyone was begging for the last of Joan's lemonade then the twins shot off out to play and the flat was instantly quieter. Bernie watched them go from the living room window then saw Jimmy's car pull up outside. He and Marie appeared to be arguing. That meant she would be in a bad mood when she came in.

Bernie went to the kitchen.

'Our Patsy's having a baby,' Polly announced.

'Shush, I told you not to tell till I'd told your mam,' Joan scolded but she was smiling. 'Isn't it wonderful? Two years they've been trying.'

Bernie couldn't imagine her cousin Patsy having a baby. Even though she'd been married more than two years she still seemed like a big kid.

'Oh love,' Maureen ran to hug her sister. Joan beamed and everyone was laughing and smiling when Marie came in.

'Our Patsy's having a baby,' Polly repeated.

'Isn't it wonderful?' Maureen looked at Marie.

52

Marie's mouth tightened. 'Good for her,' she said and marched straight to the bedroom.

'What's got into her?' Maureen shrugged. 'Take no notice of her, Joan.'

Bernie wondered what it would be like to have a baby but that made her think of George and misery descended again. She went back to her bedroom but stopped short on the threshold. Marie lay face down on her bunk, sobbing into her pillow. Bernie daredn't ask her what was wrong. The sound triggered her own pain. Every thought of George made her feel that her heart would crack. She lay down on her own bed and began to cry as quietly as she could. A few moments later Teresa came in. It didn't take much to make Teresa cry and she too began to weep.

'What's the matter?' Bernie sat up.

'Nothing,' Teresa sniffled.

'Come here,' Bernie opened her arms. 'Don't worry, we'll get school sorted out.' She hugged her sister and stifled her own tears.

'What are you two whingeing about?' Marie's voice came from the top bunk. 'Just shut up can't you?'

'What's wrong with you anyway?' Bernie said.

Marie stuck her head over the top bunk and Bernie was shocked. She'd never seen her big sister with her eyes so swollen with crying and her mascara clotted on her cheeks.

'Did you and Jimmy have a fight?'

'Mind your own business,' Marie rubbed her face with the sheet, leaving black smears all over it.

'I only…' Bernie began but Marie flung her pillow at her and shouted, 'Get out, both of you.'

Bernie left Teresa with Polly in the living room watching TV and went to help her mam and Aunty Joan sort the fruit for duck-apple. Over and over in her mind she saw George turning the corner with the mystery girl, saw how she fitted against him as he pulled her close.

'Straighten your face, for God's sake,' Maureen said when they'd finished wiping over the apples and picking out the bruised ones.

'What's up Bernie, Marie been picking on you?' Joan asked, putting on her coat to go home.

'Nothing,' Bernie muttered.

'Teenagers,' Maureen said and she and Joan laughed.

Bernie had been looking forward to duck apple and the toffee they always made but now she just wanted to hide away with her music. Why did Hallowe'en have to be on a Saturday this year, when her mam and da would be out. She would be left in charge of the fun when all she could think about was her own misery.

'Buck up,' Maureen said after Joan had left.

Bernie did her best to smile and not spoil things for her mam. Joe took her out every Saturday to Yates's Wine Lodge in Charlotte Street. She'd already got her rollers in and while Bernie made sandwiches for tea, she began vigorously brushing the fur coat Joe had brought in off the round for her.

Later, while her da was having a nap in his armchair and her mam was getting ready in the bathroom, Bernie tried on her new shoes. She thought that would cheer her up but even then she kept thinking about George.

She'd tried to phone his aunty to get him to meet her on Sunday but no one had answered. Now she would just have to go round to his house and confront him.

The red shoes pinched her toes but she saw how they toned the muscles of her calves and made her legs look longer. She wanted to show them off to Marie but Marie lay motionless in her bunk. Bernie was sure she was only pretending to be asleep.

'There's marge and sugar in the cupboard if you want to make toffee,' Maureen told Bernie. 'Don't let any of the younger ones near the stove.'

'I won't Mam,' Bernie watched her mother putting on her lipstick. She was so different with her hair curled, her makeup on and a pair of sparkly earrings dangling almost to her shoulders. Snuggled into the rich fur coat, she looked a proper lady.

'Come on Milady,' Joe, freshly washed and shaved, offered her his arm and off they went. Bernie watched as John drove them away and she wished she was old enough to go with them. She sighed as she laid a plastic curtain and set the washing up bowl full of water down for the apples. She went to ask Marie to help her but Marie turned over and pulled the blankets over her head.

Of course, everyone got soaked and the bowl of water got kicked over. It took forever to get it all cleaned up but they had such fun that Bernie forgot her troubles and found herself laughing. The toffee was a great success and would have all been gobbled up if Bernie hadn't saved small bits for Marie and John.

Exhausted after the day's antics, the kids were allowed to sit up to watch TV but Bernie sent them to bed before their mam and da came back.

She tucked Polly and Teresa up and took a bit of toffee in to Marie, leaving it on her pillow. It wasn't like Marie to sulk for so long but Bernie was too tired to think about it. She fell into a doze in front of the telly, only waking when her parents and John came in, flushed with drink and smelling of outdoors. She said goodnight, went into her room and undressed for bed. Marie looked like she still hadn't moved but the bit of toffee had gone.

Chapter Five

On Sunday Bernie could scarcely eat her dinner, even though it was always the best meal of the week. As soon as she'd forced it down she rushed to put on her new suit and the brown shoes she'd bought on the market. She spent ages brushing her hair so it would shine and trying to style it like Cilla Black's but she didn't dare put on any makeup in case her mam noticed. She packed her panstick and mascara into her handbag, watched by Marie who was lolling on Polly and Teresa's bed.

'Lend us some eyeshadow,' Bernie begged but with little hope. To her surprise Marie got up and rummaged in her dressing table drawer.

'You want green with that outfit,' she said. 'You got a feller haven't you?' She turned and handed Bernie a small eyeshadow palette.

'No,' Bernie blushed.

'Go on, I'm not daft.' Marie sat back on the bed, took a five packet of Park Drive out of her housecoat pocket and lit one up. She kneeled up and opened the window, sticking her head out to puff out the smoke. 'Well you want to be careful, that's all.'

'What do you mean?' Bernie said.

'Don't pretend you don't know.' Marie laughed and Bernie turned away thinking of the day she'd caught her in the bedroom with Jimmy. She applied the eyeshadow and checked her hair again in the mirror.

'Oh, Crikey, here's me da.' Marie pulled her head in, spluttering as she waved her hands about to dissipate the smoke. She stubbed her cig out on the window-ledge and stuffed the butt back in the packet.

Bernie waited until her da had gone into the living room. It would be just like him to make her stay home to take the younger kids to church, something they all hated with a vengeance.

Once she was sure he was safely in his armchair, she crept out to the kitchen where her mam was dishing up his dinner.

'Don't be late back,' her mam winked.

'Thanks Mam, I won't.' Out in the street, she breathed a sigh of relief in the fresh air.

'Come in, come in – oh it's good to see you Bernie luv.' Aggie's mam's face was wreathed in a smile. 'I seen your mam last week, well you know that, but how's your sisters and them cheeky little twins?'

'Oh, they're fine.' Bernie stepped in, feeling quite at home already.

'Aggie!' Mrs Coleraine shouted up the stairs. 'She'll be down in a sec,' she told Bernie. 'She's been so excited about you coming.'

Aggie came hurtling down the stairs. 'Where'd you get the suit – it's fab.' She looked on admiringly as Bernie laughed and gave a twirl.

'It was off me mam for my birthday.'

'You girls go upstairs and play records or something while I finish the tea. Your dad'll be back from the allotment soon. I'm sure you've got lots of catching up to do.'

Bernie followed Aggie upstairs. Their house was much nicer than the McCanns' flat. Aggie had a pretty room all to herself but then she was the only child in the family. She even had a portable record player that made Bernie green with envy. Aggie's uncle owned a garage and often gave her pocket money so she could always afford the latest records.

Bernie felt awkward at first. She sat on the bed while Aggie got out her new records: Sandie Shaw and Roy Orbison's 'Pretty Woman.'

'I got you a birthday present,' she handed Bernie a packet wrapped in pink tissue. Inside was a notebook with a shiny red hardboard cover. 'It's for your songs.'

'Aw thanks,' Bernie was touched. 'I'm in the school choir at St Anthony's,' she said.

'Well, you always could sing,' Aggie said and suddenly they were chatting away as if they'd never been apart.

'Wish I'd been there,' Aggie said hotly when Bernie recounted the insults from Jacko and the fight with the Sullivan sisters.

'I wish you were too,' Bernie said. 'I wish we'd never moved there. I've hardly seen George since we went there.'

Aggie didn't answer. She got up to change the record but her mam shouted them down for their tea.

Aggie's dad had taken off his wellies and his old gardening coat. He was spruced up for Sunday tea, hands washed, clean shirt and tie, so Bernie felt like a guest of honour and was treated as such. There was a proper salad with spring onions in a glass bowl and thick slices of corned beef to go with it. There were even tinned peaches and evaporated milk for afters. All through the meal, Aggie's mam and dad plied her with questions about her family, the new flat, the neighbours and the new school.

Bernie tried to make it sound like their new life was better than the old. She dwelt on her place in the school choir, seeing that Aggie's parents were impressed.

'You should do something like that, Ag,' Mr Coleraine sat back and drank his tea. 'You should be doing extra sports, but you're too lazy.'

Aggie pulled a sulky face. 'It's boring.'.

'But you're so good,' Bernie said, 'you were always the best runner in class.'

After tea the girls went back upstairs to try each other's makeup.

'Have you seen anything of George?' Bernie asked casually although her heart beat faster.

'Now and then,' Aggie said, putting on *Pretty Woman* yet again.

'It's just I've been trying to phone him.' Bernie didn't want to say how many times she'd rung his aunty, only to be fobbed off.

'I expect he's been really busy what with the training courses and all.' Aggie sat down on her dressing table stool, tapped her feet to the music. 'I love this record, isn't it cool?'

'Training courses?'

'Didn't you know? He's getting promoted at the Post Office but it means he has to go to night school and stuff.'

'Oh.' Bernie felt foolish that she didn't know about this.

'I've seen him once or twice. He was at the youth club the other week.'

'Oh.' Bernie thought of the fun she used to have at St Xavier's youth club and again she longed for her old life. 'I thought I might call round to his house before I get the bus back.'

Aggie was silent for a moment. The record ended and the scratch of the needle was the only sound. 'No point,' she said finally, 'he's not there. He's away on a weekend course in Manchester.'

Bernie stared at her. How could that be? She'd seen him only yesterday – unless -   she must have been mistaken after all.

Aggie jumped up and turned off the record player. 'Come on, I'll walk with you to the bus stop.' She reached into her wardrobe and pulled out her coat and a distinctive grey felt hat.

'You!' Bernie gasped.

'What?' Aggie primped her hair under the hat. She glanced at Bernie in the mirror.

'I saw you yesterday, at Greaty market,' Bernie stammered.

'Oh yeah, I was there. I didn't see you.' She didn't meet Bernie's gaze.

'You were with George.' Even now a voice in Bernie's head kept saying, 'It isn't true, it was someone with the same hat, please don't let it be her.'

'Oh, er, I did bump into George.' Aggie slid into her coat. 'Sorry, I got mixed up, it was last week he went to Manchester.'

'He had his arm round you.' Pain and rage ripped the words from her.

'Don't be like that, it didn't mean anything,' Aggie said. She put a hand on Bernie's arm.

'Don't touch me. How could you?' Bernie spat.

'Oh come on Bernie. You didn't really think you could keep him interested from the other side of town?' She turned back to the mirror, gave her hair a final flick and smiled at her reflection. 'I'm sorry but you'll soon find someone else.'

Bernie's fists balled in her jacket pockets. In another moment she would smash Aggie's head through the mirror. She turned and fled down the stairs. Mrs Coleraine came out of the kitchen to see what the noise was.

'Lord save us, where's the fire?' she said but Bernie was already out and running down the street as if the devil were after her.

At home, Marie was leaning over the rail of the back balcony, smoking.

'Me da's in,' she explained, keeping one eye on the back door. 'Mam's took the kids to church.'

Marie was usually out with Jimmy and Bernie wondered why she was home but her need to be alone was pressing.

'Keep dixie for me,' Marie said as Bernie made for the back door.

The flat was eerily quiet, except for the sound of her da's teeth chattering as he dozed in his chair. She tiptoed past the living room door and entered the sanctuary of her bedroom. Tears soaked into her pillow as she lay hoping that death would take her. Her boyfriend and her best friend – she didn't know which hurt most. Although she longed for her mother's comfort, she couldn't tell her anyway. She knew nothing about George and she'd be angry that Bernie had been courting without telling her.

She felt under the pillow for her radio and turned it on low. It wouldn't do to wake her da and there would be mrder if he caught her listening to pop music on a Sunday. Despite her misery, she couldn't help singing along under her breath to the catchier numbers but when *You've Lost That Lovin' Feeling* came on, she dissolved back into tears.

'Someone to see you,' Marie came into the room with a damp towel round her head, followed by Annabel. They both looked shocked as Bernie raised a red, swollen face.

'What's the matter?' Annabel gasped.

'Nothing,' Bernie shook her head.

'Bet her boyfriend's chucked her,' Marie said. She got her hairdryer and went out.

'Is it true?' Annabel sat down on the double bed and wrung her hands in sympathy. Bernie felt too ashamed to talk about it. There must be something wrong with her for George to treat her this way – and with her own best friend! And how could Aggie do such a thing, lie about it – and still pretend they were best friends?

Suddenly it all poured out. 'How could I be so stupid? I never had the faintest idea.'

'Well I wouldn't cry over them,' Annabel said hotly. 'They're just not worth it. You're well rid of the pair of them.'

Annabel's usually pale face had taken on a warm, red blush and her eyes glittered with anger. She took Bernie's hand and squeezed it.

'Get up and come down to mine; Mam's making potato cakes for supper.'

Bernie's despair lifted a little. The Beach Boys were playing *Surfing USA* on the radio. 'Okay,' she said, wiping her face.

The two girls sneaked out past the slumbering behemoth. Marie looked up from the mirror over the kitchen sink, where she was drying her hair.

'You going out with Jimmy?' Bernie asked.

'Mind your own business,' Marie snapped.

Bernie sighed, one thing was for sure, Marie never changed.

On the stairs they met Maureen with all the kids in tow. She was anxiously testing them on the service, knowing that Joe would quiz them on the colour of the priest's robes and what he had said.

'I'm just going to Annie's for a bit,' Bernie kept her head down.

'All right, but don't be late. Did you have a good time at Aggie's?'

'Yes,' Bernie mumbled. She looked up without thinking and Maureen's expression changed as she saw her reddened eyes.

'Come on,' Annabel pulled Bernie's arm. 'Bye, Mrs McCann.' They were in the Farriers' flat and closing the door behind them before Maureen could open her mouth. Once inside Bernie relaxed, thinking how lucky she was to have a friend like Annabel.

Chapter Six

Although it felt like the world would end, it didn't. On Tuesday the longed-for choir practice came around and offered Bernie distraction from her sorrow. Being in the choir was very different from singing along to her radio at home. The fact that there were nearly forty girls in the choir made her realise what a small part she would play but maybe she would be picked to sing a solo if she worked really hard.

This thought gave her enthusiasm for the rather dreary *Under the Greenwood Tree* which was the song being practised. It was harder than she had expected, she had to sing a part and she had to follow it on a music score. It was hard to concentrate but at the end of the session she realised she hadn't once thought of George or Aggie.

She knew she had made lots of mistakes. Her voice had been tense and she'd struggled to follow the printed music and the unfamiliar words. She hung her head as the other girls filed out but Mrs Meredith caught her back.

'Well done, Bernadette; that was very good for a first attempt. Take the music home and practise and I'll see you next week.'

Bernie floated home and spent an hour in her bedroom, singing her heart out while the twins and Polly mocked her with howls outside the door.

'Maybe you really will be famous one day,' Annabel said after listening to Bernie's account of the choir practice.

'No maybe about it,' Bernie said. The two girls were sitting on the wall outside the chippy, sharing a bag of scratchings that Bernie had bought from the remains of her birthday money.

'Oh-oh.' Annabel said as Jacko Hanson sauntered up the street arm-in-arm with a red-haired girl in tight blue jeans and a biker jacket.

'Dirty totter!' he yelled as he drew close, and spat on the ground at Bernie's feet. He muttered something to the girl who looked at Bernie and laughed, before they went into the chip shop.

'Let's go,' Annabel got up and brushed off her jeans.

'We've finished anyway.'

'Did you hear anything from George – or your friend?' Annabel asked as they walked home.

'No and I don't want to. Plenty more fish in the sea.' Bernie spoke in defiance of her heartbreak but she realised it was true. 'Anyway, you're my best friend now.' Annabel's face broke into a radiant smile and Bernie linked her arm.

They were only halfway back when they met Peter. 'Mam sent me to get you,' he told Annabel, 'it's getting late.'

Bernie stole glances at Peter as they walked along. He was really nice-looking. She thought about the night he'd asked her to the pictures and now she could kick herself for turning him down. Maybe if she told him she'd changed her mind? But no, he'd be bound to knock her back.

When they came into the block, Annabel shot into the flat with a hurried goodbye. Bernie stared after her in surprise and turned to Peter.

'What's up with her?'

Peter shrugged. 'Toilet, I 'spect.'

'Oh,' Bernie turned to climb the stairs but something held her back, something in the way he was looking at her. 'Well, ta-ra then,' she said uncertainly, setting her foot on the first step.

He reached out as if to touch her arm but pulled back. 'Ta-ra Bernie,' he said, turning away and disappearing into his own home.

Thursday was Bonfire Night and it would have to fall on Mam's bingo night. Bernie had been given strict instructions not to let the younger kids out and Maureen had provided a couple of packets of sparklers and a bag of treacle toffee.

These treats kept them occupied for less than half an hour and Bernie returned from the toilet to find Polly and the twins had disappeared and only Teresa remained in the living room, watching *Take Your Pick*.

Bernie was cross already because she had to stay in when Mrs Farrier had invited her to go along to the fireworks display at their church social club. Now she would be in trouble if Polly and the stupid twins didn't come back before she got back from bingo. It wasn't fair. She could hear explosions and see rockets going up. She was missing out on all the fun.

'We ought to go out and look for them,' she told Teresa.

'I don't want to, I'm scared,' Teresa whined and stuck her thumb in her mouth.

Bernie usually felt sorry for her but tonight she felt like giving her a good slap, she was such a scaredy cat. She thought about going out to look for the others, and leaving Teresa to watch telly by herself but as if she'd read her mind, Teresa whinged, 'You can't leave me here on my own. What if the house goes on fire? A rocket might smash through the window and burn me up. Mam'd kill you.'

Bernie sighed. 'Okay, I'll make some cocoa.'

They settled down to watch a soppy film about a married woman who met a man in a railway station and wanted to have an affair with him. Marriage – it seemed so mysterious, but it didn't seem to relate to her mam and dad. How had her mam fallen in love with her da when he was so bad-tempered? Bernie kept pondering this even as she was drawn into the way the woman in the film lifted her face to be kissed. She pushed the thought of George out of her mind and practised closing her eyes and lifting her face in the same way until she almost felt the whispery touch of tender lips on her own. She got so engrossed in the film that she didn't notice time passing or the fact that Teresa had fallen asleep, until the sound of the back door slamming shocked her back to reality.

'Mam!' she thought, jumping up in panic but it was Polly's voice she could hear, high and screechy, striking terror into her.

'Bernie! Come quick, it's our Anthony.'

The twins were on the landing, white-faced and silent. Anthony had his hands behind his back.

'He's all burned up!' Polly screamed.

Teresa started to scream because Polly was screaming and both the twins began to wail.

'Let me see,' Bernie demanded, pulling Anthony's arms.

The hand was black and red, like the hearts her mam roasted on Sundays. Bernie started back when she saw it. The twins saw the horror on her face and wailed louder.

'Stop it! Stop it!' Bernie shouted, trying to think what to do.

'God save us, what's going on?' Kathleen Farrier's voice floated up the stairs.

All the Farriers stood in the lobby staring up at them. Bernie had never been so pleased to see an adult.

'Our Anthony's burned his hand,' she cried, biting back a sob, 'and me mam's at the bingo.'

'Let me see.' Kathleen ran up the stairs.

Anthony, sobbing, held out the damaged hand.

'He'd better go to Casualty,' Kathleen said. 'Wait a minute.' She disappeared and came back a few minutes later with a pound note and a few pennies. 'Annabel, go to the phone box and ring for a taxi, here's the number.'

She pushed the note into Bernie's hand. 'You go with him, I'll stay here and mind the kids till your mam gets back.'

'Oh,' Bernie was flustered at the thought of going all that way in a taxi and having to explain at the hospital what had happened. She'd only been in hospital once before when her mam had the twins and she'd been really frightened by the nurses, the noises and the smells. 'Shouldn't we put some marge on it, or wrap it up or something?'

'I don't think we should,' Kathleen looked doubtful. 'You need someone to go with you really. Isn't your Marie in, or your John?'

'No,' Bernie said bitterly. Everything always landed on her shoulders.

'I'll go with you.' Peter had followed his mother up the stairs.

'Well, I don't know,' Kathleen said, 'It should be someone in the family.' Before she could protest further, the taxi came round the corner. They all clattered down the stairs.

'Come on big man, you'll be okay,' Peter ushered the snivelling Anthony into the taxi and Bernie got in on the other side.

The casualty department was crowded. After a long wait, Anthony's injury turned out not to be as bad as it looked.

'It's mostly soot,' the nurse said as she gently cleaned the wound. Anthony sat gritting his teeth as Peter had promised him a bag of chips if he was very brave.

They had to get the bus home and only just caught the chippy before it closed. Bernie felt awkward in the taxi with Peter but he'd been so nice with Anthony and by the time they got off the bus she felt quite relaxed. The night was soft and warm for November and the smell of their chips mingled with the smell of smoke from the last embers of local bonfires as they walked home in companiable silence.

They were nearly at their block when Peter said, 'Seen much of your boyfriend then?'

Acutely embarrassed Bernie stopped. 'That's all over,' she said, 'we're finished.'

'Oh.' Peter looked unsure of what to do or say.

'It's for the best,' Bernie said. 'What are you looking at?' she snapped at the goggle-eyed Anthony.

'Me da'd burst you if he knew you'd got a boyfriend,' Anthony said through a mouthful of chips.

'Well he isn't going to find out and you aren't going to say nuthin' or I'll burst you. Anyway, it's over so I haven't got a boyfriend any more see.'

She looked up at their windows and saw her mam peering down at them. 'Me mam's in,' she pulled at Anthony's good hand, 'now we're for it; it's all your fault.'

'Does she know you had a fella?' Anthony asked.

'Shut up, just you shut up,' Bernie began to drag him towards the block entrance but Peter caught her sleeve.

'Wait a minute. What about that date at the pictures then?' He laughed awkwardly as if the whole thing was a joke but Bernie saw a glint of anxiety in his eyes.

She whispered, 'I'd really like that.'

His face broke into a delighted smile. 'How about tomorrow night?'

'I'll ask me mam,' Bernie said and pulled Anthony towards the stairs.

'What the hell were you thinking of letting them out. I told you –' Maureen was up on her feet before they even got through the door.

Bernie quailed. 'I didn't Mam, they sneaked out when I wasn't looking.' She pushed Anthony in front of her.

'Let me see.' Maureen pulled Anthony forward by his uninjured arm but there was nothing to see except the huge bandage. 'Oh my God.' She sat down and took a deep drag on her cigarette.

'It's all right, Mam,' Bernie said, 'they said to take him to the doctor's after three days to get it re-dressed.'

'You get to bed NOW,' Maureen pushed Anthony. 'Wait till your da hears about this.'

Anthony began to snivel.

'Go on, Ant, I'll come and help you get in your 'jamas,' Bernie said. It was best to let her mam calm down.

'And you can get to bed as well,' Maureen went on. 'I don't know, I can't go out for five minutes without all hell lets loose.'

'But Mam –' Bernie wanted to ask about going to the pictures with Peter.

'Go on – get, before your father comes in.'

Bernie knew better than to argue when her mam said, 'your father' instead of 'your da.' She went into the bedroom with a heavy heart.

'What do you want? Get out!' Marie was sitting on Bernie's bunk with her best friend Angela. Bernie couldn't be sure in the dim light but she looked upset. Had Mam ticked her off too for not looking after the others? Teresa and Polly were just humps under their bedclothes. If they

66

weren't asleep they were giving a good imitation. 'Go on, clear off!' Marie hissed.

'Mam sent me to bed.' Bernie said.

'Oh, for Christ's sake.' Marie jumped up pulling Bernie's bedding away as she did so. 'Come on Ange.' The two girls left the room and Bernie could hear raised voices in the kitchen as she went to help Anthony get ready for bed.

'I'm sorry Bernie,' Anthony said, wiping teary eyes on a corner of the sheet.

'It's okay, kid,' Bernie said, 'It'll be all right tomorrow, you'll see.'

She cleaned her teeth and got into her own pyjamas, then climbed into bed. She was digging out her torch and notebook from under her pillow when her mam came in.

'I'm sorry Bernie,' Maureen sat down on the bed. 'It wasn't your fault, I was just scared and I lost me rag.'

'I know,' Bernie said, 'he's all right, really Mam. You won't really tell me da will you?'

'Well, he's going to notice a blinking great bandage isn't he? Don't worry, I'll think of something. Now you'd better get your beauty sleep.'

'Mam —' Bernie took a deep breath. 'Peter Farrier's asked me to go to the pictures tomorrow night.'

'Oh has he?' A sly smile crossed Maureen's face. 'And what did you say?'

'I said I'd ask you.' Bernie waited.

Maureen felt in her pocket for her cigarettes. 'It's okay with me, long as you get back in before your da gets home — that's if you want to go?'

Bernie nodded, relief almost making her feel weak.

'That's settled then.' Maureen leaned over and kissed her on the cheek before getting up. 'By the way, what's up with our Marie, she just nearly bit my head off?'

Bernie shrugged, 'I dunno.' She was too full of delightful thoughts about the forthcoming date to think about her obnoxious sister. ''Night Mam.'

As soon as Maureen had left the room, Polly poked her head out of the bedclothes. 'She thinks she's preggers,' she hissed.

'Polly!' Bernie was shocked She shone the torch full on Polly's face, making her rub her eyes.

'It's true,' Polly said, 'I heard her and Angie whispering about it.'

Chapter Seven

Sleep was hard that night. What Polly had said couldn't be true, could it? Bernie finally dozed off only to be trapped in a dream where Mam came in the bedroom and surprised Peter in his underpants while she cowered under the bedclothes.

Her first thought in the morning was whether she should ask Marie if it was true but Marie was so touchy lately, even more snappish than usual. Bernie swung her legs out of bed but Marie was not there and there were sounds of running water coming from the bathroom.

Bernie was fully dressed by the time Marie emerged and she was shocked to see how white-faced her sister looked, with deep shadows under her eyes. Her usually stylish hair hung limp over her face.

'What're you looking at?' Marie demanded.

'Nothing,' Bernie mumbled and turned to shake a snoring Teresa. Polly's bright button eyes gazed up at her from under the blankets. As usual she was listening to every word.

'Well don't,' Marie snarled. She grabbed her clothes from the back of a chair and retreated back into the bathroom.

'Now I'll never get in there,' Bernie sighed.

'What're you wearing tonight?' Annabel was clearly excited at the thought of her best friend going out with her brother.

'Oh,' Bernie said, 'probably my suit. I got those new red shoes but they don't really go with it and I haven't got anything that does.'

'You don't seem very keen,' Annabel said, 'what's up with you this morning?'

'Oh nothing, I didn't sleep very well.'

'Too busy thinking about our Peter?' Annabel giggled. 'You gonna let him kiss you?' She pursed her lips and made slurping noises.

'Stop it,' Bernie laughed in spite of herself but soon fell back into silence. They separated at the school entrance and went to their respective classes.

All day Bernie thought about her sister's predicament. She grew more miserable as the day wore on and even her favourite music lesson failed to raise her spirits.

Mrs Meredith held her back at the end of the period.

'Bernie, you've not been yourself today, is something the matter?'

'No Miss,' Bernie turned an innocent face on her teacher. 'I'm fine.'

'You don't look it.' Mrs Meredith's gaze searched her face. 'You haven't been paying attention; I noticed quite a few wrong notes. It's not what I expect from you.'

The teacher's kind tone made tears spring at the back of Bernie's eyes. 'Can I go now please Miss,' she said, 'I have to pick up our Teresa.'

'All right.' Mrs Meredith's voice took on a more formal note and she moved back to her desk. 'But you need to do better than this if you want to stay in the choir.'

Bernie ran down the corridor, her face burning with humiliation. If she was thrown out of the choir she would die, just die. It was all Marie's fault, well, she could stew in her own juice, as her mam was fond of saying.

There was no sign of Polly or Teresa outside the primary school gates. All of the kids and their mums had already gone. Bernie and Annabel stopped, uncertainly looking round the playground then Miss Stevenson, Teresa's teacher appeared at the school entrance.

'Bernadette? There's been a problem. I had to bring Teresa and Polly in to wait for you.'

'I'm sorry I'm late,' Bernie mumbled.

'I'm afraid Polly's been fighting with the Sullivan children again,' Miss Stevenson she ushered Bernie into the classroom where Polly and Teresa were waiting.

'Katy Sullivan hit our Teresa,' Polly said defiantly.

One look at Teresa's tear-stained face told Bernie the story. A bruise was already forming on her cheek.

'This has to stop,' Miss Stevenson told Bernie.

'But it's not their fault,' Bernie said, getting angry.

'I don't want to hear any more,' Miss Stevenson said. 'The whole situation might have been avoided if you'd turned up on time to collect your sisters.'

Bernie opened her mouth but the teacher cut her off.

'I shall have to report this to the Head. Your mother will have to come in so we can discuss what to do.'

'You always pick on us, everyone picks on us. What about them Sullivans?' Bernie shouted.

'Don't raise your voice to me like that,' Miss Stevenson said. 'I'm sure Mrs Bellman will want to speak to Mrs Sullivan as well. Now you'd better calm down and take your sisters home or I may have to speak to your headmaster about you too.'

Bernie pushed her way out, Polly and Teresa tagging along behind her. She was too enraged to speak.

Outside, Annabel trotted along beside her, giving her nervous glances. Teresa started to snivel as soon as they got outside the school gates.

'Oh shut up!' Bernie shouted, 'or I'll give you a slap on the other side of your face. You great baby, when are you going to learn to stand up for yourself?'

She marched off, leaving the rest of them goggling at her. Why oh why did everything have to go wrong for her, especially today, when she was supposed to be looking forward to her date?

Bernie hardly recognised herself when Marie had finished doing her hair and makeup. Thick black eyeliner, Cleopatra style, teamed with jade green eyeshadow gave her a look of mystery and Marie even had some special mascara that made Bernie's stubby eyelashes sweep almost to her cheeks.

With a lot of pinning, poking and pulling, Bernie's unruly curls were swept into a series of rolls on top of her head. She was almost afraid to move in case it all fell down but it looked fabulous.

For once, Marie seemed in a good mood, laughing and joking. She even offered to lend Bernie her newest dress but Mam said it was too short and made Bernie wear her suit. She felt so happy she pushed the trouble with Polly and Teresa to the back of her mind. She hadn't told her mam and had sworn Polly and Teresa to silence but she'd vowed that she would give Teresa some lessons in how to look after herself. There was a chance that Miss Stevenson had just been trying to frighten them and wouldn't report them. Marie was being so nice it seemed an omen of good fortune. All that about her being pregnant must have been a misunderstanding on Polly's part. She came out of the bedroom floating on air. Maureen looked a bit askance at the makeup and the hairdo but she didn't say anything.

'Come and look at our Bernie, she looks fab,' Polly shouted to the twins.

Matty and Anthony grinned and poked each other. 'Her boyfriend won't be able to kiss her with all that lippy on.' Matthew said.

'No he'll slide off, slide all the way out of the flicks and all down the street,' Anthony chortled.

'Shut up!' Bernie said, her face burning.

'You be good now,' her mam said, handing her a two-shilling piece. 'This is for just in case.'

'Just in case?'

'So you can get the bus home if you have to. Don't be spending it on sweets.'

There was a tap at the back door and Maureen opened it to admit Peter looking very smart in suit and overcoat.

'You look the gear,' he said admiringly and Bernie blushed, too tongue-tied to respond.

'Mind you're back before eleven,' Maureen said. She turned to Bernie. 'You know what your da's like.'

Bernie felt awkward, being alone with Peter on the bus and it was only when he asked about what had happened at school that she started to loosen up. Annabel had obviously been talking about it at home and before the bus passed the Broadway, Bernie had forgotten her nervousness and they were chatting away like old friends.

'I thought we'd go to see *Goldfinger*, it's on at the Futurist – that's if you'd like to?'

'Oh, I'd love it, everyone's been talking about it at school.' Bernie's eyes shone.

'That's settled then.' His knee brushed hers and she pulled away, embarrassed.

The bus was filling up and she rubbed steam from the window and watched the lighted streets as the bus made its way down towards Scotland Road and into town.

They got off at the Empire theatre and walked up Lime Street to the cinema. Bernie thought he might hold her hand but he didn't. It was a cold, dry night and she stared around at the busy pubs, cafés and restaurants. She hardly ever went to town at night, let alone to the evening pictures but she didn't want Peter to know that so she hid her excitement.

Once the film started she was lost in it. Bond was so handsome and debonair. She pictured herself at his side in an Aston Martin then glanced

71

over at Peter. He didn't look anything like Sean Connery but he was handsome too with his blond Beatle haircut.

When his hand touched hers just as Bond opened his eyes to see Pussy Galore for the first time, she didn't object. When a minute or two later, his arm crept over the back of her seat to rest on her shoulders, she snuggled a little closer, wondering if he was going to kiss her or even try to go further.

She was a bit disappointed when he didn't but relieved that she wasn't going to have to fight him off. It was comfortable leaning back against his arm and she was engrossed in watching the glamorous Honor Blackman. She wondered if her mam would let her get her hair cut in a bob like Honor's or if her curls could be persuaded to stay in one of those straight sharp-cut styles that were the latest fashion.

When they came out, blinking at the streetlights, Peter suggested going for a coffee before they went home.

'I can't,' she said. 'I've got to be home before me da gets in.' Now he'll think I'm a silly kid, she thought, he won't ask me out again. She pulled away from him and walked stiffly to the bus stop.

'It's okay,' he said, catching her hand. The bus arrived and they climbed upstairs. He was still holding her hand and Bernie blushed, seeing a middle-aged woman watching them from the seat opposite.

'Annabel says you're really into singing,' Peter said once they were settled.

'It's my dream,' Bernie turned to him. 'I keep practising.'

'I work in Hessy's on Saturdays,' Peter said, 'I'm learning the guitar.'

'Annabel told me,' Bernie said. 'I know all the latest songs, I learn them soon as they come out on the radio. Our Marie's boyfriend is in a group and I'm going to ask him if I can sing with them but I don't think he'll let me.'

'Me and a few of my mates are putting a group together,' Peter said. 'They sometimes come in the shop on a Saturday. Why don't you come down? I could introduce you, they might give you a chance to sing.'

'You really think so?' Bernie had stars in her eyes. She forgot about Bond and Pussy Galore. She floated off the bus and across the East Lancs Road, her hand firmly tucked in Peter's. When they reached the entrance to their block she glanced up at the lighted windows but all the curtains in her flat were drawn.

He was still holding her hand and he pulled her closer, folding her to him inside his overcoat. She could smell the same *Brut* aftershave her brother wore on his nights out. Pressed against the warmth of his body, she could feel his heart beating, or was it just her own?

His lips came down softly on hers; he was so much gentler than George had been but even as she was sinking into the kiss the noise of an engine startled her and opening her eyes, she saw her da's van turning the corner.

'Gotta go!' She tore herself out of Peter's arms and legged it up the stairs to the flat. She raced through the kitchen, startling her mother who was sitting smoking at the table, and into her bedroom, slamming the door just in time before hearing her father's heavy footsteps as he came in.

Bernie prayed for rain on Saturday and for once her prayers were answered. Maureen wasn't in the best of moods, deprived of her Saturday income and with all the kids under her feet.

'Can't you take Teresa and Polly with you?' she grumbled, fighting to restore some order at the breakfast table. 'Stop that!' She swatted Anthony and Matty, putting an end to their firing spoonfuls of soggy cornflakes at each other.

'Oh Mam, I can't. I promised to take Annabel and then we're meeting Peter at the music shop.'

Bernie had invited her friend along so she wouldn't have to go in the music shop alone.

'So you're going to see Peter again?'

'They're going to kisssss,' said Matty.

'Ooh, darling.' Anthony made cow eyes and they both puckered their lips and made horrible smacking noises.

Even Maureen laughed. Bernie made a grab at both boys. Luckily Annabel knocked at the back door before there were real fisticuffs and the two girls were soon crossing the East Lancs Road, brollies raised against the rain, just in time to catch the bus into town.

They got off in Church Street and lingered outside C&A's window, eyeing the latest fashions before heading off to the music shop in Stanley Street.

There was no sign of Peter on the counter, just a superior-looking boy in a smart suit. Neither Bernie nor Annabel felt courageous enough to ask for Peter so they hung about the record department until at last he appeared.

Bernie watched his face light up when he saw her and it triggered something warm inside her. Annabel nudged her and smothered a giggle.

73

'All right if I take a turn in strings for a bit? My mates are looking at guitars.' Peter winked at the other assistant.

'Well, don't be long,' the other said huffily. He cast a disparaging glance at Bernie and Annabel and went off to talk to two older girls who were flicking through the latest releases.

Bernie's footsteps slowed as she tagged along behind Peter. Was she about to make a complete idiot of herself? She wondered if she should escape before it was too late but Annabel and Peter had already stopped in front of a group of lads sitting round with guitars.

He put an arm round her waist and pulled her closer. 'Guys, this is Bernie. I thought we might give her a trial with us.'

They all stopped playing and looked her up and down.

'Ginger, Tommy, Phil…' Peter began introducing them but Bernie barely heard him. Her face burned when the red-haired boy said, 'We never planned for a girl singer did we?'

'She can sing good,' Peter said stubbornly and Bernie looked at him in wonder. He hadn't even heard her!

'Well you would say that, wouldn't you?' Ginger sneered and one of the others sniggered.

'It won't hurt to give her a try,' the third boy said. 'What can you sing, girl?'

Bernie stood frozen unable to speak.

'What about *House of the Rising Sun*?' The boy Tommy, or was it Phil?, strummed the opening bars.

Bernie opened her mouth but nothing came out. Peter squeezed her waist encouragingly.

'Go on.' Annabel poked her in the back.

Bernie tried again but only a couple of croaks came out. Ginger burst out laughing. Bernie balled her fists, willing herself not to cry in front of them all. She pulled away from Peter, glared at the laughing Ginger and anger boiled up inside her.

She concentrated hard on the song and suddenly she opened her mouth and the anger rolled out in the lyrics. She forgot them all, forgot everything until she got to the end and the guitar stopped.

Now it was their turn to stand frozen until someone in the doorway began applauding. It was the assistant from the record counter. Peter and Annabel started clapping too while Bernie blushed but the other band members just stared at her.

Tommy put down the guitar he'd accompanied her with. 'That was good.' He smiled at her then his face turned serious. 'We need to talk about this though, eh Pete?'

An older man in a dark suit bustled in. 'What's going on in here? Jenkins – Farrier, what are you doing in here? Get back to your own department and you boys, if you're not buying, put those instruments back, this is a shop not a music club.'

'I'll see you back home,' Peter whispered in her ear. 'It'll be all right, you'll see.'

Bernie followed Annabel out of the shop, still in a daze. Where had that voice come from? Even in the school choir she'd never sung like that. The choir was so formal, controlled, but in the shop she'd been so angry and scared, she'd just let rip.

She wanted to go into Littlewoods and settle herself with a coffee but she couldn't afford to pay for them both so the two girls walked to the Pier Head and sat on a bench at the bus terminus. The cold sea breeze blew the heat from Bernie's cheeks until at last she could think straight.

Annabel was full of admiration. 'That was so groovy,' she kept saying. 'Everyone was watching you. People came in from the record shop.'

'Honest?' Bernie hadn't noticed.

'They'll have to let you in the group.'

'Oh, I don't know,' Bernie stammered, thinking of Ginger's sneers. She didn't know if she could sing like that again anyway. But then, wasn't this her chance, what she'd always wanted? Suddenly she couldn't wait to get home to her radio and her songbook. She needed to practise and practise. She jumped up, pulling Annabel with her,

'Come on, let's get the bus.'

Bernie's head was still full of dreams as she said goodbye to Annabel and ran up the stairs to the flat. The pea soup her mam always made on Saturdays smelled extra good and for a moment she forgot her future stardom as her mouth watered.

The kids were already assembled round the kitchen table watching as Maureen cut thick slices from a piece of boiled bacon. Even Bernie watched spellbound as the meat fell away from the knife. Usually the pea soup was accompanied by a ham shank, which Bernie avoided eating as she didn't like the coarse texture of the meat.

'Get a knife and butter some bread, Bernie,' her mam instructed. The ham smelled delicious but she knew the meat sandwiches were reserved for her dad, Vinny Mack and John. To her surprise Maureen piled the sandwiches on a plate and set it on the table telling the kids to help themselves while she ladled hot soup into their bowls. No one needed

75

second bidding, grabbing at the butties in case Mam changed her mind and took them back.

'We'll make another lot for the men,' Maureen said. She avoided Bernie's questioning glance until they'd finished making the second lot of sandwiches and the kids had scattered.

Maureen sat down with a cup of tea and a Woodbine while Bernie bit into her own delicious sandwich and began spooning up her soup.

'Rose let me have a bit of meat cheap,' Maureen said at last.

'Oh.' Bernie mumbled. The thought of her mother talking to Rose Hanson filled her with dread. 'Are you friends again now then?'

'Well,' Maureen blew smoke at the ceiling. 'I kept seeing her in the bingo, it didn't seem right not to speak and then she asked me to call round so we could go together. Jacko works at a butcher's. He gets a staff discount. It's good of her isn't it? She's a good neighbour even if she's a bit bossy sometimes.'

Bernie nodded but thought her mam wouldn't be so keen on Rose once the latest trouble with Polly and the Sullivan girls came home to roost.

'What did you and Annabel do in town then?' Maureen put her feet up on the opposite chair. Bernie looked at her mam's worn slippers. She'd like to get her a new pair for Christmas but she knew she wouldn't have the money.

'We went to see Peter in the music shop. He's got a Saturday job there.' Bernie glowed again with the memory. 'I sang a song with one of his group. They're going to let me have a practice with them.'

Maureen tapped her cigarette on the ashtray on the table. 'Don't be filling your head with nonsense. You need to make sure your homework gets done and you've got your place in the school choir to think about.'

'I forgot to tell you, Mam.' Bernie sat up straight. 'Mrs Meredith's putting me in for the Christmas carol concert. We're going to sing at St Clare's in Sefton Park.'

'Oh Bernie luv, that'll make me so proud.'

'I'll work hard at it, Mam, really I will.' Bernie meant this even though her dreams went far beyond singing in a school choir. She knew that practice of any kind and learning to sing with others could only help her on her way.

Maureen lit another cigarette. 'That Peter seems a nice boy.'

'I do like him,' Bernie said.

'Just you be careful,' Maureen said.

Bernie's face blazed. She thought of Marie and bit her lip.

'Don't get too serious. You're only a bit of a kid yet but I know how it can feel.' Maureen's eyes took on a faraway look and Bernie wondered if she was thinking about when she first met Da.

'Annabel asked if I could go down to theirs tonight?' She was desperate to find out if Peter had arranged a practice date for her.

'You know you're babysitting – it's my one night out.'

'Can't Marie do it?' Bernie said without much hope.

'She's probably going out with Jimmy and she's been at work all day – be fair.'

Bernie sighed.

'Why don't you ask Annabel to come up and sit with you – and Peter if you like?'

'Thanks Mam,' Bernie grinned. 'I'll run down and ask her.'

'And while you're at it, nip to the shop and get me ten Woodies.' Maureen felt in her overall pocket for her purse.

Bernie and Annabel hurried to the paper shop. Arrangements had already been made for the evening and Bernie felt excited. Peter hadn't come home from work yet so she didn't know if he would be coming too but she was sure he would.

'Hey, look at this.' Annabel stopped short in the shop doorway. A notice on the shop door read, *Saturday girl wanted –must be 15, apply within.* 'Why don't you go for it?'

'Me mam wouldn't let me,' Bernie sighed. 'I have to help her on the market.'

'I bet she would if you gave her some of the money. After all you can't count on Greaty can you, I mean if it rains?'

'But I don't know anything about working in a shop.' She quailed at the thought of being quizzed by Mr Thompson, the shop owner.

'It's only like having a stall on the market,' Annabel said. 'Come on.'

The girls went into the shop which fortunately was empty. Bernie was relieved when Mrs Thompson bustled out of the stock room . She was much friendlier than her grumpy husband.

'What can I do for you girls?'

Bernie opened her mouth to ask for her mam's cigarettes but Annabel jumped in.

'She's come about the job.'

'Can't you speak for yourself?' Mrs Thompson looked Bernie up and down. 'You got any experience?'

'Er, I help me mam sometimes. She has a stall on Greaty market.'

'Hmm.' Mrs Thompson's expression softened. 'Are you local? I don't want someone as can't get here early in the morning.'

'Just round the corner,' Bernie said. Suddenly she wanted the job more than anything.

'I suppose we could give you a trial. It's seven-thirty till four, with an hour for dinner. You'd be sorting papers and tidying the shelves to start with but we'll train you up behind the counter. It's fifteen shillings. You got to look presentable and turn up on time.'

'Oh I will, I will,' Bernie gasped.

'All right then, come next Saturday, seven-thirty sharp.'

Bernie went out, Annabel following. She was halfway down the road before she remembered her mam's ciggies. Too embarrassed to go back she sent Annabel to get them while she stood on the corner wondering what her mam's reaction would be.

Luckily her mam was pre-occupied with getting ready for her Saturday night out and the thought of the extra money coming in went a long way to getting her approval.

'Nine bob for me and the rest is yours to keep,' she said through a mouthful of hairgrips as she took out her rollers.

Bernie had hoped for a bit more but it was still better than the couple of shillings she usually got and it was regular. Anyway she didn't begrudge her mam the money, she knew how short her da kept her.

'What about me da?' she asked.

'Don't worry about him,' Maureen said. 'Best if we say nowt for the time being, if he knows there's money coming in, he'll be cutting my housekeeping.'

She went off to the bedroom to put on her best dress and pearl necklace and brush her fur coat down, leaving Bernie to reflect that she would never marry a skinflint like her da who kept all his money to himself.

--

Peter wouldn't be like her da, she thought as he sat next to her on their ageing sofa that evening. Sometimes she wondered why her mam had married her da.

She was dying to know if Peter had fixed anything up with the band but she couldn't ask in front of all the kids and Annabel. Peter produced a pack of cards and suggested a game of Strip Jack Naked.

'We're not allowed to play cards,' Polly piped up, 'only Snap or Happy Families.'

'Why not?' Peter laughed.

'Me da goes mad. Our Ant brought a pack home from school and me da threw them in the fire.'

'I want to play,' shouted Anthony.

'Me too. Me too,' shouted Matty.

Peter looked enquiringly at Bernie who shrugged. He shuffled the pack. 'Well, he's not here now, is he?' he said.

'He'll kill us if he catches us,' Polly observed but she joined in wholeheartedly.

When at last the kids had gone to bed Bernie said, 'Maybe we could have a cup of coffee.'

'Annabel has to go home' Peter gave his sister a meaningful look.

'Why?' Annabel whinged, 'It's only nine o'clock.'

'Mam said you have to be in for nine.'

'No she never, I never heard her.'

'Well she told me so you better get going.'

Annabel looked at Bernie for support but Bernie pretended not to notice. 'I'll come down and see you in the morning,' she told her friend then disappeared into the bedroom where she felt under Marie's bed for the suitcase, swiftly picking the lock with a hairgrip and taking out the prized Nescafé tin.

'She'll have your guts for garters.' Polly peeped over the covers.

'She won't know unless you tell her and if you do, I'll have yours.' Bernie snapped.

Annabel had gone when she went into the kitchen to make the drinks. Her mam had left a plate of ham butties on the table covered with a bread wrapper. Bernie knew they were for when everyone came back from the wine lodge but surely no one would notice if a couple were missing? She arranged two on a plate and took them in to Peter before making the coffee. She only dared use a few grains in each cup as there wasn't much left and Marie was sure to notice if it was all gone. She proudly carried the cups into the living room, wishing they had some of those modern glass cups that were so fashionable.

'That was a nice bit of ham,' Peter said, chewing his last mouthful. He'd left the other sandwich on the plate for her.

'Mam got it cheap from Mrs Hanson. Jacko gets a discount from where he works.'

'He knocks it off,' Peter said. 'He's been doing it for months – sells it to everybody.'

Bernie's hand went to her mouth. 'Does his mam know?'

'Dunno.' Peter yawned. 'I 'spect so.'

Bernie looked at the butty wilting on its plate. She didn't feel like eating it now. What would her mam say? Should she tell her? What if she said nothing and her mam got caught? Receiving stolen goods, it was called. She'd heard her da talking about someone at the scrapyard who'd got done.

Peter put down his cup, casually draped his other arm over her shoulder. She picked up her own cup and sank back against him, feeling her stomach turn to water as he looked into her eyes. Suddenly the back door slammed and Marie came in. She took one look at the cups and exploded.

'You've been drinking me coffee.' She shook the tin, which Bernie had left on the kitchen table, in her sister's face.

'Maybe I'd better be going,' Peter was already edging towards the kitchen. 'Bernie, I'll see you tomorrow, I've set up a practice session for Monday night.'

There was a momentary lull as Peter escaped through the back door then Bernie was thrown back against the living room door as Marie grabbed her, grasping handfuls of her hair and banging her head against the door panel.

'OOOWWW!' Bernie howled. 'Gerroff! I'll buy you some more.'

'Don't you dare touch my things, I'll swing for you, you little bitch,' Marie spat.

'Don't take it out on me 'cos you've had a row with Jimmy,' Bernie shouted. It was the only reason she could think of why Marie would be home so early.

'You cow!' Marie went to grab her again but Bernie shoved her hard and she staggered back.

'What's up, he left you in the lurch?' Bernie taunted.

'What do you mean?' Marie's eyes narrowed.

'You're pregnant, aren't you? And I bet he doesn't want to know.'

Marie lunged forward and Bernie shrank back, frightened by the desperate anger on her sister's face.

Marie pinned her against the door, her hot breath hissing in Bernie's face. 'You say one word to anyone and you're dead.' She let go and dashed out of the room to lock herself in the bathroom.

Bernie sat down and stared at the dregs of coffee in the cups. So it was true. Mechanically she took out the cups, washed and dried them. She returned the wilting sandwich to the plate, hiding it under the fresher ones. Marie was already in her bunk when she went into their darkened bedroom. She put the coffee tin on the dressing table and got into bed. She felt sure that Polly and Teresa were awake and lay sleepless herself until long after the rest of the family had come in, listening to the faint sounds of misery that Marie could no longer hide.

Chapter Eight

Sounds of retching came from the bathroom as the family sat at the breakfast table.

'Ewww – vom,' Anthony said, raising his spoon to let milk and cornflakes slop back into his bowl.

Marie came in, pale under her makeup but with her hair perfectly arranged in a chignon.

'You want to lay off the ale,' Maureen brought the teapot to the table. 'And get some proper breakfast down you.' She pushed the cornflake packet across the table.

'No time,' Marie said. 'I'm going to be late.' She tied a headscarf over her hair and escaped before her mother could say anything else.

Polly had on her important face. Bernie kicked her on the ankle under the table.

'I don't know what's wrong with our Marie,' Maureen said, ignoring Polly's howl of pain. Has she broken up with Jim? I haven't seen him around lately.'

'Dunno,' Bernie said.

Maureen looked suspiciously at Bernie as if she might be guessing the source of Marie's sickness. Bernie needed to distract her.

'You know that ham you got from Mrs Hanson? Peter says it's knocked off.'

'Knocked off?' Maureen's eyebrows rose. 'What's given him that idea?'

'He says Jacko's been doing it for months, nicking from where he works.'

'Don't believe it.' Maureen stubbed out her cig. 'Rose wouldn't be party to that.'

'Maybe she doesn't know,' Bernie said, but Peter says that everyone knows about it. He sells it all round the estate.'

'Well!' Maureen lit up another cig. 'You lot get ready for school,' she shooed the kids from the table.

'What you going to do Mam?' Bernie began to wish she hadn't said anything. The business at school with the Sullivans so far had gone unmentioned. She didn't want it all raking up if her mam tackled Rose.

82

'You just mind your own business,' Maureen said. 'Go on now, get yourself ready.'

Bernie fetched her coat and checked that all the kids had their school bags. She went downstairs to call for Annabel. At least she'd managed to divert her mam's attention away from Marie, but for how long?

On the way to school Bernie tackled Teresa.

'It's time you stood up for yourself and stopped being such a sissy. Me and Polly are getting into trouble all because of you.'

Teresa looked up at her, lower lip trembling. Bernie hardened her heart.

'It's for your own good. If that red-haired one, what's her name?'

'Sandra,' Tersea mumbled.

'If she comes near you, you just trip her up or give her a good shove.'

'I can't,' Teresa wailed.

'You can and you're going to,' Bernie said grimly.

'It's not just her, everyone picks on me,'

'Well they won't once they see you won't stand for it. You only have to do it once. Stop whining and tell me what you're going to do.'

'What about Katy and Morag?' Teresa looked round fearfully.

 Bernie said. 'You leave them to me.'

Teresa looked a little relieved.

'So what are you going to do to Sandra?' Bernie persisted.

'Kick her up the arse,' Polly said, 'then punch her in the mouth, slam, bam,' she demonstrated.

'Stop that Pol,' Bernie saw Annabel giggling and tried to stifle her own grin. 'Come on Treez.'

'I'm gonna push her over,' the little girl puffed herself up.

'That's it,' Bernie said, although she doubted that Teresa would do it. She left her sisters at the school gate and carried on with Annabel wondering how she was going to deal with the Sullivan sisters.

The day dragged as Bernie's head filled with thoughts of the band practice Peter had arranged for that evening. Her attention wandered, triggering sharp remarks from her teachers. Mrs Meredith caught her in the corridor after lunch.

'Don't forget choir practice tomorrow, Bernadette. I'd like you to try out for a solo.'

Bernie jerked out of her reverie. She couldn't wait to get home and tell her mam. She floated out of school to collect Polly and Teresa. She'd completely forgotten the lesson of the morning until Teresa ran to her, eyes shining.

'I did it, I did it.'

'What?' Bernie took in her sister's unusually happy face.

'She pulled my hair so I pulled hers back and I pushed her so hard she fell over and hurt her knee.'

'And guess what?' Polly butted in. ' Everyone laughed at her, at that Sandra and she ran away and hid in the cloakroom.'

Teresa jumped up and down. 'No one saw, Miss was down the other end of the playground.'

'Good for you', Bernie said. 'Now you can make friends with her.'

'Make friends?' Teresa's eyes were like saucers.

'She'll want to be your friend now, just wait and see.'

When they got home and Bernie told her mam about the choir solo Maureen's eyes lit up. 'It makes all the slog in that rotten shop worth it,' she said. 'Just think, you could end up singing at the Philharmonic one day.'

Bernie had other aspirations. The choir was all right for practice but there was no fun in all that classical stuff – not to mention money. She wanted to meet pop stars, go to trendy clubs, have photographers chasing after her, famous designers making her clothes, have so much money she could buy anything she wanted. Her fingers clenched as if she was already reaching out to grab her rightful future.

'I might go to bingo tonight,' Maureen supped up her tea, pushed away her empty cup.

'But Mam, I'm singing with Peter's band – he's set it up special.'

'What did I tell you?' Maureen's eyes narrowed. 'You need to concentrate on one thing if you want to get on – and that's the choir.'

'It's only practice – and any singing is good, isn't it?'

'You want to nip this pop stuff in the bud before it starts. You've got choir practice tomorrow, you need to think about that, not jollying off with some silly kids that think they're the new Beatles.'

Bernie washed up in silence. Tears threatened but she held them back until she had finished, then went into the bedroom. Her sisters were out. Bernie sat on her bed, devastated. What was she going to do now?

She was still there when Marie came in.

'What's up with you?' she asked, taking her coat off and tugging the zip at the back of her work dress. 'Here, unzip me will you?'

Bernie got up and pulled the zip down. She watched Marie pull on an old skirt and sweater over her slip. There was no sign of any baby yet.

'Well?' Marie sat down at the dressing table and started to repair her makeup.

'I'm supposed to be singing with Peter's band tonight and Mam won't let me go,' Bernie mumbled. 'She wants to go to bingo so I have to stay in and watch the kids.'

'Going to be a little pop star are you?' Marie ran her lipstick round her mouth and smacked her lips together. 'Look, about last night, I'm sorry I shouted at you. I've been a bit on edge lately.'

'It's true then?' Bernie ventured.

Marie stopped in the middle of powdering her nose. 'I don't want anyone to know.'

'What about Mam?'

'Especially not Mam, or me da.'

'Does Jimmy know?'

'Of course.' Marie took out a mascara, spit on the brush and rubbed it hard on the block.

'What you going to do then?'

'Oh it'll be okay.' Marie flashed her a smile. 'We'll sort something out.' She began brushing her eyelashes, affecting an air of unconcern. 'You just keep quiet, okay?'

Bernie nodded. 'It's not me you want to tell, it's our Polly.'

'Don't worry, I'll see to her. Look, I'm not going out tonight, I'll mind the kids.'

'But Mam doesn't want me to go anyway.'

'Well, she won't know will she? You can sneak out after she's gone – as long as you're back by ten.'

After Maureen left to catch the bus to Broadway Bernie dashed into the bedroom to deck herself out. She put on her good jeans and an old smock top Marie had given her then fished out the pièce de resistance, the red boa she'd kept hidden at the back of the wardrobe. She wound it round her neck and admired herself in the mirror.

'Wow, where'd you get that?' Marie said.

'Greaty market; I've got red shoes to go with it, they're in the coal hole.'

85

Marie laughed. 'You're gonna knock 'em dead. Here let me do your makeup.'

Bernie couldn't believe Marie was being so nice to her. She thought about it while Marie painted her face. What would Mam and Da say when Marie announced she was going to marry Jimmy? Then she wondered if Marie really wanted to get married – if she even really loved Jimmy – but she didn't dare ask her.

'There,' Marie gave her hair a final pat, 'you look great.'

'Thanks Marie.' Bernie looked at herself in the mirror. She had to admit she looked fantastic, almost like Sandie Shaw. She rushed out and rescued her stilettos from the coal hole, put them on and clattered down to the Farriers' flat.

'Gosh, at last,' Peter said, 'thought you weren't coming.' He slipped on his suede jacket and picked up his guitar. 'Luckily we're at Ginger's tonight, it's only round the corner.'

The band practice was being held in a shed at the bottom of Ginger's garden. The other group members were already assembled

'You're late Farrier,' Ginger grumbled, plugging his guitar into a small amplifier that was in turn plugged into a makeshift socket board on the shed wall. 'That's what happens when you let women in.'

'Cool it man,' Tommy said. 'Give the girl a chance. She's got a good voice.'

'Let's do a few warm up numbers,' Peter said, 'let Bernie see how we work together, then maybe we can put her on.'

Ginger's mouth twisted in a sneer but he didn't say anything. After a few false starts and tune ups the band launched into a series of Beatles numbers. At first they sounded a bit ropey but soon they got into the swing of it and Bernie was impressed. Peter was on rhythm guitar and kept a steady beat. Ginger was on lead and was also the lead singer. Bernie had to admit he sounded pretty good. It seemed an awful long time that she waited for them to call on her to sing but while she wanted a turn, at the same time she dreaded making a fool of herself. The red feather boa tickled her neck and she felt sweat springing in her armpits when suddenly Tommy said,

'Okay Bernie, come on. What do you want to sing?'

Bernie's mind went blank.

'What about, *Something Tells me I'm Into Something Good*?' Peter asked. 'We've just learned that one.'

'I'll try,' Bernie said, thankful that she'd just learned the words.

It wasn't a great success. She stammered over the bits she had to change because the words were written for a male singer. There were a few moments' silence when the song came to an end.

'Not bad,' Phil the drummer said finally.

Bernie wanted to run out but Peter said, 'You choose something you like.'

She thought quickly, only one song came to mind. 'How about, *'I Got You Babe'*?'

She'd always loved that song, dreaming about the love between Sonny and Cher, both so hip.

'I'll sing with you,' Peter said.

Bernie took a deep breath as the first bars of the tune rolled out. She looked into Peter's eyes just the way Cher looked at Sonny and this time everything was fine.

. After that they sang, *'Something Tells Me I'm Into Something Good'* again but this time in male and female parts.

'That was cool,' Tommy said when they got to the end.

'Sing something on your own,' Peter whispered.

Bernie shivered, then she remembered singing in the music shop, how people had stopped what they were doing to watch her and she took courage. But what to sing? The first thing that came into her head was *'Always Something There to Remind Me,'*.

'What key do you want?' Ginger asked and she stood speechless. She knew the basics of music from her school lessons but she hadn't a clue what key the song should be.

'You start and we'll follow,' Peter said but she saw Ginger's mouth twist, saw how he raised his eyebrows at the others as if to say, 'What d'you expect? – thick as two short planks.'

She stumbled over the opening bars, nerves making her waver off key. She plodded on but all the time she was thinking, why did I choose this one? She didn't have the swift lightness of voice that characterised Sandie Shaw. Maybe she should have taken her shoes off!

At last it came to an end. She could see that they weren't happy but they didn't want to upset her. Ginger's mouth was a thin white line but he didn't say anything.

'That song's not right for you,' Tommy said. 'You need to sing something deeper; something with a strong beat and simple lyrics. What's your favourite?'

Bernie thought of Cilla – *'Anyone Who Had a Heart,'* how often had she sung that in her misery over George? 'I don't know the key,' she faltered, but I can sing it.'

'Go on,' Peter said, 'We'll see if we can follow.'

With the first notes her voice swelled as she remembered the pain of George's and Aggie's betrayal. She forgot the band as the music possessed her. When she stopped, she looked round at the group. Had they played along with her? She hadn't heard them.

'Let's have a cup of tea,' Ginger said. There was a vacuum flask of hot water and tea-making things on a bench in the corner. Peter produced a packet of ginger nuts and they all sat round munching and drinking so that Bernie began to feel quite at home until Peter said,

'Well guys, what do you think? Is Bernie in?'

They all looked down into their cups.

'We're a lads band,' Ginger said, 'like the Beatles. She can't do Beatles numbers, wouldn't look right.'

'Your voice isn't right for some of the dance numbers,' Tommy said. He looked kindly at her. 'If we're going to get bookings, we have to do dance stuff.'

Bernie bit her lip. This was the end of her dream, stunted before it had even begun. She sat up straighter, willing herself not to cry in front of them.

'But you can sing,' he went on. 'There's no doubt about that.' Peter smiled and squeezed Bernie's hand under the bench.

'She's a ballad singer,' the drummer said. 'She'd be good for the last half hour, the waltz and all that.'

'That's a great idea,' Tommy said. 'We could give her a ten or fifteen minute slot in the first half then bring her back at the end. How does that sound to you?' He looked at Bernie. 'You could do some of your powerful stuff in the first half then finish up with some romantic numbers, slow but not too heavy.'

Bernie tried not to show her delight. 'Sounds great.' She looked round anxiously. Would the others agree?

'I think it would be fab,' said the drummer, 'and we'd be different to all the other Beatles copies going around.'

Peter nodded enthusiastically. 'What about it Ginger?'

Bernie held her breath.

'I suppose we could give her a try,' Ginger muttered.

That was it. She was in.

'We've got a church social a week on Friday,' Tommy said. 'Do you think you could be ready by then? We can get in a couple of practices.'

Bernie nodded though she didn't really know what was expected of her or how she was going to get out for practices, let alone be out all Friday night.

'You'll need to decide what to sing. Three songs in the first half and three or four at the end but make sure the last lot are in waltz timing. Peter can help you pick some songs we already know. Come to practice on Wednesday at six and we'll see how it goes.'

The next day Bernie collected Polly and Teresa and took them with her to choir practice. Mrs Meredith had said it was okay providing they sat still and kept quiet. She wasn't a bad old stick, Bernie thought, she obviously knew the problems Teresa was having in the junior school. What had happened about that last fight? She must ask Polly if her teacher had said anything more about telling their mother.

The solo was to be 'Away in a Manger' and Bernie found it a lot easier than trying to sing with Peter's band. She thought she was doing really well but Mrs Meredith kept making her redo it. By the time the hour was up she was exhausted but the teacher patted her on the shoulder.

'Well done, I knew you were the right girl for this.'

Bernie beamed with pride. For the moment her mind was full of how she would sing all alone in St Clare's church and she quite forgot her pop star ambitions.

Halfway home she remembered the question she needed to ask Polly.

'What happened about that fight you had with Katy Sullivan? Nobody's said anything to me and no letter's come for Mam. Your teacher said Mam would have to come.'

'Mrs Stephenson's not my teacher any more.' Polly skipped round Bernie. 'She's sick. She went off the day after the fight.'

'What's wrong with her?' Bernie hoped it would be something that would keep her away for a long time then felt ashamed of such an uncharitable thought.

'Pat Mooney's cousin lives near her. She said that Mrs Stephenson was preggers but she lost the baby. I 'spect she's got the baby blues.'

'How do you know about baby blues?' Bernie scoffed. 'Anyway, you can't have baby blues if you haven't got no baby.'

'Well she didn't tell no one about the fight so we're in the clear.' Polly did a pirouette as they turned into their street. 'Come on, Treez, race you home, last one's a lemon.'

--

89

Not even the mound of potatoes waiting to be peeled could damp Bernie's happiness

Everything was looking rosy: the choir solo, singing with the band, not having to worry about school writing to her mam and the prospect of her new job on Saturday. She couldn't wait for Mam to come in and when she finally heard the back door open she turned with flushed cheeks, eager to share her news.

The smile died on her lips as she took in her mam's dishevelled appearance. Maureen pulled off her coat and scarf. 'Where's the kids?' she gasped.

'Polly and Teresa are in our room. What's the matter?'

'Quick, quick,' Maureen ran to the girls' bedroom. 'Get down on the floor, all of you.'

She looked so terrifying they all lay down without question. Teresa began to blubber.

'Shut up,' Maureen hissed. 'Where's the boys?'

'They're playing out.' Bernie felt like crying herself. She rubbed Teresa's back gently to comfort her. The oilcloth on the floor was hard and cold and already her bones were complaining.

'Jesus, Mary and Joseph, pray they don't come in.' Maureen raised her head to peep over the window ledge. 'The telly man's in the street. If he sees we're in we've had it.' She poked Teresa in the back. 'Stop that snivelling, he's got ears like a shithouse rat.'

Polly smothered a giggle. Bernie lay scarcely daring to breathe. Dust from the ragged mat by the bunks tickled her nose. She must not, must not sneeze.

The next minute there was a great rat-a-tat-tat at the front door. They all held their breaths. The knocks were repeated over and over and it seemed forever that they waited, listening to the flap of the letterbox as the collector peered through it. At last they heard his footsteps retreating and Bernie could let go the sneeze she'd been struggling to control.

Maureen picked up the card the telly man had pushed through the letterbox.

'Seven days' notice,' she read out. 'They're going to take the telly away.'

'Don't worry Mam,' Bernie said, 'I get paid on Saturday remember? I'll put the money back in.'

Chapter Nine

Marie had let Bernie set her alarm clock an hour early but Bernie was awake well before six-thirty on Saturday morning. She reset the alarm for Marie and sneaked out of bed, gathering her clothes as quietly as she could.

On the kitchen table she found a sixpence with a note from her mam. 'Emergency money.' Why would she need emergency money when she was so close to home? She smiled to herself, thinking of the hollow statue where her mam salted away any spare cash. Her mam had an obsession with emergency money that Bernie had never understood, nor did she know what really constituted an emergency. Was the money owed to the telly man not an emergency or had her mam already spent what savings she had on something more pressing?

Anyway she took the sixpence. There would be no pocket money now she would be earning and her mam would get the sixpence back that evening. Hearing her father's movements as he rose from sleeping in his armchair to trek to the lav, she abandoned the idea of breakfast and left the flat, arriving at the newsagent's some fifteen minutes before she was due to start.

'Good girl, nice and early,' Mrs Thompson looked up from sorting papers into two bags for the delivery boys. 'You can start by making us a pot of tea – the kitchen's out the back.' She looked at Bernie as if she could see her empty stomach. 'There's a tin of digestives too.'

Mr Thompson joined them at the table in the back room and they drank tea while Mrs Thompson explained the job to Bernie. It felt nice, almost homely and Bernie's fears melted away.

'We'll do things gradually,' Mrs Thompson said. 'First you learn to fill the shelves, then sort the deliveries and label them, then if all goes well we'll train you up in serving and working the till. It'll be good experience for you when you leave school. You'll be able to get a good job, maybe somewhere like Blackler's or Lewis's.'

Bernie agreed though she had her sights set far higher than a shopgirl in a department store. She thought of Marie coming home with aching feet five and a half days a week. Then she thought of the dance she was to sing at the following Friday. After the last band practice she felt confident of her ability. The band had liked the songs she'd chosen; even Ginger had seemed more friendly. She was going to practise singing with Peter that night while babysitting her brothers and sisters. Happiness spread through her and the time passed quickly as she filled the racks with the correct papers and magazines.

There weren't too many customers early in the morning as it was Saturday and those not working were probably having a lie in or a lazy breakfast. She longed to flick through the women's magazines but she didn't dare. She liked arranging the crisps and sweets better. Most of the sweets were in glass jars but some were in large bags, Barker & Dobson's Chocolate Dragees which Bernie had never tasted, and Everton Mints which John sometimes brought home and shared. There were a few boxes of chocolates on the top shelf also but the shelf was already full and some of the boxes were beginning to look faded. Hardly surprising Bernie thought, looking at the expensive price tickets. When she was famous she would buy a box like that every week, with a different coloured bow each time, Dairy Box one week, Milk Tray the next. She fingered the bright pink bow on the biggest box, lost in dreams of chocolate heaven.

'Don't maul the boxes,' Mr Thompson came up behind her. 'They get dirty, we can't sell 'em.'

Suitably abashed Bernie turned away to the counter display of penny Arrow bars, sherbet fountains and licorice whips. Her mouth watered over the Mars Bars, Turkish Delights and Toffee Cups. She loved the chocolatey smells and bright colours but best of all was the crisp display. Flavoured crisps were still a novelty since Golden Wonder had started up in competiton with Smith's ready salted variety and Bernie couldn't get enough of Cheese'n'Onion whenever she had money for a packet. She'd almost finished when Mrs Thompson came out from the back room.

'You've done a good job,' she nodded approvingly 'Time you had a break. There's tea on the stove, just fifteen minutes mind.'

Bernie spent her mam's sixpence on a packet of crisps and that week's copy of *Valentine*. She poured herself a cup of tea and settled down to read the fashion page, munching her crisps with delight.

The shop didn't close at dinnertime but Mrs Thompson told her she could go home for an hour if she liked.

'I don't think anyone's in,' Bernie said, 'and I haven't got a key.' This wasn't strictly true as the key was hidden behind a loose brick in the coal cupboard but she didn't want to go home in case her dad and Vinny Mack were there getting washed before their afternoon pub session.

Vinny Mack hadn't bothered her since her mam had asked her about him but she would be roped in to making butties and running errands.

'Well tell you what, you can nip to the chippy and fetch back some chips. Next week you'd better bring a butty if you're staying here for your dinner.'

Mrs Thompson remained behind the counter serving the constant trickle of customers while Bernie revelled in the peace of the back room. Chippy chips were a real treat and she still had her magazine to keep her occupied. Her reverie was interrupted when Mrs Thompson shouted from the shop, 'Bernie there's no Victors left here. See if there's any in the back.'

There were still a few copies of the boys' magazine in the store so she hurried out thinking it must be popular as she'd filled the stand earlier.

'Here you….' She stopped short seeing Jacko Hanson staring at her in disbelief.

'Well, what's she doing in here?' he drawled, taking the comic from her with his fingertips as if afraid of catching something.

'Bernie's our new Saturday girl. Do you know each other then?' Mrs Thompson said.

'You want to be more careful who you take on,' Jacko said. 'You can't trust rag totters, that's what me mam says.'

Bernie froze. Just when things were going so well. Now Mrs Thompson would be sure to turn her off.

Mrs Thompson squared up to Jacko. 'From what I see she's a nice girl and if all you can do is spread nasty gossip and name-calling then you're not welcome in here.'

'Suits me,' Jacko snarled. He threw a sixpence on the counter. 'Keep the change, you'll need it when me mam hears about this.'

He stomped out leaving Bernie and Mrs Thompson looking at each other.

'I'm sorry…' Bernie began.

'You've nothing to be sorry about,' Mrs Thompson said. She came round the counter and put an arm round Bernie. 'It doesn't matter to us what your dad does for a living. Did you think we didn't know? We know everything that goes on round here.'

'Oh.' Bernie didn't know what to say.

'We judge you on your own merits.'

'But – Mrs Hanson…'

'Don't you worry about her; she's not the big cheese round here she thinks she is. Come on, you can help me start packing up the Echo for delivery later.'

Bernie felt a flush of respect and admiration for Mrs Thompson. Her loyalty to her employer was sealed from that moment on.

It was a long day but it was all worth it when Mrs Thompson counted out her wages.

'Fifteen bob,' Mrs Thompson, plucked a ten-shilling note and two half-crowns from the till.

'Do you think I could have some of it in shillings?' Bernie stammered. 'It's for our telly.'

Mrs Thompson exchanged the note for ten separate shillings.

'How's that?'

'Ah thanks,' Bernie slid the coins into her coat pocket.

'You did really well today, have you enjoyed it?'

'Oh yes. It's been great.'

'Then you'll come back next week?'

'Oh yes,' Bernie stuttered.

'Well ta-ra then, we'll see you next Saturday. Don't forget, seven-thirty.'

'I won't,' Bernie darted out, anxious to show her riches to her mam.

At home she found the kitchen full of people, the air thick with cigarette smoke. Her mam and her Auntie Joan were drinking tea at the kitchen table while her cousin Patsy paced up and down by the back door. She was already wearing a maternity smock although there was no sign of her pregnancy yet..

'Here comes the working girl,' said Maureen. 'Look we got a cuppa all ready for you.'

Bernie bit her lip, thinking how Marie would look when her stomach started to swell up. Marie always looked so slim and stylish. How much longer would she be able to keep her secret hidden?

'What's up with your face?' Joan said. 'Didn't you like the job?'

'Oh yes, it's great. Mrs Thompson is really nice.' She pulled the money from her pocket. 'Here you are Mam.' She counted out five shillings and the two half-crowns.

'Why's it all in silver?' Maureen asked, scooping the money into her overall pocket.

'I thought it'd be better that way – to pay the telly back. There's an extra shilling 'cos I owe you sixpence anyway.'

'Jesus, yes, I forgot, the man's coming on Monday.' Maureen smiled. 'You're a good girl, Bernie.'

Bernie thought of all the money that jangled in her da's pockets. He could easily fill the telly several times over but then he never watched it anyway. She still had five shillings left and that was more than she usually got for pocket money.

She looked again at Patsy who was now smoking a ciggy outside on the balcony. Patsy was only three years older than herself. Would she too be pregnant by the time she was eighteen – maybe married to Peter with a home of her own to look after and her dreams of being a popstar smashed to smithereens?

But no, she was going to be famous, not for her the drudgery her mam had gone through – and Peter, well Peter would probably be famous too, they would be like Sonny and Cher full of love on stage for each other.

Maureen and Joan went into the living room to feed the telly leaving Bernie alone with Patsy.

'What's it like, expecting?' Bernie asked

'What do you mean?' Patsy stubbed her cig out in the ashtray on the table. 'It's like it is.'

'You must be excited?'

''Course I am and it's nice getting all the things for the baby.'

'Aren't you scared?'

'A bit.' Patsy stroked her stomach and Bernie saw there was indeed a slight swelling under the baggy smock. How strange it must be to feel something moving inside you. When Bernie was small and her mam had been expecting the twins, she remembered her letting her feel them moving.

'Me mam says it's nothing to be scared of, after all it's natural, isn't it?'

'When does it first start to show?'

'Depends.' Patsy sat down and put her feet up. 'I'm nearly four months and see – it's showing a bit..'

Bernie tried to calculate how far along Marie might be. She was so slender she would show up quicker and she still mostly wore tight skirts and sweaters rather than the smocks that were becoming fashionable.

'It's your bust first,' Patsy interrupted her thoughts. 'It gets bigger and your nips get big too.' She laughed and hefted her bosom.

'Was you pleased when you found out?

''Course we was. Francis was over the moon, and me mam.'

'But you didn't have to get married, did you?'

'No.' Patsy looked affronted. 'Why all the questions? You got something you're hiding?'

Bernie felt her face flush but before she could say anything, Marie came in.

'What are you two chunnering about?'

'Oh just baby talk,' Patsy lit another cigarette.

Marie gave Bernie a look then turned back to Patsy. 'When are you due?'

'April,' Patsy sighed. 'I'll be glad when it's all over.'

'What you hoping for?'

'I don't mind. Frankie wants a boy.'

'Names?' Marie sat down and poured herself a cup of tea.

'John for a boy, after Frankie's da. I like Helen for a girl, like Helen Shapiro.'

'The worst'll be getting your figure back.' Marie's gaze lingered on Bernie. 'Haven't you got something to do?' she said pointedly.

Bernie took the hint, got up and went to her room to change her clothes. Perhaps Marie was going to confide in Patsy and find out what to do. As she left the kitchen she heard her sister ask,

'When did you first start to show?'

'Do I look all right kid?' Maureen smacked her lips to smooth her bright orange lipstick and fluffed her hair. She pulled her fur coat closer round her shoulders.

'Smashing Mam,' Bernie said absently. She was thinking of the evening ahead with Peter. After the kids went to bed they would be alone. Marie and John had already gone out. Her stomach fluttered. Who knew what might happen?

'Don't let the twins stay up past nine and the girls in bed by ten – and mind you behave yourself with that Peter. Is Annabel coming too?'

'I think so,' Bernie said. She knew Annabel's mam had taken her to Wavertree to see her nan but if her mam knew that she mightn't let Peter come.

'And mind he's gone before we get back.' Maureen gave a final pat to her hair.

Joe appeared in the kitchen, handsome in a fresh white shirt, his hair gleaming with Brylcreem. 'Come on girl, how much longer you going to keep us waiting?'

'Ta-ra love,' Bernie was enveloped in the warm smell of face powder and hair lacquer, the soft fur of her mam's coat brushing her arms as she leaned forward for the peck on her cheek. Then they were gone, Vinny Mack pulling the van keys from his coat pocket and winking at her over his shoulder as he went out of the back door.

Peter must have been watching because in less than five minutes he was knocking at the back door. Bernie didn't even have time to dress herself up. He came in in a cloud of Old Spice and produced a Monopoly set from under his arm.

'I thought we could all have a game.'

For a moment he was so close to her then Polly rushed into the room and he moved away.

'Monopoly, oh gear. Sandra Roper at school got one for her birthday. Can I be the Scottie dog?'

They settled down to play after some initial squabbling. Bernie thought the twins were too small to understand the game but playing together they proved to be clever little property dealers and beat the rest of them into destitution.

'Cor, wish it was real,' Anthony said shuffling all their winnings.

'When I grow up I'm going to be rich as- as- as–' Polly's imagination failed her,

'As Marilyn Monroe,' Teresa said. She giggled.

'Rich as Elvis,' Matty joined in.

'Get in your jammies now,' Bernie got up, 'then toast and cocoa and to bed.'

'Aw can't we have another game?' Anthony pleaded.

'No, it takes too long. Mam said you're to be in bed by nine.'

'They want to snog,' Polly said. Bernie aimed a swipe at her and upset the Monopoly board all over the floor. She went into the kitchen and started making the toast and cocoa.

Peter came behind her, encircled her waist and nuzzled her neck. Quivers ran all over her body. She pushed him away and gave a strained laugh.

'Stop it, you'll make me burn the toast.'

After the kids had gone to bed, there was an awkward silence as she and Peter sat side by side on the sofa. Bernie pulled her songbook from the side of the sofa where she had hidden it earlier for just this situation.

'Shall we practise a bit?' she asked, 'I'm really nervous about this social next week.'

'Why, your singing's great?'

'Oh I dunno, I feel like the rest of the group don't like me, don't want me pushing in.'.

'You're not pushing in. You bring something different to the band, make it better.'

'They don't think that.'

'They're just used to the way we were before. They'll come round when they see you bring in more bookings.'

'You really think that'll happen?'

'I know it. How are you on harmonies?'

'Well, I'm singing solo in the choir at school but I've done second part.'

'Come on then, let's have a look what's in your book.'

They tried out a couple of Hollies' numbers and one or two Beach Boys but were interrupted by sounds of caterwauling coming from the lobby.

Bernie got up and opened the door to find all four kids miaowing loudly in between fits of giggling.

'Get back to bed now!' she shouted, shooing them away.

'We can't sleep for that racket you're making,' Polly shouted back.

Bernie stamped her foot. 'Go on now before I leather the lot of yous.' She followed the girls to the bedroom and checked her hair. Marie had left her new Tweed perfume out so she put a dab behind each ear.

She went back to the living room. 'It's hopeless,' she said, flopping back down on the couch. Peter put an arm round her shoulders and pulled her close. He smelled so nice and felt so warm. She closed her eyes for the kiss and the quivers she'd felt earlier turned to shivers of pleasure. Her mouth softened and opened and as their tongues met her arms snaked around his neck and pulled him close.

It seemed to go on forever, for a second she thought how much more it was than it had been with George, then she was completely lost until he dropped a hand to squeeze her breast. Immediately she thought of Marie and her passion died. She pulled away.

'What's the matter?' Peter's voice was groggy with desire.

'Nothing.' She got up and went into the kitchen. Suddenly she felt so unhappy. What was Marie going to do? Why did love have to be so full of danger? As if on cue, Marie walked in the back door.

Bernie took in her swollen eyes and streaked mascara. Tears had made runnels through her pancake and powder too. Marie made to push past but Bernie caught her arm

'Peter's in there,' she whispered.

Marie sat down at the table and kicked her shoes off. She rummaged in her bag for a hankie and dabbed at her eyes.

Bernie said, 'Go and wash your face and I'll get rid of him.' She went back to the living room. 'I'm sorry but you better go now,' she said to Peter.

He looked stricken. 'I didn't mean to upset you …' He made no move to get up.

'It's not that. It's our Marie, something's happened to her.'

'What do you mean?' Peter stood up looking anxious. 'Someone's hurt her?'

'Not like that, she's just upset. Anyway Mam and Dad will be back soon.'

'All right, as long as you're not mad at me.'

'No.' She moved into the circle of his arms and felt his body relax as she reached up to kiss him.

'Will I see you tomorrow?' he asked when they separated.

'I might be able to get out for a bit after tea,' Bernie said. 'I'll be on the wall outside if I can.'

'Okay.' He picked up the Monopoly set. 'I'll see you then.'

Marie didn't come out of the bathroom until she heard the back door slam. Bernie finished making a pot of tea for them both.

'I need a fag,' Marie sighed, 'come out on the balcony.'

The two girls leaned over the railing drinking their tea. Bernie didn't want to be the first to speak

'I went to see Jimmy.' Marie's voice was calm. 'He doesn't want to know.'

Bernie's mind reeled. What would happen to Marie if Jimmy wouldn't marry her? She knew girls got sent away somewhere but she had little idea what happened to them. One thing she knew for sure, her da would go berserk.

'What you going to do?' she gasped.

'I don't know.' Marie looked crossly at her.

'You'll have to tell Mam.' Mam was the only person who would know what to do.

'I can't.' Marie's face crumpled. She stubbed her cig out on the railing and threw it down into the tangled garden below. 'She'll have a fit and she'll tell Da.'

Bernie said nothing. It was true, telling Da would be the worst thing. She said the only other thing she could think of

'What about Father McKenna?'

Marie looked at her as if she'd gone mad. 'That mumbo jumbo merchant?' She gave a bitter laugh. 'I've never been inside that place since we got here. What's he going to do? Last thing I need is a lecture on sin. I feel bad enough already.'

In the silence that followed they heard a car door slam and voices at the front of the block.

'It's Mam and Da,' Marie scuttled indoors. 'I'm going to bed. Don't you say anything.'

Bernie stayed in the kitchen to stop her mother from going in the girls' bedroom. John came in with their parents. They'd met up at the wine lodge and come home together in a taxi as Vinny Mack had taken the van home.

'Everything okay?' Maureen pulled off her fur coat.

'Fine,' Bernie said.

'There's some butties in the pantry,' Maureen said. 'Pop the kettle on and come and sit with us.'

'I think I'll go to bed, Mam, I'm really tired.' Bernie was always wary of her da's drunken bonhomie and tonight she couldn't stop thinking about Marie. She undressed and got into bed but as she lay sleepless she was aware of muffled weeping from Marie in the bunk above. She thought of Patsy and how her baby would be loved and wanted, born into a happy home. What was going to become of Marie's little baby?

Chapter Ten

'Marie, can I borrow your black minidress on Friday?' Bernie timed her request for the best possible moment on Sunday evening. Her da had left for the pub and her mam had gone to visit Joan. The younger children for once were playing quietly together, completing a jigsaw in the twins' bedroom.

Marie was straightening her fringe with her prized curling tongs. Bernie watched, anxiously waiting for her answer.

'What for?' Marie laid the tongs down and turned to face her sister. 'Going on a date?'

She always seemed to have a sneer in her voice, Bernie thought. 'It's not that…' she stopped as she thought that she hadn't told anyone about the church social. Could she trust Marie?

'Well what then?' There was a smell of burning wood and Marie hastily switched off the tongs, lifting them to examine the fresh scar on the dressing table. 'Now look what you made me do.' After a few seconds, she expertly pulled a lock of hair through the tongs.

'I'm singing with Peter's band,' Bernie blurted. 'I got to have something nice to wear and it'll go with my red shoes.'

'Singing? OOwww!' Marie exclaimed as her hand jerked and the tongs made contact with her forehead.

No chance now, Bernie thought but Marie just rubbed her head and burst out laughing. 'Peter's in a band? What's it called?'

'Riverbeat.' Bernie wished she'd kept her mouth shut but she hadn't been able to think of another reason for wanting the dress.

'That's a stupid name.'

'Better than Strawberry Jam,' Bernie replied before she could stop herself.

Marie's face turned sulky. 'Why should I lend it you? You'll only ruin it.'

'I won't, honest Marie, please. It's my first singing date and I got to look good.'

'Are you nuts? What makes you think you can sing with a band?'

'The band want me to; I've been practising with them.'

'It's only 'cos that Peter fancies you. You want to watch him, you don't want to end up like me..' She tossed her head. 'You'll make a show of yourself and all of us, in front of everyone. Anyway Mam won't let you go.'

Bernie knew that was the biggest hurdle she had to get over. She was supposed to be in by ten on Friday nights and the social wouldn't finish till ten-thirty.

'You haven't told her have you?' Marie got out her makeup and started touching up her mascara.

Bernie shook her head. 'I'll think of something.' Why was everything she wanted such a struggle?

'Tell Mam you're going to the late pictures with me. She'll let you go then. I might even come along to see if you can sing after all.'

'Oh Marie.' Bernie hadn't dreamt Marie would help her like this. For a moment she was suspicious then reflected that Marie was only being nice to her so she would keep her secret.

'I'll do your hair and makeup.' Marie seemed quite excited.

'Really? That's fab. Oh thanks.' While Marie was in a good mood she ventured to ask

'When are you going to tell Mam – about – you know?'

Marie put down her mascara brush and gave a careless sigh. 'Oh soon, when I've sorted things out with Jimmy.' She picked up a pink lipstick and ran it round her mouth with earnest concentration, avoiding Bernie's gaze in the mirror.

All week Bernie was too excited to think about anything except the church social on Friday. At the same time she froze with fear each time she imagined getting up on stage but she had to get over that if she wanted to be famous. Marie had fixed it with their mam for them to go to the cinema together. Maureen was pleased to see them getting on so well. Bernie felt guilty about deceiving her mam but consoled herself with the thought that her career must come before everything.

It was hard to concentrate at school. What was the point of learning French or Biology when you were destined to be a popstar? Music still held her attention though, especially the rehearsals for the Christmas carol service.

Thursday evening she was supposed to have a final rehearsal with the band but her mam chose to go to bingo that night so she had to stay home with the kids.

'It doesn't matter, you'll be fine,' Peter said as they sat on the wall outside the flats.

'It's not fair.' Bernie looked down the street, keeping an eye on Polly and Teresa who were playing skipping with some other girls. No sign of the Sullivans, in fact since the school fight she hadn't seen them. Maybe they'd had a telling off from their mother too.

Peter put an arm round her shoulders but she shrugged him off. 'Not here,' she mumbled. 'Everyone can see.' Since Saturday night something had changed so that every touch, even the space between them, was charged with electricity. Was this love? Bernie thought of all the love songs she knew. She wanted him to kiss her so badly but not here where there were prying eyes – and what if her mam looked out of the window?

Just then Marie came through the entry, teetering on her high heels and carrying her big handbag as if it were full of bricks. She looks so tired, Bernie thought, feeling sorry for her.

'What's up with you two – lost a tanner and found a penny?' Marie stopped in front of them.

Bernie saw how pale she looked under her makeup. 'You're late home,' she said.

'Stocktaking. My feet are killing me.' She hoisted herself on to the wall and kicked off her shoes.

This was a different Marie to the one who swanned in and out, taking no notice of the rest of the family. Bernie was beginning to like her and for a moment she was glad that Jimmy had disappeared until she remembered the trouble Marie was in.

'Tonight's final band rehearsal for tomorrow,' she said, 'and Mam's going to bingo.'

'Oh is that all?' Marie rubbed her feet. 'Go on, shove off, I'll mind the kids.'

'But…' Bernie began. She wanted to say how tired Marie looked and that maybe she should rest but then thought of her mam's old saying – never look a gift horse in the mouth. She stood up. 'Are you sure?'

'I wouldn't say it would I?' Marie fitted her feet in her shoes, stood up and pulled her coat closer round her shoulders. 'Go on, clear off. I'll tell Mam you've gone to the youth club. Be home before she gets back, mind.'

As Bernie went down the street with Peter she wondered if there would be a price to pay for her sister's favours. Once round the corner

103

Peter took her hand and she let him. Later she knew he would find a quiet shop doorway or corner of the flats lobby to kiss and cuddle and she couldn't wait. Her body already knew his touch and longed for it.

It was there in her singing and she knew the band sensed it. Although they didn't know what had changed in her they could feel it in the music and they looked at her with a new respect – even Ginger. But the practice was exhausting. They made her sing the catchy dance numbers over and over and over till she thought she would scream. It was only when she was allowed to rehearse her solo spot that she came into her own. With the songs she'd chosen she could take her time, let her voice roll with the words, take time to sing out the sorrow, the pain of love as well as the beauty of it and the hardships of life too weren't so far away. She wasn't conscious of thinking as she sang but afterwards her mind swam with images of her mam's dogged care for the family, of Marie's pale strained face and of her own mixed up emotions about Peter.

She and Peter were quiet during the walk home from Ginger's house. The streets were empty and she focussed only on the pressure of his arm round her waist, the way they matched their steps together. Inside the lobby of their block, he took her in his arms by his front door and kissed her. She leaned into him, eager for the touch of his lips, the press of his body against hers. She could feel the warmth of him, smell the clean scent of his hair and his Brut aftershave and she never wanted to let go of him.

'Time to come in.' a voice broke in on her feelings. Bernie gasped and slid out of Peter's embrace as she saw her mam in the doorway.

'Oh Mam,' Bernie felt her face burning but her mother just chuckled.

'Say goodnight to Peter.' She smiled at him. 'Come on kid.' She hustled Bernie up the stairs. 'You'll never guess what – I won on the bingo.'

Fifty pounds. The three of them sat and stared at the notes laid out on the kitchen table – three ten pound notes and four fivers.

'I still can't believe it.' Maureen lit up a Woodbine and poured herself a cup of tea from the pot Marie had just made.

Bernie had never seen a ten pound note except on television when they had first been issued by the Bank of England earlier in the year. 'When I saw the number come up, fifty-nine it was, the Brighton line, I couldn't open me mouth. Only the woman sat next to me shouted for me, I'd have missed it, imagine that.' Maureen blew out her cheeks.

'Didn't Mrs Hanson shout for you?' Bernie asked.

'She wasn't there. She went to watch Katy doing morris dancing or something.'

'Ha! She'll be mad when she finds out,' Marie said.

'What she don't know won't hurt her,' Maureen said. She kept reaching out and touching the notes as if to make sure they were real.

Bernie wondered if her mam had had it out with Rose about the stolen meat. Nothing more had been said though Rose didn't visit their home much any more. Maureen was getting more friendly with Annabel's mam, she'd even been down to their flat a couple of times for a cup of tea. No more extra meat had appeared on the table either. Bernie forgot all about the meat however with her mother's next words.

'Listen girls, there's a fiver each for you. Treat yourselves to something nice.' She pushed a note to each of them.

Bernie couldn't believe her ears. A whole fiver, all to herself! 'Aw Mam, 'she managed to say. 'Are you sure?'

'What you never had you never miss.' Maureen folded up the rest of the money and tucked it into her handbag. 'You're good girls, you deserve a treat. Not a word to your da. Like I said, what you don't know won't hurt you.'

Marie looked stupidly at the note lying on the table in front of her. Suddenly tears welled up in her eyes and trickled down her face.

'Well God save us, give us it back if that's how you feel.'

Marie laughed through her tears and picked the note up before Maureen could snatch it back. 'Thanks Mam, I'm just tired – having to work late.'

'And left to mind the kids while your sister's spooning with her boyfriend.'

Bernie blushed.

'I think I'll get to bed,' Marie stood up, still clutching her fiver.

'Well, you can both have a good night out tomorrow. Go for a nice meal before the pictures or even afterwards. Your da won't get in till late and I'll fix it with him even if he does get in before you.'

When Marie had gone into the bathroom and they heard the sounds of running water, Maureen got up to check the steak and onions simmering in the oven. 'What's up with her?' she said casually.

'Dunno.' Bernie kept her eyes down.

'Is it Jimmy? They've broken up, haven't they?'

Bernie said nothing, if Mam got a whiff that Bernie knew something she would have it out of her in no time.

'What you going to do with the money?' she asked to distract her.

'Well, we can finish all the decorating for a start.' Maureen was all too easily led off on the path of imagining spending all that lovely money. 'I might give Greaty a miss on Saturday and get the rest of the paint and paper. Joan will come round and give us a hand.'

'Won't you buy yourself something nice Mam?'

'We'll see.' Maureen gave a tired smile. 'About our Marie...'

'I'm going to bed too, Mam,' Bernie jumped up before she could be quizzed further.

In bed she pressed the five pound note against her heart under her pyjamas. It seemed to radiate an excited heat of its own as she thought of what she might buy with it. If only Mam had won it last week she could have bought a really nice outfit for her first show with the band.

'What you going to buy with yours, Marie?' she whispered but there was no answer. Marie was either asleep or pretending to be. Probably have to spend it on maternity clothes Bernie thought sadly.

She tucked her fiver under her pillow and closed her eyes. Her head streamed with images, new dresses, makeup, shoes, herself singing to an adoring crowd, herself being booed off stage at the church social. She began to drift and then she was dreaming, buying up all the lemon smock dresses in C&A.

Chapter Eleven

Friday was a blur that seemed endless. Bernie couldn't sit still. She had butterflies in her stomach and twitches in her legs. She longed for the day to be over, for the night to come with the promise of her dreams but then her thoughts raced to ideas of escape, of running somewhere to hide. Why had she let herself in for this? She got told off several times in class for not paying attention and when lunchtime came she could barely eat a bite.

'What's up with you today?' Annabel said, looking at Bernie's untouched shepherd's pie.

'I'm just so nervous about tonight.' Bernie pushed her plate away.

'Don't be,' Annabel said, 'you'll be okay, Pete will make sure of that. You'll be great. And I'll be there. Mam says I can go and your Marie's going, isn't she?'

Bernie nodded. 'Mind you sit at the front so I can see some friendly faces.' She forced a smile.

After school she and Annabel rushed home, Polly and Teresa dawdling along behind them. Bernie opened the back door to find Rose Hanson ensconced at the kitchen table as if she owned the place.

'Eh up, here's the Bash Street kids,' she said but the way she said it, it wasn't funny.

'Well, what you gawping at girl? Rose said.

Maureen was standing by the sink, her arms wrapped round her waist. The atmosphere was tense, this clearly wasn't a friendly visit. Had Polly been fighting again? Rose's next words explained everything.

'I can't believe you wasn't going to tell me. Did you think I wouldn't find out?'

'Give me chance,' Maureen muttered. 'I only won it last night. You never said nothing about sharing before, not all the times we've been.'

Bernie huffed. So that was it. Trust Rose to come sniffing round like a dog at the smell of meat. As if her mam didn't need the money much more than her. 'She doesn't have to share it with you, you weren't even there,' she burst out.

Rose tightened her mouth and folded her arms to lift her bosom. 'If that was my kid I'd teach her a few manners.'

Bernie opened her mouth but before she could speak her mam said quietly, 'That's enough Bernadette. Go to your room, it's none of your affair.'

Bernie knew better than to argue. She trailed her sisters to the bedroom, sat on her bunk and seethed.

'She's a nasty old crow,' Polly sang and capered up and down, cawing. Bernie smiled despite herself.

'Is she going to take Mam's money?' Teresa ventured.

'I hope not,' Bernie said grimly. She lay on her bed and turned on her radio to distract herself while Polly and Teresa bickered over a colouring book. A bit later she heard the back door go and looked out of the window to see Rose Hanson retreating down the street to her own block. A few seconds later, Marie came in.

'What was that old trout doing here?' she asked.

Bernie explained what had happened.

'Coo,' Marie said, 'good job we got our fivers first.'

'You got a fiver?' Polly piped up. 'Buy us some sweets then.'

'Shut up, Big Ears.' Marie tossed off her coat and examined her face in the mirror.

'You don't think Mam's given her the money do you?' Bernie couldn't bear the thought of Rose triumphing over the family yet again.

'Wouldn't surprise me. Look I got a new lipstick, Pink Kiss.' She opened the tube to show Bernie. 'You know our mam, anything for a quiet life. Come on, you'd better start getting ready for tonight.'

Bernie was speechless when Marie had finished with her. Her hair was piled up on top of her head in huge shiny rolls and Marie had put in a tiny jewelled comb that just looked so with-it.

'The eyes are a bit dramatic.' She looked uncertainly in the mirror at the dark drawn eyebrows, heavy eyeliner and green eyeshadow.

'It's got to show up from a distance.' Marie smoothed Bernie's face with a powder puff. 'You don't want to look like a ghost.'

Bernie stood up and admired herself. The black dress clung where it touched and the feather boa set it off perfectly. Good job the butterflies trembling in her stomach couldn't be seen.

'Come on,' Marie said, 'we don't want to be late. We're off, Mam,' she shouted and rushed Bernie through the kitchen before her mam could see her, but all in vain.

'Bit overdressed for the flicks, aren't you?' Maureen took in Bernie's outfit.

'What's wrong with looking nice? I thought I'd do her makeup for her,' Marie said giving Bernie another push towards the door.

'Aye well,' Maureen sighed. 'Enjoy yourselves. What are you going to see?'

The girls stared, they hadn't thought about that. '*Goldfinger*,' Bernie said quickly falling back on the film she'd seen with Peter.

'Shut the door quick,' she told Marie once they were out on the balcony. She didn't want Mam to see her retrieving her red stilettos from the coal hole. The two girls clattered down the steps giggling. Bernie knocked once on Peter's door then she and Marie hid in the next street until Peter and Annabel joined them according to their pre-arranged plan while they waited for Tommy to pick them all up in his van.

The van was old and dirty and the girls had to fit in amongst the other band members and their equipment. Bernie worried that her dress and careful makeup would be spoiled but Marie couldn't stop giggling. It was good to see her looking happy for once.

They arrived in good time to set up before the doors opened and Bernie didn't feel so bad sitting chatting with Annabel and Marie over orange squash supplied by the vicar's wife. It was when she saw the teenagers starting to come in that the collywobbles started up again. She looked up at the stage and wanted to sick up the squash and the few chips she'd eaten at tea-time.

Couples were already jiving and twisting to the records that were playing. Tommy climbed down from the stage and came over to their table.

'We're going to start the set in five minutes – Shadows first then Beatles, just like we practised, so when you hear *Roll Over Beethoven,* you get ready to come on. Pete'll introduce you, okay?'

Bernie nodded although she was petrified.

'You'll be okay,' Tommy said, 'just don't look at the audience and you'll be fine.'

Bernie swallowed, her mouth too dry to answer. Her hands sweated all through the band's early numbers. They seemed to go on forever and she just wanted to get the whole thing over so she could go home in disgrace.

At last the moment came. She saw Peter wink at her then he took the microphone

'And now, I'd like to introduce you to a new member of our band. She's going to sing a few songs for you and I know you're going to like her – here she is, Miss Bernie McCann.'

Bernie stood up but her feet seemed nailed to the floor. Everyone in the room was looking at her. There were a few half-hearted claps and some whistles as they all waited for her to get on stage but she couldn't move.

'Go on!' Marie hissed and shoved her in the back. Someone tittered and then there was an impatient shuffling. Bernie got up on the stage and looked at Peter for reassurance.

He grinned at her, 'Ready?' he said under his breath. She nodded, waited for the opening bars, took a deep breath and launched into *Save the Last Dance For Me*. For a few seconds she was unaware of what she was singing or what came next, then the beat of the band behind her steadied her, her voice came automatically, she had practised the song so often. Only then did she look out onto the floor and saw that nearly everyone was dancing and taking no notice of her at all. Only a few boys hogging the back walls were actually watching her. She looked across at Peter, knowing her face showed her happiness. His smile back meant everything to her and the next number, *My Guy*, she sang only for him.

At the end of the set Bernie stepped down to a storm of applause.

'Well, who'd have thought it?' Marie said as Bernie sat down, her cheeks flushed with her success. Peter joined them but the rest of the band stayed on the stage, checking their equipment.

'You were fab,' he said, taking her hand. He sat down between Annabel and Marie. Bernie felt wonderful; no one had admired her for anything much before except her mam.

'Let me get you girls a drink.' Peter went off to the trestle tables where orange squash and tea were on offer.

A couple of girls came over and asked for Bernie's autograph so she really did feel like a popstar . After they'd gone an older girl came to the table, very fashionable in bell bottoms and a fringed jacket.

'Could I have a word – I'm from the Daily Post – Cathy Brown.' She put out a hand and Bernie stared at it stupidly. 'I'm doing an article about up and coming artistes. Can I ask how long you've been singing?'

'I'm in the school choir,' Bernie blurted.

'So you're still at school? Which one?' She pulled out a notebook and pencil.

'St. Anthony's, but I really want to sing pop.'

Cathy smiled and that made Bernie feel a bit easier. 'How long have you been singing with Riverbeat?'

'It's my first time – in public,' Bernie stuttered.

Cathy's eyebrows rose. 'You gave a really polished performance. I thought you were groovy.'

'Thanks.' Bernie muttered. Although she was pleased, the praise made her feel uncomfortable.

'You've got a really powerful voice. Have you done any solo singing?'

'I'm singing a solo in the carol concert at St Clare's.'

'Oh, when's that?' Bernie watched as Cathy wrote down the details.

'So when you leave school, what are your career aims?'

'I just want to sing.' Bernie couldn't think beyond that.

'What kind of music do you like best?'

'I do like ballads, I think they suit my voice best, slow stuff, bluesy you know?'

'Have you considered becoming a solo artiste, cabaret, supporting bigger acts at concerts, that kind of thing?'

Bernie opened her mouth to say that she longed to be a pop star in her own right then she saw Peter standing behind Cathy, holding a tray of drinks.

'But I'm part of the band,' she said. 'I haven't thought about anything else.'

Cathy snapped her notebook shut and produced a camera from her large shoulder bag. 'Can I get a photo?' She began fiddling with the camera lens. 'Just turn your face a bit to the left, away from the lights.'

Bernie started to comply then she saw Ginger glaring at her from the stage.

'Don't you want a picture of us all together?' she said.

'I'm not really interested in them,' Cathy said, oblivious to Peter listening behind her. 'My article is about opportunities for young girl singers, girls just coming onto the Mersey scene. I'll get a picture of you all together on stage in the second half.'

Bernie posed this way and that as the camera's flashbulbs went off, drawing attention to her. People were staring at her and as the bright light flared she saw the other band members, Peter now among them, watching her as they took up their instruments.

'Wow, you'll be famous, picture in the paper,' Annabel said as the music started up again.

'Hope it doesn't show up your big conk,' Marie said with a touch of her old nastiness.

Jealous, Bernie thought then regretted it – her sister had so much trouble to deal with while she herself seemed to be sailing into a bright future. She was thrilled at the thought of having a newspaper article written about her, and in the Daily Post. Mam would be so proud. Then she remembered Mam's thoughts about pop singing and how she had deceived her to get to the social anyway. She saw that even as the group were playing Ginger was still giving her daggers and she began to have an uneasy feeling that there might be trouble ahead.

The second set was much easier. The evening was winding down with the slower music that Bernie liked best. There was some smooching on the dance floor although nothing too serious under the vicar's watchful eye.

There was an undercurrent of emotion in the room that accorded well with Bernie's feelings as she launched into her first song, *Will You Still Love Me Tomorrow*. It was the most wonderful night of her life and she gave the song all she'd got, thinking how she would end up later in Peter's arms. For her final number she'd chosen Cilla's *You're My World* and she smiled across at Peter while she sang. She could have sung all night but as the applause and whistles died down Peter took the microphone.

'That's it everyone. We hope you've enjoyed our music. Don't forget we'll be back here in two weeks' time so we hope to see you all then.'

He barely got this out before the vicar switched off the stage lights and soon everyone was piling out of the hall while the vicar and his wife cleared away the refreshments and cleaned the tables.

In the van everyone was full of excitement.

'That was a great gig,' Tommy said. 'You went down really well, Bernie.'

'Especially with that reporter,' Ginger growled.

'She just asked me…' Bernie began but he cut her short.

'Don't act the little innocent, we all saw you. You couldn't get in front of the camera quick enough.'

Marie jumped in. 'Don't you talk to her like that. That reporter just came up to us – and she wanted to talk about girls, not blokes. You're just jealous because she's a better singer than you and better looking too.'

Phil the drummer burst out laughing and all the others followed suit except Ginger who just glowered.

'Seriously Bernie, the group needs to stick together – press interviews should be a joint thing.' Tommy's voice was kind despite the rebuke.

'Come off it, Tom, no one from the press has ever come near us before,' Phil said and everyone laughed again.

'It's still good publicity,' Peter said. 'You never know it might get us a bit more notice. We could do with some better gigs than that crummy church hall.'

Tommy dropped the four of them off round the corner from the flats and Peter sneaked an arm round Bernie's waist as they walked back behind Marie and Annabel.

'We never even spent any of our money,' Marie said over her shoulder. 'I'm going shopping with mine after work tomorrow.'

Bernie remembered that she had to go to work in the morning. She'd never get the chance to spend her fiver at this rate.

In the block lobby Marie turned and winked at her. 'Don't be long or our mam will be out looking for you.' She started up the steps but Annabel still hung about outside her front door.

'Go on in Annie, I'll be in in a tick.'

Annabel smirked at Bernie. 'See you tomorrow,' she said, letting herself in with the key she had round her neck.

At last Bernie and Peter were alone. He pulled her into the shadows under the stairs. Bernie's thoughts had returned to the humiliation she'd felt at Ginger's words.

'I'm sorry about the reporter,' she said, 'I must seem really stupid but all this is new to me.'

'Shhh' Peter drew her into his arms. 'It wasn't your fault. Forget about it.'

'But will they forget about it?' She looked up into his eyes, saw the softness there.

'Forget about them,' He bent his head and rested his forehead against hers as his arms tightened their hold.

She reached up to clasp her arms round his neck. The emotion that had brewed in her all night boiled up and she opened her mouth to his kiss.

113

Chapter Twelve

The next morning the shop was busy with people coming in for ciggies, papers, lemonade and their weekend sweets. The job seemed much easier this time now Bernie felt more settled and she took pride in making the sweet displays neat and attractive.

Peter came in just after eight to pick up a copy of the New Musical Express before getting the bus to his Saturday job. He cornered Bernie by the magazine rack

'I just wanted to see you.' He reached for her but she moved away.

'Stop it, you'll get me into trouble.' She remembered the night before and her insides started to melt all over again.

'You buying that paper or what?' Mr Thompson grumbled from behind the counter.

'Course I am Mr T.' Peter handed the money over. 'Will I see you tonight?' he whispered to Bernie.

'I don't know.' She pretended to re-arrange some Mars bars. 'I'll probably have to babysit.'

'I can come up?'

'I'll have to ask Mam.'

'Let me know when you get home.' He winked at her and touched her hand before swinging out of the shop.

'Don't stand there gawping,' Mr Thompson said, raising his eyebrows to the customer he was serving. 'If you haven't got anything to do, go and help Mrs Thompson in the stock room.'

'Was that your boyfriend?' Mrs Thompson asked later over their tea and biscuits.

'Er – yes.' Bernie said. She hadn't thought of them as a steady pair until last night but acknowledging him to her employer made it sort of official. She hadn't realised how deep her feelings for him were becoming and Peter seemed to feel the same way.

'He's a nice lad,' Mrs Thompson looked at her over the rim of her cup. 'Nice family; his dad comes in here most mornings for his fags and his paper.' She got up. 'Come on, I'll show you how to sort and label the

114

papers for the afternoon delivery. If you get on with it okay you can do them every week.'

It was another small step towards being accepted into the adult world and Bernie couldn't have felt happier.

Bernie arrived home looking forward to lying on her bed and reading her new copy of Valentine but when she got there a busy scene greeted her.

Maureen was pasting sheets of wallpaper on the kitchen table and shouting to Joan who was hanging them in the living room. Polly, Teresa and the twins were supposedly helping but were mostly having hysterics sticking paste and bits of paper all over each other. The whole scene was presided over by a huge woman in pink crimplene that overflowed each side of the kitchen chair she sat on, ham-like legs planted widely apart.

.Nan!' Bernie's eyes lit up. She hadn't seen her nan, Maureen's mother, since they left Toxteth. She ran to give her a hug, losing herself in the familiar embrace of those meaty arms and the huge bosom behind them.

'My, you've grown into a proper young lady since I last saw you.' Nan held her away and examined her. Her blue eyes crinkled in the creased fat of her face. 'Your mam says you're going to sing in St Clare's.'

'Will you be able to come Nan?'

'We wouldn't miss it for the world.' Joan came to wash her hands in the sink. 'Charlie'll bring your nan along too, I'll see to that.'

'Charlie's a good lad, you married a good 'un there,' Nan said, 'I'd never have got here if he hadn't brought me. Them buses are too much for me now.'

'Well, he knows what's good for him,' Joan said.

Bernie thought how easy it would be for her da to send John over with the van to bring Nan up now and then but her da wouldn't put himself out like Joan's husband.

'Bernie love, put the kettle on. We'll pack up now before your da comes in. I could murder a cuppa. Get out of it!' She shooed Polly and Teresa away and kicked out under the table at Matty and Anthony who were down there sniggering at Nan's varicose veins and the red blotches on her shins from sitting too close to the fire.

Once the kids had gone out to play, Bernie made the tea while Maureen and Joan cleaned the table and put away the wallpaper and paste. They were all chatting companiably when Marie came in loaded with carrier bags.

'Hello Nan.' She dropped her shopping and went to give the old lady a perfunctory hug.

'My you've plumped up since I last saw you.' Nan looked her up and down.

Marie gave a nervous smile and sat in the only vacant chair.

'Gosh, I'm shattered.' She eased off her shoes.

She certainly did look tired, Bernie thought, and pale too, with dark shadows round her eyes showing through her makeup.

'Well, it's not what she eats here,' Maureen said. 'She turns her nose up at everything.'

'It's all that greasy fried stuff, makes me feel sick. Is there any tea left in that pot?'

'It's good food,' Maureen said indignantly. 'You should appreciate what you're given.'

'Your mam's a good cook,' Nan spoke up. 'I taught her myself.'

'Oh what's it got to do with you?' Marie burst out.

'Don't you talk to your nan like that,' Maureen and Joan said together.

'Oh for Jesus' sake,' Marie rolled her eyes heavenwards.

Nan tutted . 'Taking the name of the Lord in vain.' She shook her head sadly.

'Oh leave me alone. Everyone picks on me.' Marie jumped up and flounced out to the bathroom.

Maureen gaped. 'I don't know what's got into that girl.'

'Don't you?' Nan said. 'Haven't you got eyes in your head?'

'What do you mean?' Maureen gawped at her.

Bernie put her head down and busied herself at the sink but she couldn't stave off what was coming.

'That girl's pregnant, sure as my name's Bridie Flynn.'

There was a dead silence then Maureen roared, 'MARIE!!'

The cups rattled in Bernie's hands as she brought them to the table.

'More tea?' she said weakly but everyone ignored her.

Maureen hammered on the locked bathroom door 'Get out here this minute!' She kept it up till Marie opened the door.

Maureen seized her arm and dragged her to the kitchen. 'Is it true?' she yelled into her daughter's face. 'Tell me,' she raised a hand but Joan jumped up and stopped her.

'Take it easy,' she said. 'Come and sit down Marie,' but before anyone could move Marie whirled and ran out of the back door.

'I'll swing for her,' Maureen yelled and made to follow but Joan restrained her. In the melée Bernie slipped out and ran round the block, looking for her sister.

She found Marie in the next street sitting on the wall outside a block of flats and sobbing with her face in her hands. A knot of children stood staring in front of her and as Bernie got closer she realised they were her brothers and sisters.

'What's up with her?' Matty asked Bernie.

'Never you mind,' Bernie said.

'I know,' Polly said importantly.

'Oh make them go away,' Marie moaned.

'You just shut up.' Bernie advanced on Polly. She emphasised each word with a poke at Polly's skinny chest. 'One word and you're dead. Got it?' She finished with a final shove that sent Polly reeling.

'And that goes for the rest of you. Now clear off,' Bernie shouted. They stood uncertainly for a moment then as she lunged towards them, yelling, 'Didn't you hear me?' they turned heels and ran.

Bernie sat down beside Marie. She found a none-too-clean hankie in her cardigan pocket and handed it to Marie.

'What am I going to do now?' Marie muttered, wiping away her tears.

'You'd best come home.' Bernie said.

'I can't. Mam's going to kill me. Da'll kill me.'

Bernie didn't know what to say. It was true their da probably would kill her but surely Mam wouldn't be that bad? 'It'll be all right,' she consoled although she wasn't sure anything would ever be all right again.

'I'm not going back there while me nan and Aunty Joan are there, looking down their noses at me.'

'They won't...' Bernie began but Marie overrode her

'—and me da'll be in in a minute with our John – oh I can't stand it.' She burst into a fresh bout of sobs.

'Stop it, you'll do yourself an injury.' Bernie flapped her arms as if to embrace her sister but Marie had never been the cuddling kind.

'I'm going to Angie's.' Marie got up suddenly. 'I'm not coming back till Mam and Da have gone out.'

'What if they don't go out?' Their mam never missed her Saturday night out but Maureen wasn't one to leave a fire to smoulder and if she refused to go out Da would know something was up.

'Then I won't come back at all.' Marie jumped up and ran off in the direction of her friend Angie's home.

Bernie sat on the wall wondering what she meant. Did she plan to run away or –surely she wouldn't think of harming herself? She felt cold all over and she wanted to go home and tell her mam but was that being disloyal to Marie?

After a while she got up and headed home, feet as heavy as her heart. Her steps slowed even more when she saw her da's van parked outside the flats. She stood at the foot of the lobby stairs, listening for sounds of argument but all seemed quiet.

The Farriers' door opened and Peter popped his head out. 'Are we on for tonight?'

'Oh don't ask me now,' Bernie snapped. She ran up the stairs without looking back at him and opened her back door. The kitchen was empty.

Her da and John were in the living room eating ribs with their pea soup. The savoury smell mingled with the aroma of wet wallpaper and paste. Da nodded at her as he sucked on a rib bone. Mam hadn't said anything to him then, he looked in a good mood. Bernie breathed easier.

John winked at her. 'What you up to Spud?'

'Nothing much,' Bernie said. 'Where's Mam?'

'Getting tarted up,' Joe said, starting on another rib.

Bernie withdrew. She hovered outside her parents' bedroom door but apart from some rustling there was silence. Joan and Nan must have gone and her mam must be going out as usual if she was getting dressed up.

The door suddenly opened. Her mam was standing there in her slip, half her head topped by big foam rollers. 'Thought I heard you.' She grabbed Bernie's arm. 'Come and help me do my hair.' She pulled her inside, shut the door and sat down at her dressing table, handing Bernie the brush and indicating the pile of rollers waiting to go in,

'Your da's not to know,' she hissed. 'No one's to know. You hear me?'

Bernie nodded. She brushed a lock of Maureen's auburn hair. It was hennaed now but she'd always loved her mother's hair. She wound it smoothly onto a roller and secured it with a hairgrip.

'Polly knows,' she said. Standing close she could feel her mother's anger and tension, see the fear on her reflected face in the mirror. 'She heard Marie telling Angela, ages ago.'

'Ages?' Maureen's eyebrows shot up. 'I suppose you knew too, did you?'

Bernie nodded miserably.

'And never told me? I'm the last to find out?'

'I – I was scared,' Bernie mumbled ' – and our Marie…'

'…threatened to batter you I suppose,' Maureen said. 'Stop snivelling can't you? I can't think straight. How do you think I feel having to find out like that – in front of your nan and our Joan?'

'I'm sorry,' Bernie mumbled She stroked a lock of her mother's hair, preparing to roll it up.

'What about Jimmy? What's he got to say about it?' Maureen's mouth twisted bitterly.

'I dunno,' Bernie mumbled. 'I don't think they're speaking.'

'No, I suppose he thinks he'll get away with leaving her in the lurch. Do you know where he lives?'

'No,' Bernie said blankly. As far as she knew Marie had met Jimmy in town on a night out with her friends so no one knew his family.

'So where's she gone now?' Maureen reached for her cigarettes.

'She went to Angie's. She was dead upset. Oh Mam, she's too frightened to come home – I think she might run away – or- or do something?'

'Do something? Don't talk daft.' Maureen shifted uneasily on her chair. There was a short silence while Maureen smoked and Bernie carried on rolling up her hair. When the last roller was in she reached for the squeezy bottle of *Bel Air* and gave her mother's head a good spray to set the curls. 'What are you going to do?' she ventured.

'I'll have to think about it,' Maureen stubbed out her cigarette. 'Leave our Polly to me, the nosey little cow. You can go over to Angela's house and tell our Marie to come home, once me and your da have gone out.'

'You're still going to the pub then?'

'Don't think I want to.' Maureen bit her lip and Bernie saw a suspicion of tears in her eyes. How bad was that? She couldn't remember ever seeing her mother cry.

'Your da mustn't suspect anything.'

'But won't he have to know?' Bernie shuddered.

'I don't know, I don't know.' Maureen's composure slipped and for a second she looked completely lost. 'I'll just have to think. Go on now, call the kids in and give them their tea. – it's all ready.'

Bernie moved towards the door.

'You're a good help to me Bernie – don't let me down now.'

Bernie went out with a twinge of pride but it was dampened by the thought of what lay ahead. Oh why did Marie have to cause so much trouble, just when things were looking up?

Minutes stretched into hours and still Bernie's da wasn't ready to go out. While he was snoozing in his armchair everyone had to be quiet. John was in the boys' bedroom. He'd picked up a model steam engine on the round and he was showing the twins how it worked.

Bernie cleared away the tea things. She hadn't been able to eat anything herself. A huge lump seemed to be stuck in her throat. Would she ever be able to sing again? It was a terrifying thought.

She sat on her bed and went through her song book, trying to pick out numbers she might perform with the band but she couldn't concentrate and Polly and Teresa made it worse, squabbling over the clothes they were putting on their Sindy dolls.

Bernie put the book away and sighed. She looked up at the poster of Cliff and the Shadows on the wall by her bunk. They looked happy; they wouldn't have to put up with clearing up after their families or worrying about their problems.

At last her da was ready to go out. Bernie realised there was no one to mind the kids while she went to tell Marie the coast was clear. She daren't leave them on their own, God knows what they would get up to. She didn't want to ask Annabel or Peter – this was family business but in the end, imagining the twins setting fire to themselves with John's latest toy, she decided to ask Peter. She would have to think of some explanation for going after Marie.

As soon as John had driven off with Mam and Da in the van she ran down the stairs to the Farriers' flat.

'Will you just come up and sit with the kids? I have to go a message for me Mam.'

Peter looked puzzled. 'How come?'

'I have to get our Marie, Mam said. I don't know why.'

'Is it a big secret?' Peter teased but Bernie was in no mood for games.

'Are you coming or not? She turned away from him.

'Okay, okay, just let me get my jacket.'

Bernie left him and ran round to Angie's house. Marie was in Angie's bedroom, her eyes swollen with crying.

'Mam says you're to come home. She sent me round to get you. She said it will be all right.'

'How can it be all right?' Marie poked at her eyes with a tissue. 'Me da…'

'Da doesn't know. Mam's not going to tell him till she's thought what to do. They've gone out now anyway.'

Marie burst into fresh tears. 'I can't.'

'You'll have to go home sometime,' Angie said. 'You can't stay here, our Susan'll be home and me mam's getting suspicious. You don't want everyone to know do you?'

Marie shook her head.

'Come on, let's go home.' Bernie pulled Marie up and put her coat round her shoulders. The two girls walked home in silence.

Bernie thought back to the day she'd caught Marie and Jimmy in the bedroom. Marie had been so cocky then but look what had happened. Bernie told herself she'd never ever let this happen to her.

Marie sneaked into their bedroom when they got home.

'I can't be doing with the kids,' she whispered as they went in.

'Peter's here anyway,' Bernie said, wishing for once that he wasn't.

She joined the others in the living room where a game of Monopoly was already set out.

'We've been waiting for you,' Polly bounced up and down.

Bernie sat down but she couldn't concentrate, worrying about what would happen when her parents came home. As usual the twins won.

'They're going to grow up to be tycoons,' Peter laughed ,clearing the board and putting the pieces back in the box.

'What's a tycoon?' Anthony asked.

'It's a big wind, like you, you fart,' Polly said, dodging the kick he aimed at her.

'Get your jamas on,' Bernie said. 'I'll make the cocoa.'

They all trooped off to the bedrooms but the next minute Polly was back in the kitchen trailing Teresa. 'Why's our Marie in bed?'

'She's not well,' Bernie said.

'She's crying,' Teresa said.

''Cos she's not well,' Bernie snapped. 'Don't you be bothering her.'

'Is it 'cos she's up the duff?' Polly asked.

'No,' Bernie said, 'and don't say that. Where did you hear that?'

'Janice Lyons told me her sister is up the duff.'

'Well you're not to say it. If our mam hears you…'

'All right then, she's got a bun in the oven.'

Bernie slapped Polly across the back of her head. 'Just shut up,' she shouted. 'Our mam'll kill you and so will our Marie.'

Polly went off with a sniffle to get undressed.

'There's nothing in here,' Teresa said, opening the oven door and peering inside.

It was hard sitting with Peter after everyone else had gone to bed and pretending nothing was wrong. The *Sullavan Brothers* show was on the telly and Peter slipped an arm round her shoulders but immediately she tensed up.

'What's wrong?' Peter pulled back and looked into her eyes.

'Nothing,' Bernie muttered.

'Something's up, I can tell. Come on, what is it?'

'I can't tell you. Don't keep asking me.'

Peter took his arm away and moved to the side of the sofa.

'Is it me? Do you want us to finish?'

'No!' Bernie almost shouted. 'It's nothing like that, not about you. It's a family thing. I can't say.' Tears suddenly ran down her cheeks.

'Hey, hey.' Peter pulled her into his arms.

It felt so good to lay her head against his chest and cry into his mohair sweater while he shushed and rocked her like a baby. Gradually she relaxed, comforted by the warmth of his body until he murmured in her ear,

'Do you want me to go home?'

'No.' She sat up, drying her eyes on her cardigan sleeve. She didn't want to be left alone to deal with Marie and her misery.

Peter moved to get up. 'Okay, I'll make some tea. I can find the things.' He clattered about in the kitchen while she stared at the TV screen, fighting off dread of her parents' return.

In the soundtrack of the drama showing on screen, Fred Astaire and Ginger Rogers were singing, *Let's Call the Whole Thing Off* and Bernie remembered her plan to get Peter to sing with her.

'I bet we could do that,' she said as he returned with the tea. She took her cup and set it on the coffee table.

'That's a corny old thing.'

'No, I mean we could sing something hip, *I Got You Babe* or some of the Beatles' harmony numbers.'

Peter frowned. 'We need to get away from Beatles stuff. Every band on Merseyside copies them.'

'Well, there's lots of songs we could do, Springfields, Beach Boys – I don't know. I can look some up. Can't we try?'

'Mmm, it's an idea.' Peter started humming, *I Got You Babe*. Bernie began singing the words in second part then he joined in. She could tell they sounded good together and the family problems faded away as she put her emotions into the song.

'See,' she said, filled with excitement.

'I don't know how the rest of the band would feel,' Peter said.

'But it sounds so good. They're bound to be cool about it – it makes the group a bit more different.'

She gabbled on, trying to convince him. She didn't say that already she was seeing herself and Peter as a duo, with the rest of the band just as back-up, if not disappearing altogether.

When it was time for Peter to go, she'd almost persuaded him although his loyalty to the group still made him doubtful.

'I wish I could stay longer, we've hardly had any time together.' He pulled her into his arms at the back door.

'I wish you could too but Mam and Da'll be back soon.'

'When are you going to tell your dad about me?' he nuzzled her ear while his hands roamed over her back.

'Soon,' she murmured, turning her face up to be kissed. His lips came down on hers and she was lost in a sea of sensation where every part of her longed to be touched. At some point she heard the sound of a car door slamming and voices jolted her back to reality.

'Quick, it's me da,' she hastily pulled away and straightened Peter's rumpled jumper. 'Go on.' She gave him a push.

'Why is your dad such a pain in the neck?'

'I don't know, just go. I'll see you tomorrow.'

He grinned at her. 'See you tomorrow,' and ran lightly down the stairs.

When the rest of the family came in, Bernie was tidying up the living room. Her father and John were full of bonhomie.

'Didn't tell you he's got a new girlfriend, did he?' Joe clapped John on the back 'She's a looker too.'

John laughed but blushed a little. Bernie thought it must be serious, John took lots of girls out but no one ever knew who they were. If only she could just tell Da about Peter but she quailed at the thought, especially now.

She went into the kitchen to wash up the cups and Maureen followed her out.

'Is she in?' she asked anxiously.

'Yes,' Bernie said, 'but oh Mam don't shout at her, she's dead upset.'

'I'm not going to shout,' Maureen said, 'and I'm not telling your da, not yet anyway.'

'What are you going to do then?'

'Just leave it with me.' Maureen went into the girls' bedroom. Bernie waited a bit but could hear nothing so she took the usual plate of prepared butties in to her da and John. When her mother appeared in the living room she just said, 'Better get to bed now Bernie.'

123

Bernie nodded, 'Night, Da, night John.' She went into her bedroom but all was silent. In bed she tried to calm herself by mentally running through numbers that might suit her and Peter. It was a long time after the rest of the family went to bed that she fell asleep.

Chapter Thirteen

Bernie was peeling the potatoes for the Sunday roast and Maureen was stuffing lambs' hearts when Marie came into the kitchen with her coat on.

'Just going to Angie's.' she announced.

'Oh no you're not, Madam, you just sit down there,' Maureen pointed with the knife she'd been using to trim the hearts. 'We need to talk.'

Marie didn't sit but stood sulkily by the back door.

'Bernie, go to your room.'

Bernie put down her knife and went to the bedroom. Polly and Teresa were pillowfighting but they stopped and joined Bernie when they saw she was listening at the closed door. Snatches of conversation came through.

'So what's happening with Jimmy? No wonder he hasn't been round lately.'

Something inaudible from Marie.

'Is he going to stand by you or not? How far gone are you?'

Another mumble.

'What do you mean, you don't know? Haven't you been to the doctor?' Maureen was shouting then her voice sank to a hopeful note. 'Maybe it's a false alarm. If not, you'll need to get married right away.'

Bernie just made out Marie's reply. 'Jimmy said he's too young.'

'Too young?' Maureen's voice rose again. 'Not too young to land you with a kid though. I can't believe you could be so stupid, ruining your whole life. Well we'll see about that. You tell me where he lives and we'll go round there tomorrow, see what his parents think about it.'

'I don't know where he lives and if I did I wouldn't go there. I'm not going begging.' Marie's voice was defiant.

'Don't know where he lives and you're having a kid to him?'

'Oh leave me alone,' Marie screamed. The back door banged and then there was silence for a moment until they heard their mam rush out and shout down the stairs,

'You come back here this minute.'

125

Bernie turned to the window, saw Marie running down the street. She, Polly and Teresa looked at each other with varying expressions of shock. Teresa's lip began to tremble.

'Come on,' she said, 'You can have my old *Valentines* for cutting up but no squabbling mind.'

She got out her magazines and handed them over. Marie's bags of shopping, still stood on the floor by her bed.

After a reasonable time had elapsed she ventured into the kitchen where her mam was ramming stuffing into the last of the hearts and sat down to finish the potatoes.

'Yuk, they look disgusting,' she eyed the hearts.

'Oh, not good enough for you?' Maureen adopted a jokey manner but Bernie could tell she was trying to hide her bitter hurt. 'What are you going to do when you get married?' she went on, 'Suppose you'll have a lady's maid and a cook?'

Well I won't be eating hearts, I'll make sure of that, Bernie thought but she said nothing.

There was a companiable silence while they both saw to their respective tasks. Bernie felt emboldened to ask.

'Mam can I go to town after school tomorrow? I want to buy a present for our John's birthday and now I'm at work I can't go Saturdays.'

'I don't see why not but don't go spending all that money I gave you on presents for other people, it's for you to buy something for yourself.'

'I won't Mam.'

'You needn't rush back.' Maureen got up to put the roasting tray in the oven. 'I'll see to the kids' tea when I get back from the shop. Leave the carrots. Why don't you run down to see if Annabel can go with you. I'll finish the dinner.'

Bernie didn't need second bidding.

'Oh please Mam, can I go?' Annabel's eyes gleamed with excitement.

'I don't see why not.' Kathleen Farrier looked pleased. She noticed Bernie was looking round her to see if Peter was there and chuckled. 'Peter's playing football. Do you want to come back later – after dinner?'

'Oh yes,' Bernie said. She danced happily upstairs, forgetting Marie till she opened the back door and saw her mam sitting at the table staring into space, the carrots still unpeeled in front of her.

'Mam?'

Maureen shifted, looked at her as if she was an alien then sighed and got up.

'Finish them carrots, there's a good girl,' she said and went to her own bedroom.

When all the veg was done Bernie went to her room and listened to her radio. She began to wonder why her mam had agreed so readily to her shopping trip. Usually she relied on Bernie to look after the younger ones till she got home.

Dinner was the same as every Sunday except that Joe came in late. As usual he ate sitting in his armchair and promptly fell asleep afterwards. Vinny Mack had dropped him off and John was absent. Bernie supposed he was with this new girlfriend and she idly wondered what she was like. Marie returned but only picked at her food and even the other kids were subdued, sensing that something was wrong.

'Is it okay if I go and sit with Annabel for a bit?' Bernie asked as she finished her meal.

'Er, yes, all right, after the washing up's done' Maureen said. 'I'll take the kids to mass and Marie can come with me.'

'I'm not going,' Marie looked up, eyes flashing.

'Oh yes you are,' Maureen hissed.

'I'm not.' Marie stormed off to the bedroom, leaving her half-eaten food.

'Coo,' Matty said, 'can I have her meat?'

Bernie followed Marie who was smoking out of the bedroom window.

'Why don't you go?' she said. Rubbing Mam up the wrong way wasn't going to help.

'Oh don't be such a goody-goody,' Marie burst out. 'I'm not going. Mam only wants me there to have Father McKenna ramming sin down my throat. No thank you.' She puffed viciously on her cigarette.

Bernie gave up. She helped her mam with the washing up before going down to the Farriers' flat where she spent a couple of hours playing cards with Annabel and Peter and tried to forget about her family.

The next morning Marie was sick and didn't go to work. The school day dragged by while Bernie spent most of the time daydreaming about all the things she was going to buy, trying not to think about Marie. Even when Mrs Meredith stopped her in the corridor she could barely pay attention.

'Don't forget, Bernadette, it's the final rehearsal for the carol concert after school tomorrow.'

'Oh no, I won't,' Bernie said. She would have to drag Polly and Teresa along with her but Mrs Meredith was okay about that. She knew about the problems with the Sullivans.

'After that we're having a performance in assembly the week before the actual St Clare's concert – a sort of practice run.'

Once the thought of standing up in front of the whole school would have terrified Bernie but her success at the church social had given her confidence.

'That sounds fab,' she smiled at the music teacher.

'Well off you go then,' Mrs Meredith smiled back and Bernie hurried to meet Annabel in the dining hall. It was potato pie for lunch, one of Bernie's favourites. Life was good except for the cloud on the horizon that was Marie.

The two girls landed in town at four o'clock which gave them a delightful hour and a half to spend Bernie's money. They headed straight for C&A where Bernie thought her dream of owning the lemon smock was about to come true. To her dismay the store models were now displaying new lines in autumn and winter colours. She looked dispiritedly at racks of tweedy skirts and woolly pinafores.

'This is nice,' Annabel fingered a botany wool twinset.

'Too old-fashioned,' Bernie turned her nose up. 'It's got to be something mod.'
She spied a floaty georgette frock in swirls of pink and red. 'That's more like it.'

'It doesn't look very warm,' Annabel giggled.

'It doesn't have to be. It's for wearing on stage.'

How wonderful it was to try on a lovely new dress instead of poking through someone else's cast offs from her da's round. The fabric gathered nicely under her bust and fell softly to just above her knees. It wouldn't go with the red stilettos but maybe she could manage with the brown granny shoes till she'd saved enough for some new ones.

Next stop was Woolworths where she bought white pantyhose and a Miners pink lipstick. She treated Annabel to one too and one for Marie to cheer her up. She bought an Italian style striped tie for John and the slippers she wanted to get for her mam's Christmas present. There was just enough left for coffee in one of the new cellar coffee bars.

Both girls tried not to be alarmed by the hissing coffee machine. They looked at the black liquid in the tiny glass cups. Bernie wanted to ask for milk but seeing none she took her cup meekly and they went in search of seats. The cellar was dark with stark brick walls and bearded faces peered at them out of the gloom. Two girls with white faces, pale lipstick and long hair giggled as Bernie and Annabel passed and Bernie wished they'd had time to change out of their school uniforms.

They perched on small wooden stools. Bernie sipped the bitter coffee and spooned in lots of sugar to make it taste better.

'Isn't it fab?' she said and Annabel nodded eagerly. Conversation was impossible with the loud blues music that pounded through the room. Bernie felt out of her depth but she wasn't going to let Annabel see that. She made herself finish her coffee, watching to make sure Annabel drank all hers too before heading off to catch the bus home.

It was almost seven when they got back. Bernie could hear voices coming from the living room. Opening the door she knew something was dreadfully wrong. Father McKenna was sitting in her da's armchair.

'And is this boy a Catholic?' he said.

Maureen was sniffling into a hankie. They both looked at Bernie.

'Your tea's in the oven,' Maureen said. 'Go and eat in your room, Father and me are talking.'

The last thing Bernie wanted was food. She went out but stood behind the door, waiting for their voices to start up again.

'Nearly four months gone,' her mam said. 'I've had her to the doctor this morning and she won't tell where this boy lives.'

'He's not in my parish then? And there's no time to waste. Hmm.'

There was silence for a minute then the priest's deep voice sounded again. 'Well if she won't tell there's only one thing to do.'

Bernie walked into the bedroom and stopped short in the doorway. Marie was sitting at the dressing table. She'd taken off all her makeup and was carefully plucking her eyebrows. Her full cosmetic kit was laid out on the dresser, ready for a fresh application. The skin above her eyelids was flushed pink where she'd pulled out straggling hairs, matching the pink of her eyes still swollen from prolonged crying.

Polly and Teresa were sitting on their bed, watching in silence. It was such an odd scene, Bernie almost laughed with fright. She put down her shopping bags and rummaged in them.

'Look, I got you a present,' she handed the lipstick to Marie and gave Polly a bag containing two gobstoppers. Even that didn't break the silence. Polly and Teresa popped the sweets in their mouths. Marie opened the lipstick, examined the colour and tried it on her lips but they were all straining their ears to hear what was being said in the living room. No sound could be heard.

'Is this a joke?' Marie held the lipstick out to Bernie showing the name printed on the bottom, *Baby Doll*.

'Oh,' Bernie flushed, 'I didn't mean…'

Marie shot a warning look at Polly and Teresa, then her voice softened. 'Well, thanks anyway.'

'I spent all my money,' Bernie said to cover her embarrassment.

'Let's see then,' Marie said admiring her eyebrows in the mirror as if she hadn't a care in the world. Bernie delved into her bags to show what she had bought but they all froze at the sound of heavy feet coming down the hall, accompanied by the soft slap of their mam's slippers on the lino. The unfamiliar squeak of the rarely used front door marked the priest's departure. They heard Maureen returning , the scrape of a kitchen chair, the rasp of a match and then silence.

Marie's face was white. She picked up her panstick and daubed dots round her face before starting to smooth them together. Polly and Teresa sucked their gobstoppers and looked at Bernie. Bernie could stand it no longer. She left her bags and went to the kitchen where her mam was smoking a Woodbine; her face looked grey but was set in stern lines. She sighed heavily, stuck the cigarette in the corner of her mouth and got up to light the gas under the kettle.

'Send our Polly and Teresa out to find the twins and bring them in for supper and tell our Marie to come out here.'

Bernie followed her instructions with her heart pounding.

'I'm doing my makeup,' Marie carried on applying her foundation.

'Mam said now,' Bernie warned.

'Oh for Christ's sake,' Marie got up and went into the kitchen. Despite the defiance in her voice, she looked shrunken. Bernie followed.

Maureen waited until the younger girls had put their coats on and gone out then turned away from the stove, bracing her back against the sink.

'Father McKenna is going to arrange for you to go away to have the baby,' she said.

Marie stared at her, the uneven makeup standing out as her face turned ashy grey.

'Away?' she stuttered.

'To the nuns,' Maureen's voice was clipped. 'It's for the best.'

'Nuns?' Marie sat down. Bernie sat down too. 'Why?' Marie said. 'Can't I stay here?' It was the saddest thing Bernie had ever heard and tears prickled her eyes.

Marie looked at her and began to cry also.

'It's no use bawling now,' Maureen said. 'You made your bed, you got to lie on it.' She filled the teapot and brought it to the table. 'This way, no one will know, not even your da. We'll tell everyone you've gone to work away.'

'But the baby..' Marie said.

'The baby will be adopted,' Maureen said. 'You don't want to be left with a baby when you've no husband do you? And you wouldn't be able to stay here. Your da wouldn't hear of it. You wouldn't be able to look after a baby.' She poured out the tea, put it in front of Marie, stirring several spoons of sugar into it. 'Come on, drink this up.'

'When?' Marie whispered.

'Fairly soon,' Maureen said. 'Father McKenna is going to get it all organised.

'Where?'

'I don't know but Father says we'll be able to visit. It'll soon pass over, you'll see, then you'll be able to get back to normal.'

Marie got up and went into the bedroom.

Bernie stared at her mother.

Maureen lit a fresh cig. 'Don't look at me like that. She's ruined her own life, I'm just trying to make the best of it.'

'But sending her away?' It was the most awful thing Bernie could think of.

'What else can we do? She can't keep it. It's not just the shame on the family, how could she support it, she can barely keep herself and she wouldn't be able to work and then who'd want to marry her? Not that dirty eejit who's put her in that way and no one else neither. So what's she going to do? Her life won't be worth living if your da finds out.'

The back door flew open and her brothers and sisters piled in, noses red with cold, lively and laughing. Freezing air rushed into the room.

'Cocoa and toast, then bed,' Maureen got up. Bernie rose too. 'Not a word to anyone,' Maureen muttered as she passed.

Bernie went into the bedroom. Marie was putting on her makeup as if nothing had happened. Bernie sat on her bunk and watched as Marie applied a thick band of eyeliner.

'I'm sorry..' she started.

'Don't be,' Marie said carelessly. 'Mam's right, it's for the best.'

Polly and Teresa burst into the room.

'Guess what,' Marie said, 'I'm getting away from you lot. I've got a job at Butlin's.'

Both younger girls stopped still and stared.

'What about…?' Polly began.

'Shut up!' Bernie said, 'You just shut up.'

Chapter Fourteen

Tuesday morning Bernie was rushing between classes when Mrs Meredith popped out of the music room and waylaid her.

'I want to see you Bernadette. Come here after your lunch, quarter to one, all right?'

Bernie nodded but before she could ask what was wrong the teacher had bobbed back into the classroom and shut the door. Bernie carried on, her steps slowing as she worried. Mrs Meredith had looked really stern.

Time dragged till lunch. In the dining hall a ball of apprehension clogged her throat, stopping her from eating or talking. At last the dining hall clock showed one-forty and she hurried to her rendezvous.

Mrs Meredith was sitting at her desk with a newspaper in front of her. 'Sit down, Bernie I want to talk to you about this.'

She turned the paper and pushed it across the desk. Bernie looked down, puzzled and saw her own face smiling back at her next to the headline, 'A Girl to Watch' by reporter Cathy Brown. Heat rushed to her face as she scanned the first few lines.

> Up and coming teenage singer Bernie McCann made her debut singing with local band Riverbeat last Friday and wowed the crowd at St Philomena's church social.

The print blurred before her eyes. Now Mrs Meredith was sure to throw her out of the choir and she would have to tell her mam and Mam would kill her. She looked up and saw that Mrs Meredith was smiling.

'Well I didn't know you had a musical alter ego, famous already,' she chuckled.

Bernie wasn't sure what an alter ego was but at least Mrs Meredith didn't seem to be cross. 'You – you don't mind?' she stuttered.

'I think it's marvellous,' the teacher said. 'You see, it's not just me who thinks you have a great voice. Mind you, I don't want this to go to your head and I don't want it to take the place of your position in the choir. The two roles can complement each other – you'll gain practice in public performance and different forms of music while your choral work will train your voice and give you knowledge of music theory.'

'Yes Miss,' Bernie said.

'You'll need to work very hard and not neglect your studies.'

'Oh I will, I mean I won't. Oh thank you Miss.'

'Okay, I'll see you tonight for your choir rehearsal. Maybe you'd like to keep the newspaper cutting?'

'Oh thank you.' Bernie picked up the paper and stowed it away in her bag to savour later. 'I'll work really hard, it means so much to me.'

'Off you go then,' Mrs Meredith smiled again, 'and let me know next time you're singing with your pop group. I may come along to see you.'

At the rehearsal Bernie sang as if her heart would burst. Mrs Meredith was pleased and congratulated the whole choir.

'I'm so proud of you all and I know you'll be fine when you sing in front of the whole school next week. After that we'll just have a refresher run through before the St Clare's concert to make sure there are no problems.'

Polly was fidgeting to go home but Teresa still sat dreamy-eyed. 'You sang lovely,' she said shyly as Bernie swelled with happiness.

She hadn't had time to read the newspaper article properly and it burned a hole in her bag all the way home. She hadn't told anyone about it, not even Annabel. If her mam found out what she'd been getting up to there would be hell to pay. Anyway her mam had enough on her plate dealing with Marie at the moment.

Her happiness slipped for a moment as she thought of Marie's immediate future. Marie wasn't going to be there to cover for her any more so somehow she would have to win her mam over to her singing with the group. Her worries were blotted out by excitement once she reached home and was able to lock herself in the toilet to read the article properly. It filled almost a quarter page of the *Daily Post*'s music section.

Riverbeat has been on the scene for a while now gigging around North Liverpool's church socials and youth clubs. The addition of McCann's powerful voice promises to take the band into more exciting territory.

In the first set McCann came on for just fifteen minutes, competently performing the usual dance numbers with Riverbeat keeping up a steady backbeat.

It was in the second set that McCann came into her own with an emotionally charged rendition of *Summertime*, followed by *You've Lost That Lovin' Feeling* and finishing up with *Will You Still Love Me Tomorrow?* – just right for that last smooch.

It was a stunning performance that left everyone calling for more. Bernie McCann certainly qualifies for inclusion in our list of new female artistes to watch. We look forward to seeing much more of her on the Mersey scene in future.

Underneath was a smaller photo of the group with Bernie at the mic. She wondered which song she had been singing, her heart overwhelmed by such praise. Reality suddenly intruded with a banging on the toilet door.

'Come out, I need to wee.' Polly's anguished voice ripped into her dream world.

She stuffed the paper into her schoolbag and emerged to change her clothes and start making the kids' tea.

Maureen was late so Bernie had to make the sandwiches for her da, John and Vinny Mack.

'Where's your mam?' Joe growled as she served up the plates and mugs of tea.

'I don't know Da,' she said. She was beginning to worry when at last Maureen came bustling through the back door. Bernie was surprised to see Marie behind her. She looked pale but her face wore its usual uncaring expression.

'Stay in your room till he's gone out,' Maureen said and Marie nodded as she made a beeline for the bedroom.

'Where've you been?' Joe grumbled.

'You'll never guess,' Maureen put on a chirpy voice. 'I've been with our Marie to a job agency. She's got a job working away at Butlins in Wales.'

'Yer what?' Joe's eyebrows almost met as a deep frown wrinkled his forehead. 'Who says so?'

'Oh don't be like that, Joe, it'll be really good for her. She'll be working in the restaurant, learning the catering trade. She'll be there over Christmas, she'll get loads of tips.'

'Won't be all she'll get,' Joe muttered, 'I've heard about them places.'

'It'll do her good,' Maureen persisted. 'Mary Sloane where I work, her girl opened a snack bar after working there for a couple of years.'

'Hmph,' Joe said. He seemed inclined to say more but noticed on looking at his watch that the pubs were open again. It was time to be off. He drank the last of his tea and got to his feet. 'Just as long as she knows she's not bringing no baby back here.'

'As if,' Maureen said lightly, following him to the back door.

Bernie was stunned. She was destined to be a singer but her mam had missed her way, she should have been an actress. She made her way to the bedroom where Marie was sorting through her clothes.

'I can't take much with me,' she said. 'Mam says you have to wear a uniform. These won't fit me much longer, you might as well have them.' She pushed an armful of clothes at Bernie.

'But you'll want them when you come back.'

'No I won't. They'll be out of fashion by then. I'll keep the newer ones. You can borrow them if you like but mind you look after them.'

'I will,' Bernie couldn't believe Marie was really being sent away. 'Where – where are you going?' she hiccupped.

'Don't start blubbing, or you'll have me at it,' Marie said. 'Friday – Father McKenna's going to take me in his car. I don't know where it is but he says it's near enough to visit.'

'So soon? I wish you weren't going,' Bernie mumbled, thinking of all the times she'd fallen out with Marie, wished her a million miles away.

'It won't be for long,' Marie said.

Bernie turned away, sick at heart. She went to the kitchen and saw her mam sitting at the table staring into space.

'Mam,' she said uncertainly, 'shall I make a cup of tea?'

Maureen shifted. 'No, it's okay,' she said then got up and started clearing the dirty dishes. 'Come on, let's get this lot washed up.'

There wasn't much sleep for anyone that night and by morning Bernie had almost forgotten about her newspaper fame.

'What's up with you?' Annabel asked as they walked to school. Bernie couldn't tell her the real source of her misery.

'Our Marie's going away to work at Butlins,' Polly informed Annabel, 'and bloody good riddance too.' She jigged round and round, pulling Teresa with her.

'Stop that and don't swear.' Bernie aimed a smack at her head but missed.

'Is that what's up? I thought you didn't get on.' Annabel looked curiously at her.

'I know but…' Bernie waved a hand helplessly, feeling tears mist her eyes.

They walked on in silence but as they approached the school gates Bernie sensed whispers, giggles and funny looks from some of the other kids going their way.

The assembly that morning was the story of the buried talents and the pupils fidgeted as the Head droned his way through it. Bernie wriggled her bottom on the floor, trying to get more comfortable when she was frozen by Mr Masterson's next words.

'I chose this parable for today for a special reason as it's come to my attention that we have among us a spectacular example of someone utilising her talents. Bernadette McCann, would you come up on the dais please?'

Bernie cringed but had no option but to climb up on the stage, She blushed as Mr Masterson waved a copy of the Daily Post and read out the article about her. She stared out at the sea of faces but saw only pink blobs on the maroon background of school uniforms.

'…and not only is Bernadette developing herself as a pop singer, she is a valued member of St Anthony's choir – the featured solo singer of this year's carol concert. I think we should all show our appreciation, Bernadette is a great asset to St Anthony's and a fine example to you all.'

There was a burst of clapping then Bernie was allowed to escape and retake her place.

'Wow,' Annabel poked her in the ribs, 'you kept quiet about that.'

'I didn't want me mam to find out,' Bernie muttered 'You won't tell her will you? And don't tell your mam either.'

After assembly she gained lots of admiring glances and congratulations from her classmates but also some sniggering and slyness from those who were jealous of her success. At breaktime Morag Sullivan waylaid her in the playground, surrounded by her hangers-on.

'Suppose you think you're someone now,' Morag spat.

'Leave her alone,' Annabel piped up from behind Bernie.

'Shut up, short arse,' Morag gave Annabel a shove and Bernie instinctively jumped forward to protect her friend.

'Come on then, think you're somebody? Think you're hard? Well you're not, you're just a dirty totter.'

Bernie's fists clenched then she remembered her mam's injunction and taking Annabel's arm she walked away, ignoring the raucous laughter that followed them.

That evening Bernie's mam was getting ready for bingo.

'I'm going with Kathleen,' she said happily.

Bernie was glad her mam was getting friendly with Annabel's mam instead of Rose Hanson but she hoped that Mrs Farrier hadn't seen the newspaper article. Fresh horror struck her as she thought of Peter. Perhaps he'd seen it and he would be sure to tell his mam about it.

As soon as her mam had gone out, Peter came flying up the stairs and Bernie's worst fears were realised.

'Guess what?' he shouted as she let him in. He was waving a copy of the paper.

'I know,' she said. 'I've already seen it.'

'No, no not that. We've been offered a gig at the Back Alley club. We're to be the warm-up for Rory Storm and the Hurricanes. We've got to audition first but it's a cinch.'

Bernie's mouth fell open. Rory Storm was well famous and the Back Alley club was a popular spot for teenagers, not far from Mathew Street, home of the Cavern.

'How?' she stuttered.

'The manager saw the piece in the paper. He rang the church and got Ginger's address from the priest. This is it, Bernie, Riverbeat is going places.'

Bernie began to laugh, her head turned by her new fame: first the accolade in front of the school and now this.

Marie had gone out to Angie's but the other kids crowded round, grubby fingers pawing the newspaper Peter had left on the kitchen table.

'Look, our Bernie's in the paper,' Teresa crowed.

'Let me see,' Polly fought her out of the way. 'Bernie's a popstar,' she shouted.

'Let us see,' the twins clamoured, grabbing at the paper till it ripped right across the picture of Bernie's smiling face.

'Pack it in and calm down,' Bernie shouted. 'You're not to tell no one, our mam doesn't know, nor Da. Get ready for bed now.'

When the kids had gone to their rooms to get into their pyjamas Peter pulled her into his arms and kissed her.

'Who'd have thought it, us playing with Rory Storm?' he murmured in her ear. 'But you're going to have to tell your mam and dad. Surely they'll be glad for you?'

'Me mam just wants me to sing in the school choir. She thinks pop singing is nonsense. She'll go mad if she finds out – and as for me da he's against anything that's fun. When is the gig anyway?'

'Two weeks on Saturday,' Peter said and Bernie's heart sank. There was no way she could get out on a Saturday night.

'I don't get it,' Peter said, 'my mum and dad are thrilled to bits.'

'Your mam knows?' A chill struck Bernie's bones.

'Of course,' Peter said, 'Dad saw it in the paper and they were both there when Ginger come round with the news.'

'Was Ginger all right about the article?' Bernie was momentarily sidetracked.

'He was a bit mad about them not giving the rest of us any coverage but it's the article that's got us the gig after all.'

After the kids had gone to bed she and Peter kissed and cuddled on the sofa but Bernie's mind kept going to the problem of how she was going to get out for the gig. Peter was right, she would have to tell her mam but now wasn't the right moment. Her mam was already upset about Marie but she would have to know soon

However, matters were taken out of her hands. The back door slammed and she pulled hastily out of Peter's arms before her mam came into the room with a face like a thundercloud.

'What's all this about singing with a pop group at some youth club last Friday?'

Bernie paled. 'Mam, I wanted to tell you…'

'But you didn't. You went behind my back, you and our Marie …a pack of lies about going to the pictures. I suppose this is your doing?' She turned on Peter.

'But Mrs…' Peter began but she cut him off.

'I told you Bernadette, I don't want you doing this, you haven't got time for it, not with your school work and the choir.'

'But Mam…'

'I told you before, you was to forget about that pop stuff and I haven't raised you to lie through your back teeth to get your own way.'

'Mrs McCann,' Peter broke in, 'she's too good to let it drop. She went down a bomb at the church dance, that's why the reporter from the paper wanted to interview her.'

'Mr. Masterson read the article out to everyone in assembly. He said I'm an asset to the school. And Mrs Meredith thinks it'll be good practice for me, you know performing in public and all that.' Bernie hoped this might cool her mother's temper.

'And I'm the last person to know. The whole city knows about it but not your mother.'

'I was too scared to tell you,' Bernie said.

'Have you seen the article?' Peter asked. Maureen shook her head. 'Show it to your mam, Bernie,' he went on.

Bernie fetched the torn newspaper, smoothed it out as best she could and handed it to her mother. Maureen read it slowly. Her expression changed as she ran her fingers over Bernie's photo.

'Well,' she said at last and took a thoughtful drag on her cig.

'Mrs Meredith thinks it's great,' Bernie said, encouraged by her mam's silence.

'I still don't think it's a good idea.'

'But we've been offered a gig at the Back Alley club in town,' Peter broke in. 'We'll be playing with Rory Storm and the Hurricanes.'

'They're famous Mam, Bernie joined in, 'and it's what I really, really want.'

'I don't know – as if I haven't got enough on me mind already. How can you go singing in some club? You're only fifteen.'

'No one knows that do they?' Bernie muttered. 'And anyway, Lulu was only about twelve when she had her first hit and look at Helen Shapiro. She was only fifteen.'

'And I suppose you think you can do the same?' Maureen's face softened as she saw Bernie's pleading look. 'Well..' she said uncertainly.

'I'll still be in the choir, I'll work just as hard. Please Mam.'

'I'll look after her, Mrs McCann, I promise.'

'My girl, in the paper,' Maureen mused. 'I suppose I shouldn't stand in your way.'

'Oh Mam,' Bernie jumped up to give her a hug.

'Not so fast, when's this performance at this club?' Maureen turned to Peter. 'She's underage to be going in night clubs.'

'I'll be singing, not drinking.' Bernie said.

'Well, I'll be coming along too,' Maureen said, 'You'll need someone to keep an eye on you.'

Bernie's joy withered. The last thing she needed was her mam turning up in her fur coat.

'Don't look at me like that, Bernadette,' Maureen said.

'It'll be okay,' Peter said, 'maybe my mam'll come too.'

'That'll be good,' Maureen said with a relieved smile.

Later that evening Peter and Bernie leaned against the wall outside the chip shop sharing a bag of chips. It was a freezing night and the warmth from the fryers spread outside to where they stood.

'Maybe your Marie could get us an audition at Butlins,' he said. 'Imagine us getting a summer season there.'

'And what about me going to school? And you're still at college.' Bernie answered.

'We'll both have left by then, won't we?' Peter said.

'Me da wouldn't let me go,' Bernie said.

'Well he let Marie go.' Peter picked up a chip and teased her with it.

'That's different, she's nearly eighteen. Anyway let's get this next one over with first, I'm scared stiff about it.'

The thought of appearing at a proper club terrified her but it was nothing compared to what had happened to Marie.

'I've got a new dress,' she said.

'You'll look fab whatever you wear.' Peter screwed up the chip papers and put them in the bin outside the shop. He pulled her close and put his hands under her coat.

139

'Gerroff, you're freezing.' She couldn't help laughing then she saw Jacko Hanson approaching on the other side of the street but he contented himself with a sneer as he went past.

'I'd better get home,' Bernie said, 'I have to be in before ten.'

She felt much happier when she went to bed that night. At least she didn't have to sneak and lie any more. Marie was not in but her little suitcase was standing at the side of their bunks. For a while Bernie had forgotten her and guilt washed over her. She comforted herself with feeling the outline of her songbook under her pillow and rehearsing the tunes and lyrics it contained in her head. She was dozing fitfully when she felt the creak of the bunks as Marie crept up the ladder to bed.

'Are you okay?' she whispered.

'Yes, go to sleep,' Marie hissed.

The next day when Bernie got home from school, the suitcase was gone and so was Marie.

Chapter Fifteen

'But I never got to say goodbye.' Bernie burst into tears.

'It couldn't be helped,' Maureen said. 'Father McKenna has to go somewhere else on Friday so he could only take her today.'

'But Jimmy…' Bernie said.

'Look, we tried, Father tried but there's nowhere to start. No one seems to know him. If Marie had told me earlier, but she's too far gone now and there's no time to waste. Father says she's lucky to get the place. She's not the only one you know.'

'Where?' Bernie sat down at the kitchen table. 'Can we go and see her?'

'It's a long way,' Maureen reached in her pocket for her cigs. 'And we can't go for a while. The nuns say she has to settle in. You can write though. I'll buy some stamps. It's going to be hard, managing without her wages.'

Bernie stared at her. She got up and went to her room. Even though Polly and Teresa's things were scattered around, it seemed empty. She buried her face in her pillow, too miserable even to take solace in her beloved notebook. After a while there was a tap at the door and her mam came in.

'Peter's here,' she said.

Bernie dragged herself off the bed and went out to the kitchen where Maureen was pouring Peter a cup of tea.

'Hi,' his face lit up in a smile and for a moment the heaviness inside her lifted.

The atmosphere in Ginger's shed was fizzing with excitement when Peter and Bernie arrived with Tommy. Everyone was too excited about the upcoming gig to have anything to say about the newspaper article. Bernie's spirits rose, now she was really going to belong. In her mind she

141

saw their name in neon lights outside the Empire in town. It said 'Bernie McCann and Riverbeat' but she kept this image to herself.

She came back to reality as the group began to sort out the set for their audition on the forthcoming Friday.

'Should we dress for it, or doesn't it matter?' Phil asked.

'I think we should,' Ginger said. 'We want to make an impression and he probably wants to see what we look like on stage. You got something decent?' he looked disparagingly at Bernie's jeans and old cardigan.

'Of course she has,' Peter jumped in.

'Only asking,' Ginger gave a crocodile smile. 'Just that everyone's going to be looking at her, aren't they?'

His tone made Bernie feel uncomfortable but she shrugged it off. She bit her lip thinking that now there would be no Marie to do her hair and makeup for her. Maybe her mam would help but she didn't have much idea about the latest styles. Still she would manage somehow. The excitement was catching and she bubbled with enthusiasm through the dance numbers but when she came to her blues set, her voice almost broke, singing *House of the Rising Sun*. She thought of Marie and the only way to lose her misery was to let it out in her voice. There was silence when the song finished.

'Wow,' Tommy's eyes were shining.

'Quite.' Even Ginger looked admiring. 'If you sing like that at the audition, nothing's going to stop us.'

They were all on a high when the practice broke up but when Bernie got home   there were voices coming from the living room and her heart fluttered. Surely her da wasn't home already?

A girl was sitting on the couch next to John. One look told her that she wasn't local. She had on a beautiful smock dress that looked to have come from one of the expensive shops like *Wallis*. Her smooth, blonde hair was cut in an immaculate bob.

'This is John's girlfriend, Sandie,' Maureen said. Her voice gave no clue as to what she thought of her.

Bernie couldn't help looking at the girl's feet but they were encased in green leather granny shoes that matched the handbag on her lap.

'Me sister, Bernie,' John said.

'Hello,' the girl said, giving Bernie a smile that seemed friendly enough though Bernie thought that such a posh girl might be snooty.

'Well, I'd better be getting home,' Sandie said. She stood, swirling her coat over her shoulders. Bernie looked on enviously. It had what looked like a real fur collar that framed Sandie's beautifully made up face.

'I've got to pick Da up anyway,' John said, getting up.

142

'Nice to meet you Mrs McCann,' Sandie said, 'and you too Bernie.' She flashed another smile. 'Bye bye then.'

'Ta-ra love,' Maureen said.

Left alone they looked at each other. 'God, I'm dying for a fag.' Maureen pulled out her cigarettes. 'She don't smoke.'

'She seems nice,' Bernie said.

'She's not from round here,' Maureen said. 'Childwall.'

In bed Bernie thought that Sandie had two black marks against her already in her mother's book: not smoking and coming from a posh area like Childwall. 'God knows what she sees in our John,' Bernie giggled to herself.

Bernie herself was envious of Sandie's good looks but more of her expensive clothes and makeup. Could I look that good? she wondered then she thought of the money she would get singing with Riverbeat. She remembered Peter's words, 'It's just the start,' and her heart beat faster. She struggled to sleep, conscious of the empty bunk above her and wondering how Marie was faring but at last the sound of her sisters' rhythmic breathing lulled her. She slid into a dream of singing alone under a spotlight as an adoring audience threw roses at her feet.

Friday came too soon. Bernie was so nervous even at breakfast time that she couldn't eat anything. All day her stomach was tied in a knot, if she wasn't worrying about her singing she was worrying about how to do her hair and makeup.

'I'll do your hair,' her mam said when she got home. Bernie changed into her new floaty dress and it looked great.

'Can't I get it cut, Mam?' she asked while Maureen brushed out her long hair.

'No, you got lovely hair,' her mam said, brushing out the dark curls so that Bernie's hair lay at least partially flat. 'I'll put it up in a beehive,' she said, reaching for a handful of hairgrips.

'No,' Bernie squealed, 'that's too old-fashioned. Oh Mam, can't I get it cut like Cilla's or our John's girlfriend's?'

'No, it's a shame to cut it, you'd regret it.' She brushed energetically. 'You'll thank me later.'

Bernie sulked. 'I'm not having no beehive'

'Okay, I'll curl up the ends how's that? A bit like Lulu has hers.'

'I suppose,' Bernie said gruffly but after her mam got busy with Marie's curling tongs it looked pretty good. A generous spray of *Belair* ensured it would stay in place.

' I ought to be coming with you but I couldn't get anyone to mind the kids. Kathleen and Tommy are going out with Annabel to the pictures, it's Tommy's birthday.'

Bernie breathed a sigh of relief, then Peter was at the door. 'You look fab,' he gulped, then they were both flying down the stairs, filled with excitement. He kissed her in the lobby, holding her tight, then they ran down the street to where Tommy was waiting in the van.

The Back Alley club looked very dull and tacky with no one in it but the manager and a barmaid preparing for the evening opening. Bernie had to sit with the manager while the band set up their gear. He was called Sid Slocombe, looked even older than her da and he was fat and bald, dressed in a wrinkled suit.

'Well you're pretty enough,' he leered at her. 'If you can sing as good as you look, you'll do okay.' He puffed on a cigarette held between fingers yellow with nicotine. 'How long you been singing then?'

Bernie said 'Oh quite a while now but I've only recently joined Riverbeat.' It wasn't quite a lie, she had been singing with the school choir for some time. She did her best to appear friendly but her palms sweated with terror in case he asked how old she was. She kept him talking by asking questions about the club – whether they had special evenings for different kinds of music.

At last Peter beckoned her up to the stage and as soon as the opening bars of her first number struck up she forgot about the manager and swung into the song; it was good to let all her tension out.

She was only halfway through the first of her slow songs, *Summertime*, when the manager held up his hand with a weary gesture. Bernie stuttered to a halt. He waved them over.

'Okay, you'll do,' he said and her heart soared. 'Cut out the slow stuff though. You'll be on first. Rory comes on at nine. You'll be on eight till nine so people want summat lively to dance to. Sounds good though girl.' He winked at Bernie. 'You can maybe slip one or two in between the dance numbers. Be here for six-thirty to set up and check your sound.' He got up and went over to the bar.

They were all delighted, drunk with success. On the way home Tommy stopped at a chippy and they sat in the van eating chips and imagining the fame and fortune they were sure would come their way. Bernie felt like she loved them all, even Ginger. Never before had she had this sense of belonging, outside of her own family. Not with George nor Aggie. Their names now seemed to come from a life lived by a different girl.

After Ginger and Phil had been dropped off Peter cuddled her in the back of the van. His lips tasted of salt and vinegar and his kisses were no longer tentative but possessive, fuelling Bernie to burning point.

'Okay man, we're here.' The van jerked to a halt and she and Peter jumped out, eager for the privacy of the lobby and the shadows under the stairs where they could melt into each other.

Folded inside Peter's jacket, Bernie was conscious only of the heat of their bodies. Brian Hyland's *Sealed With a Kiss* floated through her mind as their lips burned together then Peter's tongue teased her mouth open and she felt an instant response between her legs. She fitted herself closer to him wanting his hands on her back, on her bare skin but the dress prevented that. She had to be content with feeling his touch through the filmy material. His hand brushed her breast cautiously, as if she might slap him away but her breast seemed to lean forward of its own accord, fitting itself into his hand, the nipple stiffening and tightening inside her bra.

Peter broke the kiss; he groaned and rested his chin on her head. She felt herself melting, the heat of his hand churning through her body, tingling her nipples and that spot… Everything ached for him. She turned her head and kissed his neck, running her fingers through his hair.

'Oh Bernie,' he gasped then the clattering sound of a motor pulling up broke in on them.

'It's me da,' Bernie felt a shock like a bucket of cold water. She moved to run out and up the stairs.

'No,' Peter whispered, pulling her back and kissing her once more. She heard the van doors slam then the heavy sounds of John and her da's feet approaching. She cowered back inside Peter's jacket. One set of footsteps started up the stairs, the other came closer.

'Having fun kids?' John grinned at them and Bernie sighed with relief. 'Better get in Bernie.' He winked at Peter and set off up the stairs after his father.

After a final clinch, Bernie pulled away and crept quietly up the steps. Noiselessly she opened the back door and went into the bathroom. She looked at herself in the small square of mirror as she scrubbed off her makeup. Her hair was wild, her mouth red and swollen. When she emerged looking tamed, her mam was in the kitchen.

'Everything all right? How did it go?' Maureen asked anxiously.

'We're booked,' Bernie said, edging towards the bedroom.

A smile of pride suffused Maureen's face. 'Come and get some onion gravy and tell me all about it.'

'I'm knackered Mam, I just want to get to bed.'

Maureen looked closely at her. A knowing look came into her eyes.

Bernie turned away, blushing. It was as if her mam could see the hot desire that still pulsed through her body. She got into bed and curled up, holding her songbook clasped between her knees, reliving those moments under the stairs. French kissing, she thought with delight, then she remembered Marie and Jimmy. Now she understood why.

Chapter Sixteen

The day before the Back Alley gig Bernie's nerves were tight as violin strings. It didn't help that Friday morning had been chosen for the public rehearsal of the carol concert at school assembly. Once the choir began its well-practised programme however, everything else was blotted out by the need to concentrate on her part. At the end the choir took a bow to an enthusiastic audience. Mrs Meredith, red-cheeked and bursting with pride, congratulated them all.

'Now girls,' she told them, 'just another two weeks to the St Clare's concert. We'll be going there next week to test the arrangements and do another rehearsal.'

The thought of performing in the church no longer frightened Bernie. It paled beside the pitfalls of singing in front of a crowd of critical teenagers.

At home time she collected her sisters. Teresa was walking out with the red-haired Sandra, now her best friend in school. Friendship didn't extend to Katy and Morag Sullivan who were waiting at the school gate for Sandra but apart from giving Bernie dirty looks they did nothing to stop her passing by.

'Who does she think she is?' Katy said in a voice meant for Bernie to hear.

'Teacher's suckhole,' Morag said and they both laughed.

Bernie ignored them, she had more important things on her mind. She wouldn't finish work till four-thirty the next day which would only leave her an hour and a half to get ready before Tommy collected them all in the van. She dreaded letting her mam do her hair even more than she dreaded her coming to the club to see their act but there was nothing she could do to stop her.

Later, after tea, Maureen had run out of cigarettes so Bernie offered to nip to the paper shop. Mrs Thompson was at the counter, preparing to close up when Bernie dashed in.

'Hi Bernie,' she said, 'what brings you here? Nothing wrong is there?'

'No, no, I've just come for ten Woodies for me mam.'

'Thought for a minute you were going to let us down for tomorrow.'

'Oh no, I wouldn't do that,' Bernie stammered.

'Sure you're all right? You seem a bit flustered.'

'Oh yes, I mean, I'm fine. It's just that I'm singing at a club tomorrow night and I'm trying to sort out how to get ready in time.'

'Which club would that be?'

'It's called the Back Alley. It's in town.'

'I saw the article about you in the paper. I says to Mr Thompson, look that's our new shop girl.'

Bernie blushed. 'Seems like everyone knows,' she mumbled.

'So what's wrong with that?' Mrs Thompson opened the till and started cashing up. 'Well, I wouldn't want to stand in the way of a budding popstar. How about we let you off an hour early? You can just take half an hour for lunch tomorrow and next week to make it up.'

'Oh thanks, Mrs Thompson, ' Bernie beamed.

'Don't forget your mam's cigs.' Mrs Thompson slid the packet across the counter.

Bernie pushed through the door and almost bumped into Jacko Hanson who was just passing the chip shop.

'Hey, watch it,' he grabbed her arm, turned and began walking along beside her.

'Let go,' she hissed but he held on to her easily.

'Don't be shy,' he grinned into her face. 'Just want to talk to you. Suppose you think you're too good for everyone now you've had your picture in the paper.'

He gave her wrist a twist but she wasn't going to give him the satisfaction of hearing her cry out.

'Get off me,' she spat, trying to pull her arm from his grasp.

'Don't be like that,' he laughed unpleasantly. 'You shouldn't be rude to your fans. I might ring up that newspaper and tell them what you really are – a dirty little totter.'

Tears of rage sprang to Bernie's eyes. She turned and thumped Jacko in the chest with her free hand but he didn't let go.

'Little tramp,' he snarled. Suddenly he pulled her into the alley that ran between the closed baker's shop and the pub on the corner. It was already dark and even darker as he dragged her into the pub car park where he pinned her up against the brick wall by a row of dustbins.

Bernie was too petrified even to scream and it all happened so quickly. She could smell the sweat of his armpits and a hamster smell of old blood and unwashed body.

The sickly scent of Brylcreem filled her nostrils as he lowered his head and pressed his body against her. She twisted her head and his kiss slobbered down her cheek. Her whole body crawled with revulsion as he grinned into her face.

148

'Come on,' he said, forcing a knee between her legs. 'I know you give it out to everyone,' he whispered hot breath in her ear. 'Farrier's getting it, why not a bit for me as well?'

His lips came down on her mouth, wet and rubbery as she struggled to free her arms. She could feel the heavy buckle of his leather belt pressing into her belly and he pushed his knee upwards, forcing her legs further apart. She twisted and turned, grunting in a futile effort to get away from him. It only made him laugh more, soft, menacing laughter.

Suddenly the back door of the pub opened and a woman came out, carrying a sack of rubbish for the bin and peered into the darkness.

'Who's there?' she shouted. 'What's going on?'

Startled, Jacko loosened his grip and stepped back. That was all Bernie needed. She brought her knee up sharply into his crotch and raked her nails down his face as he let go of her hands.

'Get out of there,' the woman shouted.

Bernie needed no second bidding. As Jacko doubled up with a cry of agony she fled away back down the alley and into the lamplit street.

When she got home her mam and Kathleen Farrier were in the kitchen with their coats on, ready for bingo.

'Where've you been,' Maureen chided. 'I'm spitting feathers for a fag.'

Bernie gave her the cigarettes. 'Mrs Thompson was asking me about my singing,' she managed to get out without bursting into tears.

'What's the matter with you?' Maureen gave her a sharp look. 'You look like you've been through a hedge backwards.'

'Nothing,' Bernie said. 'It's cold out and it's windy. Need the lav,' she muttered and made for the toilet.

'Well, we're going out now,' Maureen yelled from the kitchen. 'John and Sandie are here anyway.'

'Okay Mam, bye.' Bernie tried to sound normal. She went into the bathroom, sat on the edge of the bath and examined her face in the mirror. There were no marks but she felt dirty all over. She decided to run a bath even though it wasn't bath night. Her mam wasn't there to tell her off and it was the only way to get the stink of Jacko's hair cream off her skin.

She lay soaping herself till the water grew cold, asking herself over and over if it was somehow her fault. Had she given him some reason to think that she was easy? Had the way she was with Peter somehow

149

communicated itself to him? She couldn't think that Peter himself had said anything to him.

When she was dry and dressed in clean pyjamas she felt a bit better. The kids were all in the twins' room making a noise but Bernie didn't have the energy to investigate. John and Sandie burst apart on the couch when she went into the living room.

'About time,' John said, red-faced. 'We're waiting to go for a drink.'

'Well you can go now can't you?' Bernie said crossly.

'See she thinks she's somebody now 'cos she's been in the paper. That's why she's in the bath for hours, tarting herself up for this club she's singing at tomorrow.'

'Oh shut up John,' Bernie snapped. She sat down in her da's armchair and put her face in her hands.

'What's up with you?' John looked astonished. 'I was only joking.'

'I know – it's just…' She gulped. She couldn't say what was really wrong. She seized on the first thing that came into her head. 'I don't know what to do with me hair tomorrow, it's got to look good. Our Marie did it for me last time but now she's not here.' To John's amazement she began to sob.

'Thought you didn't get on with her,' he muttered.

'I'll do your hair,' Sandie said. She got up and laid a hand on Bernie's shoulder. 'I'll do your makeup as well if you like.'

Bernie looked up at her. 'Are you sure?'

'I'm not at work tomorrow. John and I are going into town in the afternoon then I'll come back with him, help you get ready. I'd love to come and see you sing too.' She smiled at John. 'What do you think?'

'If you like,' he said grudgingly and Bernie had to smile. It seemed like half her family were going to be there to see her make a show of herself.

On Saturday the shop was busier than usual and Bernie was kept on her feet. She was glad as it helped to take her mind off what had happened with Jacko. She had to try and put it behind her and concentrate on performing her best that night. In the afternoon, Mrs Thompson took her behind the counter and explained how to work the till. She was allowed to serve a few customers under her employer's supervision.

At four o'clock Mrs Thompson told Bernie she could go home. 'Go on, you've done well and I can manage now.'

Bernie breathed her thanks and got her coat. She took the time to look up and down the road in case Jacko Hanson was about before racing home as fast as she could.

In the flat Kathleen Farrier was drinking tea with Bernie's mam and Joan. The twins were running round zapping everyone with toy rayguns Maureen had brought back from Greaty market. In the living room Sandie was trying to teach Polly and Teresa to do the twist to the music on Radio Caroline.

'We want to watch you sing too,' Polly sang out as she and Teresa danced about.

'Well you can't,' Bernie said. 'Kids aren't allowed.'

Sandie had brought a small travel case. Inside was a whole palette of eyeshadows. Bernie stared enviously; it wasn't cheap stuff from Woolies: Miners or Rimmel but obviously an expensive set. Out of the case came cosmetic bags containing mascaras, lipsticks and eyeliners. Bernie had never seen so much makeup, more than Marie ever had and all of it looked like the stuff Bernie would try samples of in Lewis's or George Henry Lee's when she went to town.

'Zip – zap,' Matty and Anthony came racing in but all the merriment was curtailed by the arrival of her da with John and Vinny Mack.

'Come in our room,' Bernie urged Sandie as all the kids made themselves scarce.

'What's this, a mothers' meeting?' Joe joked gruffly at the women in the kitchen. Seeing her da, Bernie thought there was no way her mam would get out of her Saturday night out with him but she reckoned without her mam's inventiveness

'You'll never guess,' Maureen said, 'me Aunty Ann's come up to see me mam. Joan's offered to mind the kids so me and our Bernie can go and see her.'

'But it's Saturday,' Da growled.

'I know Joe but she's going back tomorrow. She's come all the way from Glasgow. I haven't seen her for years and she hasn't seen our Bernie since she was little.'

'Hmph. What about me tea?' Joe headed for the living room followed by Vinny Mack

'I've got your tea ready. John can run us over and bring me back to the wine lodge for the last hour. Fred said he'll run our Bernie home. I just really want to see her.'

'Well suit yourself,' Joe said, 'but our John'll have to run me and Vinny to town first.'

'I'll get your butties now.' Bernie heard the relief in her mam's voice and she turned back into the bedroom with a smile.

Polly and Teresa were sitting on their bed with Sandie, examining the seemingly endless collection of cosmetics in her bag.

'Isn't your dad coming to see you sing?' Sandie asked.

'No fear,' Bernie said. 'I'll get into me frock.'

When Bernie saw her finished face in the mirror she knew she was going to love Sandie forever. She was already hoping that she and John would get married so she would have a wonderful big sister. Bernie sobered for a moment, wondering how Marie was getting on and promised herself that as soon as tonight's gig was over she would send Marie a long letter telling her all about it. A few minutes later she forgot everything in the excitement of getting ready.

Peter came for her at five-thirty as soon as he saw her da leaving the block. He looked so handsome in a suit with narrow lapels and a crisp pinstriped shirt.

'John's coming back for me and your mam and Sandie,' Maureen told him. 'We should be there by about seven.'

'Me mam's dollying herself up now,' Peter laughed. 'There's not many tables in the club but I'll see if I can save you one.'

'We'll only stay for your act,' Maureen said, 'then we're going back to the wine lodge so can your mam come back with you?'

'It'll be a bit of a squash but we'll manage. Come on Bernie, Tommy's downstairs waiting.'

The club still looked dingy but there was an air of expectation as the bar staff got ready for the evening. Bernie hung around backstage in the tacky corner that was the dressing room, hoping to meet up with Rory Storm and The Hurricanes but they hadn't yet arrived.

Ginger called her out to check the microphone sound and she saw that already a few people had gathered at the bar and with the coloured lights turned on the club looked much more inviting. Shortly after, a disc jockey began to play the latest hits, more people trickled in and the dance floor began to fill.

She sat at the small table Peter had reserved and waited for her family. She was so pleased to see them she forgot her fears of Mam showing her up. Only a few minutes later Riverbeat went on stage and she watched as the lads crashed into the opening set with, *When I Saw Her Standing There*.

All too soon it was time for her to go on and she stepped onto the stage with dry mouth and sweating palms. She took hold of the microphone and launched into *I Only Want to Be With You*.

This time she had half a dozen songs and the crowd before her blurred into a mass of swirling colour as more couples pushed onto the dance floor. From the corner of her eye she saw Sid Slocombe sitting on a stool at the bar. He gave her a smile and a thumbs-up. Encouraged she closed her eyes and let her voice rip out.

In the interval she ran breathlessly to where her mam was sitting.

'Golly, you were fabulous,' Sandie gasped.

'Took the words right out of me mouth,' Maureen said.

'Talk about a dark horse.' John was grinning.

Bernie felt so high, as if she could do anything. Nothing and no one could harm her. She couldn't stop the laughter that bubbled out of her at the sight of their amazement.

In the second set she was allowed a couple of blues numbers. Even though she was conscious of her mam watching, she had to sway sensuously to *Can't Help Lovin' dat Man of Mine*. Her second number, *You'll Never Walk Alone* flowed out to appreciative silence. When she came to the end, she felt drained but also excited as Peter came forward and asked the audience,

'Let's hear it again for Bernie McCann.'

She ran off the stage to thunderous applause. After a couple more songs, the boys were finished. The disc jockey came back on with more records while Riverbeat packed up their instruments. Bernie waited backstage, still hoping to bump into Rory Storm but Peter came to tell her her mam was leaving.

'I'm so proud of you,' Maureen hugged her. 'We'll have to go or your da'll be grumbling. Don't be too late home, she called to Bernie's embarrassment as John hustled her and Sandie out.

Bernie sat with Kathleen. Even more people were coming into the club, attracted by the star act. Bernie couldn't wait to see it.

'Let me get you a drink,'

She looked round to see Sid Slocombe at her elbow.

'Oh it's okay, my boyfriend's getting me one,' she said.

'Boyfriend eh? Lucky guy. You were great tonight.'

'Thanks.' Bernie didn't want to talk to him but she couldn't afford to be rude.

'We'll definitely be booking you again. So what about that drink?'

Bernie spotted Peter coming across with a tray of glasses. 'Oh, here's Peter now Mr Slocombe,' she said.

'Call me Sid,' he looked Peter up and down. 'You did well tonight, all of you. I think we'll be seeing you again soon.'

Peter grinned and said something but the words were lost on Bernie. In the sea of faces in the room she saw someone familiar sitting at one of the tables round the edge of the room. Blood pounded in her ears as she recognised Jimmy, Marie's disappearing boyfriend drooling over a dark-haired girl in a pink dress.

She got up and moved towards him, feeling as if she was wading through water, intent only on reaching that table.

'You,' she hissed as she got near. Jimmy looked up and the smile died on his face.

'Bernie,' he said, what are you doing here?'

'Looking for you – you – bastard.' The word flew out of her mouth before she even thought it, loud enough for heads to turn in their direction.

'Who's she?' the girl said, giving Bernie a frosty stare.

'I'm his girlfriend's sister,' Bernie spat, 'the one he got pregnant and left in the lurch.'

The girl looked at Bernie like she was some insect. Jimmy raised his hands defensively. 'Now then Bernie,' he said.

'Don't you now then me,' Bernie lunged at him but someone gripped her arm and she turned to find Peter, looking horrorstruck.

'What do you think you're doing?' He pulled her away.

'You're hurting me.' She pulled back, blood rushing to her face.

A smirk crossed Jimmy's face and rage blundered through her. If she could just get at him… but Peter was holding her tight in what seemed to be a lover's embrace but felt like an iron lung.

'Stop it,' he whispered in her ear. 'Everyone's looking.'

'I don't care' she cried but she was crumpling in his arms.

'Be professional,' he muttered, ' people are watching us.'

She let him lead her back to their table where Kathleen and the rest of the group were drinking and chatting. She sipped her lemonade and pretended to join in even though she was still raging inside. There had to be some way to find out where Jimmy lived. She couldn't let him get away now. She was just glad her mam hadn't seen him.

The others were in high humour now their part of the show had been successfully completed.

'What was all that about anyway?' Peter asked. 'Wasn't that Jimmy ……..that used to go out with your Marie?'

'Do you know him?'

154

'He's in that crummy band, Strawberry Jam. I see him now and then. Is that what you were mad about, because he's with another girl?'

'Let's forget about him,' Bernie smiled sweetly but she was storing up the information that Jimmy was to be seen on the music scene and when she saw him get up and head to the toilets, she excused herself and went to the Ladies. She waited outside till he came out of the Gents.

'Oh get lost, Bernie,' he said with that lazy smile that made her want to smack him.

'What about our Marie?' Bernie spat.

'What about her? It was good while it lasted.' He grinned.

'She's been sent away and it's all your fault.' Bernie shouted. 'How could you do that to her?'

'Oh come on, Bern. It's not mine you know. There were plenty of others.'

Bernie flew at him fingers outstretched to claw his face. I'll kill you,' she screeched but someone pulled her roughly away. She turned to find Ginger pinning her arms to her sides.

'What are you doing, you idiot,' he shouted.

'Mind your own business,' she yelled back, struggling as Jimmy made a quick escape out of the club.

'It is business,' he said, dragging her away. 'There's an agent backstage wants to talk to us.'

Chapter Seventeen

From the day Bobby Charles took the band on Bernie's life changed. He was a young and enthusisatic agent and with Christmas coming up Riverbeat were getting two or three bookings every weekend. It was hard work on top of her school studies but she loved it and she was now earning upwards of two pounds a week.

Her first free Friday night she went to Miss Fifi, the best local hairstylist and got her hair cut in a straight bob.

Maureen was horrified but she mellowed when Bernie handed over a pound instead of the usual nine shillings towards her keep. Bernie didn't forget to treat her brothers and sisters either. When her mam went to bingo she sent down to the van for a monster feast of sweets, crisps and lemonade as well as some sachets of Nescafé for herself and Peter.

Bernie sent the kids to bed early, allowing them to take their treats with them to keep them quiet. She wanted to be alone with Peter but it was clear he had other things on his mind than cuddling.

'I've been wanting to ask you something.' He pulled away from her, his face serious.

'Okay, go on,' she said uncertainly.

'The other week, at the Back Alley, that bloke Jimmy you were having a go at – was it really because of your sister?'

'He did the dirty on her.' Bernie's romantic mood disintegrated.

'But she went away to work. I thought she'd finished with him?'

Bernie was silent.

'I thought… I thought maybe you and him…'

'You thought me and him? How could you? I wouldn't touch him with a bargepole.' She shifted to the end of the couch and glared at him.

'Then why'd you get so mad at him?'

Just thinking about Jimmy made her see red all over again. ''Cos he got her pregnant and ran off and left her.' It was out before she could stop it.

Peter's face drained of colour. 'But Butlins..' he said.

'She never went to Butlins. She got sent away to have the baby.' Bernie burst into tears.

Peter looked bewildered.

'He said it wasn't his. When I saw him in the club, he said she went with everyone.'

'Bastard,' Peter folded her in his arms and rocked her till her sobs slowed.

'You mustn't tell no one.' Bernie pulled away to look in his face. 'No one knows, not even the kids and specially not me da. Mam arranged it all with Father McKenna. They couldn't find out where Jimmy lived so they sent her to the nuns.'

'I won't say nothing to no one, promise, but you should have asked me. People know him on the music scene. If you'd told me earlier … maybe it's not too late. I'll see what I can find out.'

They sat in silence for a while. It was a relief to spill the secret to someone she trusted but she wasn't sure about tracking Jimmy down. Marie was probably better off without a rat like him in the long run. But then, the thought of him getting off scotfree made her blood boil.

Fancy Peter thinking she'd have a fling with that slimy pig. It made her want to laugh but she saw that he wasn't too sure of her and perhaps that wasn't a bad thing. The advice pages in *Valentine* always said not to wear your heart on your sleeve too soon.

'Come here you divvy,' she pulled Peter close, 'you know I wouldn't look twice at anyone else.'

John's birthday fell the following Tuesday. Bernie wanted to give him something more than the striped tie she'd bought him weeks before. She'd had a busy weekend with Riverbeat booked at Litherland Town Hall and again at the Back Alley so she hadn't had time to go into town. All she could do was nip round to the paper shop to buy an extra gift.

She called down for Annabel but she was doing her homework so Bernie set off alone. At the paper shop she bought a packet of Golden Virginia, John's favourite rollup tobacco. She chatted to Mrs Thompson for a few minutes. On the way home she sang to herself, happy to have enough money to buy little treats for her family. It wasn't so long ago she hadn't even had the coppers to phone that rat George. How scornful she felt now when she thought about him. She was so lucky to have found Peter. As she neared home she heard heavy footfalls behind her and, turning to look, she saw Jacko Hanson catching her up. She began to run but he was already reaching out, grabbing her shoulder and jerking her back.

'What's the rush?' he grinned.

He smelled of old blood and she gagged, seeing a bloodstained white overall sticking out of his workbag.

'Let me go,' she tried to pull away but he slid his hand down her arm and twisted her wrist viciously. She bit back a scream but just then her da's van turned the corner into the road.

Jacko let go of her. 'Don't think you got away with it. I'm going to get you,' he hissed, then walked away towards his own block, disappearing into it before John got out of the van.

John was alone, having dropped off her da and Vinny at the Crown pub further up the East Lancs road.

'What was that about?' he asked as she rubbed at her wrist where the imprint of Jacko's fingers was clearly visible. 'Has he been bothering you?'

'Don't make a fuss, John,' Bernie pleaded. 'I don't know why he's got it in for me.'

'It's not the first time then?'

'No.'

'So what happened?'

Bernie saw that he wasn't going to let it drop so she told him how he'd attacked her in the pub car park.

John's face reddened and he began to ball his fists. 'I knew he was a wanker but I didn't think...' He scowled. 'I'll see to him, don't you worry.'

'Oh no John, I don't want to cause trouble. Mrs Hanson...'

'Fuck her, and him too. Does Peter know?'

'No, I told you, I don't want no trouble and if me mam finds out or Da...'

'You just forget about it, he won't bother you no more. Leave it to me.'

The next day it was John's birthday so surely he would have other things on his mind than avenging her? She gave him her presents first thing, getting up before he left for work.

'The tie's fantastic,' he said, holding it up against his chest. 'I'll wear it tonight. I'm taking Sandie to town and we're going for a Chinese.'

At school the choir were taken by coach to St Clare's for a rehearsal. Bernie admired the beautiful old church and the girls' voices sounded so clear and pure with the jewelled light from the stained glass windows shining down on them. Afterwards she was given two tickets for her parents. The performance was scheduled for Friday evening and everyone was excited when Mrs Meredith revealed that their singing would be recorded by the BBC for regional broadcasting. Bernie knew that her da wouldn't go, the second ticket was reserved for her Aunty Joan and after a lot of pleading Mrs Meredith allowed her an extra ticket for her nan. Kathleen Farrier was going to mind her brothers and sisters. They'd all seen the carol concert already as the junior classes had been brought in for the school performance. The weekend was going to be hectic with the concert on Friday, then Riverbeat was booked at St Teresa's social club on Sunday, which at least was local.

'Mam, it's going to be hard for me to keep working at the paper shop,' Bernie said as the family ate their egg and chips that evening. There was no sign of John, Da and Vinny so she supposed John had gone to drop them off at the pub before picking up Sandie.

'You need to keep that job,' Maureen said. 'This pop lark might be a flash in the pan.'

'But it means such a rush. I'm singing every weekend now and for what I earn at the shop it's not worth it.'

'Don't put all your eggs in one basket. It's only a couple of weeks since you thought it was a fortune.'

It was true. Things had changed so fast. She would feel really bad about leaving the shop after Mrs Thompson had been so kind to her.

The back door opened and John breezed in.

'How's the birthday boy?' Maureen began but her smile faded as she saw the bloody cut on his cheekbone. 'What's happened to you?' She jumped up. 'You've been fighting.'

'Tripped on the steps,' John said cheerfully. Bernie stared at him.

'Tell that to the Marines,' Maureen said. 'What's Sandie going to think, you turning out like you've been five rounds with Cassius Clay?'

'He's not called that no more,' John said. 'You want to get with it Mam.'

'Don't change the subject,' Maureen snapped.

'Aw Mam, don't go on.' He headed for the bathroom.

'Get some cold water on it,' Maureen shouted but she didn't pursue it further. Bernie pushed away her plate. She went to her room and waited for John to come out in his finery. He looked so smart in a new shirt, his good suit and the tie Bernie had given him. The cut on his face was less noticeable now the blood was washed off but a purplish bruise was forming round it.

'What happened?' Bernie whispered.

'Told you, I fell up the steps. Don't you worry about it, you won't be having any more trouble from you-know-who.'

The next day when Bernie collected her sisters from school, Morag and Katy Sullivan pushed in front of them, blocking the way.

'We're gonna get you, you scruffbag,' Morag hissed, 'and Jacko's mates'll get your scummy brother.'

'You're goin' to be so-o-o-o sorry,' Katy drawled and they both laughed.

'Come on,' Bernie said to Annabel and she pushed Morag out of the way.

'We'll be waiting,' Morag sang out as Bernie and Annabel crossed the playground.

Polly and Teresa were just coming out. Teresa was chatting away to Sandra. Bernie looked round for another means of getting out of the school yard but the gate was the only exit; the rest of the grounds were surrounded by tall railings topped with spikes.

'Listen, Morag and Katy are after us so we have to make a run for it,' she told her sisters.

'I'm not scared of them,' Polly said. 'I can batter Katy no bother.'

'No,' Bernie said, 'not here. Mam'll get into trouble if we're caught fighting and I'll get banned from the choir. We'll make like we're doing a runner till we get away from here.'

Teresa and Sandra were lagging back so they hadn't heard the conversation. 'Right,' Bernie said, taking Teresa's hand, 'when I say run, run like hell.'

A few yards from the gate, Bernie gave the signal and took off, yanking a surprised Teresa behind her. She cannoned into Morag, making way for Polly and Annabel to follow before the Sullivan girls could react. Sandra stood open-mouthed, unable to decide whether to stay or go with her friend.

A quick look over her shoulder told Bernie that Katy and Morag were giving chase. Sandra came behind them, her spindly legs trying to keep up. Bernie led the way, racing, not towards home but to an area of waste ground. Panting, she turned to face the Sullivans.

'Come on then,' she taunted Morag and without waiting she slung her schoolbag from her shoulder and swung it at Morag's head, knocking her to the ground. She jumped on the other girl's back, forcing her face down into the mud. While Morag struggled to free herself, Polly waded in, grabbing Katy by the hair and swinging her round. Teresa started to cry but Sandra, finally catching up, attacked Polly from behind, jumping on her back and trying to claw at her face.

Seeing her sister getting the worst of it, Teresa also jumped in, trying to drag Sandra away.

'Dirty totters,' Morag hissed through a mouthful of mud and Bernie, seeing red, pulled her head back by the hair and pounded her face back in the muddy puddle.

'Take it back,' she screamed, emphasising each word with a dunk in the mud.

After a minute of useless struggling Morag caved in. 'Okay, okay, I take it back. Gerroff me,' she muttered.

Bernie got up, the red mist cleared and she saw that Morag was covered in mud all down her front. Her face was also streaked with blood from her nose and from scratches inflicted by gravel in the puddle. She looked like something from a horror film. Resisting the urge for triumphant laughter Bernie looked down at herself to see she too was splattered with mud and her shoes and socks were caked with it.

She pulled the other girls apart. 'Okay, that's it.' She held on to Polly who was still swinging punches at Katy. In the fracas Teresa had torn Sandra's skirt and blazer and she was revealed standing in her navy blue knickers. A group of older boys, passing by, laughed and pointed and Sandra burst into tears and ran off trying to cover herself with the remains of her clothes.

Katy and Morag also made off. Bernie shouted after them, 'That'll teach you to call us names,' but already she was beginning to fear the consequences. What if Mam was in when they got back covered in muck? But Annabel, Polly and Teresa were cock-a-hoop.

'Calm down now,' Bernie said trying to brush the worst of the dirt off her sisters. 'Come on, let's get home.'

Luckily they were able to get back and clean themselves up before their mam arrived home. When she came Bernie was at her usual task of peeling potatoes.

'What's all this?' Maureen looked at the row of freshly washed school blouses hanging on the kitchen maiden.

'Oh it was terrible,' Bernie lied. 'These boys came past on bikes and splashed us all over.'

'Well that's saved me a job, better get them by the fire if they're going to dry by tomorrow.' Maureen wound the maiden down, took the clothes into the living room where she arranged them on the large fireguard. Bernie breathed a sigh of relief. As long as Polly and Teresa kept their mouths shut they were safe – for the time being.

After tea Bernie went to write her weekly letter to Marie. She set the other kids to making little cards for her. She filled her own letter with all her news but she didn't write about seeing Jimmy. Some things were best left unsaid. Marie hadn't replied to her previous letter but perhaps she was busy still settling in or maybe she hadn't the money for a stamp.

She'd finished her letter and was helping the other kids finish their cards when there was a sudden commotion at the back door, then her mam yelled,

'BERNIE!!'

Her heart dropped; she shushed the kids and went to the kitchen with lagging footsteps. The only salvation was that her da had already left for the pub before Rose Hanson came round on the bounce.

Rose looked more formidable than ever. Behind her Bernie could see her sister Daisy and Morag, her usual cocky expression damped for once.

'Splashed by bikes eh?' Maureen shouted. 'You bloody little liar.'

Bernie stepped back, expecting a slap. Before she could open her mouth, Rose butted in.

'Look what she's done to our Morag. Pulled her hair out an' all. Show them Morag.'

Morag dutifully inclined her head where a patch of hair did seem to be missing.

'She's an animal,' Daisy Sullivan pointed at Bernie, 'and that other one, your Teresa.' She rounded on Maureen. 'They stripped Sandra naked in front of the whole school. Her uniform's ruined.'

Daisy was as thin as her sister was fat. She had a skinny whiny voice to go with her scrawny face and figure at the best of times but today she looked like a half-starved terrier raring for a fight.

'They're all the same.' Rose looked at Bernie like she was something disgusting on her shoe.

'Polly – Teresa,' Maureen yelled, 'in here right now.' She glared at Daisy. 'I don't believe our Teresa did that, she's frightened of her own shadow.'

Bernie kept quiet. It wasn't the time to remind her mam that she'd told them to teach Teresa to stand up for herself.

Polly came white-faced but defiant, Teresa behind her on the verge of tears as usual. 'We never started it,' Polly began but Rose took a step towards her and raised her hand.

'You're a little liar, you nasty little bitch,' she hissed but Maureen jumped in front of her.

'Don't you talk to my kids like that and if there's any chastising to be done, I'll be the one to do it.'

Maureen turned to Bernie. 'What's this all about?'

'It's because of Jacko,' Bernie muttered.

'Jacko?' Maureen looked puzzled. 'What's he got to do with it?'

'She attacked him an' all,' Rose said. 'Oh, I never said nothing at the time. I'm not one to cause trouble and our Jacko didn't want it spreading round that he'd been attacked by a girl but she went for him like a wild animal.'

'Bernie?' Mam's eyebrows disappeared into her fringe.

'He grabbed me,' Bernie said, 'and he called me a …………..' She couldn't say what had happened, not in front of Rose and Daisy with Morag's ears flapping in the background.

'Jesus, Mary and Joseph, she just tells lie after lie,' Rose burst out. 'Our Jack told me what happened when he come in with his face all scratched. 'She's been after him ever since yous moved here, well not just him, anything in trousers. She's already got Peter Farrier twisted round her little finger but he's not enough for her – and just because our Jack told her straight he didn't want to know, she went for him.'

Morag snickered and Bernie had to stop herself lunging at both of them.

'And as if that weren't enough,' Rose went on, 'she's been telling this taradiddle about being attacked so that your John jumped our Jacko the other night and battered him. That's the kind of family you've dragged up; liars and bullies, the lot of yous. You're not fit to live with civilised people.'

'I think you'd better get out now,' Maureen said, 'before I forget meself.'

Rose folded her arms across her bosom. 'I should have known better than to try to help you bring yourselves up to our level. I knew that first day you never had a pot to piss in and manners to match.'

'Out,' Maureen said evenly. She moved towards Rose and Daisy, her body full of menace.

'Don't worry, we're going but don't think you've heard the last of it.'

Maureen opened the door with exaggerated movements.

'I don't know what the council was thinking of putting totters in here among decent people,' was Rose's parting shot.

'I bet we've caught fleas now,' Bernie heard Morag shout as they went down the stairs.

'So what really happened?' Maureen folded her arms and leaned against the back door.

'Oh Mam,' Bernie couldn't help hot tears spilling down her face. 'It was all Jacko's fault, that night he dragged me in the pub car park. He was horrible.'

'What did he do to you?' Maureen took out her cigarettes and lit one.

'He tried to touch me - here.' Bernie pressed her hands to her chest, 'and he said I was doing it with Peter so why not with him. I couldn't get away. He had me squashed against the wall, then someone came out of the back of the pub and started shouting so he let go and I scratched his face and kneed him in the ...'

'Good for you,' Maureen said, her mouth tight with disgust.

'And then I ran away.' Bernie wiped her eyes,

'And you didn't think to tell me?'

'I was too scared to tell you. I thought you'd tell Da and I didn't know what he'd say and I - I felt ashamed. He acted like I was asking for it. Mam will I have to tell Father McKenna?'

Maureen stepped forward and gave Bernie a brief hug. 'You got nothing to be ashamed of. I'm proud of you. God knows what might have happened if you hadn't stood up for yourself. I seen Jacko with his face all scratched but Rose said the cat had done it. God, what a family. So you told our John instead?'

'It wasn't like that. I'd been to the shop the other day and Jacko grabbed me on the way back. He said he was going to get me and our John came by in the van and saw it so I had to tell him and then - I didn't know anything till Morag and Katy jumped on us coming out of school and well - we had to fight back Mam.'

Maureen laughed. 'I can't believe our Teresa pulling that Sandra's clothes off. Not that I'm saying it's right like but sometimes you just got to stand up for yourself. Anyway that Jacko's got his just desserts and we're well rid of Rose and her relations. Some friend she turned out to be.'

'You won't tell me da will you?' Bernie stammered. She didn't know which would be worse, telling Da or confessing to Father.

'Do I look crazy? World War Three would break out. But just wait till I see our John, fell up the stairs indeed. But don't you worry about it, I think we've heard the last of it.'

Bernie wasn't so sure. Rose Hanson wasn't one to let things lie if she could stir up trouble and it was all right for Mam, she didn't have to deal with the Sullivan sisters and Jacko on the streets. She thought about the things Jacko had said to her and the way he talked echoed the way Jimmy had spoken about Marie. Why were some men like that? She wondered about her da, John, even Peter. Did they think about girls that way, that they were all easy? She had to stop thinking about it, she would never get to sleep and she needed a clear head, In two days' time she would be singing solo in the church concert. She practised the words to the carols in her head until at last she dozed off.

But the next day her misgivings were justified. After tea she and Peter were sitting on the wall outside the flats, waiting for Tommy to pick them up for a rehearsal. Peter was quiet and she knew something was up.

'Bernie, what's going on with you and Jacko? It's all round the estate your John gave him a hiding.'

Bernie sighed. 'He tried to grab me. Our John saw him and battered him. That's it really.'

'Come on, there's more than that. You and your sisters got in a fight with Katy and Morag. Jacko's telling everyone that you let him do you in the pub car park and you cried rape to your brother.'

Bernie felt the blood drain from her face. Her mind reeled but all she said was. 'Do you believe that?'

'No, of course not but I can't believe you didn't tell me, that is if you got nothing to hide.'

'You do believe it!' Bernie jumped up. 'Well if that's what you think you can get lost Peter Farrier. Forget the band, forget everything.'

'Hey, hey!' He grabbed her arm. 'I know he attacked you but I can't understand why you didn't come to me instead of John. I would have protected you. I've been looking for Jacko ever since I heard the stories but he's keeping out of sight.'

Bernie shrugged. She would have to tell the whole story all over again when all she wanted was to forget about it. 'I was too ashamed to tell you, to tell anyone after the things he said,' she finished. 'It was only because our John saw him threatening me in the street that it came out.'

Peter put his arms around her and held her close. He kissed her gently but she pulled away, still angry and then Tommy's van pulled into the street.

Bernie was still fuming about Jacko's lies when they got to Ginger's shed. It all flew out of her head though as Ginger announced,

'Bobby's just rung up. The Mardi Gras has a cancellation on Friday night and he's got us booked in.'

For a moment Bernie shared the excitement. The Mardi Gras was well known and popular, appearing there would be a big boost for them. Then she remembered and her face fell.

'I can't go. It's the carol concert at St. Clare's. I'm doing the solo.'

'You'll have to give it a miss,' Ginger said. 'Tell them you've got a sore throat or something.'

'I can't. Me mam'd have a fit. Her and me aunty and me nan are coming to see me and I can't let the school down, we've been rehearsing for months.'

'Oh for God's sake, what's more important, singing in a crummy school choir or getting a chance at a big club like the Mardi and keeping our agent happy?'

Bernie looked sullen but stood her ground.

Ginger looked round the group. 'This is what you get for working with a schoolkid.'

'Lay off her,' Tommy said. 'It's not her fault. We'll go on without her, say she had a prior engagement.'

Ginger snorted.

'I'd rather be with you,' Bernie said, 'honest I would but I can't let them down, it's going to be on the radio.'

That night in bed she felt torn between singing with the band and doing the choir solo. Was Ginger right? Should she pretend illness? It still wasn't too late - but she would be letting Mrs Meredith down as well as telling a serious lie. The thought of telling lies reminded her of Jacko. She wasn't going to tell her mam or John. There'd been enough trouble already. If she kept quiet maybe it would all die down.

That was a vain hope. The next day at the end of Assembly, Mr Masterson called for Bernie, Morag and Katy to come to his office.

'I don't need to tell you what this is about.' His stern voice said it all. 'You've been warned before about fighting outside school.' Although he addressed all three he looked straight at Bernie.

'She started it, Sir,' Morag began.

'That's not true,' Bernie cried.

'Quiet!' Mr Masterson thundered. 'Not only did you engage in this attack,' he said to Bernie, 'You encouraged your younger sisters to take part as well in a most disgusting manner. Mrs Sullivan has been to see me and I couldn't believe what she told me. Is it true, Bernadette that your sister pulled off Sandra Riley's clothes and ruined her uniform?'

Bernie stood in silence, she couldn't deny the accusation but Mr Masterson wouldn't let her tell what had happened.

'There may have been some provocation,' he stared hard at the Sullivan sisters, 'but we can't have pupils acting like savage animals. I'm surprised at you Bernadette. You have great talent which you seem intent on throwing away. You must learn to control your temper if you want to succeed in life.'

Bernie remained mute, the blood rising to her face as she saw Katy and Morag smirking.

'So what have you got to say for yourself?'

'Sorry Sir,' she muttered.

'For something like this I'd normally suspend all of you from school and I certainly wouldn't allow you the privilege of performing with the school choir.'

'I don't care about singing in the choir,' Bernie was unable to stop her anger bursting out. It was so unfair of the Head to blame her and not them and after all she was doing them a favour by singing in their rotten choir while she'd given up a paid job to do it.

'Don't be impertinent.' Mr Masterson said. 'It's too late to find another soloist so you will perform as planned but after that you will be excluded from the choir for as long as Mrs Meredith sees fit, if not permanently. As for you,' he turned to Morag and Katy, 'if there's any more of this, make no mistake, you will be suspended. Now off you go.'

Bernie pushed out and rushed away before the Sullivans could follow and torment her. It was always the same, everyone was willing to believe the worst of her because her da was a rag-and-bone man. Well, it solved one problem for her. From now on she would concentrate solely on her pop music career. School and the choir could go to hell.

She didn't feel like that however when the moment came for her solo at the carol concert. Mrs Meredith hadn't mentioned her exclusion and she'd begun to hope that Mr Masterson had changed his mind. The church was jolly with the joyful atmosphere of Advent, everyone looking forward to Christmas no matter how little they had to spend.

There was a hush as Bernie took her place for the solo and suddenly everything changed. She felt the sweet benevolence of the ancient church, its very stones soaked in the song of centuries of believers. As she sang the opening bars of *Away in a Manger* she forgot about the presents and nice food that characterised Christmas for her. In her mind she was carried to the silent landscape of the carol, a calm, dark open

167

land, a touch of frost in the air and the bright star lighting the cattle shed with the warmth of the animals and of love within. She forgot the congregation in front of her, her mother, her nan and aunty, forgot the choir behind her, Mr Masterson, Mrs Meredith, forgot everything as her voice soared up into the rafters above.

She came to the end of the carol like a bird coming down to land and looked around her, drained of energy. She looked for her family in the sea of faces but couldn't see them as tears blurred her eyes. After a farewell speech by Mr Masterson people got up to leave and her mam and Joan rushed forward.

'Ah, Bernie love...' Maureen seemed speechless. She enveloped Bernie in a hug that squeezed the breath out of her.

'Wasn't she magnificent?' Mrs Meredith came from behind Bernie. 'You excelled yourself tonight.' She smiled sadly. 'I'm so sorry to be losing her,' she said to Maureen.

'Losing her? What do you mean?'

Oh no, Bernie thought, dread flushing away her happiness.

Mrs Meredith looked from one to the other. 'You haven't told your mother, Bernadette?'

Bernie stayed silent. The blood rushing to her head made her dizzy.

'Told me what?' Maureen bristled.

'We've had to exclude Bernadette from the choir for the foreseeable future. She's been warned before about fighting. I'm really sorry about it. It wasn't my decision but the Head is right, we can't tolerate that kind of behaviour.'

'That kind of behaviour?' Maureen shouted. 'It's them Sullivans should be punished, they started it.' People turned as her voice rang out.

'Don't Mam,' Bernie plucked at her sleeve.

'Where is he?' Maureen wheeled round, looking for Mr Masterson but he'd already left the church.

'I suggest you take it up with him at school on Monday if needs be,' Mrs Meredith said, 'it's not the time nor the place Mrs McCann.' She turned away to round up the stragglers who were still getting their coats leaving Maureen fuming.

Nothing was said while they went to fetch Nan from her seat so as not to spoil the old lady's pleasure but once Uncle Charlie had collected her and Joan in his car, Maureen let rip.

Everything was ruined, Bernie thought as she listened to her mam going on about Mrs Meredith, Mr Masterson, Rose Hanson and the Sullivans all the way home. But the next night Riverbeat, having successfully survived the Mardi Gras without her, were gigging at the

Back Alley. The venue was starting to feel like a second home to Bernie as she headed up the band. The crowd was lively, everyone enjoying the happy dance music. Bernie was caught up in the atmosphere, part of the group behind her. This was where she belonged.

That night she and Peter sat on the wall outside the block cooling down after the excitement of the evening. Peter took her hand.

'There's something I have to tell you.'

Her mood sank at his serious tone.

'I didn't want to spoil things earlier on.' He paused

'What?' her heart lurched.

'It's Jimmy. I found out where he was living, sharing a flat with some of the lads I know.'

'Was?' Bernie relaxed a little. For a moment she'd thought he'd been going to finish with her.

'He disappeared last week. They reckon he's gone to sea.'

'Do you think it's true?' Bernie thought Jimmy's pals would probably say anything to protect him.

'They're good blokes. There were a few ships in last week, it's possible isn't it, one of the best ways for a scouser to disappear?'

'What about his family, would they know where he is?' Bernie knew she was clutching at straws.

'Nobody seems to know about them,' he shrugged. 'They said he didn't get on with them.

So that was that, Bernie thought. Mam always said every cloud had a silver lining. For Marie's sake she hoped so.

Chapter Eighteen

On the Tuesday before Christmas Bernie and Annabel went shopping for gifts for their families. Bernie treated Annabel to egg and chips in Littlewoods café while she quizzed her on what to buy for Peter.

'He wants a new watch,' Annabel said, 'but I think me mam and dad are getting him one.'

'Let's go and have a look anyway,' Bernie said.

They hurried to H. Samuel and gazed at the watches in the window. Most of them were more than she could afford so she picked out a small silver St Christopher medal and chain. The assistant put it in a nice box for her and on an impulse she also bought a tiny silver crucifix and chain for Marie. Word had come that they could finally visit and she and Mam were going on Christmas Eve. She felt sad thinking of Marie having to spend Christmas away from the family. However nice the place was it wouldn't be like home. As they left the shop Bernie couldn't help looking longingly at the engagement rings sparkling in the window. One day someone would put a beautiful ring on her finger. Would it be Peter?

She'd almost finished her Christmas shopping. She had the slippers she'd bought her mam weeks earlier. She'd also bought tobacco for John, a Monopoly set for the kids and chocolates for Annabel from the paper shop at staff discount but she hadn't anything for Sandie. She looked doubtfully round Woolworths as Annabel was buying bath cubes for her mam but Sandie was too posh to be given gifts from Woollies. Eventually in George Henry Lees, she spent most of the money she had left on a box of Coty *L'Aimant* dusting powder with a pink puff on top.

'Aren't you getting anything for your dad?' Annabel asked as they neared the bus station where John had arranged to pick them up. 'I got mine some new gardening gloves.'

'Da doesn't believe in Christmas; he doesn't buy any presents, me mam does all that. He's a proper skinflint.'

Annabel didn't say anything. Bernie wondered if she knew how jealous she was of her lovely dad. She imagined them all sitting down for Christmas dinner together, pulling crackers while their da carved the turkey. Christmas Day was fun in her own home too but only after her da had come back from the pub and passed out in his armchair after eating his dinner.

'Here's our John,' she cried. Sandie was with him in the cab so Bernie and Annabel had to sit on the floor in the back on some newspapers John had spread to keep off the worst of the dust and muck left by the scrap. They chatted excitedly about the presents they would give and hopefully receive. Bernie longed for a record player but knew it was far more than her mam could afford. Maybe after Christmas she would be able to save up for one herself. In the meantime she hoped for new tights, maybe a sweater. She wondered if Peter would get her something nice but she was distracted by John suddenly exclaiming, 'Fuck me,' and yanking the van to a halt as they turned into their street. Peering over his shoulder through the windscreen she saw a tangle of fighting bodies blocking the entrance to their flats.

John jumped out and ran towards the melee.

'Let us out!' Bernie and Annabel shouted, banging on the back doors of the van. Sandie jumped out, ran to the back and opened the doors. As she tumbled out, Bernie could see Peter being held by Jacko while two other boys took turns punching him. He was fighting as best he could with his arms held but he was no match for the three of them. He fell to his knees as Bernie ran forward screaming but John was there before her, knocking one of the assailants flying with a single blow.

Peter scrambled to his feet, dodging a punch from the other boy but Jacko was still holding his arms. Bernie jumped on Jacko's back and sank her teeth into his right ear, ignoring the powerful smell and taste of Brylcreem that filled her mouth and nose. Jacko screamed with pain and rage. He let go of Peter, shaking himself like a rat in the attempt to dislodge Bernie but someone else was beside her, someone wielding a granny shoe and whacking Jacko over the head with it - Sandie!

Bernie almost laughed but couldn't let go of Jacko's ear until Peter was completely free. She could see John and the other lad still fighting but the third one had run off, seeing they were outnumbered. In no time it was over. Jacko and his henchman limped away, jeered by the small knot of kids who had gathered to watch the fight.

'You'll be sorry,' Jacko muttered over his shoulder, wiping blood from his nose on his jacket sleeve.

'Just crawl back to your hole Hanson,' John yelled. He turned to the girls. 'Come on, let's get inside. Coming up Pete?'

'Thanks,' Peter said. 'I couldn't fight them all at once.'

'Cowards,' Bernie spat. She took her handkerchief out of her pocket and wiped the blood from his mouth.

171

Annabel went into her flat to let her mam know she was home but no one was in. John opened their back door to find their home was empty too. There was a note on the kitchen table to say Maureen and Kathleen had taken the kids to Broadway to buy their Christmas presents.

'Better get cleaned up before they come back,' John said, diving for the bathroom.

Sandie sat down and examined the shredded feet of her tights. 'They were new on this morning,' she said sadly. Her soles were bloody too where the gravel of the street had scraped them. Bernie wet the corner of a clean teatowel and gave it to her to bathe her feet.

'You were great, I can't believe what you did,' she said. Who would have thought it of her, she looked such a dainty little thing, Bernie would have bet she'd never seen a fight in her life before.

Sandie just grinned. 'Better see to Peter,' she said.

Bernie rinsed the towel and started on Peter. Bruises were already swelling his face and one eye was puffing and closing over. She was close to tears as she gently cleaned the wounds.

'What happened anyway?' Annabel demanded.

Peter's words were muffled by his swollen lips. 'I went looking for him, told him I'd kill him if he went near you again. He said some rotten things about you and I went for him but he ducked off into the pub. I was nearly home when he jumped me with them other two.'

'Bastard,' Bernie said but part of her was proud that Peter had defended her.

John came out of the bathroom clean but there were tell-tale bruises already forming on his face and his lip was split. 'I'm getting out of here before Mam comes back, Let's head back into town.' He grinned at Sandie.

'I'd better make meself scarce too,' Peter got up.

'You'll have to get something on that eye,' Bernie said. 'We've got a gig on Christmas Eve, you can't go on looking like that.'

'Witch hazel,' Sandie said. 'We can stop off at a chemist and get you some.'

'Yeah sure,' John said. 'Come with us, Pete, you look like you could do with a drink?'

'Go on,' Bernie said. 'You're best getting out of the way, my mam'll only go on and on, and yours too. I'd better stay here, Mam'll want me to help with the kids.'

'Sure you don't mind?' Peter took her hands and kissed her gently - in front of everyone!

After they'd gone she and Annabel tidied up.

172

'I couldn't believe that Sandie,' Bernie said, ' I thought she was a snob and a bit nesh.'

'She ripped all her tights,' Annabel said. It was a sobering thought. Tights were expensive.

They laughed about it but Sandie had gone up still higher in Bernie's estimation. By the time Maureen came back with the kids everything was back to normal.

'What are you two giggling about?' Maureen said, untying her headscarf. 'What have you been doing?'

'Oh nothing,' Bernie got up and filled the kettle. 'I'll make us a cuppa Mam.'

Wednesday passed without incident although Bernie's heart was in her mouth. All day she expected Rose Hanson to turn up. She was also keyed up about the visit to Marie the next day and found it hard to take part in the usual fun as all the kids helped decorate the flat for Christmas. John and Da had brought in a real Christmas tree to everyone's excitement. No one asked where it had come from, they were too busy squabbling over the boxful of old baubles Maureen fetched out from the bottom of her wardrobe. Mrs Thompson had given Bernie some tinsel left over from decorating the shop and soon the living room looked festive with a cheery fire going and their home-made Christmas cards on the mantelpiece.

Even Bernie began to look forward to Christmas Day when she would be able to give all her gifts. That evening Maureen went to bingo and everything was perfect as she and Peter cuddled in front of the fire, the decorations and tree baubles glinting in the firelight.

On Christmas Eve morning Joan arrived to look after the kids while Maureen and Bernie visited Marie. First they took a bus to town then another that trailed through unfamiliar districts before reaching open countryside and great flat fields of vegetables. Bernie had never seen such landscapes; her trips out of the city had been only to Formby and Crosby beaches and the occasional ferry over the water to New Brighton.

After getting off the bus in a small town called Ormskirk they had a long walk past big houses with lovely gardens. The day was dull, dark and damp. Bernie's feet were freezing in her thin shoes.

Maureen said, 'That must be it over there.' She nodded towards a huge wrought iron gate set into the stone wall they were walking alongside.

'Let me get a fag before we go in.' Bernie saw her mam's hand was shaking. Bernie hopped from one foot to another trying to keep warm. Through the big gate she could see lawns and bushes and between the tops of the trees behind the wall several pointed roofs poked up into the sky. It must be a very big place, Bernie thought, and posh too to have such big gardens but there was something about the silence and the looming bushes that made her shiver.

During the walk up the long drive she tried to shrug off her sense of foreboding. Squirrels ran up and down the huge trees that lined the driveway, making her smile.

'Look Mam,' she pointed them out but Maureen seemed lost in her own thoughts. A few yards from the imposing front door she ground her cigarette under her foot and squared her shoulders.

'Come on,' she urged Bernie and marched up to the door and rang the bell.

After a long wait a slot in the door slid back and a white face appeared.

'We've come to see Marie McCann, Sister.' Maureen put on her polite voice. 'I'm her mam and this is her sister Bernadette.'

The door opened, revealing a small body to go with the face. 'Come in please.' She had a face like sour vinegar but her voice was sweet with a soft Southern Irish lilt.

'Follow me please.' She led the way to a set of double doors opposite the front door. genuflecting and crossing herself before a large crucifix hanging on the wall as she did so. Bernie was surprised to see her mam do the same so she followed suit although her mind was taken up with the strangeness of this house. There were huge heavy old pieces of furniture pushed against the walls, the like of which Bernie had only seen on telly. Everywhere smelled of furniture polish, the walls were pristine white and the floor was tiled black and white. Everything was spotlessly clean but there was no colour and it felt cold, so cold.

'Please, in here.' The nun ushered them into a little room with a table and chairs and not much else yet it seemed almost cosy with its blue velvet curtains at the windows which looked out over the front lawn. 'I'll arrange for some tea and then I'll send your daughter to you.'

'Thank you Sister,' Mam sounded almost childish. Bernie would have laughed if she hadn't felt so apprehensive. Once the nun left they took off their coats. Bernie could tell her mam was nervous too and would be dying for another fag. She wondered how Marie was managing without any cigarettes.

174

The door opened and a huge jolly-looking nun bustled in with a tray of tea things. 'I'm Sister Agatha,' she boomed, 'come to see Catherine have you?'

'No,' Maureen looked startled. 'Marie, I've come to see my daughter, Marie McCann.'

'Ah yes,' the nun chuckled. 'We don't use those given names. All the girls are allocated a saint's name. That's how they're known while they are with us.'

Bernie stared. *Catherine?* Was this woman crazy?

Sister Agatha put down the tray. 'It's better for them - a new identity. It's not always temporary, some of them never leave us.'

'Marie'll be coming home,' Maureen said. Bernie saw she was starting to bristle.

'Of course,' the nun said soothingly. 'Help yourselves to tea, I'll fetch your daughter, she's been excused laundry duty for your visit.'

'Laundry duty?' Maureen exclaimed, her voice rising.

Sister's eyebrows rose. 'All the girls have to work. It wouldn't be good for them to be lounging about now would it? And they have to earn their keep.' She smiled and left the room.

'Well,' Maureen said. She began to pour the tea from the dainty teapot. Bernie marvelled at the embroidered traycloth, the beautiful thin china teacups and saucers painted with fat pink and white roses but even as she admired them her mind was elsewhere. She was trying to picture her elegant sister skivvying over other people's washing.

The door opened again and at first Bernie failed to recognise the drab creature who entered.

'Hello Mam, Bernie,' Marie said and sat down at the table. 'Pour us a cup of that tea please Mam.'

Bernie stared. All Marie's colour was sucked away. She looked grey and old. Her hair was lank and had reverted to its natural mousy colour. She wore a shapeless grey smock and thick lisle stockings with brown lace up shoes. This person was so un-Marie that Bernie wanted to burst into tears. What had they done to her?

Marie drank her tea greedily as Bernie and Maureen watched in embarrassed silence. At last Maureen said, 'So how have you been?'

Marie shrugged. 'Could be worse.' She attempted a smile. 'I've made a couple of friends, Rosie and Dawn. That's their real names, not them daft saints' names they call us.'

'But the nuns, they are good to you?'

'They're all bitches.' Marie's eyes flashed and for a moment Bernie saw the old Marie. 'They hate us, we're just sinful to them.'

175

Maureen looked up at the crucifix hanging on the wall by the table. 'That Sister Agatha, she said you're working in the laundry ...'

'At least it's warm in there,' Marie broke in, 'but it's awful, all scrubbing and rubbing, just look at me hands.' She held them out, red and rough, the nails cut almost to the quick. 'And dragging those great tubs about.'

'But you shouldn't be doing that!' Maureen cried.

'They don't care,' Marie said. 'If you miscarry it's your own fault, it's because you've sinned.' Her hand went to her stomach. 'Sometimes I wish I would miscarry, then I'd be able to get out of here.' Her face crumpled for a moment then she straightened her back, picked up her cup and finished her tea.

Bernie didn't know what to say. Her mam looked stupefied. Bernie wanted her to jump up and take Marie out of there, away home with them but she realised that couldn't happen. She delved into her handbag.

'I brought you something for Christmas.' She produced the little box now wrapped in Christmassy paper printed with holly leaves and red ribbon.

'Thanks.' Marie took it carelessly but Bernie could see tears standing in her eyes.

'And I brought you a present too,' Maureen fetched a squashy parcel out of her shopping bag.

'Is it something to wear?' Marie eyed the package. 'They won't let me have it but thanks anyway.'

'There's some sweets and biscuits too,' Maureen put a carrier bag on the table.

'Give us a fag, Mam please,' Marie said.

Maureen looked appalled. 'You can't smoke in here,' she glanced up at the crucifix as if Jesus was actually watching them.

'I know but just give us one for later, and a match. Please Mam.' Marie bit her lip.

Maureen sighed. She took out her packet of Woodbines and her box of matches.

'Here keep them.'

'Thanks Mam.' A real smile appeared on Marie's face. She lifted the hem of her smock and tucked the cigarettes and matches into the waist of her white cotton knickers. There was still only a slight swelling to suggest a baby growing inside her.

'They search our pockets after visiting but they won't look down there. So how's Da and the kids?'

As they chatted Marie seemed more cheerful. Bernie had agonised for days over whether to tell her about Jimmy but had decided against it. It wouldn't help her anyway and Mam would go mad because she hadn't told her about it.

When time came for them to leave Marie became the old careless Marie. 'Don't worry about me, Mam, I'm fine,' but Bernie could see the deep unhappiness in her eyes. As they emerged Bernie felt like she was leaving some strange dream world and she welcomed the biting cold of the fading afternoon.

They were silent on the trudge back to the town. Maureen bought fresh cigarettes and matches at the paper shop by the bus station. Upstairs on the bus she puffed furiously but neither of them spoke much, both lost in their own thoughts. As the bus pulled into Liverpool Bernie remembered it was Christmas Eve. The streets were thronged with shoppers and everywhere twinkled with Christmas lights.

'They never even had a flaming Christmas tree,' Maureen said, lighting up a fresh Woodbine.

Later Bernie felt guilty joining in the Christmas Eve excitement but the kids' mood was infectious and she didn't want to spoil their fun. She followed her mam's example and put on a smiling face.

Once Da had gone out there was a party tea with sandwiches, crisps and mince pies then the ritual of leaving milk and a mince pie for Santa. It was the one night of the year that the children were happy to go to bed early. Bernie wanted to see Peter but she didn't like to leave her mam alone after the day's experience. She helped her fill the kids' stockings with nuts and tangerines then they finished wrapping the last of the presents while watching carol singing on the telly. Bernie kept thinking about Marie and how different her Christmas would be.

'They'll be at Mass most of tomorrow,' Maureen said as if she could read Bernie's thoughts. She went into the kitchen and came back with a bottle of sherry and two teacups. 'Won this on the bingo last week. Come on, it might cheer us up.'

Maureen stoked the fire, they both put their feet up and sipped sherry with the last of the mince pies. The drink was sweet and sickly but the mince pie helped it go down. There was silence till Maureen said,

'You know if I could have brought her home I would. '

'I know,' Bernie said but she was thinking, if it was up to me I'd have fetched her home and blow me da and everybody else.

She lay awake in bed haunted by the memory of her sister's wan face, remembering her as she used to be putting on her makeup and painting her nails. Polly and Teresa kept interrupting her thoughts with whispers of, 'Has he been yet?' At last they fell asleep but Bernie was still awake when John tiptoed in with the Christmas stockings. At last she slept only to be roused at five-thirty by screams of delight as her sisters rummaged through their gifts.

After breakfast Bernie was able to run down to give her gifts to Annabel and Peter.

'Merry Christmas, Bernie,' Kathleen Farrier welcomed her in. 'Tell your mam to pop down after dinner for a cuppa and a bit of Christmas cake.'

'I was just coming up to yours,' Peter beamed. 'Look what I got.' He showed off a large Timex watch with a posh imitation crocodile strap.

'Me too,' Annabel appeared. She had a smaller watch with a pretty pink strap. 'It's just what I wanted. What did you get?'

'Tights and a dressing gown.' Bernie said. 'I wanted a record player really, but I suppose Mam couldn't afford one.'

'Never mind,' Peter said. 'You'll be able to buy one yourself soon the way our bookings are going. Come in here,' he tugged her into the living room where a tiny sprig of mistletoe hung from the central lampshade. He pulled her under it and kissed her long and deep. Everything round her disappeared as he held her tight and she responded without thinking, pressing closer and letting her mouth open to his tongue. At last he pulled back slightly and tilted her chin with his finger so she had to look up at him.

'I think I'm falling in love with you Bernie McCann.'

The words made her melt but before she could respond she heard a discreet cough. They pulled apart to see Tommy Farrier grinning in the doorway. Peter flushed to the roots of his hair and Bernie also felt her face flame.

'Tommy---coffee,' Kathleen called from the kitchen and Peter's da winked at them

'I'll leave you two lovebirds alone, but don't do anything I wouldn't do.' He laughed.

Peter folded her in his arms again. 'I've got something for you.' He let go of her to fish in his pocket then produced a tiny box. Inside was a small silver cameo ring. It was the prettiest thing Bernie had ever seen and fitted perfectly on the middle finger of her right hand.

'One day I'll give you a proper ring,' he murmured as she clung to him. 'Maybe next year?'

'I've got something for you too.' She pulled away to find his gift in the carrier bag she'd brought with her. When he saw the St Christopher medal nestling on its blue silk cushion he smiled at her tenderly.

'Put it on for me.' He ducked his head so she could fasten the chain round his neck and then he kissed her again.

In the evening when Da had gone out Peter and Annabel came up. John had returned with Sandie who cooed over the powder puff and gave out selection boxes to all the kids. They settled down to play with the Monopoly set while Maureen watched Morecambe and Wise on the telly and drank the last of the sherry.

In bed that night Bernie kept admiring her new ring. She would never take it off if she could help it. She kept repeating Peter's magic words to herself. Falling in love – was that what was happening to her? It felt so good but then she remembered Marie – she too had fallen in love and look what had happened to her.

Under her pillow was the tiny diary the kids had clubbed together to buy her. She was tempted to write down her thoughts but there was always the risk of someone reading it. Anyway it was too small for more than notes but perfect for filling in dates. And that was something she was going to have to do now that bookings were coming in thick and fast.

Chapter Nineteen

January twelfth was Maureen's birthday and John and Bernie took her out for a meal in a Chinese restaurant. Sandie and Peter were invited along too and Kathleen Farrier had promised to mind the kids.

Maureen had never eaten a Chinese meal before. She kept looking round the restaurant and fingering the faux pearl necklace Bernie had given her for her birthday.

The restaurant was a popular one in the Chinese quarter, frequented by many of the area's residents.

'Always a good sign,' John said, making suggestions as to what they might order. Bernie hadn't realised her brother was so well up on restaurants and menus. Before he'd met Sandie he had always been a pub and chippy man, like their da..

'That was lovely,' Maureen said when they'd finished the meal. ' I didn't think I'd like it but I really enjoyed it, even that curry.'

'This is going to be a great year for us,' Peter said to Bernie as they drank jasmine tea to complement the food.

'It's been the best Christmas and New Year I've ever had,' Bernie whispered. She squeezed Peter's hand under the table. The restaurant was warm and she felt mellow as she leaned against him on the banquette where they sat. She could see the year opening out in front of her: money in her pocket, leaving school forever, her career taking off and Peter by her side. Right now she wanted him holding her tight more than anything. As they trudged down the icy street to the van she couldn't wait to get home for a kiss and a cuddle.

Back at the flats Maureen went straight up to relieve Kathleen from babysitting duty.

'Don't be long,' she winked at Bernie and Peter, 'it's bloody freezing out here.'

As soon as John and Sandie had driven off to fetch Joe home, Bernie and Peter set about warming each other up under the stairs in ways they thought only they knew how. Peter's hands were inching up her tights when Kathleen and Annabel came clattering down the stairs.

"Night, Bernie,' Kathleen called as Bernie and Peter broke apart and a smothered giggle from Annabel made her blush. She ran up the stairs, her heart full to bursting, the imprint of Peter's fingers burning on her thighs while his final kiss still stung her lips.

Maureen was smoking at the kitchen table. 'You took your time,' she said but she was smiling.

'Just saying goodnight to Annabel,' Bernie muttered. 'Did you have a nice birthday?' she kissed Maureen on the cheek, hoping she didn't smell of Peter's *Old Spice* aftershave.

'Lovely,' Maureen said, 'you both spoiled me.'

'Didn't you spoil me on my birthday? If anyone deserves it, it's you Mam.'

She sat down. She could see her mam had something on her mind.

'I been thinking,' Maureen began. 'Did you notice how quiet Sandie was tonight?'

Bernie hadn't, her eyes had been too full of stars.

'She's having a hard time at home.' Maureen let out a stream of smoke.

'Sandie is?' Bernie couldn't imagine Sandie having any problems. She had everything a girl could wish for and so much style.

'Her mam wants her to go away to university but she likes her job and her da thinks our John's no good for her. He told her she's got to stop seeing him. She says they're on her back all the time.'

'Not good enough?' Bernie cried, 'Our John's as good as anyone else.'

'I can see she's a different class,' Maureen went on, 'but I think they really love each other. Our John's never been serious like this with a girl before. He's a fast learner and he works hard. He'd look after her that's for sure. I didn't take to her at first, thought she was a bit of a snob but I've got to like her, she's a nice kid.'

'Oh I like her too,' Bernie said. 'What can we do?'

'What if we said she could stay here, have our Marie's bed while she's away?'

'But she's posh,' Bernie said. 'I bet she's got her own room with fitted carpets and one of them dressing tables with frills on it an' all that.'

'At least she'll have peace here, time to sort herself out.'

'But what about our Marie?'

'It'd only be till she comes home. Would you mind?'

'No,' Bernie said uncertainly but when she lay in bed later it seemed that they were betraying Marie by putting Sandie in her place. It would be fun to have Sandie all the time, she would be able to pick her brains on clothes and makeup but she was used to being the pampered only daughter, how would she take to the rough and tumble of the McCanns' family life? As she dozed off Bernie wondered if Sandie would take a turn at peeling the spuds for the family's tea.

When Bernie came home from school on the following Friday her mam and Kathleen Farrier were drinking tea but one glance told her something was seriously wrong. After shooing her sisters into the bedroom to change their clothes, Bernie joined them to find out what was going on.

There was a break in the conversation when she came in. Maureen lit up a cigarette and squinted at her.

'You had any more bother with Jacko and them Sullivans?'

Bernie shook her head. 'Haven't really seen any of them since Christmas. I've seen Morag and Katy round school but only in the distance.'

'Kathleen says Rose has been going round everyone in the street saying things about us.'

What's new? Bernie thought. 'What sort of things?' she asked.

'Like we're not fit to live here: that me kids are like animals, that your da and John can't get proper jobs because we're tinkers.'

Bernie shrugged. 'Isn't she always saying things like that?

'Just be careful,' Kathleen said. 'It's not idle gossip, she's up to something. Mrs Shimmin in the next block, she's been getting her washing pinched off the line: all her boys' good jeans. Everyone knows it's probably them Jacksons upstairs but Rose has convinced her it's your family's to blame.'

'Us?' Maureen flushed. 'Cheeky bitch. I'm not that hard up I have to go robbing, nor my kids neither.'

'I know that, you know I do.'

'I've a good mind to go round there now and pull her up,' Maureen raged.

'Just be careful,' Kathleen said again. 'She's a nasty old cow but people round here are scared of her. Something's brewing, mark my words.'

'Well what can she do?' Maureen laughed uneasily. 'I don't talk to her any more anyway, thank God. You just keep away from the lot of them,' she said to Bernie, 'and make sure the others do the same. I'll have a word with our John.'

On Saturday afternoon Bernie was working in the shop as usual when Rose Hanson marched in. She chose a couple of magazines and the football Echo, then headed to the counter and asked Mrs Thompson for a quarter of Everton Mints. She cast a baleful glance at Bernie who was sorting the evening deliveries.

'Surprised to see her still here,' she said to Mrs Thompson. 'Wouldn't trust her as far as I could throw her. You know what totters are like. Suppose you do know the kind of family she comes from?'

Bernie felt her face flame but she pretended not to have heard.

'Bernie's been here several months now. We think very highly of her.' Mrs Thompson tipped the weighed sweets into a paper bag and thrust it into Rose's hand.

'Once she's got into your good books she'll have her fingers in the till and no mistake. Thieving's second nature to them sort.'

Bernie fumed behind her papers. She longed to run over and punch Rose but she knew she couldn't do that in the shop.

Mrs Thompson rang up the amounts on the till. 'Mrs Hanson, I've already had to bar your son from my shop. If you don't like my staff you're welcome to shop elsewhere as well.'

Rose puffed herself up. 'Don't you speak to me like that.'

'Then don't come here insulting my staff.'

The two women faced each other across the counter. Bernie watched fascinated.

'Well it's good to know whose side you're on,' Rose hissed. She threw her money on the counter. 'You should be supporting local people what pays your wages, not sticking up for them as isn't no better than animals.'

'I think you'd better leave.' Mrs Thompson pushed Rose's change across the counter.

'Well you'll be the one as'll be sorry, not me.' Rose picked up the coins and snapped her purse shut. 'I've got a lot of friends round here what comes in this shop. We'll see what they think when they find out about this.' She took up the paper bag containing her sweets and papers and swept out.

Mrs Thompson blew out her cheeks and looked at Bernie.

'Maybe she's right,' Bernie mumbled. 'Maybe it'd be better if I left.'

'Don't be so daft,' Mrs Thompson said. 'You're the best girl we've had, a real treasure.'

'But if she's going to cause trouble for you, lose you customers because of me?'

'Don't you worry about it. If people listen to her rubbish then they're not the kind of people I want to serve in here.'

Bernie carried on with her work, feeling subdued although it was wonderful that Mrs Thompson thought so much of her. At least she and Kathleen Farrier weren't listening to Rose's muckspreading. She was still thinking about it as she made her way home but on arriving she forgot the events of the afternoon. Sandie was sitting at the table sobbing her heart out.

'It'll be okay, they'll come round,' Maureen was saying but Sandie just cried all the more. Bernie put the kettle on without stopping to take off her coat. Tea and sympathy were obviously the first priority. Sandie wiped her eyes, leaving runnels of mascara down her face.

'No they won't,' she looked from Maureen to Bernie. 'You don't know what my dad's like. Oh I hate him.' She buried her face in her dainty white handkerchief.

Bernie plonked a cup of tea in front of her and stirred in a couple of spoons of sugar. She wanted to say there was nothing to worry about, that Sandie could stay with them but it was up to her mam. She took her unopened pay envelope out of her pocket and gave it to Maureen. Now she was earning more money with the band she could afford to turn over the whole of her Saturday wages. It meant her mam didn't have to stand on Greaty market in the worst of the winter weather.

'I've told Sandie she can stay here,' Maureen said, 'and that you don't mind sharing.'

''Course not,' Bernie said, 'It'll be great.'

'But you've got a houseful already,' Sandie wailed.

'One more won't make much difference,' Maureen said, 'and you'll be paying for your keep won't you?'

Bernie felt the corners of her mouth twitch. Extra cash was always welcome in her mam's struggle to provide for the family.

'Anyway it might only be for a few days,' Maureen went on. 'Once your mam and dad realise you're not coming home they'll change their tune, you wait and see. I wouldn't encourage anyone to leave home but at least you'll be safe here.

'She's been to see some grotty bedsit,' she said to Bernie before turning back to Sandie. 'And your mam and da will know where you are and that you're somewhere safe. It'll give you all a bit of breathing space and once they've calmed down they'll want you to come home.'

'You really think so?' Sandie managed a watery smile. 'Daddy said he'll disown me.'

Bernie'd never seen Sandie's parents but she imagined a right pair of snobs. Someone else looking down on the McCanns. Maureen patted Sandie's arm.

'People say things they don't mean in temper.'

'He told me not to come back.' Sandie dissolved into tears again.

'What about your mam?' Bernie asked.

'She just sides with him. She's more worried about what the neighbours will think and what the people at the Conservative Club will say. She's on the committee there.'

Bernie stared. She wasn't sure what the Conservative Club was but any mam who put other people before her own daughter couldn't be much of a mother. She looked at her own mam in her shabby old jumper and skirt, her face worn with care lines and screwed up against the smoke from her fag, and felt a powerful tug of love. No matter how hard up they were their mam would always protect them and think the best of them.

'Our John'll take you home when he comes in. If your dad's still mad you can pack a few things and come back here.'

'Come on,' Bernie said, 'Let's go and sort your bed out.'

When John and Sandie didn't come back Maureen said to Bernie, 'See, her mam and dad have probably made it up with her now.'

Bernie hoped so although she'd quite been looking forward to having Sandie stay for a few days. For once the band didn't have a Saturday night booking so after her mam and da had gone off in a taxi with Vinny Mack she settled down to watch telly with the kids. When she heard the back door bang she thought it was Peter but it was Sandie with John carrying a suitcase and an assortment of bags.

Sandie was still tearful. Her dad hadn't been home and her mother had told Sandie to stay away till she came to her senses, refusing to speak to John at all. She soon cheered up though when Bernie helped her unpack as the other kids ran around examining her belongings in high excitement. She'd brought so much stuff! Even Bernie gasped in amazement at all the outfits that couldn't be squeezed into their little wardrobe. There were piles of lovely underwear and endless bottles and jars and makeup kits that had to be stuffed on the dressing table. Much as she admired Sandie Bernie couldn't let her use Marie's special drawer. That would be a betrayal of her sister so she kept the key hidden in her own underwear drawer.

Best of all Sandie had brought her small portable record player. Bernie felt like jumping for joy when she saw it. Sandie soon brightened up, catching the general mood of excitement as they all laughed and giggled

185

together. Bernie thought how nice it was. She had never got on with Marie like this. Immediately she felt guilty. She pictured Marie in that horrible place with the coldhearted nuns and vowed she would be nicer to her when she came home.

Later when Peter arrived and the kids had been packed off to bed, the four of them settled down to listen to records. Sandie had the latest Kinks and Rolling Stones numbers and John had bought a bottle of sherry. Nestled in Peter's arms Bernie felt in seventh heaven. Having Sandie here was going to be such fun. Peter bent to kiss her and seeing John and Sandie similarly entwined, she responded, banishing the lingering ghost of Marie to the back of her mind.

Chapter Twenty

Valentine's night saw Riverbeat back at St Aloysius church hall, where Bernie had made her singing debut. It meant a nice relaxed Friday night and it held good memories for her even though the band had gone on to bigger bookings. The room was decked out with red balloons and paper roses. Earlier Bernie and Peter had exchanged cards and her heart was beating fast with thoughts of the kisses they would share later that night.

The room was already pretty full when they arrived and tonight the floor was crowded with couples. There were spot prize dances going on as the DJ warmed everyone up while the band set up. Bernie was in the dressing room cupboard next to the toilet when the vicar appeared at the door.

'Someone asking to see you, you must have a fan.'

Bernie laughed but she was curious. Maybe it was another reporter.

'It's a young man, said he knows you.'

Bernie's heart thumped. Maybe it was Jacko come to pester her. 'Do me a favour Mr. Winters,' she said. 'I'll come out but stick around and keep an eye out for me, it could be anybody.'

'All right.' He drew himself up to his full six foot three and Bernie felt reassured. Mr Winters taught boxing to the local lads and nobody with any sense would pick a fight with him. She gave him a smile and went out into the hall but did a doubletake when she saw who was standing there - George!

It was so long since she'd seen him that she wasn't sure it was him till he smiled and she remembered how her heart used to leap at that smile. She turned away but he took her arm.

'Bernie - don't go, I just wanted to see you.'

'What for?' Bernie pulled free but stood irresolute. Memories of her time with him, both sweet and painful, washed over her.

'I - I saw you in the paper - and I've seen your name up at some of the clubs. I couldn't forget you - I wanted to come before but - I thought - I mean I know I didn't treat you right. I wanted to say I'm sorry. I made a mistake.'

'Okay you've said it,' Bernie looked over to the stage where Peter and the rest of the band were tuning their instruments.

'I've been stupid,' George went on; ' I didn't realise how much you meant to me.' He tried to take her hand but she clasped her hands behind her back, rubbing the silver ring on her right hand with the fingers of her left.

'Took you a long time, didn't it? And what about Aggie, my so-called best friend?'

'That's long over,' George looked shamefaced. 'It was just - a fling.'

'Well you can go fling yourself at someone else, George,' Bernie said. 'I've got someone new, someone who really cares for me, so you and Aggie did me a favour.' She walked away with her nose in the air. Mr Winters gave her a wink as he moved away from the bunches of balloons he'd been arranging and went off to help with the refreshments.

Scrambling up on stage she hissed to Peter, 'Change of plan, start with *I Got You Babe*.'

'That's at the end,' Peter whispered.

'No,' Bernie insisted. 'Now, do it now.'

Peter shrugged, muttered to the others, then announced, 'Valentine's night, when romance is in the air, what better song to start with than *I Got You Babe*. Let's go.'

Bernie stood close to him, centre stage. She slid her arm round his waist and turned him to face her and sang only to him. During the instrumental break, she turned to look at the couples smooching on the dance floor and saw George glaring at her from the far wall where the single guys gathered to check out the talent. She clasped Peter even tighter, delighted when George dumped his glass on the nearest table and stalked out.

At the end of the night Bobby Charles popped in to see them. 'Listen guys, I haven't just come on a friendly visit. I've got a gig for you at the Jungfrau next month, part of the warm up for the visiting band. 'Course you'll be bottom of the bill but you think you can handle it?'

The Jungfrau - one of Manchester's top venues. A stir of excitement ran through the group. Ginger kept his cool, 'I don't see why not. Who's the guest band?'

'Nashville Teens,' Bobby said casually.

Five sets of feet hit the floor and their mouths dropped open. Bernie choked on her orange squash.

'You should see your faces,' Bobby burst out laughing.

'You're having us on, aren't you?' Peter looked disappointed.

'No, I'm not. Look, you're ready to go places. I'm going to try to get you out to Hamburg in the summer. This is just the start for you.'

The boys broke into whoops and cheers but Bernie felt suddenly chilled. How could she just go off to Germany? She'd never been away from home, she didn't have a passport.

'But I've got my exams,' she said. 'I never get to do my revision as it is.'

'Well there's a choice,' Bobby said. 'Get a few CSEs and a boring job in some typing pool or take a chance on making it big time doing something you love and having fun along the way. Anyway you'll have left school by the time I'm planning to send you out.'

Bernie was still thinking about this when Tommy dropped her and Peter off outside the flats. Bobby was right - did she really want a life married to someone like George - a lifetime of passing post office exams while she spent her time washing and cleaning and bringing up kids like her mam?

These thoughts left her when Peter took her in his arms and kissed her. All the heat and romance of the evening flowed between them and she wanted him more than ever before. What would it be like, to go a bit further? But always Marie was there, her pale face sending out a warning. She returned to the reality of their dark hidey hole under the stairs as Peter held her away from him and looked into her eyes.

'By the way,' he said, who was that bloke you were talking to at the club?'

Towards the end of the month the band was booked at St Philomena's social club which was attached to Bernie's local church. It should have been an easy night but when Bernie walked in and saw Morag Sullivan on the dance floor with her cousin Charmaine, she knew that trouble was brewing.

'We can't go on,' she whispered to Peter, panic-stricken.

'Don't be daft,' Ginger said. He glared at Morag and Charmaine. 'They're just a couple of birds.'

'We can't not go on,' Peter said. Don't let them bug you.'

Bernie went to get ready but she seemed to feel dagger stares coming through the walls. She didn't come out till the band was announced and the first thing she saw was the Sullivan girls whispering and giggling at the table closest to the stage. She thought about telling Bert the manager that Morag was underage but saw she was only drinking Coke anyway.

189

She faltered through the opening bars of her first song then professionalism kicked in, she closed her eyes and forgot about them.

The first half went fine, Bernie relaxed and the dance floor was crowded. The band slipped backstage in the interval while Peter went to fetch drinks.

'What the hell was up with you at the beginning?' Ginger demanded.

'Those girls at the front,' Bernie said. 'They got it in for me and my family. I thought they'd come to cause trouble but it's all right now.'

'Don't be so sure.' Peter came through with the tray of drinks. 'Take a look out front.'

'What?' Bernie peered through the curtains. Jacko Hanson and his cronies were making their way to Morag's table.

'What is it man?' Ginger and Tommy at Bernie's white face.

'There might be trouble.' Peter filled them in on the Hanson family.

'Oh Christ,' Ginger said, 'that's all we need.'

'We'll just have to ignore them,' Peter said. 'Maybe it will be okay.'

They were all jumpy when they came back on stage but they went straight into their routine Bernie was conscious of Jacko's contemptuous stare as he slouched with his hands in the pockets of his leather jacket. The others at the table sniggered but didn't do anything disruptive so she began to breathe easier.

She'd just begun her bluesy set with her version of *Summertime* when something hit her in the face and exploded wetly. She stopped singing and opened her eyes. Something trickled down her cheeks. The band faltered to a stop. There was a moment's silence then Morag and Charmaine burst out laughing. Through blurred vision Bernie saw Jacko's arm move then a second tomato hit her in the chest and slid down the front of her dress.

Peter slung off his guitar, jumped off the stage and seized Jacko by the throat. Jacko staggered up, pushing Peter so that he fell onto a nearby table, knocking over all the drinks on it. A girl screamed and the burly boy at the table jumped up, swinging punches at both Peter and Jacko. The next minute the fight spread like wildfire. Girls ran screaming to the toilets and the bar staff quickly brought the shutters down.

Bernie froze till she noticed the other band members had joined in to rescue Peter who was getting the worst of it. She saw Morag and her cousin dragging him down on the floor while Jacko kicked him and she dived off the stage and onto Morag's back, getting an armlock round her neck. She yanked viciously, at the same time trying to kick at Jacko. Morag fell, bringing Bernie down with her. All around were sounds of

190

breaking glass and splintering wood. Bernie heard Peter shout her name and looked up then something hit her head and she went out like a light.

It was after two when Bernie got home. They'd spent ages backstage while police and the club staff had cleared the place. Bernie had a lump on her head but otherwise felt okay. The boys had bloody noses, cuts and bruises but no one was seriously hurt. They peeped through the curtains to see what was going on but there was no sign of Jacko and his gang.

'I hope they've arrested him,' Bernie said. 'It was all my fault.'

Tommy leapt to her defence. 'Bernie, they were just out to cause trouble.'

'Yes but it was me they were getting at.' Bernie struggled not to cry.

'You landed a good one on that Morag,' Phil said and suddenly they were all laughing.

'One thing for sure, no more gigs at this dump,' Ginger said.

The back door was still open when Bernie got home. She sneaked in with Peter behind her for back up only to find her mam smoking in the kitchen. She could hear her father grinding his teeth in his sleep from his armchair.

'Oh Mam, you're still up,' she faltered.

''Course I am.' Maureen got up and switched on the light. 'Where the hell have you been?'

'There was a fight - at the club,' Bernie stammered. 'We had to wait till the police had cleared the place.'

'A fight? I told you that no good would come of all this pop singing. Them places aren't safe.'

'No Mam, honest, it wasn't our fault.'

'I don't care whose fault it was. You wouldn't get this singing in the choir.'

'Mrs McCann it was Jacko Hanson and the Sullivans,' Peter broke in. 'They started throwing tomatoes and stuff and then it just sort of spread.'

'Lord save us.' Maureen clutched her chest. Her expression softened. 'Are yous all right?'

'We're okay. We hid backstage till it was all over.' Bernie wasn't going to tell her mam she'd actually been in the fight and been knocked out for a few minutes.

'Well you'd better get to bed now. Thank God your da never noticed you wasn't in.' Maureen turned to Peter. 'And you better get home, your mam will be worrying where you are.'

Bernie followed him out for a lingering kiss on the balcony but she was utterly exhausted and so glad to climb into her pyjamas and the comfort of her bed.

Chapter Twenty-one

Saturday passed quietly at the paper shop although Bernie was a bag of nerves, expecting Jacko or Rose Hanson to storm in. At the end of the day Mrs Thompson handed her her pay packet. 'You've been quiet today, is everything all right?'

'Yes, fine.' Bernie put on asmile. 'I'm just a bit tired, we were singing late last night.' She hoped the local gossips hadn't heard of the fight and spread the news round the district.

But when she got home Father McKenna was sitting in her da's armchair balancing a cup of tea on his cassocked knees. Bernie's legs began to shake. She could see her mam was a bundle of nerves because Joe was due home any moment.

'Oh ho, here's the villain of the piece,' Father said.

'It wasn't her fault, Father,' Maureen said, 'those Hansons and Sullivans have got it in for our family.'

'They're not in my congregation, are they?'

'They're proddy dogs,' Bernie said, terror making her defiant.

'Orange,' Maureen corrected, flashing a warning look at Bernie.

'Hmm,' Father said. 'Nevertheless there's a great deal of damage done. There'll have to be an insurance claim.'

'We was just singing. They started throwing tomatoes then everyone started fighting.' Bernie reached into her coat pocket. 'Here Father, you can have my wages towards it.'

'That won't make much difference,' the priest said but he produced the cloth bag in which he kept money collected on his visits and the fifteen shillings disappeared into it. It's some time since I've seen you in church. How long since you've been to Confession?'

'I don't know, Father,' Bernie mumbled.

'She's been so busy with all this singing,' Maureen tried to make excuse.

'Devil's work if you ask me,' Father said.

'I'll make sure she's there tomorrow,' Maureen promised.

'I sincerely hope so,' Father got to his feet. 'I'll say no more for now but you know the police had to be involved. They may want to speak to Bernadette.'

Bernie ran to her room and burst into tears. Polly and Teresa gaped in surprise and Sandie tried to comfort her but Bernie was inconsolable. The thought of the police was terrifying but even worse was the prospect of confession. Would she have to tell Father McKenna that she'd let Peter put his hand inside the top of her tights?

They had no booking that evening so Bernie was minding the younger children but after her mam had gone out Peter came up solemn-faced to say that Bobby Charles was coming to see them at their Sunday night slot at the Back Alley.

'So what's wrong with that?' Bernie'd been grateful that the Sunday night gig would excuse her from going to church and stave off the dreaded confession.

'He rang Ginger up. The club manager complained about the fight and he's furious.'

'Oh no!'

'We'll have to hope he'll listen to our side of it.'

Just when things were going so well the Hansons had to spoil everything. Even after the kids had gone to bed and she snuggled up against Peter, her mind kept replaying that awful moment when the rotten tomato splattered in her face.

'Don't worry, it'll be okay.' Peter turned her face to his and lifted her chin to kiss her but suddenly there was a huge crash as the living room window caved in and a brick landed on their old dining table.

Bernie screamed, they both ran to the window but there was no one in the street. A moment later Tommy Farrier ran out of the block.

Peering up at the McCanns' window, he yelled, 'What happened?'

'Don't know, someone threw a brick,' Peter shouted through the jagged opening.

Tommy ran down the street and Peter hurried to join him. The kids were all frightened and crying and Bernie struggled to calm them. She knew very well who was responsible for this but what would happen when her da and John came home? She put on a smile for the children's sake but inside she was gripped with fear as she fetched a pan to collect up the broken glass. Wind and rain whipped into the room making the fire smoke erratically.

The kids were still blubbing on the couch when Peter came back. 'No sign of anyone,' he said.

'Well, we don't need to look far,' Bernie sniffed. She went to pick up the brick.

'Don't touch it,' Polly shouted. 'It's evidence. Like on telly. There might be fingerprints on it. Leave it for the police.'

'Never mind police,' Peter muttered, 'I'll go round there and drag Jacko Hanson out now.'

'No don't,' Bernie clutched his arm, 'Not on your own. Wait till our John comes in. I don't know what we're going to do. It's freezing in here. Me da's going to go berserk.'

'My dad's got some boards he's been saving to make a shed. He's bringing one up to fix it for now.'

Tommy Farrier appeared with a large board and his toolbag and the hole was soon secured.

'I'll stay till your mam and dad come back, explain what happened,' Tommy said and Bernie was too relieved to refuse. She made tea for Tommy and Peter and persuaded the kids to get in their beds although there wasn't much chance of them going to sleep.

Not long after, her mam burst into the kitchen. 'What's happened to the window?' Her face was white.

'What's going on?' Joe glared at the unexpected sight of Tommy Farrier in his armchair.

'Someone chucked a brick through it,' Bernie said.

'We had a look round but we couldn't see anyone,' Tommy said. 'Maybe you should get the police.'

'We don't want police round here,' Joe said. 'I'll settle this me own way.'

Tommy shrugged and began collecting his tools. Bernie burned with shame for her father's rudeness. She didn't dare say anything but her mam spoke up.

'Come on Joe, Tommy's gone to the trouble of coming up and boarding the window.'

'Yeah, well, thanks,' Joe muttered then marched off to the lavatory.

Tommy and Peter left and Maureen sat down heavily with her head in her hands. Bernie knew that Maureen knew who was responsible but she would never tell their da - he would be too quick to blame the rest of the family for the feud.

Joe came back into the kitchen. 'So who was it?' His face was turkey red and his eyes glittered - a blind stare due to rage, drink or a mixture of both. Bernie's tongue stuck to the roof of her mouth.

'You tell me or by Christ I'll...' His eyes looked ready to pop out of his head and he raised a meaty fist.

195

'Stop it Joe, she don't know.' Maureen pushed in front of him. Bernie was gobsmacked at her mother's daring, the way her skinny body was braced like a fighting cock against her da's brawny muscles.

'Hmph!' Joe glared stupidly at them for a moment then turned on his heel and went out of the back door. They both ran to the other living room window to see him emerge onto the street.

'Come out you bastards!' he shouted, swinging his fists and turning in circles.

'Oh no!'Maureen wailed.

They watched terrified as he ranted and cursed. Curtains twitched at windows but no one ventured out. Bernie feared her da would start smashing windows at random in revenge. Luckily the van came round the corner and John jumped out. He began trying to get Joe back into the block. There was a commotion in the lobby as he and Sandie herded Joe back up the stairs. Bernie thought Peter might come out to help but no one emerged from the Farriers' flat.

Joe was still cursing but the rage was dying out of his voice as drink overpowered him with sleepiness. Eventually he allowed John to lead him back to his armchair where he slumped, looking round at them all with bloodshot eyes.

'I'll swing for 'em,' he muttered, 'you just tell me who it was.'

'Da, it's late, we'll find out tomorrow. We'll sort it then.' John knew well how to placate their da and within a few minutes Joe's eyes began to flutter. As Bernie listened to him grinding his teeth in his sleep she wondered what would happen next. Her da would rage for a bit but John was a different kettle of fish. Bernie knew he would exact revenge.
The next day she also had to face Bobby Charles and sleep wouldn't come as she worried. She heard her mam padding into the kitchen for tea and cigarettes and although Sandie made no sound from the upper bunk, the snuffles from her two younger sisters told her they too were still awake.

On Sunday morning Joe was still on the rampage, convinced they all knew who had thrown the brick. Thankfully Vinny Mack called to take him off for their Sunday breakfast and follow on pub session. John didn't go and after they left all hell broke loose in the kitchen.

'I'm going round there now and smash every one of their windows.' John was already pulling on his jacket.

Maureen grabbed his arm. 'No, you mustn't. We don't know for sure it was them.'

'Oh Mam, get with it. Who else would it be?'

'Don't you talk to me like that,' Maureen held on to his sleeve.

'I'm sorry Mam, but we can't let them get away with it. Tell her Bernie.'

'I don't know,' Bernie looked from him to her mam. Like John, she couldn't bear letting the Hansons walk all over them but they had to live together. Getting revenge would mean all-out war. 'What do you think?' She turned to Sandie, thinking she would have good advice. Sandie was clever, worked in an office. She was used to solving problems and John might listen to her rather than to their mam.

Sandie stirred her tea. 'I think you should report it to the police. You don't have to say who you think did it but you're going to have to get the council to fix it and they'll want to know what happened. It'll look better if there's an official police report.'

'I dunno,' Maureen said, 'Joe won't hear of going to the police.' She let go of John's arm. 'You just calm down me laddo and let me think on. I'll see about it in the morning. Put the kettle on Bernie, my head's fair cracking. And then we better get the dinner on.'

'What do you think she'll do?' Sandie asked later when she and Bernie were trying on makeup.

'Dunno,' Bernie said. She and Peter were going for a walk in Walton Hall park after dinner and she would be glad to get out. She talked it over with Peter as they walked through the park in the cold, crisp, winter air.

'Of course it was Jacko,' Peter said. 'You know I wanted to come back last night when your dad was out in the street but my dad wouldn't let me.'

'I don't blame him,' Bernie said, 'not after the way my da spoke to him.'

'Never mind, as long as you didn't think I wasn't protecting you.'

'There'll be more trouble from Jacko if we don't do something to put a stop to it,' Bernie said but she couldn't think what to do. Trying to talk to Rose seemed unlikely to succeed and despite anything she or her mam said, she knew John would be plotting his next move.

Their talk moved on to the forthcoming evening, they still had to face their agent.

When the group met at the Back Alley that evening they were all apprehensive but they put their worries to one side when they went on stage. Their set was going well but Bernie kept glancing round the dance floor for signs of Jacko or the Sullivans. Her heart flapped when she spotted Bobby sliding into a seat at the back of the room and she sang out of beat for a moment. Ginger gave her a warning look and she closed her eyes to concentrate. In a second she was steady again and finished the set without looking out at the crowd.

197

When they came off they reluctantly squeezed round Bobby's table.

'Well, I suppose you know I've had Father McKenna on the phone?'

The boys hung their heads but Bernie spoke up. 'It wasn't our fault.' Her eyes flashed.

'But you all took part,' Bobby looked at her, 'even you.'

'What did you expect us to do?' Peter said. 'They were throwing stuff; they were out to make trouble.'

'You should have just left the stage. Look, it's not just yourselves you made a show of, it falls back on me and my other acts. If I get a reputation for handling troublecausers who's going to come to me?'

Bernie's heart sank. Bobby was going to drop them and her dreams of a singing career were going to go up in smoke.

Bobby's voice softened. 'I know you're young, you still don't know the ropes but you're good. You're better than these dives you're playing but you got to learn to be professional . No matter how provoked you are, you carry on and if it gets too bad you get backstage fast.

'If you were just some fill-in group I'd be telling you to walk on right now but I got plans for you so I'm going to let it go this time, but no more, you hear?'

They all relaxed, smiles of relief and sheepish grins on their faces, but they weren't off the hook yet.

'No more gigs in your local area,' Bobby said, 'and this lot that's after you, do they come into town?'

'I expect so,' Peter said. 'doesn't everybody?'

'Maybe it'd be best to stay out of Liverpool for a while, at least till this all dies down.'

Bernie opened her mouth to protest. Why should they have to hide? It wasn't their fault. She couldn't bear the thought of missing their regular sessions at the Back Alley and weren't all their fans here in Liverpool?

Bobby held up a hand. 'No arguments. We'll concentrate on Manchester, maybe Southport, even Preston, if that battered rustbucket you call transport can cope. I might be able to get you into some of the holiday camps or pier shows for the summer season and by the time you've left school,' he raised a questioning eyebrow at Bernie, 'I'm planning to put together a German tour in the autumn and I'd like Riverbeat to be part of it.'

'Just think Bernie,' Peter murmured as they cuddled under the stairs of the block later, 'we're on our way, leaving all this behind. It's a dream come true. You and me together in Germany.' He squeezed her breast and began to unbutton her blouse as she squirmed against him and clung closer. Despite the heat that rose to her face that was as far as she was going to let him go and after a prolonged kiss she gently pushed him away.

In bed she thought about the future Bobby Charles had mapped out in front of them but although it was exciting it was frightening too. Her dreams of stardom had been just that, the best she'd really hoped for was a steady job and the opportunity to sing in the city's pubs and clubs at night. If Riverbeat was going to travel to other towns and cities she might have to be away till the early hours of the morning, maybe even stay out overnight. Sooner or later her da would find out and what would happen then?

She drifted into sleep only to be roused by a sudden commotion outside. Recognising her father's voice she jumped up and rushed to the window. Someone was screaming and Bernie saw it was Rose Hanson trying to pull her husband away as Joe swung punches at him. The little man was no match for Joe's brawn and went down under the blows.

'Go on Da, get him,' Polly yelled behind Bernie who turned to see Teresa and Sandie also standing there.

In the street, John was trying to restrain their da. He shouted, 'It's not him Da,' but Joe was beyond hearing anyone.

'Break my windows will yer, yer bastard,' he roared, dragging the defenceless Mr Hanson up for another smash in the face.

Lights were going on all along the street. Sandie let out a gasp as Jacko, dressed only in striped pyjama bottoms flew out of their front door and jumped on John.

Bernie ran to her mam who was pulling on her coat. 'No Mam, don't,' Bernie begged but before Maureen could respond they both froze at the sound of a police siren. They ran down the stairs as a panda car zoomed to a halt alongside the fight. Peter and his dad were coming out of their flat but two policemen were handcuffing Joe before shoving him in the back of the car where he carried on raging and swearing. John grabbed the door handle to release him but he was restrained by one of the officers.

'Let them go! Maureen yelled. She lunged forward but Bernie held her back. Jacko knelt beside his fallen father. 'Dad, Dad,' he cried and Rose joined in sobbing hysterically and wailing, 'Bert, Bert.' Between them they got Mr Hanson to his feet.

'Attacked - we was just coming back from the pictures, minding our own business,' Rose appealed to the officers. Maureen gasped as she saw Bert Hanson was bleeding quite heavily from a cut above his eyebrow and a split lip.

'Is that true?' one officer took out his notebook. Mr Hanson nodded mournfully and Bernie felt quite sorry for him. He probably had nothing to do with all this. Trust her da to pick on the wrong person.

'Animals,' Rose spat. 'You should lock them up and throw the key away.'

Mr Hanson plucked at her sleeve. 'Let's just go home, Rose. I don't want it to go no further.'

'We're taking him in anyway,' the officer put away his notebook. 'Let him cool his heels till morning. The rest of you better get indoors.'

John started to protest but the policeman turned on him. 'You want to come too? Any more out of either of you' - he pointed at Jacko, 'and you'll be spending the night in the cells too.'

'Come on Dad,' Jacko took his father's arm and Rose took the other. Together they helped him into their flat.

The McCanns stood by as the officers got into the car. 'Domestics,' one said to the other in a disgusted voice as he slammed the door.

'I'll take the van down to the station, ' Peter said. 'Maybe they'll let him out after a ticking off.'

'Want me to come?' Peter offered.

'No but thanks for coming out. No one else did.'

Peter gave Bernie a quick hug before following his dad back to their flat. Bernie and Maureen went upstairs to find everyone still up. There wasn't much sleep for any of them and Bernie eventually slipped into a doze to be woken at four when John brought her da home. He'd been released with a caution and a warning to behave in future.

Chapter Twenty-Two.

On Monday Maureen reported the broken window but days went by and it was still boarded up. Bernie never found out what happened between her mam and da after he came back from the police station. She hoped it would all die down without any further trouble but despite the lull at home there was an uneasy atmosphere as if something needed to be settled.

On Friday Bernie came home from school to find her mam in floods of tears at the kitchen table. Her aunty Joan and Patsy were there too, trying to comfort her. Polly and Teresa gawped in the doorway, Teresa's eyes already filling with tears in sympathy.

'Go and get changed.' Bernie shooed them out. 'Whatever's the matter, Mam?'

'Housing's been round,' Joan said.

Maureen wiped her eyes. 'I thought they'd come about fixing the window.'

'That bitch,' Joan said, 'that wicked old cow.'

'Mrs Hanson?' Bernie's heart thumped. Rose, it had to be Rose.

'She took a petition round, to get us evicted,' Maureen mumbled.

'A petition? What about?'

'Said we're aggressive, dirty. She said my kids are bullies. And she said things about Joe, about totters being robbers. Oh my God, Joe'll go berserk…'

Blood pounded in Bernie's ears. 'And people signed this – this pack of lies?'

Maureen shrugged. 'Not the Farriers, but nearly everyone else. You know how bossy Rose is.'

'But you told her it was all lies, how she's got it in for us?' Tears of anger burned Bernie's eyes.

'It didn't do no good,' Maureen said. 'She was nice about it but she said there was evidence of fights, at the school and now your da's had a caution… She said it would be better for everyone if we moved away, had a fresh start.'

'But I don't want to move!' Bernie shouted. 'Why should we?'

'We haven't got no choice,' Maureen said.

'She's promised yous a proper house.' Joan said. 'Maybe she's right – a new start.'

'Bernie felt the ground falling away beneath her. 'What about school?' She wanted to say, 'and Peter' but changed it to, 'and Annabel, she's my best friend.'

'It's not so far away, only Norris Green,' Joan said.

'Nice houses in Norris Green,' Patsy rubbed her belly. 'We'd jump at one if we got the chance.'

Bernie ran out of the back door down to the Farriers' flat. Peter wasn't home yet so she sat on the wall with Annabel and poured out the whole story.

'She's a nasty old cow,' Annabel said, 'I bet me mam sent her packing.'

'Oh I don't want to go,' Bernie wailed, 'it'll mean changing schools again – and what about Peter and the band?' She glanced down at the little silver ring on her finger and burst into tears.

Annabel waited while Bernie composed herself. 'I was coming up to yours anyway to tell you,' she hesitated.

'Tell me what?' Bernie sniffed. Nothing could be worse than what had already happened.

'Why it's been quiet, why no one's seen Jacko. Someone gave him a kicking on Monday night, put him in hospital. He only came home yesterday.'

It had to be Da or John but there was no time to find out more – it was the night of their debut at the Jungfrau club in Manchester. Bernie's excitement about singing at the famous venue and meeting The Nashville Teens was spoiled. Not only would she have to move away from Peter and Annabel but her da and her brother might end up in a prison cell.

'Don't worry,' Peter said. 'Norris Green's not far away and it's not going to make any difference. The band needs you and you don't think I'm going to let you get away from me, do you?'

She reached up to kiss him. Feeling his arms around her gave her strength to voice her fears. 'It's not just that, it's me da and our John.'

'You don't actually know what happened to Jacko, do you?'

She shook her head.

'It looks like Jacko hasn't said anything, hasn't told anyone.'

'But the police…'

'If he'd told them, they'd have been round. Maybe it was someone else, there's lots of people don't care for Jacko.'

Bernie drew back and scrutinised him. 'Did you know anything about it, tell me straight now?'

'I don't know anything,' Peter said and looked out of the van's rear window.

At the club Bernie forgot everything. They were all nervous walking on stage but the floor was rocking already, everyone out for a good time and their first number, *Louie Louie*, sent the crowd wild. Bernie's troubles dropped away as she was swept along in the heady atmosphere and at the end of their forty minute set she was barely tired at all.

The crowd showed appreciation but everyone was clearly eager for the stars to appear. There 'd been no sign of them although their roadies had been doing sound checks when Riverbeat first arrived. It was only as Riverbeat were making their way out that The Teens themselves came flying in.

'Hey guys, great warm up,' one yelled.

'Yeah, come see us backstage after the show,' another called over his shoulder.

'They weren't even here,' Bernie said.

'I know,' Peter said as they listened to the excited roars as the group went on stage.

Bernie was disappointed that they couldn't stay to see the show and meet the band. It was a pain still being at school and having to get home before her da came in. It was just another thing she had to blame him for. Would she ever be able to escape?

On the Monday someone came to inspect the broken window. Bernie heard all about it when she came home from school.

'Bloody cheek!' Maureen was still fuming, even though the man had called in the morning before she left for work.

'Why won't they fix it?' Bernie set to peeling the potatoes . 'It's their window, not ours.'

'He was a proper snooty bugger. Wanted to see a police report number and then wanted to know why we hadn't reported it, made out we'd done it ourselves..'

'Why would he think that?' Bernie felt bewildered.

'Well we're already down as troublemakers aren't we?' Maureen said bitterly.

203

'Sandie said you should have got the police.'.

'You know your da wouldn't hear of it. The bloke said we'd have to pay for it ourselves.'

'Well me da should pay for it then,' Bernie said.

'Ha, he won't cough up. I've got a bit put by, I was saving for birthdays and such. I'll just pay it meself, it'll be easier.'

Bernie bit her lip. It wasn't fair, her mam had little enough while her da always had money for the pub and for his pals.

Maureen said, 'It could be worse I suppose.'

'Can't we just leave it, if we're moving anyway?'

'We've to leave the place in good condition, they come round to check before they give you the new keys.'

'Are you happy about the new house?' Bernie had hardly given a thought to her mam's feelings, she'd been so upset about the move herself.

'It's a proper house with a garden front and back. There might even be a driveway for your da's van. I always wanted a real house, never thought I'd ever get one. It's nearer to our Joan's as well.'

'What does Da think?' Bernie wondered how he had taken the news, surely he would have been on the bounce to the Hansons, caution or no caution.

'I didn't tell him about the petition. I just said I didn't want to stay here any more and I asked the council for a transfer. He's happy anyway, it's nearer the Crown.'

Bernie went to her room and took a pound and ten shilling note from the stash under her mattress.

'Here Mam, I've been saving up too.'

Maureen looked at the notes. 'No Bernie. You got to buy new clothes and get your hair done and all that.'

'Don't be daft Mam, take it, I want you to.' Bernie folded the notes into her mam's hand.

Maureen scraped a hand across her eyes.

'When do you think we'll be moving?' Bernie asked to cover her embarrassment.

'They don't give you much time once you've signed up.' Maureen glanced round the kitchen. 'When we came here I thought it was going to be great after all those years in that fleapit in Toxteth but I can't say I'll be sorry to go. We had better neighbours in Toccy than here, except for the Farriers.'

Bernie would miss being so close to Peter and Annabel but after all the trouble here it would be good to get away from the Hansons and the Sullivans.

'We're getting a four-bedroomed,' Maureen went on. 'You and Marie'll be able to have a room of your own. I rang the nuns yesterday, we can take her birthday presents on Wednesday.'

The idea of the four bedrooms was tempting but Bernie wondered what Marie would be like when she came home – and what would happen to Sandie?

The convent driveway was lined with daffodils nodding their heads in the spring breeze and the lawns were greening up after their winter sleep. Everything seemed bright and hopeful until the door clanged behind Bernie and Maureen and the silence inside engulfed them.

They followed the nun's swishing skirts and again were shown into the parlour and treated to the tea tray with its china cups and plate of biscuits. Neither of them felt like eating when they saw Marie. She was huge and shapeless in a grey cotton smock and cardigan. Bernie looked at the thick stockings her sister was wearing and thought how she must hate every stitch of her outfit. Her hair hung lank, her complexion was pasty as if she never saw the sun and there were dark rings under her eyes.

Maureen crossed herself but Bernie put a smile on her face for her sister's sake.

'Lord what's been happening to you girl, you look awful?' Maureen said.

Marie said listlessly ' I'm so bloody tired all the time. It kicks all night and keeps me awake and it's work, work, work all day. Pour us a cup of tea Mam and pass them biscuits if you're not eating them.'

Bernie and Maureen watched as Marie gobbled up all the biscuits.

'I brought some chocolate.' Bernie put a paper bag on the table. Marie pulled out a Mars bar and tore off the wrapper.

'Best eat it now,' she said with her mouth full, 'in case they take it off me.'

'Surely they're not that bad?' Maureen whispered.

'There's so many things to get punished for,' Marie said. She drained her cup. 'Ah, that's better.'

'Still, not long now is it?' Maureen put on a smile.

'Another month.' Marie reached for a Bounty bar. 'Some birthday I'm going to have.'

'Won't they do anything special for you?' Bernie asked

'You get sent to Mass, and you get a card with a religious relic inside, to do with your saint's day, mine's St Victor. You still have to work and everything. I'm on ironing now. God, it's so hot and standing up all the time. If it wasn't for the other girls I think I'd have killed meself by now.'

'Marie!' Maureen crossed herself. 'That's a terrible thing to say and with a life inside you as well.'

'Well, I haven't done it have I?' Marie munched her chocolate.

'Are you scared?' Bernie asked. 'You know, having the baby?'

'What do you think?' Marie finished the chocolate and screwed up the wrapper. 'At least it will be over.'

But it wouldn't be over, Bernie thought. There would be the baby to think about and how would Marie feel after it was born? She'd often thought about what it would be like to have a baby and the idea had terrified her ever since she discovered how they got out. She thought babies must be made out of the deepest love, why else would you put yourself through that? Poor Marie, to go through all this and then have the baby taken away and given to someone else - how would she bear it?

'We're moving house,' she said to cover her thoughts.

Maureen smacked her forehead, ' I'd forgotten all about it with coming here.'

Marie looked startled. 'How come?'

'Don't worry, your bed'll be safe.' Maureen explained about the feud and the housing department's offer with Bernie chipping in.

Marie's eyes flashed. 'Wish I'd been there,' she said as Bernie recited the tale of the attack in the club. 'I'd have shown them a thing or two.'

All too soon Sister Agatha returned to say their time was up. They hadn't given Marie her birthday gifts so had to leave the bag of presents on the table. Bernie had wanted to see Marie open them; she was worried the nuns might confiscate them before she even got to see what they were. She hadn't known what to get. It was no use bringing tights or makeup that Marie wouldn't be allowed to wear so she'd brought the usual boring stuff, a box of handkerchiefs and some bath cubes but tucked underneath the hankies was a pack of five Park Drive and a few matches. What if the nuns should find them?

Maureen had brought sensible gifts: a new hairbrush and cotton underwear. On the way home Bernie reflected that her sister's birthday wouldn't be much fun that year. She resolved to start buying some little treats to make it up to her when she came home.

There wasn't much time to think about anything as Maureen began organising the family for the move. The younger kids were excited with the prospect of making new friends and having a garden at home to play in.

Bernie was allowed to stay at St Anthony's as she would leave in July anyway. It meant she would still see Annabel every day. She shed a few tears while packing up her possessions. She would miss running down to the Farriers' flat or sitting on the wall with Annabel - and what about the lovers' hidey hole she shared with Peter under the stairs?

Sandie came in and saw her crying. 'What's the matter with you?' She plopped down next to Bernie.

'Oh it's just all this - moving,' Bernie sniffled. 'Everything's going to change.'

'You're not worried about Peter are you?' Sandie put an arm round her shoulders.

'Last time we moved, I lost my boyfriend and my best friend.'

'That was last time. Peter loves you, anyone can see that.'

'Do you really think so?'

'Of course. If you were old enough, he'd be putting a ring on your finger right now.'

Bernie giggled through her tears. 'What about you and John? Seems like you're getting pretty serious.'

'Oh well, I dunno.' A faint blush spread over Sandie's cheeks.

'You wouldn't let him down, would you?'

Sandie shook her head. 'I'm not sure how he feels,' she confided, '- and there's my family...'

'Will you go back home, when our Marie comes home?'

'No fear.' Sandie stood up and began tidying the girls' bed, folding the school uniforms they'd left strewn about.

Bernie wondered how hard it must have been for her at home to make her leave her well-off life to come and live with them.

'It must be different for you living here,' she said, remembering the early skirmishes over missing makeup and borrowed clothes.

'But I've loved it.' Sandie turned round. 'You've all been so good to me. just so warm and friendly. You've got no idea what my house is like – and my dad…'

'Well what about my da?' Bernie said

'Yeah, but he's hardly ever here, is he?'

'When we move we might have more space, till our Marie gets back.'

'Actually, I'm not coming to the new house. Where I work, there's an office upstairs lets out flats and houses. They've got a little bedsit that'll just suit me.'

'Does me mam know?' It felt like she was losing another sister.

'I haven't definitely got it yet. I'm going to see it on Friday and sign up for the rent book and then I'll tell her.'

And so on Friday evening Sandie waited till Joe had gone off with Vinny Mack before breaking the news that she'd rented the bedsit.

'But... you're too young!' Maureen spluttered, choking on a lungful of smoke.

'I'm eighteen,' Sandie pointed out. 'Lots of girls my age have flats.'

'Not on their own.' Maureen scowled. 'This is something you've cooked up between you.' She glared at John.

'I'm not going, Mam, I'm staying here.'

'Well, I'm telling you, any stopping out all night and out you go for good. I'm not having no shenanigans going on, people gossiping and all.'

Bernie hid a smile. Many a night she'd heard Sandie creep out of the top bunk, not to return for an hour or more. She hoped she and John were more careful than Marie and Jimmy had been.

'You're going to need the room anyway when Marie comes home,' Sandie said.

'The new house is bigger,' Maureen said. 'We can fit an extra bed in.'

'I don't think that would work,' Sandie said calmly. 'Honestly Maureen, it's time I moved on.'

'What's your mam and da going to say?' Maureen demanded.

'I'm old enough to look after myself.'

'Well I don't like it.' Maureen stood up. 'I'm not having nothing to do with it and don't come crying to me when it all goes wrong.' With that she swept out to get ready for bingo.

'Phew!' Bernie sat down at the table.

'I didn't think she'd take it so badly,' Sandie said. 'I thought she'd be pleased, what with you all moving out and your Marie coming back.'

'She's mad because she's going to lose the keep you've been paying her,' John said.

'Oh, I never thought of that,' Sandie looked crestfallen.

'Me neither,' Bernie said but she thought it more likely her mam had grown fond of Sandie as the rest of them had.

'Never mind,' John said. 'I'll give her an extra few bob.'

'I will too,' Bernie said.

'Anyway, we're going somewhere special tomorrow,' John squeezed Sandie's hand, 'so Mam might get a surprise when we get back.'

Chapter Twenty-three

On Saturday morning Bernie went to work with a troubled mind. She was building herself up to telling the Thompsons that she would be moving in just over a week. She didn't really need the work but she felt like she would be letting Mrs Thompson down. Perhaps they would still let her keep the job, it wasn't so far away; it would just mean getting up that bit earlier.

She waited for Mr Thompson to go out to the wholesaler; she was a bit wary of his brusque manner and Mrs Thompson always seemed more relaxed when he wasn't there. That morning there was a rush of customers and Mr Thompson came back while Bernie was taking her break.

Mrs Thompson came into the back room 'Arthur's minding the shop while I snatch a breather.' She plonked herself down. 'You're very quiet today, penny for 'em.'

Bernie sighed, 'I've been meaning to tell you. We're moving to Norris Green.'

Mrs Thompson sat back, stirring sugar into her tea. 'Well, I heard about the petition on the grapevine. There's some miserable beggars round here. Don't you let them get you down. What about your mam, how's she taking it?'

'She was upset at first, but we're getting a proper house, not a flat.' Bernie's eyes were filling up at Mrs Thompson's kind words. 'But I just got used to being here- my friend – and my boyfriend…'

'But you've had trouble here. You'll see it'll be better for you away from those bullies and your friends will stick with you. Norris Green's only up the road.'

Bernie brightened a little. It was true Norris Green wasn't far away like Toxteth.

'And I hope you're not going to leave us?'

Bernie looked up. 'But you always said you wanted someone local?'

'Don't be daft.' Mrs Thompson reached across the table and squeezed her hand. 'How many times have I told you you're the best Saturday girl we've had? Arthur and me have been talking. When you leave school this summer we'd like you to come and work for us full-time. We're going to lease another shop in Kirkby and we'll need another pair of hands here. We could train you up as manager in a couple of years.'

Bernie didn't know what to say. It was sweet flattery to hear her employers thought so much of her. How could she say she had her sights set so much higher? And did it make sense to give up this chance for the uncertain hope of making it on the pop scene?

'You'll still be able to do your singing,' Mrs Thompson said.

'But I might have to be away sometimes, our agent's trying to get us some seaside bookings; he's even talking about sending us to Germany.'

'Well, I didn't realise you were doing so well. I'm sure we can work round it between us. It's always as well to have something to fall back on – music and acting, nothing is guaranteed you know. We'd like you to stay with us.'

'I'd love to – and I'm really grateful,' Bernie said. 'It's just – oh everything's so upside down what with moving and leaving school – I don't know what I want.'

'Well there's no rush. You just have a good think about it, the offer's there if you want it. We'd be really sorry to lose you.'

Bernie was tidying the magazine racks, still mulling over the Thompsons' offer when Peter rushed into the shop. 'You'll never guess what,' he shouted.

'Sshh,' Bernie said as Mrs Thompson and the customer at the counter stared in surprise. 'What is it?' She'd never seen him so excited.

'Bobby phoned Ginger. You have to come now.'

'I can't.' Bernie frowned. 'I'm working, can't you see? What's so important?'

'We've got a gig, at Prestatyn – at a holiday camp, for the Easter weekend.'

'Wow, that's fab,' she said, then the meaning of his words struck her. 'You mean we'd have to stay there?'

'Yeah, just think, a whole weekend away by the sea, lots of cool kids and music – but we have to say yes right now.'

'Oh,' Bernie's excitement deserted her. How could she go off for a whole weekend? She was sure that her mam wouldn't let her go away with a gang of lads even if Peter was one of them. And there was her da…

'Come on Bernie, the others are in the van outside.'

'Go on love,' Mrs Thompson nodded, 'but don't be too long.'

Bernie followed Peter out of the shop 'Me mam'll never let me go,' she stuttered as Ginger wound down the passenger window.

'Now you look here,' he said, 'you're in this with us and it's too late to back out now. I never wanted you in the band in the first place. If you let us down now, you're out for good Bernie.'

Heat flooded her face. A retort sprang to her lips but died as she realised deep down that he was right. Somehow she had to go.

'But me mam,' she still hesitated.

'Look, I'll get Bobby to ring your mam and explain,' Ginger rolled his eyes heavenward.

'Ring me mam?' Bernie echoed. 'How?'

'Oh for Christ's sake. Can't you fetch your mam round to mine and she can ring him from there?'

'She's not home,' Bernie felt near to tears, 'she's at Greaty market.'

'Come on Bernie, we haven't got time to piss about. Bobby wants an answer.'

There was only one thing for it. 'Okay, I'm in.'

Ginger's face split in a grin. 'Attagirl,' he said, 'what a chick.'

Peter planted a smacking kiss on her lips and swung her round in a circle. Suddenly they were all laughing and for the moment Bernie believed anything was possible.

'We'll go tell Bobby now.' Tommy started the engine up and Peter jumped in. 'I'll be round at seven,' he shouted as the van pulled away.

Bernie went back into the shop. Somehow she was going to make the gig but as her euphoria wore off she grew more and more fearful of breaking the news to her mam.

But when she got home it was clear that a celebration was going on. A box of cream cakes stood on the table amid the usual clutter of teapot and cups. Bernie stared at this rarity as she took off her coat and the next minute all the kids streamed in jumping like frogs with excitement.

'Our John and Sandie's getting married.' Polly did a handstand threatening to knock the precious cakes off the table.

'Get away.' Bernie swatted them aside and rushed into the living room. Her mam, John and Sandie were drinking coffee from the china coffee set Maureen kept unused in an old display cabinet Da had brought in off the round. Bernie's eyes widened; she'd never seen that set used before.

Sandie sat like the Queen of Sheba on the couch, John by her side. She lifted her cup carefully so as to show off the tiny diamond sparkling on the third finger of her left hand.

'Oh wow!' Bernie said. She sat down in the one vacant chair. Her mam was grinning from ear to ear.

'Would you like some coffee, Bernie?' Sandie said graciously.

'Yes please,' she took Sandie's hand. 'Let me see. Oh, it's lovely. Congratulations.' She looked at John. 'When you said you were going out for something special, I never thought...'

'Me neither,' Sandie laughed and squeezed John's arm. Of course we won't be getting married for quite a while.'

'I'm glad about that,' Maureen said, 'that's sensible, give you time to save up.' This was a tacit declaration that Sandie wasn't pregnant, much to Bernie's relief. They'd enough to cope with with Marie.

The kids burst into the room, the cream round their mouths showing that they'd polished off the rest of the cakes.

'Oh you greedy eejits,' Maureen said, 'our Bernie hasn't even had one.'

'Are you still going to live with us when you're married?' Anthony asked.

'You can't stay in our room 'cos it's all boys,' Matty said and they both turned red and smothered giggles.

'They can have your room and yous can sleep in the coalhole,' Polly said. She and Teresa burst out laughing.

'Stop it the lot of you,' Maureen said but she had a twinkle in her eye. 'They'll be getting their own place away from you nosey parkers.' She collected the precious coffee cups. 'I'd better get your da's butties before him and Vinny come in.'

'What do you think me da'll say?' John frowned.

'Oh I expect he'll be pleased,' Maureen looked vague and hurried off to the kitchen. Bernie made to follow her when a rentman's knock sounded at the front door and froze them all where they stood.

'You answer, Bernie,' Maureen whispered, 'and whoever it is I'm not in.'

Bernie went to the door and drew the bolts that squealed with disuse. The door creaked open and there stood Bobby Charles. Bernie gaped at him.

'I thought I ought to come and see your parents about this booking at Tower Beach,' he said, smiling at her. 'You know, with you only being fifteen.'

'You'd better come in,' Bernie stood back although she could barely get her thoughts together. 'Wait there.' She left him standing in the hall outside the lavatory door.

Her mam was hiding in the kitchen. 'Mam, it's Mr Charles, the band's agent. He wants to see you about a booking we've got.'

212

'See me, whatever for? What you been up to?' Maureen straightened her clothes and smoothed her hair.

'Nothing Mam, honest.'

'Well, put him in the living room, I won't be a tick.' Maureen started putting the precious coffee cups in a bowl of soapy water. 'See if he wants a cuppa.'

Bernie returned to the hall where all the younger children were standing in a row staring at Bobby. 'Won't you come through?' she said shooing the kids away into their rooms. She led him into the living room where he sat in her da's armchair. 'This is our agent, Mr Charles,' she told John and Sandie.

'Pleased to meet you.' John got up and shook his hand. 'Our Bernie going to be a pop star is she?' he joked.

Bobby laughed politely. 'Well, she's got some talent.' He smiled at Bernie and she blushed. 'Would you like some tea?' she asked to cover her embarrassment.

'Yeah, that would be nice,' He relaxed in the chair and glanced round the room.

'We're about to move house,' Bernie said as if that would make up for their shabby belongings.

'We'd better be going,' John said, pulling Sandie up off the couch. 'We'll see you later, Bernie.'

'Coming to see the band play tonight?' Bobby asked.

'Maybe,' John said, 'we're going out for a meal first, celebrating. We just got engaged.'

'Oh congratulations,' Bobby said as Maureen entered with a battered tea tray. She had the air of a posh waitress as she poured the tea and Bernie would have giggled if she hadn't been so afraid of what was coming.

'I thought I'd better come and see you about this Easter booking,' Bobby said, taking the cup from her. With Bernie being under sixteen I wanted to reassure you that she will be properly looked after and to answer any questions you may have.'

'What are you on about?' Maureen forgot her gracious manner. 'Bernie what's all this about?'

'Mam, the band's got a booking for the Easter weekend but it's at a holiday camp in Prestatyn. I - I said I'll go.'

'Oh no.' Maureen's eyebrows disappeared into her hair. 'No, I'm not having that. She's too young to be going off - and with a pack of lads too. You know her and Peter are...' she broke off and glared at Bobby.

Bobby put his cup on the arm of the chair. 'Let me assure you, Mrs McCann, it's a purely professional engagement.'

'Professional my foot,' Maureen said. 'Who's going to keep an eye on her?'

'Mam!' Bernie was in an agony of embarrassment. 'I don't need keeping an eye on, honest.'

'That's what we thought about your sister,' Maureen shot back then bit her lip.

'She'll have her own accommodation, I'll see to that,' Bobby said.

'That's no guarantee, is it?' Maureen said. 'You know what these kids are like and them camps - drink - drugs, no supervision.'

Bernie was ready to burst into tears. 'But -'

'Don't you but me my girl. It's out of the question and that's that. What do you think your da would say?'

There was silence for a moment then Bobby spoke up.

'Mrs McCann, your daughter's got a real talent and I think the band can go places with her singing up front. Surely you don't want her to give up a chance of making a good living that way rather than slaving in a factory or a shop?'

Maureen didn't answer. Bernie saw she was struggling between pleasure at this praise and her suspicions as to Bobby's motives. While Maureen was still gathering her wits John poked his head round the door.

'We're getting off now,' he said, 'but we heard what you were saying. How about if we book into the holiday camp for Easter? We could do with a break and then we can keep an eye on our Bernie.'

Maureen looked taken aback but her face softened.

'Well, I don't know. I suppose - I mean I don't want to stand in her way.'

'Oh thanks Mam, you won't need to worry, honest.' Bernie threw her arms round Maureen almost knocking her off her feet.

John and Sandie left for town and Bobby Charles took his leave shortly afterwards. Bernie glanced out of the window to see her da's van pull up in front of the block just as Bobby came out. A couple of minutes later her da and Vinny Mack came in.

'What's been going on here?' Joe eyed the crushed remains of the cake box, 'and who's that bloke I saw on the stairs?'

'What bloke?' Maureen said. 'Must have been someone visiting them upstairs.' She picked up the cake box, flattening it to go in the bin. 'John and Sandie bought the cakes. They've got engaged. I thought he would have told you already.'

'Nobody tells me anything,' Joe growled but a slight smile creased his face. 'He could do worse, I suppose.'

'She's a lovely girl,' Maureen said.

'He'll have to work a bit harder if he's going to get married,' Joe said. 'Anyway what about our butties?'

He went off to get washed and Vinny Mack settled himself in the living room in front of the telly. Maureen scurried to make the sandwiches and Bernie stayed to help, the living room with Vinny Mack in it was a no-go area.

'What's me da going to say about me going away for Easter?' she asked as she put slices of ham onto the bread her mam had buttered.

'Don't you worry, just leave that to me. I can't believe it, you going all that way to sing.'

'If this one goes okay, Bobby says we'll get more through the summer.' Bernie didn't mention the idea of going to Germany. 'This might be just the start - and I'll make sure you get some of the money, Mam.'

Bernie was still bubbling with excitement that evening after Maureen and Joe had gone out with Vinny Mack. Maureen had agreed that Annabel could babysit as Bernie and the band were playing a social club in St. Helens.

Tommy picked her and Peter up at six-thirty. They were all in high spirits, singing all the way to the gig and on stage there was no stopping them. At the end of the set the crowd howled for more and they had to play several encores before they could finally get away.

'If it wasn't for your old man we could stay later,' Ginger grumbled, 'have a few drinks.'

Bernie was too worried about getting home late to pay much attention to Ginger. When she did get home her mam was already in, warming a pan of bacon ribs on the stove and Annabel had gone home.

'Where've you been?' she hissed. 'Go and get your jamas on, your da thinks you've been in all night.'

Bernie hurried to change and wash off her makeup. Back in the kitchen she took the steaming bowl of ribs her mam passed her.

'Take this in to your da. I've told him you and Sandie and John are all going to Butlins to see our Marie so just stick to that if he says anything.'

Bernie carried the bowl to the living room. Da was in his armchair, his face actually broke into a smile when he saw her but he was always in a good mood when he came back from the pub.

'Going off to Butlins eh? Quite grown up now aren't you?' He took the bowl and poked a finger in the contents.

Bernie nodded. 'Yes Da.'

'Our Marie doesn't seem to keen to come back and see us now, does she?'

Bernie shook her head but didn't reply. Despite his good mood he had a habit of taking things you said the wrong way.

'Mind you behave yourself,' he pointed a sucked bone at her.

'Oh I will, Da,' Bernie blushed. 'It's only a couple of days.'

'Only that our John's going, otherwise I wouldn't hear of it.'

'I know, Da, we just want to see Marie.'

'Hmph' Joe said. 'I know what you kids get up to at them camps but you're a good girl. I'll give you a few bob spending money before you go.'

'Thanks Da,' Bernie said but she doubted this would happen. Anyway she had her own money now.

'Better get off to bed then,' Joe dismissed her. Mo, what you doing out there? 'C'mere and give us a kiss.'

Bernie went into the kitchen. Maureen had left a bowl of ribs on the table for her. 'Get them down you,' she said, picking up two cups of tea for herself and Joe.

'Thanks Mam.' Bernie sat down to enjoy her supper, savouring the thought of a whole weekend away with Peter. She'd never had a holiday and it seemed like a dream come true.

On Sunday all their belongings had to be packed up ready for the move. In the evening she sat on the wall outside with Peter and Annabel.

'Don't worry,' Peter squeezed her shoulders, 'it'll be okay,' but later, as they cuddled under the stairs, she clung to him like they were parting forever.

'Hey, come on, look I'll be round tomorrow night after college, it'll be just the same.'

She knew she should trust him but how could she be sure he just wouldn't drop her like George had done? What if he only wanted her because she sang well with the band.

In the morning she bid a tearful farewell to Peter, Kathleen and Annabel, before taking the younger children to their new school. She was staying off school to help with the move. Maureen had taken the day off from the shop to get settled in. Joe grumbled because he had to let John use the van to shift their possessions. He and Vinny Mack repaired to the transport cafe on the East Lancs road until John finished moving their stuff.

When everything was in the van Bernie and Maureen walked through the empty rooms checking that nothing was left behind.

'All that money gone on new wallpaper and such,' Maureen said, fingering the still fresh paintwork on the boys' bedroom door. If I'd known we was only going to be here five minutes, I'd never have started.'

Five minutes? Bernie thought. It seemed like an age to her since they'd left Toxteth, so much had happened - she was a different girl to the one who'd run up the steps so many months ago.

Outside John honked the horn and they went out gazing up for a last look but within ten minutes they arrived at their new home. It was in a quiet cul-de-sac with a tiny front garden bordered by a low green fence and gate and she could see her mam was delighted as she explored the house she'd only briefly seen before. It didn't even need decorating, every room had nice wallpaper and clean paint.

'It's a little palace,' Maureen breathed, 'maybe our luck's changed at last.'

They started carrying in the furniture which looked shabby in the neat rooms lit by bright sunshine.

'At least it's not up loads of steps.' John said.

'The kids'll love the garden,' Bernie looked out of the kitchen window at the patch of overgrown grass. 'Do you think Da might get us a swing - and a paddling pool?'   They went outside to inspect the garden. 'They'll all want to play in that henhog,' Bernie peered into the tunnel passage that separated their house from the one next door and gave access from the back to the front of the terraced houses. It wasn't so long since she had played house in similar alleys in Toxteth with Aggie but of course now she was far too grown up.

Once everything was unloaded John went off to pick up Joe and Vinny for their day's work. Bernie and Maureen got to work. The gas and electric were on and the furniture in place by the time Bernie picked the kids up from their new school. She had no worries about Matthew and Anthony as they fitted in anywhere and when the school doors opened they came barrelling out with a crowd of other boys. But how would Teresa have fared? Bernie waited full of apprehension as the girls failed to appear but at last they straggled out and Bernie saw Teresa's face was wreathed in smiles.

'Wow, you should see my teacher,' Polly hogged the limelight as usual. 'She's so beautiful, her name's Miss Pomfrey and she looks like that girl on *Ready Steady Go* and I'm going to have my hair just like hers when I get older. She gave me a sweet 'cos I got all my spellings right.'

'That's great,' Bernie said, 'how did you get on Treez?'

'I've got a friend, her name's Ruth. She sits next to me. She's got a cat called Prudie.'

She looked so happy, Bernie felt happy too and hardly minded them dawdling along behind her all the way home.

At their gate, the front door of the next house opened and an old lady with a stern face came out. Behind her was an old man looking equally grumpy.

'Behave you lot,' Bernie hissed at the kids who were pushing and shoving in their excitement to get into the house. 'Hello,' she said in her best voice. 'I'm Bernadette McCann and these are me brothers and sisters.'

'You're the new ones then are you?' The couple looked them up and down.

'Bernie nodded. 'Have you met me mam yet?'

They shook their heads.

'Well, I better get these in. If you'd like to meet me mam, I'm sure you can come round.'

To her surprise the elderly couple came out of their house and followed her down the passage as she herded the kids in front of her. Maureen was in the kitchen, her hair all dishevelled, surrounded by heaps of dishes, pots and pans that she was trying to fit into the kitchen cupboards.

'Mam, these are our next-door-neighbours,' Bernie stammered.

Maureen turned and put a hand up to her hair. 'Lord, sorry everything's upside down.' She turned on the kids who were staring at the neighbours. 'Go and get changed, Bernie see if you can find their things.' The kids shot off to explore the house while Bernie went to the girls' bedroom where all the bags of clothes were piled. She dragged the bags onto the landing where she could hear what was going on in the kitchen.

'Ivy Morgan,' the old lady was saying, 'and this is me husband Fred. Well, we just wanted to introduce ourselves.'

She sounded kinder than her face had looked. Bernie thought maybe they weren't going to be so bad after all. She found the kids' play clothes and took them down to the bathroom that was by the kitchen.

'Won't you have a cup of tea?' Maureen said but Ivy shook her head.

'You got enough to do,' she said. 'We just wanted to say if you need anything be sure to give us a knock, we're at number 45 and the Jones's

218

live at 49 but they're still at work. They're nice people, their daughter's about your girl's age.' She smiled at Bernie.

The kids ran in and dashed out to the back garden where they began trying to climb the single tree in the middle.

'Tell you what,' Ivy said, 'I was just going to make some jam tarts for tea. Why don't you send the kids round to help me, get them out of your hair while you get sorted out?'

'And maybe the lads'd like a kick about in the park down the road?' Fred said.

'Oh there's no need,' Maureen sounded embarrassed.

'Don't be daft,' Ivy said, 'we've got grandkids of our own you know, we're used to kids.'

'Well, if you're really sure?' Maureen called the kids in and told them of the plans. 'Oh wow, jam tarts,' Polly jumped up and down. The boys were torn between thoughts of football and sticky jam.

'What's your name then, sweetheart?' Ivy bent down to Teresa.

'Teresa,' the little girl whispered, 'but you can call me Treez.'

'Okay Treez, do you want to come and make jam tarts with me?'

To Bernie's surprise Teresa nodded and put her hand into Ivy's.

'Well,' Maureen said after they'd all gone, 'that seems like a good start.'

'I thought they didn't like us by the way they looked,' Bernie said. 'I can't believe they're so nice.'

By the time the children returned, everything was shipshape, the butties made for Da, John and Vinny. and chips frying for the kids' tea. Bernie thought the new house felt like home already as they ate the jam tarts Polly and Teresa brought back. Happy, sticky and tired out, all four kids had a bath and fell into bed without a murmur. Later that evening Joan came round. She only lived a few streets away so Maureen was pleased that she would see much more of her. This evening Joan was fizzing with excitement.

'Our Patsy's gone in. Baby should be here by morning. I've just come from Walton but they said to go home till tomorrow.'

Maureen and Bernie exchanged glances. They were happy for Joan and Patsy but they immediately thought of Marie. Joan left promising to let them know as soon as she had any news.

When Peter arrived, he and Bernie sat in the kitchen listening to the pop charts on Radio Luxembourg. When it was time for him to go home Bernie realised she did had a use for the hen hog' it was perfect for cuddling yet she could still see if her da's van pulled up at the other end of the entry.

In their bedroom Polly and Teresa were fast asleep in the double bed. In Bernie's room the bunk beds were set out side by side and Bernie looked at the empty bunk next to her own. She was already missing Sandie and she thought sadly of her sister still buried alive in that horrible convent. Snuggled under the covers though she couldn't be sad for long - for her the world seemed full of promise.

Chapter Twenty-four

The weeks till Easter flew past. Maureen got a new part-time job in the Co-op shop at the top of Utting Avenue which meant she got home in time to pick the kids up from school. Patsy gave birth to a baby boy and Bernie bought a tiny cardigan and booties for the new arrival. She was sad that she wouldn't be able to buy such things for her own niece or nephew

Despite her misgivings about moving, everything seemed to be fine, her mam was happy, the kids were happy, her da was just the same as always and Sandie came round several times a week with John. Ivy and Fred Morgan popped in and out and Bernie'd made friends with Jackie Jones next door but she couldn't take Annabel's place as her best mate. She still saw Annabel every day at school and either she would walk up to the Farriers' or Annabel and Peter would come down to Norris Green two or three nights a week. It made no difference to their gigs and band practices, Tommy just detoured round to pick her up.

Soon it was the week before Easter and Bernie still couldn't believe she was going to the holiday camp. Only when her da brought in an old suitcase off the round and she had packed all her outfits and makeup, did it start to feel real.

On Good Friday the boys picked her up after eleven. John and Sandie were going to the camp by bus. In the van their mood was crazy. None of them had been out of Liverpool on holiday before except Phil who'd been on a school trip to Colomendy years earlier. This was going to be a proper holiday and just looking out of the van's windows at the unfamiliar countryside confirmed that. They all cheered at the first sight of the sea and arrived at the camp delighted that the wheezy old van had got there without any trouble.

Bernie was bemused by the sheer size of the camp. Crowds of brightly dressed people strolled the avenues and everywhere kids were playing in the parks. She thought how her brothers and sisters would love it. All the colours were dazzling against the sky and the bluecoat who welcomed them was handsome and friendly. Bernie felt tongue-tied and she hung back while he went through arrangements with the lads.

The band were allocated three chalets in the staff blocks. They were a bit shabby but to Bernie her little room seemed like heaven with its chintzy curtains and single beds. Bobby Charles had arranged for Sandie to share with Bernie and John to bunk in with the rest of the band.

Bernie longed to explore the camp with Peter but first they had to rehearse in the ballroom. Afterwards they went back to their chalets where John and Sandie had now arrived and then they did the rounds of the camp, stopping for ice cream at one of the kiosks. It was freedom Bernie had never known, a crowd of kids having fun. She wanted Peter to kiss her more than anything. Sandie was sitting on John's lap, nuzzling his ear. Bernie willed Peter to make a move but he didn't and the moment passed. Next they headed for the boating lake where she and Peter shared a rowing boat. The rest of their gang split into three boats and they spent a few minutes weaving their way in and out of the other boats, chasing each other and splashing till the attendant told them off. Tommy, Phil and Ginger took the boats back and disappeared into a nearby pub. Bernie saw Sandie and John, their boat idly floating near the rear of the island, locked in a passionate kiss but Peter was concentrating on rowing backwards and never noticed them. Bernie sighed, pulling her cardigan round her as they came to the far side of the lake where trees blocked out the sun. Peter drew the boat to the edge and shipped the oars. He turned to her and tilted her chin up for a kiss. How deep that kiss went in the silence. Her whole body reached up to receive it and she opened her mouth to take in his tongue. The chill of the air disappeared, replaced by the burn of his hand through her dress, only to reappear as fingers of ice played along her spine. She was nothing but sensation, it seemed forever, then a bump on the side of the boat dragged her back to the lake and the gloomy trees. She pulled out of Peter's embrace to see John and Sandie grinning at them from their boat.

'Been looking for you,' John called, 'coming to the pub?'

The Queen Vic was cosy with its dark décor and beery smells. The boys had only a couple of pints as they needed to stay sober for the evening performance. Bernie stuck to lemonade but Sandie knocked back several Cherry Bs and was quite tipsy when they left for their evening meal. The dining room was another delight for Bernie, where you were waited on, had a choice of sweet and had tea brought to your table, even if it was in a plastic cup.

Back at the chalet, Sandie produced a bottle of sherry and poured it into the toothglasses from the bathroom.

'Go on,' she urged, 'no rules and regulations here.'

'No, not now,' Bernie said. She knew how important this gig was.

'Spoilsport.' Sandie pulled a face and drank both glasses.

When she saw the seething crowd filling every inch of the dance floor in the big ballroom, Bernie felt terrified. Clusters of men lined the bar at the back of the room. The din of chatter and laughter broke over the loudness of the records and a pall of cigarette smoke hung over everything.

'Just close your eyes and pretend you're at The Sink,' Peter whispered.

Bernie took his advice; as the band crashed out the first bars of *Needles and Pins* behind her she stuck out her hip, swung into rhythm and belted out the lyrics. The crowd was like an animal. If it went the wrong way it would attack but everyone was in holiday mood and out to enjoy themselves. The young children and their parents were all in the family theatre and this venue was strictly for adults. Soon Riverbeat had the whole place swinging. They could do no wrong and at the end of the set the applause was deafening.

Bernie came backstage, her hair plastered down with sweat, melting the lacquer she'd applied earlier and her pale green smock had dark stains under her arms. She and Sandie dashed back to the chalet so she could change while the boys got the drinks in. Sandie was stumbling and staggering, after more Cherry Bs while the band was on stage but Bernie was just drunk with the success of the set. Back in the ballroom she and Sandie danced to the records until the smoochy numbers came on, when Peter and John joined them. She saw John had to practically hold Sandie up and smiled to herself as several girls flocked around Phil, Ginger and Tommy. They'd never had so much attention.

Losing herself in the music, she moulded her body against Peter, her head under his chin. She drank in the warmth, the smell of him and again felt that wanting that was becoming so hard to resist. There was so much romance in the room, so many couples dancing close, feeling happy.

Was it just that that made Peter whisper in her ear, 'You do know I love you, Bernie McCann?'

A rosy glow spread through her but she played hard to get. 'Of course,' she lifted her mouth for his kiss.

'And?' he tilted her head to look in her eyes.

'And I love you too,' she murmured.

'Let's get out of here,' Peter took her hand and pulled her out of the ballroom into a cold, dark night. Fairy lights and glowing lamps along the paths created a magical atmosphere as they passed the dark waters of the boating lake. Along the way he stopped to kiss her every so often and she moaned as his hands roamed her body. He was leading her back to the chalets and something in her mind began to protest but his kiss, his touch was so sweet.

Her chalet door was open when they got there; the overhead light shone on Sandie, lying on her bed. John was wiping her face with a flannel but she was completely out.

'She's been sick everywhere in the bathroom,' John said.

'Oh no!' Bernie hurried to the communal bathrooms at the end of the block. John had tried to clean up but hadn't done much of a job. Using yards of toilet paper Bernie got most of the mess wiped up and down the toilet, flushing away her romantic feelings at the same time.

When she got back Peter and John were still hovering over Sandie.

'She'll be all right,' Bernie said, 'just leave her, I'll stay with her. You can go back to the pub.'

'Think I'll turn in,' Peter said. 'It's been a long day.'

'Me too,' John grinned, 'been great though, hasn't it?'

Bernie got into her pyjamas after they left. She looked at Sandie's grimy face, smeared with tears and mascara, her lipstick rubbed off and her hair all over the place. Her dress was rucked up to her thighs, one strappy sandal hung off her foot, her tights smeared with mud and laddered to ribbons. Bernie carefully removed the sandal so as not to wake her, took the counterpane from her own bed and covered her up.

It was chilly with only the sheets and one blanket on her bed and the sounds of many revellers returning from the bars kept her awake. She kept wondering what would have happened if no one had been in when she and Peter had come back but there was a warm soft ball of happiness inside her that smoothed all worries away. Peter had said he loved her.

Early Saturday morning Sandie bounced up as if nothing had happened.

'God, what a mess,' she regarded her face in the little mirror over the sink in their room.

'You should see what you did in the bathroom,' Bernie said but she hadn't the heart to be cross.

They were all in high spirits and after a good breakfast they headed into the seaside resort of Rhyl which was crowded with Easter holidaymakers. They spent most of the day at the funfair, eating candyfloss and hotdogs. It was one of the best days of Bernie's life, free from responsibilities, with money to spend on the fairground stalls and rides. Peter won her a small teddy bear at a darts stall and she cuddled it all day, knowing she would never part with it.

'I'm going to call him Bobby,' she said.

'Talk about sucking up to your agent,' Ginger said and everyone laughed. She wasn't so sure it was meant to be a joke but they were having too much fun to spoil the day. She screamed on the Mad Mouse and the Big Dipper but all too soon they had to return to prepare for the Saturday night show. They were warming up for Herman's Hermits, the star turn that night. Riverbeat had played with them once or twice round Manchester but now they were really famous.

'Maybe that'll be us by next year,' Tommy said, looking at the big poster outside the ballroom.

'If this goes all right,' Ginger said. 'No one better make a balls of it.'

Bernie sensed him looking at her but she kept her back turned. She had on a special dress for the gig, covered in silver sequins with silver spangled tights and sandals to match. Sandie had straightened her hair, then brushed it till it fell like a dark waterfall and she knew she looked good.

That night they were more confident. They knew they could make the crowd their own and they left everyone yelling for more, even though they'd really come to see the Hermits.

After their set they stayed for the rest of the show and watching Peter Noone singing *I'm Into Something Good* Bernie felt as if the song had been written especially for her. Sandie was again getting merry, though nowhere near as bad as the night before. Suddenly she tipped something into Bernie's lemonade.

'Only a drop of vodka,' she laughed, 'do you good.'

Bernie looked round guiltily. 'I'm under age.'

Sandie just laughed. 'Who's to know? Go on, don't be a baby.'

Where's the harm? Bernie thought. She took a sip and it tasted good. She took another; she wasn't a schoolkid any more, she was grown up. Soon she felt a lovely glow, everything seemed wonderful, the lights, the music, the good feeling in the room. She wanted Peter to take her in his arms but he was at the bar fighting to get more drinks and a fat bald man took his seat.

'Hi, I'm Sam Lomax,' he flipped a business card on the table. 'You were good tonight, where are you from?'

'Liverpool.' Ginger spoke up. 'And you?'

'Chester.' Lomax said. 'You guys need an agent?'

'We've got one,' Bernie said. She didn't like the way Lomax was looking her up and down.

'Well, like I said, you were good, really good. If you ever need another agent, give me a call.'

'Thanks.' Ginger picked up the card.

'Just a word of advice,' Lomax stood up. 'get some Motown into your act - and you darling,' he winked at Bernie, 'show a bit more,' he demonstrated with his hands, 'and a bit more leg.' With that he walked off.

'What a horrible man,' Bernie gulped her drink.

'We can keep the card anyway,' Ginger stowed it in his jacket pocket.

'We are staying with Bobby?' Bernie persisted.

'Sure,' Ginger said and then Peter came back with the drinks.

Bernie scarcely noticed when Sandie and John disappeared. She was enjoying the music and dancing close to Peter so much. The Hermits had long gone off and the lights were dimmed for the last few slow records. She could feel the muscles in Peter's back under his shirt and she relaxed as he held her tight, bending his head to kiss her every so often. Soon they were walking back to the chalet but this time when they arrived, there was no one in.

Closing the door, she leaned against it as Peter kissed her in the dark and all her longing for him reared up again. She leaned in close, pulling out his shirt so she could touch the soft skin on his back. His lips were on her neck and his hands caressed her breasts over the rough fabric of the sequinned dress. Her head reeled as something inside her said 'no' but another voice was saying, 'just a little bit more.' His hands were under her dress now, on her thighs and she trembled as he touched that yearning place, lightly, so lightly.

In a flurry of movement they slid to her bed and she felt his erection through his trousers, hard against her leg. Her fingers went to his belt as if she'd always known what to do but he stopped her, sliding her dress up to her waist.. She cried out at his touch on her tenderest flesh. Her body no longer seemed to belong to her, filled with flowing and beating sensations and she buried her hands in his hair, holding him close. It went on and on and she thought she would die if he didn't stop and she thought she would die if he did and then the backs of her thighs suddenly strained as orgasm burst over her, wiping away all thought.

Afterwards she opened her legs to him, reached for him but he stopped her.

'You're too young, Bernie,' he said gently, 'get some sleep now.' He kissed her softly and left her there.

She didn't know whether to laugh or cry. He'd given her the most precious thing but she couldn't give him anything back. She knew she wouldn't have resisted going the whole way, she had really wanted it. Did that make her some kind of slut? What she had done was a lesser sin, but was it venial or mortal? The thought of confessing it made her shiver. And Peter must have known how much she wanted him, would that make her dirty in his eyes? After all most lads would have taken the advantage. These thoughts chased round her head but she was exhausted. Cuddling Bobby bear, sleep caught up with her and she never heard Sandie creep in hours later.

Not much was said over breakfast. Bernie felt she was changed forever and that her newfound experience was written all over her but no one else seemed to notice. It was time to leave and they were all a little sad.

'I had a wonderful time,' Bernie said, looking sympathetically at Sandie who was badly hung over.

'So did I.' Peter smiled secretively at her.

Bernie knew she was flushing pink but no matter. She knew she was bound to him forever after the joy he'd given her. She was still reliving the pleasure she'd felt when she got back home. She composed herself as she went up the jigger to the back door but her mouth dropped open as she went into the living room and saw Father McKenna sitting there.

'Marie's had the baby.' Maureen started up as soon as Bernie came in the room.

'What?' Bernie was thinking that somehow Father knew what she'd done with Peter and had come round to confront her. As the news sank in, all thoughts of Peter were blanked out.

'It's too early, isn't it?' She sank down on the arm of the couch. 'Is she all right?'

'It's a bit early,' the priest said, 'or maybe she wasn't right about the dates. The child is a bit small but almost six pounds - a fine healthy boy.'

'And Marie?' Bernie asked.

'She's fine too,' Father seemed in a better mood than the last time he'd come round.

'Can we go see her? Mam?'

'Well now, that's not such a good idea,' the priest said. 'You'll upset yourselves about the child and you know it's to go for adoption. Anyway the baby's to stay in hospital for a few more days, till he puts on a little more weight. I'm sure your daughter'll be glad of the rest Maureen, before she comes home.'

227

'She'll be coming home so soon?' Maureen whispered.

'Well, within the fortnight. There's no point in prolonging it.' He shifted uncomfortably. 'It only makes it harder to give up the child. The child will have a good start in life and the mother has a chance to make amends and make something of herself.'

Maureen's eyes were full of tears. 'Has she named him?'

'Joseph James,' Father McKenna beamed. 'A fine name.'

'After her da,' Maureen breathed, ignoring the fact that the child's second name was for its father.

So Marie still carried a torch for Jimmy, Bernie thought. She remembered the night before, how she'd felt about Peter, how passion had taken her over. She blushed even more for thinking about this in front of the priest. Had Marie felt that kind of love and did she still feel it even though Jimmy had abandoned her? Unlike her mother she had no tears, only rage at the priest and the nuns who could so coldly cast Marie into sin and take away her own baby.

'Will we never see him?' she asked after the priest had gone.

'It don't look like it,' Maureen said grimly. She had retreated into her usual hard shell. She went into the kitchen to finish the Sunday dinner which had been interrupted by Father's visit.

Bernie had no appetite for the meal and all the joy of the weekend had turned to ashes. She sat in her bedroom looking out of the window at the new leaves bursting out on the tree in the garden. Tomorrow was Easter Monday, the day of Jesus's resurrection. Did Our Lord really think unmarried mothers were sinful and should have their babies taken away?

Chapter Twenty-five

Marie was never far from Bernie's thoughts during the following week but they heard nothing more so she was glad of their gig at Manchester's Twisted Wheel club on the Friday night. Riverbeat was the only band playing so they had two long sets. In the interval Peter and the rest of the band went to the pub across the road, leaving Bernie to chat with some girl fans over a glass of lemonade. She took no notice when a young man in a snappy suit came to her table; she was used to them trying to chat her up.

'I'm Terry Donoghue.' He broke into the conversation. 'I've been watching your act.'

She looked up and saw his eyes, almost violet blue, staring at her with an intensity that made her catch her breath.

'I'm a talent scout for Class Act Management.' He put a business card down in front of her. She was still thinking about the contrast of his sooty eyelashes with those eyes when the meaning of his words dawned on her.

'You're pretty good.' He sat down, crossing long legs, full of confidence. Bernie wasn't going to let him see that she was impressed.

'Thanks,' she said carelessly.

'You got an agent?' He smiled at her and her insides melted. 'How long you been singing?'

'Oh ages,' Bernie said, 'we've done the Jungfrau, the Mardi Gras and lots of Liverpool clubs. The Sink's one of our regulars and so's the Back Alley. Our agent is Bobby Charles.'

'Maybe I could do something for you. I think you could do better than this but you need grooming.' He leaned across and put a finger under her chin.

She pulled back angrily, her face on fire. How dare he make her feel as if she was just a silly kid. He didn't look old enough himself to be anyone important. She looked away and saw Peter making his way through the dance floor.

'What's going on?' Peter looked suspiciously at Donoghue.

'Terry Donoghue - scout for Class Act Management.' He stood up, shook Peter's hand and gave him another card.

Peter's expression turned to one of respect. 'Class Act?' he breathed. 'You got some great bands.'

Donoghue flashed that smile again. 'I was just telling the young lady here -'

'Me name's Bernie McCann,' Bernie interrupted.

Donoghue turned the smile on her. 'As I was saying,' he spoke over her head to Peter, 'I really liked the act. Could you give me your agent's phone number?'

Peter wrote it down on another of Donoghue's cards. Terry slipped it in his breast pocket.

'Got to go now, tell your agent I'll be in touch.'

Peter was cock-a-hoop as they went on for their second set. 'Class Act,' he enthused, 'they got some top stars on their books.'

'We get in there, man, we're made,' Ginger said.

'This time next year, London, New York, who knows. Come on Bernie tell us everything he said,' Tommy looked at her eagerly.

'Mmm?' Bernie murmured. She was still thinking about those violet eyes, that heartbreaking smile. No one should be that handsome.

Back at school after the Easter holiday, Bernie no longer had any interest in her classes. The only good thing about school now was the time she could spend with Annabel.

On the third day her teacher kept her back after registration.

'Bernie I need to have a word with you.'

Bernie had a good idea what was coming.

Miss Tracey tried to catch her eye. 'Some of your teachers are getting really concerned. Your work's gone straight downhill since Christmas. You were a promising student when you came here last year. What's happened? You don't pay attention, your work is slipshod - messy.'

Bernie shrugged and looked out of the window.

'And this attitude, like you're not listening when anyone talks to you. You've only got a few months left here...'

'Thank God,' Bernie muttered under her breath.

'What did you say?'

'Nothing.' Bernie shuffled her feet. 'Can I go now Miss?'

'No you can't. Don't be insolent.' Miss Tracey adopted a softer tone. 'Look I know you probably feel you're too old for school and longing to leave but if you don't get a good report you won't get a good job?'

'I've already got a job,' Bernie said.

230

'Oh? Where?' Miss Tracey looked taken aback.

'In the shop near where I used to live. I've been working there Saturdays and they're going to train me as a manager.'

'Then you need to keep your maths up to scratch, don't you?'

Bernie's temper rose. 'Anyway I'm going to be a pop singer, so school reports don't matter.'

Miss Tracey burst out laughing. 'Oh Bernie ...'

'It's true.' Bernie wanted to slap the grin off the teacher's face. 'Me and my band are going to Germany.'

Miss Tracey stopped laughing and looked serious. 'You can't rely on these daydreams. Every girl your age dreams of being a pop star. I know you've done a bit of singing locally but-'

'You don't know nothing,' Bernie shouted and she turned and fled down the corridor.

That evening the band practised in Ginger's shed. They were excited about the talent scout but there was still a tinge of resentment towards Bernie.

'How come people always come to her for interviews and stuff?' Ginger said.   'She's the front man,' Tommy said, 'she's the one everyone's looking at on stage. Don't suppose anyone's heard anything yet?'

'Bobby'll get in touch soon as anything comes through. I'm the only one on the phone,' Ginger said and after that they settled down to practising a few new numbers.

When Tommy dropped her off at home, Peter jumped out too.

'I'll walk back, it's not far.'

'Okay,' Tommy winked, 'be good children.'

The van zoomed away and Peter and Bernie melted into the dark passage.

'I miss our place under the stairs,' Bernie whispered.

'It's still there,' Peter nuzzled her ear. 'waiting for when you come over. Anyway, this is just as good.'

'But what if me da comes home?' Bernie giggled but forgot all about that as he bit softly on her earlobe.

When he finally released her she watched him walk away till his figure blended into the darkness. Her breath had calmed and her hot cheeks returned to normal by the time she clicked the latch on the back door.

'Oh there you are,' Maureen was in her usual position at the kitchen table. 'Our Marie's coming home tomorrow.'

When Bernie came home from school the next day, Marie was already there. Maureen had taken the day off to welcome her back and she'd brought in some nice cakes for tea but there seemed little to celebrate.

Marie was in the bedroom putting on her makeup when Bernie arrived. Her clothes had been stored in bags while she was away but Bernie had unpacked and pressed them and hung them up in the wardrobe. She saw that Marie had already been riffling through them and was wearing the newest dress, one she'd bought just before she went away.

'Lend me the money for a hair dye?' Marie said without even saying hello. 'I don't want to ask our Mam.'

'Yes, all right,' Bernie said, 'how much is it?'

'Ten bob'll do; you're earning it now aren't you?- singing and all that.'

Bernie got her purse and gave Marie a ten-shilling note. 'Will you go back to your old job?'

Marie tucked the note in her cardigan pocket. 'That's well gone, I'll have to find something else. Don't worry, you'll get your money back.'

Bernie wanted to comfort her sister. She'd expected tears but Marie seemed to be just the same hard person she'd been before she left. 'I'm glad you're home,' she ventured.

Marie flashed a quick smile as she applied her mascara. 'At least there's a bit more room in here, no more climbing up that ladder. You still knocking about with that Peter Farrier?' She put aside the mascara and gave her lips a liberal coating of *Orange Fire* lipstick. 'Where did that come from?' She pointed at the teddy bear sitting on Bernie's pillow.

'Peter won him for me on the fair at Rhyl, his name's Bobby. Did Mam tell you, we had a booking at Prestatyn holiday camp? Peter and me, we're sort of going steady.' She thought Marie might be excited about the band's success and want to know all about the Prestatyn weekend but she only said,

'Well just be careful, you don't want to end up like me.'

'I'm sorry about the baby.'

'Yeah well, it was for the best.' Marie pulled at wayward curls in her hair which was now its natural mouse brown. 'God I hate this colour.'

'I'd love to have seen him,' Bernie said, 'didn't you get a photo?'

'No,' Marie snapped. She began shovelling makeup back into the drawer. 'Where's the key for this?'

'Oh,' Bernie fetched the key from her purse. She was wondering how those nuns could be so cruel, to take a child from its mother and leave her with nothing to remember it by - and what about the family? She

232

was the child's auntie, and was never to see her nephew. She thought how unhappy her mam must be at losing her first grandchild yet she still harboured some resentment - it had been her mam's choice to send Marie away.

'That seems really unfair,' she said, handing Marie the key. 'It must have been hard for you having to give him up like that?'

'Stop going on about it, can't you? I don't want to talk about it.' Marie slammed the drawer shut and twisted the key viciously.

'I'm sorry, I only meant...'

'Just leave me alone.' Marie jumped up and Bernie saw there were damp patches on the front of her dress. She was puzzled for a few moments until she realised what had caused them. Marie clattered down the stairs with Bernie in pursuit. She stormed through the kitchen, surprising Maureen who was enjoying a fag, a cup of tea and Bernie's latest copy of *Valentine*.

'I'm going to walk to Angie's,' Marie shouted and banged the back door as she went out.

'What've you said to her?' Maureen put down the magazine, 'I've been on pins with her all day.'

'Nothing,' Bernie said and sat down to peel the potatoes.

The next afternoon after school, Bernie found Father McKenna sipping tea in Da's armchair while Maureen dabbed her eyes with a hankie.

'What's the matter?' Bernie sank onto the couch next to her mam.

'Our Marie,' Maureen sniffled, 'she spoke to Father terrible and now she's stomped off out. I'm so sorry Father.'

The priest gave a gracious smile. 'My only intention, as you know, was to help her.'

'It must be her hormones, Father,' Maureen mumbled.

He looked uncomfortable. 'Well, Maureen, the job offer is still there if you can make her see sense. And what about Bernadette?' He looked Bernie over. 'She's due to leave school isn't she? I expect there's an opening for her too, if I put in a word for her.'

Bernie thought he looked like a toad, swelling out of his cassock, his face puffy with sly eyes swivelling in search of prey. And why talk about her as if she wasn't there?

'What job?' she asked.

'Father's kindly arranged a job for Marie at St Augustine's nursing home.'

'Is it run by nuns?' Bernie imagined her sister's horror.

'The sisters of Mercy, a very caring order,' the priest said. 'She'd have a good start there. You too,' he smiled at Bernie.

'What do you think, Bernie luv?' Maureen asked hopefully.

'I've got a job to go to already,' Bernie muttered.

Father McKenna looked displeased. 'I'd think it over if I were you.'

'I will,' Bernie said and left them to it. In her room she vowed she would never ever work in a place like that and she just hoped that Marie too could avoid such a fate.

Marie came banging up the stairs an hour later. 'Well, I've got a job,' she said, flinging her coat off and examining her face in the mirror. 'Start on Monday, trainee machinist at the Jacobs Paula factory in Aintree - making swimsuits for Marks and Spencer.'

Bernie was glad to be away from home on Saturday in the paper shop but her peaceful mood evaporated in the afternoon when Morag Sullivan came in and started rummaging through the magazines. After a few moments she looked slyly over her shoulder at Bernie who was stocking the chocolate rack.

'You still here?,' she sneered. 'Thought we'd chased you lot out for good.'

Bernie said nothing, conscious of Mrs Thompson serving a customer at the counter.

Morag picked up a copy of *Jackie* and flicked through the pages. 'Hear your sister's turned up again. Dropped her sprog, has she?'

Bernie's face burned. 'She's been working away.'

'Oh yeah? Everyone knows your Marie got knocked up and had to go away.'

'Are you buying that magazine?' Bernie's fists balled at her sides.

'It's true though, isn't it? 'Our Jacko says she had it off with all the lads on the estate. That's why your mam had to send her away, she didn't know whose kid it was.'

That did it. Bernie snatched the magazine and swiped Morag in the face with it.

'Come on then,' Morag's eyes lit up and she poked Bernie in the chest.

Bernie pushed her so hard that she staggered against the rack, showering papers and magazines everywhere. She shoved Bernie so that she fell onto the chocolate shelves. Mars bars, Crunchies and Turkish Delights clattered to the floor. Bernie grabbed at Morag's sweater and they both went down, scratching and kicking. Through a red fog of rage Bernie felt something dragging her upright in a firm grip.

'Stop that right now!' Mr Thompson bellowed, holding each girl at arms' length. The elderly lady at the counter made a beeline for the door as he shoved Bernie towards the back room. 'You get in there,' he shouted, 'and you,' he turned to Morag, ' you get out.'

'Don't worry, I'm going,' she shouted back. 'You wait till me Aunty Rose hears about this.'

Bernie sat down at the table. She heard the click of the bolt on the front door and knew Mr Thompson had shut the shop. Now she was in for it.

'Fighting in the shop, in front of customers!' He glared at her. Mrs Thompson was behind him.

'It was Morag started it,' Bernie said.

'I don't care who it was,' he shouted. 'Look at the damage, ruined magazines, squashed chocolates -'

'You should have just come in the back and ignored her,' Mrs Thompson said. 'Poor Mrs Saunders was terrified. I'm very disappointed in you, Bernie.'

'I'm not having that kind of behaviour in my shop.' Mr Thompson thumped the table.

'Calm down Arthur,' Mrs Thompson said.

'Calm down? Look at the mess she's caused.'

'I'll go and clear it up,' Bernie stood.

'No you won't, you're finished here.' Mr Thompson barred her way. 'You can get your coat and go.'

'Arthur...' Mrs Thompson protested.

'No Margaret, it's too much of a risk. I can't take the chance of that happening again. You need to control your temper, Bernadette.'

Bernie just stared at him. Red spots danced before her eyes. She couldn't speak.   'Bernie, you know you can't pick fights in the shop - but -' Mrs Thompson looked pleadingly at her husband.

' I don't care how good her work is, she's unpredictable. She can't be trusted to behave and that's that.'

Bernie felt the rage returning. She had to get out before it burst out again. Grabbing her coat she rushed through the shop but while she struggled with the bolt, Mrs Thompson called her back. She took Bernie's wage packet from the till and handed it to her.

'I'm sorry Bernie, I know you were provoked but Arthur's right, you have to learn to deal with it. Give him time to calm down, I'm sure I can talk him into taking you back.'

Bernie couldn't answer. She was hot with shame and only after she'd crossed the East Lancs road and was out of the area did she give way to tears. She was still crying as she neared the house and saw Bobby Charles sitting outside in his little red MG sports car.

'There's no one in,' Bobby leaned across and opened the passenger door.

'Me mam's probably at Greaty market.' Bernie's tears had stopped in the surprise of seeing Bobby but she knew her eyes must still be red.

'Get in,' Bobby said. 'What's wrong with your face?'

'Nothing,' Bernie muttered. '

Bobby said. 'I wish your parents would get a bloody phone.'

Bernie got in the car, took her hankie out and blew her nose. 'What is it then?' she asked. 'Couldn't it wait till the gig?' Her mind was still running on her humiliation in the shop.

'I need to speak to you on your own. You remember the scout who saw you at the Twisted Wheel?'

Bernie nodded, recalling those violet eyes.

'He wants to be your manager. He reckons with some training you could have national appeal, maybe get work in television.'

'Bernie's heart jumped. 'Really? Oh that's fab - the band'll be thrilled, just wait till I tell Peter.'

'The thing is ...' Bobby shifted in his seat to look her in the eye. 'He doesn't want the rest of the band, Bernie, only you.'

Bernie's joy deflated instantly. She couldn't leave the band. They'd given her a start and anyway the thought of singing alone terrified her. And what about Peter? 'No, no,' she whispered, shaking her head.

'Bernie this is your big chance, you can't let personal feelings get in the way.' Bobby took her hand. 'Loyalty is groovy but don't let it destroy your future. You're too good for Riverbeat. They're only ever going to be just another Merseybeat group.'

Bernie thought of the fight in the shop, of all the trouble with Rose, Jacko and the Sullivans. Was this a chance to get away from all that? The next minute all thought left her as her da's van came round the corner and pulled up behind Bobby's car.

'What's all this? Joe said, jumping from the passenger seat.

'Mam's not home yet,' Bernie said.

'So who's this then?'

Bernie quailed. Her tongue stuck to the roof of her mouth.

'I'm Bobby Charles, Bernie's agent.' Bobby smiled and extended his hand. 'Pleased to meet you Mr McCann.'

Joe looked at the hand and scowled. Bernie wriggled, trying to think of a way out of this.

'You needn't look like that, girl,' her da roared. 'You must think I'm stupid if you think I don't know what you've been up to. D'you think I haven't seen the paper with your picture plastered all over it, or the posters all over town? I suppose you and your mam think I don't know what's been going on with our Marie either. I'm not as daft as I might look and if you and your mam think you can pull the wool over my eyes, you got another think coming.'

Bernie stayed silent. It was no use trying to reason with Da when he got a rant on. Her mind was reeling with shock at the realisation that Da had known about Marie and about her singing all along. Why hadn't he said anything?

Bobby tried to say something but Joe shouted over him. 'Bringing kids up is women's business, but your mam's just been letting you do what you like.'

Bernie fired up at this. 'But Bobby says I could sing on telly, work in London,' she said.

'Oh does he?' Joe sneered, spittle forming at the corners of his mouth, his face turning redder than it already was. 'Filling your head with nonsense. What do you think he's after? Come on, out of there.' He dragged at the car door handle.

'It's true, Mr McCann,' Bobby said calmly. 'Bernie could be making a good deal of money this time next year.'

'Money?' Joe stared at him.

'She's got a rare talent. Surely you don't want to take that chance away from her?'

Joe seemed stumped for words. Bernie saw Vinny Mack gawping from the driver's seat of the van. Joe turned to him.

'You better take the van up to the Crown and come back in an hour or so. Mo'll be back by then and there'll be summat to eat.' He turned to Bobby. 'You'd better come in.'

They trooped into the house.

'Come in here,' Joe ordered Bobby into the living room. 'Bernie go make some tea and see if there's summat for a butty for me and Vinny - and don't come in till I call you.'

Bernie didn't protest. She found the cold ham her mam had left in the larder and set about making sandwiches and a pot of tea with shaking hands. She could hear their muted voices. They were talking about her, making decisions about her as if she was a piece of meat on the market. Well, even if Da agreed to her singing, she wasn't going anywhere without Peter. She dithered about the rest of the band, after all, Ginger never wanted her there anyway but Peter - no that would be a betrayal and she couldn't do it to him.

The back door opened and her mam came in with Polly and Teresa. She dumped her loaded shopping bags on the floor and took off her headscarf. Polly and Teresa rushed to the bedroom to try on the clothes their mam had bought at the market.

'What's going on?' She looked at the plate of butties.

'Da's home early,' Bernie said.

'Well don't sit there like a lummox. That tea'll be getting cold, take it in. Where's the van anyway?'

'Me da knows,' Bernie said.

'Knows what?' Maureen fussed round getting cups and milk. 'I'll take these in,' she grabbed the plate.

'You can't go in.'

'Why ever not?'

'He's in there with my agent. Mam, he knows about me singing, he's known all along - and he knows about our Marie.'

'Jesus, Mary and Joseph.' Maureen sat down suddenly. She rummaged in her pockets for her Woodbines. 'Pour us a cup of that tea.'

Bernie had to go through the whole story while her mam smoked and drank two cups of tea.

'Bobby says it's only me the new manager wants, he says the rest of the band aren't good enough, but I'm not leaving the band.' Bernie blinked back tears.

'Well your da'll probably put the kibosh on it anyway, I'm surprised he hasn't sent that Mr Charles packing already.'

'His ears pricked up when Bobby said there was money in it.' Bernie said. She fell silent at the sound of the living room door opening and her da appeared.

'You can come in now.' He even had a smile on his face. Bernie saw Bobby was smiling too and she relaxed a little.

'Your father has agreed to Class Act Management taking you over,' Bobby said. 'There'll be a proper contract, arrangements made for you to finish your schooling and to make sure you're chaperoned if you have to travel.'

Bernie felt her temper rise. They'd decided all this without even asking her. 'I'm not going on my own.' She braced herself. 'I want to be with the boys.'

'Don't be silly,' Bobby said, 'honestly you're never going to get anywhere with them.'

'I don't care,' Bernie snapped. 'We go together or not at all.'

'Bernie, your potential is as a solo artist not a band singer.'

'Then I'll go solo and they can be my backing group.'

'It's not going to happen, Bernie. The deal is just for you.' Bobby shrugged and looked at Joe.

'You listen to what Bobby here tells you,' Joe said. 'You got to look out for yourself in this world. I always thought you had talent mind.'

Bernie thought, as if he knew anything about her. He was always in the pub or out on the round. She bit her lip to stop herself shouting back at him.

'Bernie luv, I think Mr Charles knows what he's talking about. I think you should listen to him.' Even her mam was against her.

Bernie swallowed her anger, kept her voice calm. 'I'm not going on my own. Okay, I'll leave the band but not Peter. We make a good duo. You can tell Mr Donoghue it's both of us or neither.'

She saw her da's face turn red but even though her knees were knocking she stood her ground. She turned her back on them and through the living room window she saw Matty and Anthony and a couple of their pals climbing in and out of Bobby's car and fiddling with the steering wheel and controls.

She turned back to him and said, 'Maybe you ought to go downstairs to see what's happening to your car.'

Chapter Twenty-six

The band were playing the Manchester Cavern that night and Bernie's singing wasn't up to scratch but she couldn't pull herself together. She knew she should tell the others what had happened but she couldn't, even on the way home. She was sure they would hate her. She decided to wait until Bobby took her ultimatum to Terry Donoghue and see what happened.

'What's up with you?' Peter frowned as she pulled away from him in the alleyway outside her house. 'You've been funny all night.'

She invented the first thing that entered her head. 'I'm worried about our Marie. She's hardly got out of bed since she came home and you can't say boo to her without her giving out.'

Marie *had* been acting strange. Every time Bernie or her mam tried to talk to her they either met a brick wall or got their heads bitten off.

'She'll be all right when she gets used to being back at home and gets a new job,' Peter said.

Bernie bit back a retort; after all he was a man and men just didn't understand.

'She's got a job to start Monday,' she said, 'and she's still got her mate Angie.'

'She'll soon settle down,' Peter reached for her again.

'I hope so,' Bernie tried to relax in his arms. If only Marie was the only thing she had to worry about.

Bobby had told her to ring his office on Monday afternoon so after school she found a phone box and dialled the number he'd given her with shaking fingers.

'Hi Bernie,' Bobby sounded cheerful. 'Good news, you'll be pleased to hear. Terry has fixed up a studio audition for you and if that goes okay he wants to make some demo tapes to send round the record companies.'

Records? She might make a record? Her mind whirled then she remembered the band. 'What about Peter and the rest of the band?'

Bobby sighed. 'I had to work hard to get it but he's agreed to give Peter an audition with you, maybe as another solo singer. He doesn't think there's anything in it as a duo.'

240

Bernie felt weak with relief. She and Peter were going to make it big time. All her dreams were going to come true. 'Oh Bobby, that's great,' she gasped.

'Well, okay,' Bobby said. 'We'll fix up a date and I'll let you know what's happening.'

That night Bernie went round to the Farriers' flat as she and Peter had arranged. They sat together in the kitchen listening to Radio Caroline.

'I talked to Bobby this afternoon,' she dived right in.

He stopped singing along to *She's Got a Ticket to Ride*. 'You did?'

'He asked me to ring him. He came to see me last Saturday.'

'Why would he do that? And why didn't you tell me, or the rest of the band? Has there been more trouble with Jacko Hanson?'

'It was about that scout, Terry Donoghue.'

'Scout? Why didn't he ring Ginger? He's going to take us on?' He looked excited and puzzled at the same time.

'Peter..' Bernie's voice faltered. 'He doesn't want the rest of the band, only me - and you.'

'Doesn't want the band?' he repeated.

'He's setting up a studio audition for us both. Bobby said he's thinking about making records.'

'We can't leave the band.'

'It's our big chance. I know how you feel but...'

'We've been playing together for over a year, long before you came along. I can't just go off.'

'I feel the same,' Bernie said, 'but Bobby says I have to do it and my da...'

'Your da?'

'He's known all along,'

'But he's never said anything.'

'I know, I don't get it meself but he was here when Bobby came last week and as soon as he heard there was money to be made he was all for it.'

'I don't know what to think. What if I don't go, what'll you do then?'

'I don't know,' Bernie said, 'don't make me decide.'

Silence fell and for the first time Bernie felt awkward with him. Soon she made an excuse to leave. He walked her home but he didn't hold her hand or put his arm round her shoulders. Outside her house he gave her a brief kiss.

'I'll let you know tomorrow,' he said and walked away without looking back.

In the kitchen Maureen was ironing school shirts for the morning. Bernie sat down. 'I told Peter about the scout.'

'And?' Maureen set the iron back on the table.

'He doesn't want to leave the band - and I don't want to leave him.'

'Don't be a fool. You stick to your guns. He'll go with you, you'll see.'

'Do you think so?' Bernie brightened a bit. 'He's going to let me know tomorrow.' She was thinking that her mam never stuck to her guns, never stood up to her da.

As if she was reading her thoughts, Maureen said, 'It's different for you young girls. In my day you went straight from your da to your husband, you didn't have much say over anything. I suppose it was a bit different in the war but my da didn't go away to war and he never let me or our Joan move.'

'How come Da never let on he knew about me singing?'

'I don't know luv, I thought he'd go berserk but he seemed to think it was funny that we all tried to kid him.'

'But why didn't he say anything?'

' I suppose he expects me to deal with anything to do with the house, as long as things go smoothly and he doesn't have to interfere. It's probably because he never had a home. He's used to being out all the time, being with other men.'

'Never had a home?' What did Mam mean? Was that why he never acted like other people's fathers?

'Your da was brought up in an orphanage. Never had no mum or dad, doesn't even know when his proper birthday is. He ran away to sea when he was thirteen.'

Bernie imagined having no mam, no family. Even Marie's little baby would have a family, though he would never know he had another real one.

'Is that why he's so grumpy?' she asked but her mam was hanging up the clothes on the maiden, signalling that the conversation was over. Bernie couldn't figure it out. Was her da hurt because he had no family or was he jealous because their family was close?

'Don't you say nothing to the others,' Maureen said. 'I shouldn't be telling you. But you just stand your ground with Peter. You can't let a chance like this go by.'

In their bedroom Marie was under the covers reading a *Honey* magazine and eating chocolate.

'Want a bit?' It was a rare offering Bernie couldn't refuse.

'How's the job?' she sat on her bed in her pyjamas.

'It stinks,' Marie said. 'Bloody boring.'

'You'll make some nice friends soon,' Bernie said then changed the subject as Marie shot her a venomous look. 'I got the sack from the shop.'

'How come?' Marie rolled over, showing some interest for once.

Bernie explained what had happened.

'Want me to flatten that Morag?' Marie offered.

Bernie shook her head. 'I can fight me own battles, thanks.'

'Well never mind, you still got the band.'

Bernie spilled out all that had happened. Tears rolled down her face as she recalled Peter's coldness earlier. 'I don't know what to do,' she finished, 'I can leave the band but I can't leave Peter.'

'Don't be a booby.' Marie put down her magazine. 'You got to look after number one in this world. Men – they're not worth it. They're all bastards.' She turned over and pulled the covers over her head, leaving Bernie to turn the light out and climb into bed.

The next day she couldn't concentrate at school, wondering what Peter would decide. She felt like running to the Farriers' flat with Annabel but she remembered Marie's advice, 'Don't you run after him, let him come to you.'

Time crawled by as she prepared tea for the kids, till her da came in and went out again, till Marie got home from work, ate her tea and hid in the bedroom.

'What's up with you tonight?' her mam said, 'You're like a cat on a hot tin roof.'

'Nothing,' Bernie said. She didn't want to talk to anyone except Peter.

At last he came but one look at his face told her he wasn't happy. It was a fine evening so they were able to walk. Peter kept his head down, kicking at pebbles as they walked past the cemetery towards the East Lancs road. The silence became unbearable. At last Bernie put a hand on his arm. He stopped and turned towards her, leaning back against the cemetery wall.

'I've thought and thought,' he said, 'and I don't like it but you're right. We can't pass up a chance like this. I will come with you.'

He pulled her close and kissed her and all her worries and fears dissolved in that embrace that sealed their togetherness.

'You're under my skin, Bernie,' he murmured against her ear, 'you know I can't be without you.' His lips trailed her neck and although her knees felt weak she felt a surge of power. Her mam and Marie had been right.

She reached up and kissed him, welding her body to his till a honk from a passing motorist reminded them they were in public view.

'Let's go and tell my mum,' Peter said and they wandered on hand in hand. Peter's dad was out at a darts match but Annabel and Kathleen were thrilled to bits.

'What about the rest of the band?' Kathleen asked as they celebrated with tea and crumpets. 'What did they say?'

'They don't know yet,' Peter said. 'I suppose I'd better tell Ginger.'

'Let's tell them together,' Bernie said. She dreaded the band's reaction but she could do anything with Peter beside her. They had a gig the next night. 'We'll tell them then,' she was already taking charge, 'and I'll ring Bobby in the morning and tell him we're ready to go with Class Act.'

The next morning she rang Bobby but when she got in the van for the gig she was shaking. They were all quiet and their performance was lacklustre. It was as if everyone knew there was something bad in the air.

After their set the atmosphere was tense. Bernie sipped a Coke and wished it was all over with but she couldn't bring herself to speak.

At last, after some false banter, Peter said, 'Bernie and me have got something to tell you.'

'Surprise - yous are getting married. Is she up the duff?' Ginger quipped.

Bernie blushed and Peter gave him a dark look.

'We're leaving the band.'

'You what?' Ginger's mouth dropped open.

'But we're just starting to go places,' Tommy said.

'That's just it,' Peter said. 'That scout, the one who was at the Twisted Wheel, Bobby says he's interested.'

'There you go,' Tommy sat back. 'That's great - so why...?'

'It's her,' Ginger said, she's got some cock and bull idea about doing duets with lover boy.'

'It's not me,' Bernie said, blood rushing to her face. 'Bobby says the scout, Mr Donoghue, only wants me and Peter.'

'That's bollocks,' Ginger had also turned bright red.

'No,' Bernie protested, 'I tried to get him to take all of us, honest.'

'It's true,' Peter said, 'and we had to make a choice.'

'Look after number one and shit on your mates,' Phil said.

'After we bent over backwards to give you a start,' Ginger sneered.

'Come on,' Peter said, 'it's thanks to Bernie we've done as well as we have.'

244

'Well you would say that wouldn't you?' Ginger glared at him. 'She's leading you round by the dick, that's for sure.'

'I'm not listening to this,' Bernie got up and went to the Ladies where she rinsed her burning face in cold water. It was worse than she'd imagined . 'So what?' she told her reflection in the mirror, it was done and tomorrow everything would be different.

When she returned to the table everyone got up to leave. No one spoke till she and Peter got out at her house.

'We'll honour the gigs we've already got booked,' Peter said but the only answer was a snort from Ginger.

As Peter got his guitar from the back of the van, Tommy got out of the front.

'Look, I'm not happy about this but I'd do the same if I was in your shoes. Best of luck mate.' He clapped Peter on the back. 'And to you Bernie, you deserve it.'

Bernie still felt like she'd betrayed them but she set her mind on the future. It seemed so exciting, uncertain but full of promise - and at least she wouldn't go into it alone.

Bernie had come to look on Bobby Charles as a sort of big brother but Terry Donoghue frightened her. Terry was sharp and businesslike, looking her over like an item of stock in a shop. And he was so handsome; she couldn't stop sneaking looks at him. She squeezed Peter's hand, glad he was there to steady her although she knew he was just as nervous.

'I'm going to hear you sing separately and together,' Terry told them. 'If all goes well, we'll make some demo tapes. Okay?'

They both nodded, too green to ask questions. Bernie was first to sing. The empty stage made her even more nervous.

'Just relax,' Bobby said as she went up, 'You'll be fine.'

'What shall I sing?' she asked and her voice came out tiny and tremulous.

'Whatever you like,' Terry said.

There was no backing, no band behind her. Bernie closed her eyes. She just couldn't do this; it was stupid to think there was any future for her here, she was just another front of band singer. Already she could feel tears gathering at the corners of her eyes.

She remembered the night at Pontins when she'd been so scared and Peter had told her to imagine she was back at The Sink, then she remembered what had happened that night, how her feelings about Peter had deepened. Before she knew it *Anyone Who Had a Heart* came rolling out of her. She'd sung that song so many times, tormenting herself with thoughts of how she would feel if Peter finished with her or two-timed her like George had done.

There was silence when she got to the end.

'That was good, thank you,' Terry said but he didn't sound too enthusiastic.

Peter got up to sing but he was unsettled by singing without his guitar or the rest of the band. He chose *You've Lost That Loving Feeling* but even Bernie felt the poor quality of his performance.

Together they sang *I Got You Babe*. It was their best number and she knew they did it well.

Terry didn't comment on their singing. 'Let's take a break,' he said and went off to the coffee machine in the foyer.

Bernie found her way to the toilet. Now the audition was over she should have felt more relaxed but her nerves were still wound tight. On her way back she passed Terry's office door.

'But can't you do something for him?' she heard Bobby say and she stopped to listen.

'He's not good enough,' Donoghue said. 'I'm running a business not a charity. I can't take on every shit vocalist that comes through the door.'

'But she won't come without him,' Bobby said. 'You know what kids are like; think they're in love, think they're the only ones.'

Bernie bit down on her lip as her temper flared. Peter was good, he was just nervous. As she walked back to the studio she reassured herself that Bobby would hold out for them; he'd promised they would be together. Peter would be fine when they did the demo tapes.

He was still sitting by the stage. 'I was rubbish,' he muttered as she came close.

'No you weren't,' Bernie said. 'I always think I sound rubbish when I'm singing, then people say it was great. Don't be grumpy. You'll be okay, you'll see.'

But making the demo tapes was a nightmare. It was nothing like singing with the band. The musicians were complete strangers and it was a while before they managed to produce something reasonable between them. Terry made her do the song over and over again till she felt ready to break.

At last he was satisfied. 'Great, you were great.' He looked her over, saw how exhausted she was. 'Take another break. Back in ten minutes.'

Bernie thought if this was what the music business was like, maybe she didn't want to be in it. She looked round for Peter but he'd disappeared. She felt a little hurt that he hadn't stayed. She found him in the foyer drinking a coffee from the machine. She'd never seen him look so miserable. She put a smile on her face.

'That was really tough. Not like singing with the band.'

'Sounded good to me.'

'Our turn together next. Come on we'd better get back.'

Bernie's heart was beating so fast she thought she would choke when Terry and Bobby came into the room but she tried to smile nonchalantly.

'That's a good demo,' Donoghue said, 'I'll take it to London next week.'

'But you haven't done Peter's, and we're singing together.' She moved closer to Peter and slipped her arm through his. Heat flooded her face and neck as she sensed what was coming before Donoghue opened his mouth.

'I won't be taking you on,' he said to Peter. 'I'm sorry but you're just not good enough.'

Bernie saw Peter shrivel as the words hit him. 'You promised,' she shouted at Bobby. 'Both of us or neither of us.'

Peter's eyes widened in shock. She would never forget the look he gave her. He got up and walked out without a word. Bernie jumped up to follow but Terry gripped her wrist and pulled her back. At the touch of his fingers a shiver ran through her. A retort died on her lips as she looked up at him. His eyes were dark, shadowed and seemed to look right through her.

'Don't be a fool,' he said. 'You're so much better than him. With some decent makeup, a good hairdo and some nice clothes, you'll be a top of the bill act, on your own.'

She pulled back and he let her go. She rubbed her wrist, so furious she could barely speak. 'I don't want to be on my own,' she ground out.

'He won't stand in your way - if he cares for you.' She turned away and went to look for Peter. He was outside in the street, leaning against the wall and staring into space.

'Let's go home.' She took his arm.

'You knew they only wanted you, didn't you? ' He couldn't hide the pain in his eyes.

'I wanted us to be together,' Bernie said. 'I didn't think this would happen.'

They walked to the bus station in silence.

247

'Anyway, they can get lost,' Bernie said at last. 'We'll stay together with the band. It'll be like it was before.'

'It won't be the same,' Peter said.

She fell silent. What could she say against this brooding?

As they climbed on the bus, Peter said, 'You have to go, they're right, you've got what it takes and I haven't.'

It was the only thing he said for the rest of the journey. The silence between them was painful and she didn't know how to make it better. At her house he kissed her on the cheek before turning away but she caught his arm.

'I won't go Peter, I'm staying with you and the band.'

'You have to do what's best for you. I'll be okay.'

He started to walk away and she knew she should run after him but she couldn't; there was just too much to think about.

No one was home when she went in. She went to her room and lay down on her bed, her nose pressed into Bobby Bear's fur. She told herself she'd made the decision to stay with the band and she should stick with it but if Bobby and Terry were right, she'd be giving up the chance she'd always dreamed of. *Maybe it's not just that,* a little devil spoke up in her mind. *Maybe it's Terry Donoghue's sexy smile, those eyes and the way he looks at you.* Immediately she felt ashamed. Was she ready to betray Peter in more ways than one?

No! She pounded the pillow with her fist. She sensed a dangerousness in Donoghue and his invitation into his world was an entry into strangeness, uncertainty. Peter was familiar, comfortable and there would always be a place for her in the band she had come to feel part of. Or would there? Maybe she had already burned her boats by betraying them.

Her thoughts were interrupted as she heard the children come in. She got up and went down to the kitchen.

'Well?' Maureen said, a Woodbine dangling from her lip

'They made some tapes of me. Mr Donoghue says he thinks I could make a record.'

Maureen gaped. 'Well, I don't know.'

'I'm not doing it Mam.'

'What?' Maureen's eyebrows rose into her hair.

'They don't want Peter, only me. Oh Mam it was awful. They said he wasn't good enough.' She sat down at the table and burst into tears.

'Oh luv,' Maureen stared at her for a moment then came and put her arms round her shoulders.

'That Mr Donoghue was horrible.' Bernie gasped.

'Don't let that throw you,' Maureen stroked her hair. 'Peter'll understand.'

Bernie lifted her head. 'I can't do it without him, and I won't.'

'Don't be so bloody daft,' Maureen's voice hardened. She moved away and began   peeling potatoes.

Bernie wanted to die. She jumped up to go to her room and hide but there was a knock at the back door and in came Aunty Joan followed by Patsy carrying a snowy white carrycot festooned with blue ribbons.

Maureen was beside herself. 'Oh sweet Jesus, will you look at him?' She peered into the cot as Patsy proudly set it on the table.

Maureen hastily shifted the ashtray and the teapot and, putting out her cigarette, washed her hands at the sink. 'Oh let me look.' She lifted the lacy cover away from the baby's face. Her fingers looked huge next to the child's tiny fist curled on the pillow.

'Don't disturb him Aunty Mo,' Patsy hovered anxiously. 'It's a miracle he's actually asleep.'

Bernie marvelled at how grown up Patsy had suddenly become. She also looked rosy with health although there were lines of tiredness in her face.

'Conan's a nice name,' she said, 'I've been dying to see him. I've got him a present.' She rushed upstairs to fetch the package. The other children followed her back down and began pushing and shoving to see the baby.

'Shoo, go on out to play, you'll wake him up,' Maureen scolded.

As the door banged behind them the baby stirred and woke, mewing like a kitten. Patsy lifted him out of the cot and took off his woolly hat revealing a shock of black hair. Although he'd managed to work one arm out, the rest of the baby's body was swaddled in woolly shawls. A line of sweat beaded his nose.

'Mam, you've put too many blankets on him, he's roasting,' Patsy complained, unwrapping the child like a prize in a game of pass the parcel.

Joan was unrepentant. 'Got to be careful, they can soon get cold.'

Conan turned his head towards Bernie and opened startling blue eyes. For a moment Terry Donoghue's face flashed before her, then she held out her gift to Patsy.

Patsy handed the baby to Maureen and unwrapped the little blue cardigan. 'Oh it's lovely. Try it on him, Aunty Mo.' She watched protectively as Maureen expertly fitted him into the cardigan. Bernie wondered at his stick-thin legs dangling from the wider holes of his white romper suit. He began to grizzle and his face turned an alarming dark red.

Such fine skin, Bernie thought. 'Can I hold him?' she asked.

Patsy took the baby from Maureen. 'Let me show you,' she said, cradling the baby's head as she put him into Bernie's arms. 'See, you got to keep a hand on the back of his head so it don't fall back.'

Bernie didn't say that she'd had plenty of experience of holding babies with her younger brothers and sisters. Anyway that now seemed such a long time ago, she'd quite forgotten what a new baby felt like. He was surprisingly heavy and she felt stiff and awkward. She rocked him hopefully but his wails intensified, his mouth a ring of woe showing toothless gums. His head bumped around searching for something.

'He wants feeding,' Bernie said, her memory kicking in.

'I'll take him in the bedroom.' Patsy lifted him and rested him against her chest, patting his back. She went upstairs and a few moments later the wailing stopped. They were sitting round the table talking about how easily Patsy seemed to be taking to motherhood when the back door opened and Marie came in from work.

'Hello Aunty Joan. God, I need to get out of these things, I've been sweating like a pig in that factory.'

She crossed the kitchen and ran up the stairs. Bernie jumped up to follow but before she reached the bedroom door Marie rushed out, ran past her and down the stairs to the bathroom.

Bernie heard the bolt shoot home but she followed her and rattled the door anyway. 'Come on Marie, we forgot you were coming home.'

'Get lost, just go away,' Marie yelled. Her voice dissolved into terrible sobs.

Bernie ran back upstairs as Patsy came out of the bedroom, Conan still attached to her breast. 'What's the matter?' she asked white-faced. The baby let go of the nipple and started to cry. Maureen and Joan were standing at the top of the stairs.

'Come in my room, finish feeding him,' Maureen said.

'It's my fault,' Joan looked miserable, 'I should have thought on.'

'Never mind,' Maureen said. 'She's going to have to get used to it.'

They all went into Maureen's room and Patsy sat down on the bed, to give Conan her other breast.

'You better tell her,' Maureen said.

'Tell me what?' Patsy looked mystified. 'What are you all on about?'

When Maureen explained, she was devastated. 'You should have told me, Mam, I'd never have come if I'd known.'

'We didn't want everyone to know,' Maureen said. 'We thought the less people knew, the better.'

'We'd better go,' Patsy detached Conan who was falling asleep and began wrapping him up in his various shawls. 'Poor Marie,' she said to Bernie, 'it must be awful for her.'

At some point after they'd gone, Marie came out of the bathroom, went upstairs and got into her bed, turning her face to the wall. That was how Bernie found her when she went in after the younger kids had their tea. Nothing she or Maureen tried would get her to respond and then Joe came in with Vinny and John and attention shifted to getting them fed.

After her mam had gone to bingo and the younger ones were in bed, Bernie sat staring at the telly without seeing the screen. All the enthusiasm and energy she'd felt about making the tapes that afternoon was gone. What was the point when life was so horrible? She couldn't help Marie and she was destroying Peter and the rest of the band.

Chapter Twenty-seven

Two days went by with no news. Bernie felt as if she'd imagined the whole audition scene. She was still going to school, peeling spuds for tea and minding the kids while her mam went to bingo. She half-hoped nothing would happen, so that she could go back to just being Bernie and loving Peter. He hadn't been round and she was too afraid of being knocked back to go round to see him, even though Annabel kept saying Peter was just as miserable as she was.

But on Thursday night, after her mam had gone to bingo, she was surprised by a knock at the back door and opened it to find Peter looking hangdog.

'I've been thinking,' he said, following her into the living room. 'You need to do it, Bernie. I'm sorry about before and I don't want to lose you.'

She pulled him to her, melted in his arms. 'You won't lose me,' she whispered, 'I won't let that happen.'

They sat on the sofa and he held her while she cried against his chest.

'I was afraid,' he murmured. 'You'll be famous, you'll go away, forget us all - forget me.'

'Never, never,' she lifted tearful eyes.

He held her face in his hands and kissed her lips. All the magic was still there.

'You won't leave me?' his mouth moved against hers.

'Never, never,' she repeated, the desire in her body fuelling her kiss.

The next afternoon, Bobby's sports car was outside her house when Bernie got home from school. A mixture of fear and excitement filled her. Bobby was in the living room with her mam, drinking tea from one of the best coffee cups.

'What is it?' Bernie flung her coat off.

'I'm just telling your mother she needs to get a phone in. It's no good me having to chase round here every time I've got something to tell you.'

252

'What is it?' Bernie repeated, her voice rising with excitement.

'Good news. Terry wants to see you tomorrow. Sounds like he's got someone interested.'

'In recording?' Bernie sat down, her eyes fixed on him.

Bobby shrugged but she could tell he was excited too. 'That's all he said, we'll find out tomorrow.'

So at ten on Saturday morning Bernie waited anxiously for Bobby to collect her. She'd got up early to persuade Marie to do her hair and makeup and she was dressed in her best with a headscarf to protect her hair from the wind in the open car.

Terry Donoghue was waiting in his office and Bernie's stomach gave that flip again as she felt his assessing gaze.

'I won't keep you in suspense,' he said when they were seated. 'Parlophone are interested. I took your photo and the demo tapes and they're provisionally offering a contract with £1000 advance. Of course they want to see and hear you before they sign you so I'll be taking you to London on Monday for two nights. You're not old enough to sign yourself so one of your parents will need to come too. In the meantime you need to smarten up. Get your hair done properly and make sure you wear something decent.' He opened a drawer and pulled out a wad of five-pound notes, counted out ten and threw them across the desk. 'Here.'

Bernie stared at the money. She'd hardly heard anything he said. She looked at the fifty pounds and thought it was more than her mam and Marie earned in a month.

'Okay kid, any questions?'

She shook her head, too dazed to think.

'Be at Lime Street station for seven on Monday morning. I'll meet you there. We need to be at the studios for one o'clock. Get a taxi.'

Bobby was cock-a-hoop in the car on the way home but Bernie was still in a dream. Bobby talked as he drove, unfolding the delights of London and all the exciting people she would be able to meet but all she could think about was leaving her family behind - and Peter.

'It's not too late to change my mind, is it?' she asked as the car pulled up at her house.

Bobby looked at her aghast. 'What?' The colour drained from his face.

Bernie felt stricken, it was cruel of her, after all he had done for her. Suddenly her dream punctured. Whatever she did was going to hurt someone. She just wanted to sing and be happy. She jumped out of the car and ran round to the back door so Bobby wouldn't see her tears. Indoors, she ran up to the bedroom and threw herself on her bed clutching Bobby Bear. She could hear voices from the kitchen and realised Bobby had followed her in. She put the pillow over her head.

After a while her mam came into the room. 'Here,' she set a cup of tea on the floor by the bed, sat down on Marie's bed and lit up a Woodbine. 'So, we're going to London on Monday.'

Bernie raised her head. 'I don't want to go, Mam.'

'It's a big thing, I know, a big thing for a little girl. That's what you are still you know - to me - but I can see now you're growing up and you got something special, something more than any of us has ever had. It's something you can't afford to waste, not just for us and yourself, but think of all the pleasure you can bring to other people, listening to you sing.'

'But I don't want to leave everyone.' Bernie sat up and rubbed her eyes.

'Lord save us, it's only a couple of days, we'll be back home Wednesday. Our Joan and Marie will look after the kids and your da. I've never been to London, and it's a free trip. You don't want me to miss out on that, do you?'

Bernie laughed through her tears and Maureen smiled. 'That's better. I know I was against all this pop singing at first but I see now this is what you're made for. Don't you know how proud we are of you, even your da telling everyone in the pub about his famous daughter? Don't let us down now.'

Bernie couldn't imagine her da taking interest in anything she did. Her heart lifted. It wouldn't be so bad going to London with her mam beside her for support.

'I have to get my hair done and buy a new outfit.' She pulled the fifty pounds from her handbag and showed her mam.

Maureen's eyes rounded. 'Miss Fifi will fit you in tomorrow. I better get mine done too and get the dry cleaner's to give my fur coat a brush up.'

'Forget that, we're both going to Ellison Lea and then up Bold Street for a decent outfit each. There's plenty here,' she crumpled the notes. It gave her a thrill to see her mother's face full of wonder at the thought of going to the best hairdresser's in the city and she began to see some of the advantages money and success could bring.

But Bernie's stomach churned all day at the thought of telling the band about the trip to London. Was it all really worth it if it was just going to make her miserable? She thought of her cousin Patsy, so happy with her husband and baby. Wouldn't it be better just to settle for that?

Predictably the gig didn't go well. Bernie kept trying to raise her spirits with thoughts of the shopping spree the next day but she wasn't up to par for the dance numbers. She had a bluesy slot in the middle and when she sang *Summertime* all her misery poured into her voice. On the line about the bird spreading its wings her voice broke but she finished the song like the professional she was learning to be.

Afterwards as they sat with a drink there was a tense atmosphere. Bernie had told Peter the news earlier but now she had to face the others. They took it in silence then Tommy and Phil wished her good luck but Ginger muttered

'Some people will crawl under a snake's belly to get on.'

'There's no need for that,' Peter glared at him

'I suppose you're going too?' Ginger taunted. 'Going to do a little Sonny and Cher act together?'

'They don't want me either,' Peter said and Bernie's heart twisted. 'Look guys, we all know Bernie's got something special; we don't want to split with bad feelings do we?'

Bernie smiled gratefully but she saw that, despite his bright grin, his fingers were tearing the beer mat in front of him to shreds.

Phil gave a sheepish smile. 'No hard feelings Bernie, hope you make it big, girl.'

'Don't think you can come crawling back when you don't.' Ginger kicked his chair back and marched out.

'He'll get over it, take no notice,' Peter said. 'Come on, let's get home.'

They were all quiet in the van. Ginger ignored her but Tommy and Peter wished her a subdued goodbye.

'We'll still see each other?' Bernie asked and they smiled and nodded but there was a falseness between them now. She knew that whatever happened she would never sing with them again.

Back home she and Peter cuddled in the passageway but sadness overcame her as she leaned against the warmth of his chest.

'I wish you were coming to London too.'

'So do I, but don't be sad, you should be excited. I'm going to take you out to celebrate tomorrow night. Be ready for seven o'clock. Okay?'

'All right.'

With a final kiss he pushed her gently away. 'Go on now.'

Was this a sign that he was moving away from her, ready to let her go? She hurried in worrying at this thought to find her da and John already home and slurping down their steak and mash suppers.

'Here she is, our little songbird.' Da's voice was thick with drink and he had a sentimental look in his eyes. 'All grown up, going to London...' he went on. 'You mind now you do us proud.' He waved his fork at her.

'I will Da,' Bernie promised and escaped to bed.

On Saturday there was no time to think, only to enjoy the luxury of having money to spend. Bernie and Maureen lost no time in hitting the Bold Street boutiques. Bernie splashed out on a purple minidress with a pink Beatle neck jacket and matching bag and kitten heel shoes. Maureen tried on a smart crimplene two-piece but looked shocked at the price tag.

'It really suits you Mam,' Bernie searched the shelves for a handbag to go with it.

'Oh it's too much. Really I'd rather wear me fur coat.'

'You're not wearing that old thing. Look there's plenty of money, that's what it's for, so we won't look like....' She stopped short. 'Anyway it's too warm for fur.'

At the hairdresser's Bernie's bob was expertly cut into a sharp geometric crop that fitted close to her head. Maureen looked on in awe as her own hair was curled in a flattering bubble cut. Tired and hungry, they enjoyed a lavish lunch in Lewis's restaurant.

Afterwards they browsed the cosmetics counters. Bernie insisted they both get a free facial and she bought for Marie a bottle of Worth's *Je Reviens* perfume and a Revlon mascara wand. After buying sweets for the kids they made their way home laden with packages.

Marie was still in her pyjamas. She took Bernie's gifts with listless thanks. Bernie began unpacking her new clothes. Marie opened the perfume and rubbed some on her wrist. The delicate scent filled the bedroom with an air of luxury.

'Suppose I'm babysitting again?' she said.

'I've got a last date with Peter before we go away. He said he's taking me somewhere special,' Bernie said happily then looked up and saw Marie's face. 'Oh, you don't mind do you? I thought - well, you don't go out much now?'

'It's okay,' Marie gave a twisted smile. 'Angie's going out with her boyfriend. I think they're going to get engaged soon. That's a fab hairstyle.' She touched her fingers to Bernie's sleek Mary Quant style.

Bernie felt awful. As she got ready she thought that Marie really needed something to gee her up, get her back to her old self. Maybe she could get Peter to fix her up with a blind date, they could go out as a foursome. She'd mention it to him but she wouldn't ask Marie yet, she was so prickly and after what happened with Jimmy she was probably not ready to start up with someone new just yet.

'You had your hair cut.' Peter stared at her head as he handed her into the taxi waiting outside her house.

'A cab!' she exclaimed, settling into the leather seat and feeling like a princess. 'Last time we were in a cab we were taking our Ant to the hospital, remember?'

He laughed. 'You'd better get used to it. I expect you'll be using cabs a lot in London.'

'Don't you like my hair? Terry Donoghue told me to get it done.'

'Ye-es, it's - stylish, but I liked it longer.'

'Where to mate?' the driver interrupted.

Peter gave him an address and they were whisked away. Bernie felt special, cosseted in the cab with Peter's arm around her as dusk fell and city lights began to glimmer. The taxi pulled up in the Chinese quarter and Bernie was pleased to see the restaurant was small and cosy. Although it was in a quiet area, the place was already half-full of Chinese people eating which Peter said was a sign of good food.

'You've been here before?' Bernie asked as she sat down at the table he'd reserved by the window.

'Once or twice. It's my favourite, when I've got the time and the money.'

'You bring all your girls here?' Bernie joked.

'Only my best one,' he took her hands in his, his face rosy in the glow from the small candle in a red glass bowl between them.

The waiter came and Peter ordered a bottle of Sauternes.

'It's only table wine, you can have some,' he filled her glass.

She sipped it and tried to relax as they waited for their first course. Peter seemed nervous or maybe it was her fault: she was on edge about going to London. She nibbled at the prawn crackers the waiter had brought, glad of something to do.

The food was fabulous and the wine and general good humour of the other diners softened their mood so that soon they were chatting away as they always did together. Peter ordered coffee and toffee fruits for dessert but once their main course dishes had been taken away another

257

nervous silence developed. She toyed with the candle bowl and after a minute, Peter moved it to the edge of the table and took her hands in his again.

'Bernie, I need to tell you something. I'm so scared I'm going to lose you, that you'll forget me once you go away.'

She moved to protest but he silenced her. 'No, listen, soon you'll be sixteen and I want - I want more than anything to make you mine, ask you to marry me but I can't till then anyway.' He turned her hand over, examined her palm like a fortune-teller. 'It wouldn't be fair. You've got enough to think about with the recording contract and everything but I just want you to know how much you mean to me.'

Tears glistened in Bernie's eyes. 'I do know,' she said. squeezing his fingers. He withdrew his hand and reached into his inside pocket.

'I bought you this,' he offered a small leather box. 'I only ask you'll wear it so that while you're away it'll remind you of me.'

Bernie opened the box. Inside nestled a gold and silver eternity ring studded with marcasites.

'Oh,' she gasped, 'it's beautiful. She made to put it on her wedding finger but Peter took it from her.

'On here,' he slipped it onto the third finger of her right hand. 'There'll be one for the other hand soon, God willing.'

It was more beautiful and obviously more expensive than the silver ring he'd first given her but Bernie knew she would never take either of them off.

In the taxi home Bernie never saw the Saturday night crowds or the streetlights. Wrapped in Peter's arms she soaked up his kisses and caresses. For once, desire was only the undercurrent to the love between them. If she had ever doubted his love before, now she was sure and with that surety came the confidence to face whatever lay in store for her.

Epilogue

Bernie sits on the train in her pink jacket and purple dress. Next to her, her mam fidgets, tugging her crimplene skirt down over her knees. Bernie knows her mam is dying for a ciggy but their compartment is non-smoking. There is an old lady with a moulting dog in one corner and the other seats are taken up with men in suits with briefcases on their laps, reading the Times or the Daily Express, papers that weren't on sale in the shop where Bernie worked, unless you put in a special order.

Terry Donoghue stands out in his sharp mohair suit but fits in with his leather document case. He has taken out some papers and fiddles with his gold-topped pen. He is younger, smarter, more hip than the other men, even though when Bernie examines them some of them are not really that old. Terry looks up and gives her a slow, lazy smile that makes her stomach somersault. She looks away, hoping her face isn't as pink as her jacket, and thinks of Peter.

Her mam gets up and goes out to the corridor. Bernie watches the countryside flying past. Her world is going to grow into an unknown expanse but the train is like a time bubble between what she leaves behind and what lies ahead. She watches the buddleia bushes beside the tracks. They have found their way up through stony ground, yet thrive on it, bursting with brilliant purple flowers, flaunting their joy in life to the sky.

Inside herself the same stream of energy bubbles and builds, waiting to explode into blossom. It's the same feeling she gets on stage when the music, the sound, just has to come out of her. This is all she has to do, what she's meant to do.

She smiles and Terry glances up, smiles back. It's an ordinary, genuine smile between friends. Bernie can see her mam in the corridor looking out of the open window as she puffs on a Woodbine. Under her breath, Bernie starts to hum *Something Tells Me I'm Into Something Good.*

End

About the author

Carol Fenlon was born and raised in the Midlands and moved to Manchester with her parents in the early 1960s. She met and married a Scouser, moving to Liverpool in 1964. Much of the background setting and detail in *A Liver Bird Sings* is drawn from her experiences in this period. Carol later moved to Skelmersdale where she has lived for the last 40 years.

Carol has written five other books. Two short story collections *Plotlands*, set on the North wales coast, and *Triple Death* are dark tales with touches of macabre comedy. Her first novel, *Consider the Lilies* won the Impress Novel Prize in 2007 and her second novel, *Mere* was published by Thunderpoint publishing in 2018. Both novels are dark chillers set around Carol's home landscape of West Lancashire. She has also written two non-fiction books, *Skelmersdale - A New Town in the Making*, a partial history of her home town and *You Can't You Won't*, written jointly with Gary Skyner, thalidomide victim, scouse comedian and motivational speaker. This autobiography recounts his fight to succeed despite physical disability and his tireless efforts to get justice for UK thalidomiders.

A Liver Bird Sings is the result of a longheld desire to revisit those wonderful times in Liverpool in the swinging sixties. Carol hopes readers will enjoy joining her on this journey back in time as much as she has enjoyed writing it.

Lightning Source UK Ltd.
Milton Keynes UK
UKHW040835041219
354754UK00003B/813/P